Looking for
Lucky
By
Shirley Kennedy

Desert Sky Publishing
Las Vegas, Nevada

ISBN 978-0-9769238-3-1 (Paper)
ISBN 978-0-9769238-2-4 (Ebook)

Dedicated to animal lovers everywhere and
with fond remembrance to the animals I was
privileged to know and love in my life.

Dogs: Tippi, Butch, Prince & Hot Shot

Cats: Sierra, Anabelle, Caesar, & Romeo

Horses: Heathcliff & Handsome Joe Bar

Feathered friends: Tiburon & Featherly

Books by Shirley Kennedy

Deadly Gamble, Inkspell Press

The Last of Lady Lansdown, Camel Press

Heartbreak Trail, Camel Press

Three Wishes for Miss Winthrop, Signet

Lady Flora's Fantasy, Signet

The Irish Upstart, Signet

The Selfless Sister, Signet

The Rebellious Twin, Signet

The London Belle, Signet

Lady Semple's Secret, Ballantine

Chapter 1

Santa Marta, California

Doctor Harvey Linderman was in an especially fine mood as he backed his red Lincoln MKZ out the driveway of his suburban Santa Marta home. Heading for Linderman Laboratories, he tuned in a classic music station on his satellite radio, settled into the multicontour seat, hummed to a Mozart concerto as his brain darted from one pleasant thought to another.

Finally the sun, thank God, after dreary days of coastal fog. Wintry weak but welcome just the same…

At last the New England Journal of Medicine had published his article in the April edition, just out. This morning he'd be flooded with congratulations from his colleagues. He would play it casual, of course. Modesty was always the key…

Today the new funding from the National Institutes of Health would be approved. New money. New experiments. More recognition…

Last night, what a triumph. Nothing could be more prestigious than being the main speaker at The Western Medical Research Association's annual banquet. Hectic, but he loved the flurry and hustle of it all. The quick flight up to San Francisco, reception committee at the airport, the Hilton, cocktails, dinner, splendid introduction.

To those of you who have been exposed to the brilliance of his research, Doctor Harvey Linderman needs no introduction. Physician, pathologist, virologist, Director of Linderman Research Laboratories, distinguished staff member of Santa Marta General Hospital, Doctor Linderman is a recipient of NIH grant support for his work in pathology as well as other grants from The March of Dimes, The American Heart Association and The American Cancer Society….

The applause, long and loud, still rang in his ears. Just one thing wrong. One item was missing from the introduction and it really pissed him off. Where was *Member of The International Academy of Sciences?* Talk about an outrage. The most prestigious scientific society of all and he wasn't a member. By everything holy, the distinguished scientists on the election committee should have nominated him for membership long ago, but for reasons unknown, they had not.

Distinguished shitheads. What more was he supposed to do? If anyone deserved to be a member, he did. He had published, published, and published some more. Still they wouldn't give him the recognition he was due. Well, forget it. Just keep publishing. Sooner or later they'd accept him or he'd know the reason why. Meanwhile, the sun was shining, good things were happening...

Connie.

Why, why, why? Dammit, every time his mood lightened and his spirits began to soar, he had to think of his wife. Well, by God, this time he wouldn't let her ruin his day. Absolutely not. So what if another maid quit? He didn't care anymore. Actually, this latest fiasco was so off-the-wall it was amusing. What was this last maid called? Juana? Juanita? Whatever. He couldn't remember their names, they came and went so fast, all looking alike—short, dark and foreign. When they quit, and they always did, they simply took their wages and disappeared without notice, without an explanation, except Juana—Juanita—whatever.

He could almost admire the determined way she'd marched into his den, suitcase in hand, black eyes sparking with anger. "I no work for you no more." Hell, she could hardly speak English. An illegal, fresh from Mexico. Ought to be grateful to have a roof over her head. "Senior Linderman, I leave. *Su esposa esta loca.* She scream at me. She pee her bed. I no change sheets..."

Su esposa esta loca. Jesus Christ, what next? The maid could go and good riddance. Plenty more where she came from. They sneaked across the border by the thousands. Only...not even the frigging wetbacks would work for Connie long.

That did it. From now on, if she wanted that rat's nest of a bedroom cleaned, she could do it herself. He'd tell her tomorrow at breakfast, that is, if she was sober again. Come to think of it, that was strange...

This morning, for the first time in months, Connie appeared at breakfast not soused as usual. What had gotten into her vodka-soaked brain? He'd been so startled he hadn't thought to mention the maid. Connie was downright civil, almost like the girl he used to know except she looked terrible. Gray-faced and shaking, clothes stained and wrinkled, as if she'd spent the night in a dumpster. Why had she postponed her first little nip of the day? She couldn't be out of vodka, not when he always made sure the liquor cabinet was full. Grey Goose. Nothing but the finest for old Connie, in remembrance of the good old days if nothing else. They'd had a good marriage once, long ago before Christie died, before Connie's drinking got out of hand, before the nightmare memories that still made him cringe...

His humiliation when his wife fell fully clothed, into the swimming pool at Doctor Clarence Osborne's Silver Anniversary party...

His agony of embarrassment at the awards banquet when she screamed "Go fuck yourself!" at the president of the A.M.R.A. when he, in all kindness, suggested she go lie down.

That was years ago, back when he was so worried she'd ruin his career he nearly divorced her, before he realized his colleagues and their wives not only understood but sympathized. *Poor Harvey. What a terrible thing that was, losing his little girl and all the fault of that awful wife of his. Where does he find the patience? He deserves a medal. Most men would have dumped her years ago. She drinks, you know.*

How the mighty had fallen. Constance Stanhope Linderman, once proud, haughty, beautiful. Stanford grad from snobby Burlingame. Disgusting lush. Dammit, let her change her own wet sheets.

But why should he be upset? Connie didn't embarrass him anymore. She hardly ever left the house now, or her bedroom, for that matter. She just holed up and drank. Fine. Now he could do as he damn well pleased. That meant women, all he wanted, more than he could use, the way he attracted them. "You're a soap opera doctor," one called him. Yeah, he was. He had it all—money, power, polish, prestige. At fifty-five, he looked forty-five with his year-round tan, his full head of silvery hair, his tall, trim body, fine-tuned three times a week at his health club.

Best of all…if the woman of the moment looked into the depths of his sky-blue eyes, she would discover the hint of tragedy he tried so bravely to hide. Almost. How it wrung her heart. What a marvelous excuse for never getting serious. The scenario was always the same. "Please, please try to understand, darling. God, how I love you, how I want you!" (Grip her arms brutally tight. Gaze with desperation into her pleading face.) "But how can I leave my wife? It broke her heart when…(choke up) forgive me… (bite lips and look away) even now, after all these years, I can't bear to talk about my little girl. It breaks my heart, darling, but I'm simply not free."

Harvey began his turn from Fifth Street onto Elm. Those lines had earned him invitations to more beds than he cared to count. Of course, lately there was only one bed he cared to be in. *Ah, Gretchen…* That rosy, soft young flesh, slender waist, shimmering golden hair. Those big, lusciously rounded breasts. Perhaps this weekend he'd take her to San Francisco, only a two hour drive up the coast. They would stay at the Stanford Court on Nob Hill. Or better yet, the San Francisco Marriott at Fisherman's Wharf. They would dine at Jai Yun where he'd order the poached chilled duck for them both, or perhaps they'd dine at *Fleur De Lys* where his French would impress her. They would spend plenty of time in bed.

Ahead lay the main gate of Linderman Research Laboratories. As always, a tiny thrill of pride gripped him at first glimpse. All his own creation, begun in one small room and expanded over the years by dint of his hard work, talent, and, yes, brilliance. Now it was a huge facility with over five hundred employees. Located not far from Santa Marta General, the sprawling, five-story building sat amidst a park like setting of sculptured pyracanthas and trimmed privet hedges. Stately trees dotted unblemished lawns where no employee with thermos and brown bag lunch in hand would ever dare to sit.

A guardhouse stood by the front gate. An eight-foot welded mesh fence with three strands of barbed wire running across the top surrounded the facility. They were eyesores, jarring, ugly contrasts to the beautiful buildings and grounds, but, of necessity, there. He hated them, yet each morning managed to ignore and look beyond. The first gratifying view of his laboratory always gave him a boost even on the worst of days when he headed into a hornet's nest of problems. An experiment failed, board of directors down his neck, funding cancelled or cut back. But this morning all was well. In fact, a new experiment was taking shape and…

"Son of a bitch."

Completing the turn, his eyes narrowed as he looked ahead. There they were, the idiots from WEELA, come again to ruin his day. He slowed the car to a near standstill and began creeping the short block to the main gate. *We Especially Love Animals*, WEELA. What right had they to be here? But there they were, at least thirty yelling and hollering fools, parading in an untidy circle in front of the main gate. Some waved signs in the air. Others wore signs over their bodies. Off to the side, a crowd of at least a hundred spectators watched curiously. In addition, wasn't that…Jesus Christ…a panel truck with KMAR Channel 4 painted on the side. The media. His hands clenched the wheel. He scanned the crowd and spotted a young Chinese man with a camera on his shoulder and a skinny, dark-haired woman with a microphone in her hand, both wearing Channel 4 blazers.

The signs. They'd outdone themselves this time. As he rolled towards the entrance, a slender blonde girl waved a Stop the Abuse sign and screamed, "This means you, Linderman!"

A young man with chipmunk teeth held up *Laboratory Animals Never Have a Nice Day* while he shouted, "Can you read, Doctor Linderman?"

A white-haired old lady, red socks and blue tennis shoes clashing with her matronly coat and dress, screamed unintelligible words as she charged his car shaking a *Stop Murdering Animals* sign.

For one grim, indulgent moment, he considered gunning

his Lincoln MKZ straight ahead. How the bodies would fly. Was *he* here? Ah yes, of course. The head of WEELA, dressed in faded jeans, windbreaker, well-worn tennis shoes, wearing a ridiculous sandwich board, strolled towards the car. Shafted by Travis Kerrigan again. Gritting his teeth, Harvey pulled up to the front of the gate and turned off the ignition. The demonstrators gathered around his car. With deliberation and a deep breath, he climbed out, straightened up slowly and smiled at the man in the sandwich board who stood waiting. "Ah, Travis, what a delight to see you again. Tell me, what devilment are you up to today?"

"Good morning, Doctor." Travis Kerrigan smiled as if he had just encountered a dear old friend. Fairly tall, in his mid thirties, he had intelligent, bluish-gray eyes and dark hair hanging nearly to his collar, just a tad short of hippy length. Touches of humor lurked around his mouth and near his eyes as he extended his hand, requiring an extra second to reach his arm around the sandwich board. His gaze swept with genuine admiration over Harvey's Harris Tweed jacket, cashmere slacks, genuine crocodile moccasins, gold cuff-linked shirt, and muted maroon silk tie. "You're looking your usual splendid self today."

Harvey shook Travis's hand. "Why, I'm feeling fine, too, Travis, that is, unless—" he glanced at the demonstrators gathered around listening to his every word, "—you're planning on blocking the gate with another of your, uh, sitins as you call them."

Travis's face broke into a wide grin. "Like last time? That was rude of us, wasn't it? But you must admit it got your attention."

The doctor nodded in agreement. "Oh, absolutely. It did indeed. What happened after the four policemen carried you off?"

"Not much. Booked and released. I never saw the inside of a cell."

"How fortunate."

"I knew you'd think so."

Harvey stepped back, directing his attention to Travis's

sign. "Well done, Travis. It puts your point across beautifully. The beagles are adorable and the words a real attention-getter." He stepped back farther, nodded his head in admiration, slowly read aloud: "Destined for Death at Linderman Laboratories. My, my, that's strong stuff. Channel Four has got its shots?"

"Yes, indeed, Doctor. The back is different. Would you like to see?"

"Of course."

Travis turned around. On his back was the picture of a monkey screaming in agony. The caption read *End the torture at Linderman Laboratories*.

The corners of Harvey's mouth tightened. "What are you planning, Kerrigan? What's brought you down from San Francisco this time?"

With his thumbs securely hooked to the pockets of his windbreaker, Travis turned and answered, "We've been so busy over at Berkeley that we thought you might feel neglected. This is only a brief visit, Doctor, not a sit-in, unless...?" He looked inquiringly towards a heavyset young woman with long brown hair who stood in the crowd. "Terry, were you planning on chaining yourself to the fence today?"

"Not really," the woman called back lightheartedly. "It's too cold."

"I didn't think so." As the Channel Four crew came in close, Travis's smile disappeared. His eyes looked into Harvey's with piercing directness. "You know what we want. We've asked before and we ask again. We want to come in and inspect your laboratories. All of them and all the animals. Mice, rats, rhesus monkeys, rabbits, chimps, goats, dogs, and whatever else you've got in there."

Harvey carefully folded his arms and bowed his head, as if he were giving the request serious consideration. If only the Channel Four guy and the bitch with the microphone would leave. How he would love to give Travis Kerrigan a swift kick in the ass. He'd do it too, by God, if he weren't being recorded. He pursed his lips, rocked back and forth a few times on his toes and heels. Finally, he shook his head with regret. "I can't let you do that, Travis. I admire your zeal, misguided though your motives may be, but you cannot come in and disrupt the routine of my laboratories."

"Let us in, Doctor," Travis said in a measured, reasonable tone.

"Absolutely not. What you're doing here is nonsense. You know we're inspected under the Animal Welfare Act. There's nothing for you to see. You're a lawyer, aren't you? Surely you know the law."

"Let us in, Doctor."

"You people are irrational. You don't understand what we scientists are doing. Our research might someday save the lives of your children. Such an unnecessary fuss."

The crowd began to chant, "Nothing to hide? Let's go inside…nothing to hide? Let's go inside…nothing to hide? Let's go inside…"

Their voices grew louder, grating on Harvey's ears. He pointed a finger inches away from Travis Kerrigan's face. "Let me tell you something—"

Travis shoved the offending finger aside with the back of his hand. "Don't push your luck, bucko."

Bucko? Harvey sensed a red blush of fury creeping over his face. His heart pounded with rage. The camera whirred. Channel Four had a microphone practically under his nose. My God, he'd better get out of here. He whirled and headed back to his car. "I don't have to listen to this. Get away from the gates. I'm calling the police if they haven't been called already." He leaped into his Lincoln, slammed the door and turned on the ignition.

Everyone backed away. Travis raised his hand in a friendly salute. "Have a good day, Doctor."

A wave of applause and gleeful laughter swept the crowd as the Lincoln MKZ sped through the gate. Travis waved in appreciation. "Thanks, Sparrow," he called to the young man with the chipmunk teeth. "You were fine, Mrs. Bagley," he said to the little old lady in red socks and blue tennis shoes.

"You did it again, Travis," said a slim young woman in her

early twenties.

"You think so, Krista? Thanks. And thanks for coming all the way from Berkeley."

Terry Woodard, the heavyset young woman with the long brown hair, detached herself from the laughing crowd and flung her arms around Travis. "Way to go." She hugged him tight, signboard and all. "I loved it when the great doctor lost his cool. He sure didn't like it when you called him bucko. Too bad Latonia wasn't here."

A regretful smile flitted across Travis's lips. "Yeah. She'd have loved it. I hated to tell her to stay away, but if you're black, beautiful and six feet tall, you might get noticed, and we don't want that, do we?"

Terry shook her head. "Lord, no. Not if she's going to be working here."

"Looks like she will be, which is good because the truth is, we got nowhere with Linderman today."

"We'll get there, Travis, and when we do we'll want more than a tour. We'll liberate every animal in the place."

"Right. But until then…" Travis looked up at the Linderman Research Laboratories, beyond the welded mesh fence and immaculate lawns, to the fortress-like five-story brick building. "I hate to think what's going on inside." He turned and his gaze swept the crowd. "Okay everyone, that's it for today. Thanks, you did great. We will be back."

Harvey burst into the office of his assistant, Doctor Clarence Osborne. "Did you see those idiots out there?"

Seated at his desk, Doctor Osborne, short, bald and cherub-faced, nodded calmly. "I could hardly have missed them, Harvey."

"Call the police."

"They're leaving." Doctor Osborne, whose office faced the front entrance, moved to his window and pointed. "Look, they're going quietly, as you can see."

"Why not? They've got their pictures. No doubt I'll be starring on the six o'clock news tonight."

"Surely not. The media has more important matters to report than animal liberation. Channel Four might give them a few seconds, but so what?"

Harvey began pacing the room. "What really bothers me is what if those fools get in here? That's what they want, you know, to get in here and 'liberate' our animals."

Clarence returned to his desk and sat down. "Calm yourself. Be reasonable. We've beefed up security to the point where this place is a fortress…almost."

"What the hell do you mean, almost?"

His assistant sighed. "You've spent thousands on security. Magnetic sensor cards—mercury switches on the fence—badges with photo ID's—time recording locks. And what have you got at the front gate? One damn Mexican, Harvey, that's ridiculous."

"I have no control over what Safe-T-First Security Services gives us. As it is, the guards are the most expensive part of our security."

"But what kind of quality are we getting for ten dollars an hour? That's what they're paid, you know, the minimum wage. If you're worried about security, you should go biometric. Fingerprint readers, hand and eye scanners, that sort of thing."

"Forget it. Too much money." Linderman continued to pace. "Have you met Travis Kerrigan? I wouldn't put anything past that bastard."

"He's well-intentioned, as they all are. He simply doesn't understand what you're trying to do."

"Exactly. From those signs and the way they talk, you'd think I'm some sort of sadistic monster."

"We all know that's not so."

"Of course it's not so. I'm not cruel. When I was a little tyke, I always had a dog."

Doctor Osborne sighed and leaned back in his seat. "You don't have to defend yourself. They're gone and no harm done. For heaven's sake, let's forget it and change the subject. Did you know the whole lab's buzzing?"

"No, by God, I won't be sidetracked."

"The New England Journal of Medicine? Your article on the alteration of rat brain catecholamine metabolism? They're saying it's brilliant, Harvey. Quite a feather in your cap."

Harvey knew manipulation when he heard it. But perhaps, for the sake of his blood pressure...he sat down abruptly in one of the guest chairs. "Is that what they're saying?"

"Absolutely. And another thing, don't forget we get the new funding from NIH today. A substantial grant, Harvey. Think of it. What about this new experiment you've been talking about?"

He was relaxed now, his pulse back to normal. "New experiment? On again, off again. I'm still not sure we'll do it."

"What animals will we need if we do it?"

"Mmm...dogs, I think."

"Conditioned?"

"No. Forty trash dogs will be fine."

Chapter 2

Winter Park, Colorado

Jillian Dahl sped down the mountain, her honey-blonde hair flowing out from beneath her blue ski cap as she skimmed gracefully over and around the steep moguls of the Drunken Frenchman run. She wore bright blue boots, yellow tinted goggles, and a one-piece silver ski suit that fit snugly over her long, lean form. *Best run of the day. Where's Tom?* Her glance swept the slope and spied her fiancé's navy blue jacket and flashy orange boots. He stood waiting near the bottom, by the side of the tree-lined trail. *Damn but he's handsome.* Broad shoulders—ski-tanned face—powerful legs. She changed course. As she wedged her skis to a stop beside him, the sun made a sudden, dazzling appearance after lurking all morning behind gray snow clouds. It warmed her face, set off a million brilliant sparkles in the snow.

"Finally the sun." She stabbed her poles into the snow. "Now the day's perfect."

Tom grinned. "What could be better than snow like butter and no wait at the lift lines? So what are we waiting for? Let's go."

"We'd better wait for Tish and Karlin and Dennis."

"Not me." With one smooth shove Tom cut to the middle of the slope and called back, "Old Tom doesn't waste ski time."

"Go ahead then." Jillian watched him speed off and disappear around a turn. Tom could be so impatient sometimes. Something she'd have to deal with. She wiggled her fingers, feeling the unfamiliar press of the two-carat diamond ring inside her mitten. Engaged a week now. She held her breath, waiting for the thrill to hit. Nothing. Well, it just hadn't sunk in yet. She inhaled a lungful of chilled, fresh, ten-thousand-foot Colorado air and looked back up the trail, searching for the green of

Tish's jacket and Karlin's dark blue. Where were they? Naturally she would beat Tish down, but Karlin? Her younger sister usually flew down the hill in the flashy-fast style that only a twenty-year-old expert skier in top shape could have. Karlin never stopped to view the scenery, mess around with buckles and bindings, decide which trail to take. Karlin just simply skied.

Jillian raised herself up on her poles, bent forward, and rapidly flexed her knees. *Come on, Tish, come on, Karlin.* She swung her skis uphill and scanned the mountain. Here came Tish. She was easy to spot, not only by the brilliant green of her jacket and warm-up pants but by her bulldozer style—a five-foot-ten, one-hundred-seventy pound brick wall moving with wide, ungraceful, yet majestic, swoops down the slope. Tish wasn't a flashy skier. Rather, a formidable skier. You wouldn't want to get in her way, even if you were a tree.

Tish skidded to a stop, planted her poles, and lifted her goggles. "Not a bad run." Her deep voice boomed over the slope. "Ain't it great when the sun comes out?"

Jillian nodded. "Where's Karlin?"

"Wiped out on Outhouse. Dennis is with her."

"That's twice today. I wonder what's wrong with Queen of the Slopes this morning." Karlin had skied since she was four, won a World Cup bronze at Lake Placid when she was seventeen, could have easily made the U.S. Women's Olympic Ski Team had she not decided pre-med studies came first. She hardly ever fell, at least not off the slalom runs, and never on a well-groomed slope like this.

Tish looked her up and down. "So is that your new fifteen hundred-dollar ski outfit?"

"Fourteen-ninety-nine. It's a Bogner. Do you like it?"

Tish sniffed. "You look like a Texan in that thing."

"Thanks loads." Tish liked to bring her down to size. What better way than to compare her to the Texans, those pitiful creatures from the flatlands who looked great in their fancy Nieman-Marcus outfits but couldn't ski worth a damn. Still, she valued Tish's opinion. Too bad Tom couldn't understand why this big, brusque woman was her best friend. "Why do you put up with her?" he once asked. "She's simply not your class. That makeup—all that blue gunk on her eyelids—that awful junk jewelry. Really, Jillian, doesn't she embarrass you?"

"No, she doesn't. So what if she has a rough edge? She cuts through all my bullshit and tells me where I'm really at. She's the best friend I ever had."

Tom's remarks were annoying, but she could see where he was coming from. He grew up in Cherry Creek, the "old money" neighborhood of Denver, the only son of wealthy, indulgent parents. He inherited his father's chain of sporting goods stores, ran them well, and now, at forty-two, was rich and successful. In contrast, Tish was raised by her widowed mother in a tiny house in northeast Denver, not the best section of town by far. She grew up tough and ambitious, put herself through Colorado School of Mines. Now in her mid-thirties, she was one of Alpha Oil's top geologists.

"Let's wait for Karlin and Dennis." Tish dug into her jacket pocket for a handkerchief, pulled off her goggles, and began to polish the lenses. "So you've been engaged a week now?"

"Yes, a whole week."

Tish polished vigorously. "Still thrilled and excited?"

"I'm not all bubbly, if that's what you mean."

"You sound less than thrilled. Everything okay? Nothing's happened to the big romance, has it?"

Jillian stabbed the snow with both poles. "It isn't just that Tom is fun and does exciting things. He's a fine man and I love him. I want us to spend our lives together."

Tish looked off over the mountain. "Hmm."

The time had come. Jillian had suspected for a while but hadn't asked, didn't want to know. "You don't like Tom, do you?"

Tish remained silent for a long moment, tipping her head to one side, carefully observing the few skiers who swished by. "How could I not like Tom? He makes piles of money. He's handsome enough to make Hugh Jackman look like a troll. He skis like Ted Ligety, owns a condo at Aspen, and...oh, yeah, how could I forget his season tickets to the Broncos?"

"On the forty-yard line."

"Well, there you go. Tom is a marvelous catch. How could you be so lucky?"

"You don't like him."

"No."

Somehow the day wasn't perfect any more. Funny, how Tom's opinion of Tish didn't bother her in the slightest. Tish was her best friend and that was that. But Tish's opinion of Tom? That mattered. "So why don't you like him?"

Tish frowned in thought. "'Don't like' is maybe the wrong term. Tom's a bigot and a snob, but I don't hold that against him. That's how he was raised. The poor man doesn't know any better. I think he's wrong for you. You're as spoiled as he is, but you've got a heart. You care about people, but Tom? That guy is shallow. He's got all the depth of a pizza pan. Sometimes I think his main concern in life is someone might scratch his Mercedes." Tish wrinkled her nose. "Besides, I don't think you love him."

"I just told you—"

"Aw, come on. You're single, almost thirty. Your biological time clock—"

"That has nothing to do with it."

"Oh, really?" Tish gave her friend a long, cool stare. "You've never stuck with any man you didn't think was super perfect. My God, just since I've known you, you've gone through—" she started enumerating on gloved fingers. "Let's see—"

"I know, one man after another. Makes me sound like a fool, but this time I'm serious. Do you think I want to be a career girl forever? Do I want to end up a moldy old lady with a bunch of cats for company?"

Tish shook her head with disgust. "Boy, are you hard to figure. At work you're so efficient and well-organized and professional, but when I listen to you here, away from the office, I think, this woman is all messed up."

Jillian caught a glimpse of blue and a spot of red cresting the hill above. It was Karlin in her bright red ski hat, her boyfriend, Dennis, close behind. "Here she comes. I'll think about what you said, Tish." She turned fond eyes on her sister, a delight to behold with her skis tight together, knees flexing as she skimmed each mogul, darting like a hummingbird down the slope, confident, precise, and smiling. When she was born, their parents called her "our little surprise." Jillian was ten then, a spoiled only child, nose more than a little out of joint because of the new arrival. But Karlin was such a cuddly, jolly baby that Jillian soon grew to love her.

"Hi, guys!" Karlin skidded to her usual snow-spraying stop. "Such a great day, all sunny and nice. Perfect for the race." Anyone could tell she was Jillian's sister. She had the same wide-set brown eyes, dimpled smile and determined chin that frequently, like Jillian's, was set at a stubborn angle. There the resemblance ended. Jillian was the tall beauty of the family, a willowy five-feet-nine. At five-feet-three, Karlin was "the runt" and merely pretty, a fact she resented when she was growing up. "Why can't I look like Jillian? Why is my hair mousey brown and straight when Jillian's is blonde and thick? Why is my nose bigger? Why does it have a bump in it when hers doesn't? How come she's got big boobs and I'm flat?"

Now, jealousies forgotten, Karlin was her own person. A premed student at the University of Colorado, she was earning all A's and had such a lively, friendly personality that no one noticed she wasn't as beautiful as her older sister, or if they did, didn't care.

Jillian gave her a scornful glance. "Look who's finally here. I hear you've been leaving your sitzmarks all over the hill."

The hint of a worried frown crossed Karlin's face, quickly replaced by a rueful smile. "I'd better not fall this afternoon. I can't let the team down."

Dennis skied up behind her. Karlin had done well with this latest boyfriend. They were a perfect match, both slim, in great physical shape, both in premed. Karlin was already looking ahead to after they graduated. They'd get married and set up a practice together.

"That last spill was a killer." Dennis cast a concerned look at his girlfriend. "Skis, poles, gloves, glasses scattered halfway down Outhouse. Man, did you wipe out."

"How come you fell?" Jillian asked, mildly curious.

Karlin shook her head. "The first time, I don't know. I just fell. The second time, not that I'm making excuses, but my right leg was hurting, right at the knee. Maybe I pulled a muscle."

"How does it feel now?"

"Okay...well, it still hurts a little, but it's all right."

"Maybe you shouldn't race this afternoon."

Shock filled Karlin's eyes. "Not race? For the Rocky Mountain Championships? If I don't race today, it'll be because either I died or I got carried off the hill in a deep coma."

"So you're okay?"

"Of course. I'm fine. And I can ski circles around you, big sister, any day in the week."

"Get out of here!" Jillian stabbed a pole in her sister's direction.

Laughing, Karlin hopped her skis parallel to the slope and bent backwards until her back touched her skis. With an effortless move, she stood up again, not even using her poles to push. "Come on, Dennis." She shoved off and headed down the hill. "See you guys at the lodge."

Tish looked after her, shaking her head. "How does she do it? If I lay back on my skis like that, they'd have to haul me up with a crane."

Jillian couldn't resist. "How does she do this, you mean?" She laid clear back on her skis like Karlin had done. Using the strong muscles of her legs and stomach, she sprang up with ease. "I thought everybody could do that." Before Tish could answer, she pushed off to the center of the slope. When she picked up speed, she did a one-hundred-eighty degree turn and continued down the mountain backwards. "And this!"

"Turkey!"

"I know!" Jillian turned another one-hundred eighty degrees and headed down the mountain. The day was gold, pure gold again. Why had she felt a little depressed back there? Oh, yes, Tish's opinion of Tom. That hurt but she'd live with it.

There was something else, too, that cast a slight shadow over her fine mood, but as she cut across the moguls and headed towards the lodge, she couldn't think what it was.

Chapter 3

Santa Marta, California

In the fashionable Westwood Oaks section of suburban Santa Marta, in the bedroom of her six thousand square foot home, huddled in a pink velvet armchair, Connie Linderman shook with misery.

Never had she felt or looked so bad. Her shoulder length hair hung uncombed and lifeless, a grown-out tangle of gray roots blending into a jarring mismatch with the faded blonde remains of her last trip to Mission 6 Salon in Palo Alto. Her sunken, dark circled eyes were bloodshot, eyelids drooping beneath unplucked brows. Her colorless lips pressed into a downward curve, highlighting the tiny vertical lines that ran upwards towards her nose. A cold sweat glistened over the yellow-tinged pallor of her skin. Her pink silk negligee was spotted with food and drink stains, dotted with cigarette burn holes and torn in several places along the lace edged hem. The pink high heeled slippers that matched were long since gone, replaced by a pair of gray wool socks that belonged to Harvey, far too large for her size four feet, but lying handy in the hamper when her feet got cold.

The beauty of the rich, traditional style furniture was lost amidst the disarray of dirty clothes, overflowing ashtrays, smudged glasses, a TV dinner barely touched, an empty vodka bottle lying in the corner, scrunched up tissues and crumpled cigarette packages. The queen-sized bed was stripped. Blankets, pillows, stained sheets; a pink and turquoise quilted bedspread lay tangled together on the floor.

Across the room on a big flat screen, a fat, rosy-cheeked lady leaned forward to spin the wheel of fortune while Vanna, gorgeous in a tightfitting gown of gold lamé, smiled, clapped, and waited to flip letters. Connie wasn't listening. She had, in fact, turned the volume so low there was no sound.

Connie wasn't watching, either. With a cigarette clutched

in her fingers, she bent forward, hugging herself tightly, rocking back and forth and trying to control her violent shaking. She fought to hold down yet another wave of nausea. Good God, what was left to throw up? She hadn't eaten all day. What could her stomach possibly do but dry heave, and dry heaves were the worst of all.

Why couldn't she just die? No, she didn't want to die. On second thought, yes, she did. Who would care? Nobody. *Alone, alone, alone.* Harvey didn't care anymore. No friends anymore. No family either, now her parents were gone and her little girl dead.

Oh, Christie, Christie. Oh, how I need a drink.

Well, she wasn't going to have a drink. Absolutely no. But where was Harvey? Why wasn't he home yet? She had to talk to him. He had to help her. Last Friday was the worst day of her life. Well, not quite. The day Christie died was the worst. Last Friday was second worst. First, the scene with the maid, then the horrible visit to the doctor's office. All she had wanted was a new Valium prescription. It was always so easy, with Winslow whisking her in and out in no time. He'd prance into the little examining room in his starched white coat, playing his kindly old doctor routine to the hilt. He'd ask after Harvey, so stupid because they played golf together every Wednesday. Then he'd tell a couple of his unfunny jokes, do a little "tsk tsk" because her blood pressure was a bit high, tell her to cut down on salt, and renew her prescription. Simple, only Friday it hadn't turned out that way.

Connie closed her eyes and shivered. Just about everything went wrong, starting from the moment she woke up feeling really, really rotten, worse than ever before. Finding she'd wet the bed again didn't help. Definitely she needed a drink, but never had she taken one before her appointment with Winslow. Friday was different, though, especially after the maid walked out and upset her even more. She hated to break her rule, but after all, what would it hurt to be flexible? Truly, she had no choice. How could she drive to Winslow's office if she couldn't calm her nerves and stop the shaking? So she took one little shooter. Well, two. No, actually three, but she really needed them. Besides, it was vodka. Who could tell?

As it turned out, the shooters didn't help. When she tried to get dressed, she had a terrible time. How long had it been since she'd gotten into her fancy underwear and her Donna Karan suit, or, for that matter, any suit? She couldn't remember the last time she'd even put on a dress. Or panty hose. Whoever invented panty hose should be shot. They were nearly impossible to get into. No problem getting one leg in, but when she tried to climb into the other leg, she kept losing her balance and falling over, even when she braced herself against the wall. She finally lay on her back on the bed, legs in the air, and managed to pull them on. Only then did she discover the runner, but too late. She would have died before she took them off and started again.

And then, as if that weren't enough, she couldn't get into the skirt of her Donna Karan. For some reason, her stomach was swollen, so she ended up digging clear to the bottom of the Good Will box and dragging out her old skirt with the elastic waist. The black knit didn't exactly match the brown tweed jacket, but time was flying and she had no choice but to wear it anyway. As for the cream satin blouse that went with the Karan, it was entirely the maid's fault it was wrinkled. Juana had to be the one responsible for letting it fall off its hanger and lie crumpled on the closet floor for God knew how long. And then, because the maid was stupid enough to quit over a wet bed, for heaven's sake, she wasn't there to iron it. Well, phooey on her. The jacket covered most of the blouse anyway. The wrinkles hardly showed.

She completed her outfit with her red calfskin Salvatore Ferragamo pumps she'd bought years ago in Maiden Lane (some things were timeless). Though they were tight, perhaps because her feet were a teeny bit swollen, she wore them anyway. She even remembered to toss her fox stole over the suit. And because her hair was absolutely impossible for some reason, she put on one of her marvelous old Halstons, the brown felt with the jaunty red feather and the smart, wide brim that dipped low over one side of her face. She had remembered to brush off the lint, hadn't she? She wasn't sure. Had she put any makeup on? She couldn't remember. Surely she must have.

The bottom line read she looked perfectly fine when she walked into Winslow's office and up to the window. Why did Reba gasp? Such rudeness, totally uncalled for.

Reba Davies, Doctor Winslow Hart's nurse, office manager and onetime red-hot lover, opened the little glass window, peered out, gave her that quick, shocked look. "Mrs. Linderman, are you all right?"

"Of course, I'm all right. Why? Is something wrong?"

"Oh, no, nothing. How nice to see you again. You did know Doctor's out of town?"

That surprised her. Winslow was always here. Except for emergencies, never in twenty-five years had he not been here. "Out of town?"

Reba raised a finger in a "just a minute" signal, closed the glass window, and opened the waiting room door. Back in the day, before she gained at least fifty pounds, she always looked darling in her white cap and crisp white uniform, the gold "R.N." pin perfectly aligned on her collar. Nurses didn't do that anymore and neither did Reba. Now she wore slacks and a tent-like top that looked like it came from Target and couldn't begin to hide those rolls of flab. "Doctor's gone to Palm Springs." Her low modulated tone indicated a special confidence, granted only because Connie was a doctor's wife and not just anyone. "But come in. His new partner is here."

Stepping inside, Connie remembered the Reba Davies she used to know—slender, full bosomed, red-haired, sassy, and madly in love with Doctor. From what Harvey said, their affair lasted for several years, but of course led nowhere because Doctor was married to the daughter of one of Santa Marta's leading families and most certainly would remain so.

What Reba never knew was that Doctor Winslow Hart bragged about his conquests to his locker room buddies at the Santa Marta Town and Country Club, who in turn brought the lurid details straight home to their wives. The entire medical community knew that Reba Davies would, in an instant, hike up her white starched skirt and get boffed between patients on the infamous black leather couch in Doctor's office. Not only that, Miss Starched Efficiency would go down for a quickie whenever he asked. Well, it really wasn't all that funny. To this day the poor woman probably didn't realize what a great and fickle swordsman Doctor was. Now, looking at the stout, middle-aged woman in front of her, so prim and dignified in her Landau Comforts with the rubber soles and her rimless glasses, Connie could hardly imagine a wild, wanton Reba flinging her panties to the floor, climbing onto the fine leather couch, riding with mounting passion astride Doctor's…

"Let's get you weighed, dear."

Connie climbed on the scale. When had it ended? Probably when Reba's jowls started to sag and when the little roll of fat collected on her upper hips and when underneath-her-eyes got baggy.

"Hmm. Ninety-two pounds. Shame on you, Mrs. Linderman. You've been losing weight, and you're tiny enough already."

Connie faked a concerned expression and climbed off the scale. *Men.* They liked their women young. Winslow was messing around with a twenty-two-year-old blonde now. Well, wasn't that typical? Poor Reba spent the best years of her life waiting, fool that she was, for Doctor. Now she was unmarried, alone, and likely to remain so. "I didn't know Winslow had a new partner."

"Oh, yes, Dr. Tessler. Now, look, if you want to reschedule, it's okay."

"No, that's all right." There were a couple of things she had wanted to mention to Winslow. They could wait, but not the Valium. "What's he like?"

"Dr. Tessler?" Reba rolled her eyes. "Wait 'til you see him."

What could it be? Had Winslow…? Oh, no, not that. "Is he…" Connie lowered her voice to a discreet whisper

"...black?"

Reba burst into a merry peal of laughter. "Black? Oh, that's funny." She put a hand over her mouth to stifle herself. "Come on, let's get you in the examining room. Just wait. You've got to see for yourself." She led the way down the hall and into the room. "He'll be right in." She rolled her eyes again and left.

In the white blandness of the tiny room, Connie sat down to wait, annoyed with herself for having asked such a stupid question. Had she thought, she'd have realized Dr. Winslow Hart would slow broil in hell rather than be an equal opportunity employer. Law or no law, he'd get around it some way. She glanced around. No magazines. Doctor was as cheap as ever. She reached into her purse for her cigarettes and lit one, not easy the way her hands were shaking. She'd have to hide them when Doctor...what's-his-face came in. She inhaled deeply, exhaled, blowing her smoke towards the small THANK YOU FOR NOT SMOKING sign on the wall. Winslow hung it there a couple of years ago, pressured by all the antismoking nuts. But the rule certainly did not apply to the wife of one of his most esteemed colleagues. She waited, puffing impatiently on her cigarette. She crossed her legs, extending her top leg, rotating her foot until she remembered the runner, saw it had spread and practically her whole leg was laddered. She recrossed her legs, extending the other. Oh, no, another runner! *Well, poo. Who cares what I look like? Just give me my prescription and let me out of here. Where is this character anyway?*

The door opened. There he stood, big smile on his face, her folder in his hand. "Hi, Mrs. Linderman. I'm Doctor Tessler."

This was a doctor? He was incredibly young, dewy fresh young, the kind of firm jawed, clear-eyed, rosy-cheeked young that disappears forever before you even hit thirty. He was good-looking, too, well-built and slender, blond hair clipped short on the sides and, for God's sake, spiked on top. No white coat, just Dockers and a gray knit shirt. No stethoscope. And on his feet, sandals. Incredible. What was Winslow thinking of?

He sniffed. His smile faded. He frowned. "Put it out."

She gazed up at him, her eyelids fluttering. "I beg your pardon?"

"The cigarette, put it out. Here, I'll take it." He stepped briskly into the room and plucked the cigarette out of her upraised fingers. Holding it at arm's length, he spun quickly around to the tiny sink, doused it with a splash of water and dropped it in the trashcan. "There." He rubbed his hands in a "good riddance" gesture, raised his eyes to the sign. "No smoking means no smoking, Mrs. Linderman." With a graceful, easy swing he perched himself on the edge of the examining table in the center of the room, crossed his arms, and looked down at her. The smile returned. "Now, what can I do for you?"

For a brief moment she sat stunned. Winslow would certainly hear about this. "Well!" She started to register a further protest but changed her mind. *Just give me my Valium so I can get out of here.* She pulled herself up straight, tucked her laddered legs underneath her, and clasped her hands tightly in her lap. "I have simply come to get my Valium prescription renewed, Doctor...?"

"Tessler."

"Yes, well, the drugstore renews it five times, and then Winslow makes me come in. Why, I don't know. It's not necessary."

"Why do you need Valium, Mrs. Linderman?" He was flipping through the pages in her folder.

"Why? Depression. I'm depressed."

He remained silent, continuing to study her records.

"I've had a terrible tragedy in my life. I couldn't get through the day without Valium."

Inquisitive gray eyes peered at her over the top of the folder. "Tragedy?"

Young fool, what could he know of tragedy? She'd give him tragedy. "My little girl died when she was two in a terrible accident."

His face softened. "I'm sorry, how long ago did it happen?"

"Christie would be eighteen now." Was it really sixteen years ago? It seemed like yesterday.

He glanced through her records again. "I see Doctor Hart has diagnosed depression...and anxiety. He's gone through a lot of combinations, hasn't he? Tranquilizers, sedatives, antidepressants...had you on Librium and Nembutal for a while, and even…" he looked up, raising an eyebrow… "Dexedrine?"

"Yes. Well, the Librium was to calm me down during the day, and the Nembutal was to help me sleep at night, and then the Dexedrine was to get me going in the morning, after the Nembutal. But all that's before he put me on Valium."

His look was inscrutable. "Okay, I'll need to examine you."

"What?" She raised a hand from her lap in protest, saw it was shaking and quickly returned it. "I didn't come here to be examined. All I want is my Valium. Winslow never—"

"For one thing, you need a pap smear."

"Really? Oh, that can't be. I'm sure I had one not too long ago."

"According to your records it's been three years. Doctor Hart must have overlooked it."

"Well, even so...look, I really don't have time now. I've got loads of things to do today. I'll make another appointment, all right? Meanwhile, if you'll just give me my Valium?"

"No, Mrs. Linderman. You really do need to be examined." He hopped off the table. "I'll send Reba in." He was gone before she had a chance to reply.

The examination was complete. Why had he poked and prodded her so thoroughly? At least now he looked more like a doctor, had his white coat on when he came back in and carried a stethoscope like he was supposed to. This time their positions were reversed, he in the chair and she sitting on the edge of the table in a paper gown, clutching a paper sheet around her, wishing she could run and hide. It wasn't that she was embarrassed by the examination. She'd had too many pelvics for that. It was all because of the hat. Getting undressed, she'd been in an agony of indecision. She pictured herself lying on the examining table in her white paper gown, feet in the stirrups, the Halston on her head. She would look ridiculous, but what if she took it off? Then her horrible hair would show and she'd forgotten her comb. That seemed the better of two miserable choices, though, so she took off her hat, ashamed he would see the uncombed mess. She didn't know why she should care what he thought, but somehow she did.

She also had to remove the panty hose, and that was a real calamity. How would she ever get them back on? The shaking was getting worse and her balance wasn't too hot either. So now here she sat, not at her best, still waiting for Young Doctor Smartass to give her the prescription. "Well, did I pass inspection?" She managed a gay, flirtatious smile. "Do I get my Valium now?"

He sat relaxed, ankles crossed, resting an arm on the tiny table next to the chair, idly dangling the stethoscope from his hand, looking at her in a strange, piercing way. "No, Mrs. Linderman, you do not."

"I beg your pardon?" She could hear her voice shake. "I came here for Valium. Winslow always—"

"Winslow's not here. You're dealing with me now, not your husband's golfing buddy, and I say no more Valium."

"And just why not, might I ask?"

He dipped his head. She could see him take a good deep breath. He looked back up, gazed squarely into her eyes. "Because pills and alcohol don't mix."

His words hit her so hard she flinched. Every fiber of her being quivered with indignation. Nobody had ever... "Are you inferring that I drink?" His reply was a silent nod. "Then you are mistaken, Doctor. Very, very much mistaken."

"No, I'm not. I'm not inferring, I'm telling you flat out you've got a drinking problem."

"And just how do you know that?"

"The examination and the way you look, for one thing. For another, you've got liquor on your breath and it's nine o'clock in the morning."

Vodka wasn't supposed to smell, dammit. "Well, Doctor Tessler, you are wrong. I will most certainly take this up with Winslow when he returns." She started to get off the table. "Since you won't give me any Valium, I'll get it someplace else."

He raised a restraining hand. "Don't go yet. Sit back and talk to me. Let's start back at square one, shall we?"

She sat back down. She hadn't really wanted to get off the table. It was hard to be highly indignant when you were wearing a flimsy paper gown tied with a piece of string. "Very well." She looked down her nose at him.

He hunched his shoulders forward and clasped his hands together. "Okay. Now tell me, do you ever take a drink?"

She tossed her head. "Of course I do. I'm not a teetotaler, for heaven's sake."

"Good. Now, how much do you drink?"

She crossed her legs, looked up at the ceiling, the top leg jerking up and down.

"How much?" he repeated.

"How should I know? A social drink now and then."

"One drink a week?"

"Maybe a teeny bit more."

"One drink a day?"

"Yes."

"Yes, one? Yes, more than one?"

Her leg jerked faster. "Well, sometimes more than one."

"Two? Three? More than three?"

Why was he hounding her? Well, she would show him. "How about a fifth?"

"A fifth of what?"

Her leg stopped its erratic bouncing. "A fifth of vodka, dammit! I drink a fifth of vodka every day."

He nodded his head as if confirming something to himself, sat back in his chair and let a few seconds pass by. "How long?"

"How long what?"

He sighed a patient sigh. "How long have you been drinking a fifth of vodka every day?"

"I was just kidding you."

"No you weren't."

Hell and damnation, she didn't have to tell him a thing. Silent moments passed. He settled in and crossed his arms, as if he was preparing for a long wait. Well, maybe she'd answer. Strange, all those years of drinking, and nobody else had ever asked. "It's been a while. Years, I guess. Ever since Christie, my little girl, died."

"So sixteen years maybe?"

"Something like that, I suppose."

"Do you know what you're doing to your body?"

"I haven't a clue and I don't want to know."

He stood up abruptly and looked down on her with an expression so stern she forgot how young he was. "I wish you could tour the alcoholic ward at Santa Marta General, Mrs. Linderman. A person in the advanced stages of alcoholism is not a pretty sight. We're talking irreversible impairment of the liver, congestive heart failure, nerve degeneration and brain damage. There's edema. Sometimes abdomens that are grossly, unbelievably swollen. There's gastritis, creatitis. And then there's the withdrawal syndromes—grand mal seizures—hallucinations—delirium tremens, the worst of all. That's when they see the rats, bats, snakes, and they scream a lot. They shake. They do a lot of shaking."

She absolutely did not want to hear this. She put up a hand. So it shook, so what? "Please stop. What has this to do with me?"

A pained expression crossed his face. "What I'm trying to get across to you is that you are seriously ill and you need medical attention. Mrs. Linderman, you are suffering from acute alcoholism."

The urgency in his voice was frightening, but what he was saying was just not true. "Look, you've got it wrong. So I drink a little, so I'll cut down, that's all. It's not a serious problem. I don't have to drink a fifth of vodka every day. I just do, that's all. I can stop any time I want." She tilted her nose in the air and glanced at him sideways, an impish look she used to use back when she was a gamin-faced flirt and everyone said how adorable she was.

He put his hands on his hips, rocked back on his heels, looked her up and down and pursed his lips. "I look at you and do you know what I see?"

"No, what?" She braced herself.

"I see a woman who looks fifty-five, maybe sixty, only her chart says she's forty-five. She's got a lot of class, well educated, married to a doctor, but her clothes are a mess, her breath smells of booze—vodka probably because she thinks nobody can tell. She's shaking badly, her blood pressure is sky-high, and her abdomen is swollen. She's here for Valium, which leads me to believe she's cross addicted—likes pills and booze."

How dare he? She opened her mouth to speak.

"No, let me finish. Now, I have just examined this lady, and what I found was not good. I suspect she has one hell of a thiamine deficiency, and not only that, she's showing symptoms of the Wernicke-Korsakoff Syndrome. That's a sensory disturbance. We see it a lot in chronic alcoholics. Starts in the feet. Have your feet been tingling lately? Numb maybe? There's loss of short-term memory, ocular problems, loss of balance—have you been losing your balance lately? The thing is, the destruction is irreversible."

"You can't be serious."

"What I'm telling you is that you need treatment, now. If you keep on the way you're going, you'll be dead in a year."

Thinking back on it now, she shuddered at the scene. Dead in a year? How outrageous and how very, very wrong. After he made the ridiculous suggestion that she go to the hospital to dry out, for heaven's sake, she told him in no uncertain terms to mind his own business. And proved him wrong, too. On her way home, she vowed to stop drinking and she had. Not one drop of alcohol had crossed her lips since Friday morning before she went to Winslow's office, but the problem was, now she wanted a drink more than ever, needed one more than ever because she had no Valium to help her over the worst of it.

If only Harvey would get here.

The front door opened. Harvey at last. She hated to face him but had no choice. She extinguished her cigarette in a butt-filled ashtray and hurried to the living room.

Carrying his briefcase, brimming with anger, Harvey Linderman slammed the front door shut and walked across the marble floor of the entry hall into the living room. Damn it all to hell, it wasn't only WEELA and that sonofabitch, Travis Kerrigan. It wasn't even the unexpected delay with the NIH funds. What really galled him was the employment agency telling him to take his business elsewhere.

"So sorry, Doctor Linderman, but we can't keep sending you maids. They never stay because..."

He ought to divorce her. She was no longer any use to him anymore, like last week at the banquet in San Francisco when every member except him had a lovely, gracious wife by his side. Free as he was, there were certain events he couldn't bring Gretchen to, such as the uptight WMRA's banquet. *Damn Connie.*

"Harvey?"

He turned and saw her standing in the arched doorway of the living room in her disgusting rag of a negligee, hugging herself, looking like a sick fish, all bent and gasping.

"Harvey, I need some Valium."

"Well, if it isn't my lovely wife." He spit out "wife" like something bad tasting. "And my, my, I do believe sober. Has Bacardi's gone bankrupt? Is there a shortage of vodka? Tell me, what's the occasion?"

Connie hated it when he got sarcastic, like he was doing now. Any other time she'd match his nastiness with some of her own, but today she'd stay nice if it killed her. "Winslow's out of town. When I went to his office, this new doctor wouldn't give me any Valium. Will you write me a prescription, please? I've never asked before."

"Winslow is your doctor, not I."

"What does that matter? You could write it if you wanted to." Uh-oh, she was getting light-headed. She'd better sit down before she fell down. She collapsed into the nearest easy chair.

He came towards her with an angry stride, flinging his briefcase onto the couch, twisting his lips in a snarl. His nostrils quivered as he looked down at her. "You're asking me for favors? Do you know what you've done?"

"What have I done? Please do fill me in." She reached for a cigarette and lighter on the coffee table, put the cigarette in her mouth and snapped the lighter. Hell and damnation, her hand shook so badly she couldn't get the flame anywhere near the end of the cigarette. She threw the cigarette and lighter back on the table.

He bent closer, hunching his shoulders. "Fill you in? Oh, I'd be glad to fill you in. The employment agency has kicked us out. No more maids for us. It appears you've wet your bed one too many times."

She shriveled a little, just looking at the sneering expression on his face. Was this the man she married? Had they ever run laughing down the beach together, barefoot, hand-in-hand? Had he ever called her his adorable little bird when he swept her into his arms? Had they ever made love by the hour and sworn they would never part? But no, it never happened, couldn't possibly have happened. How could they ever have been young and in love? "My, my, we're a tad upset, aren't we?" She had to have a cigarette. She tried again, managing to light one this time on the third attempt.

He waited until the cigarette was lit, rolled his eyes in frustration at the ceiling, walked a few paces away and at the first curl of smoke, stormed back. "What did I do to deserve you? For what dark deed am I being punished? How did I get on God's shit list?"

"If you'll just get me some Valium, please, Harvey." She was begging. She hated that.

"No. And what the fuck are you doing sober?"

"I—"

"We can't have that." He stalked to the wet bar in the family room. She listened to the familiar noises. The solid slam of the pitcher on the counter—the pleasant clatter of the ice cubes—the oh-so-gratifying glug-glug as he poured the vodka and vermouth—the melodious clink clinking as he stirred. When he returned, he set the martini glass on the coffee table directly in front of her. Filled to the brim, it had a bit of froth on top. He had even added a green olive, spiked on a bright red toothpick.

"Drink enough of these, my dear, and you won't need any pills." He left the room.

She sat regarding the glass for a while before finally she picked it up and took the first sip. Ah, so good, so very, very good. As it went down, she thought about young Doctor What's-his-face and what he had said. Forty-five but looked sixty? Dead in a year? Good. No great loss. What use was she to anyone? Who needed her? The world would be better off without her. Dead in a year? She held her glass high. *I'll drink to that.*

Chapter 4

Denver, Colorado,
Pine Mountain Condominiums

Lying beside Tom on her king-size bed, Jillian wished she'd been more in the mood this evening, but she wasn't, and hadn't enjoyed their lovemaking at all.

"Was it good for you, darling?" Tom's face was flushed and covered with sweat.

A sharp "Arf, arf!" from the corner saved her from answering.

"Lucky, it's okay." She turned to Tom. "He must think you were trying to kill me."

"That's all I need, a fifty-pound black Lab taking a bite out of my ass."

"He won't. He likes you."

"Like hell he does."

Tom was right. Karlin's dog had never once been friendly with Tom. Jealousy, she supposed. What else could it be?

He asked, "Heard from Karlin?"

"Not since I drove her to the airport. Was she ever excited. Park City, the Nationals! She's certain her team's going to win."

"I still don't understand why she gave up on the World Cup."

"She hated to. This competition she's in now is small-time in comparison. But that World Cup Circuit is a killer. It takes nine months out of every year. When she decided to study medicine, she knew she couldn't do both."

"Life's full of tough choices."

"You're right, especially considering she could have made the U.S. Olympic team."

Tom raised a quizzical eyebrow. "No kidding? I never realized...she's that good?"

"Sure, even though she's small compared to most of those women. Some have thighs like fire hydrants. Karlin would have done it, though."

"She had a chance for the Olympics and didn't take it? That's crazy."

"No it's not. She wants to be a doctor, and that's for a lifetime. Winning an Olympic medal is fine at the time, but twenty years later, who remembers your name?"

Tom's head rolled back and forth in disagreement. "But the fame...the glory...the money. Look at Lindsay Vonn, Michelle Kwan. They've made fortunes off their medals. To hell with medical school, I'd go for the gold."

She gave him a jab. "You would, you materialistic bastard."

Laughing, Tom turned towards her, and tugged a lock of her hair. "Look who's talking. The greatest pleasure-seeker of them all. And because you are..." he paused for dramatic effect. "How would you like to take the honeymoon to end all honeymoons?"

"Like what?"

"How about a month in the Caribbean in our own rented yacht? Imagine sailing around the Bahamas, diving when we please, where we please. We might even find some sunken treasure, eh? All those Spanish galleons out there, yet to be discovered? The deep-sea fishing will be fantastic."

She burst into delighted laughter. "Stop, that sounds so good I can't stand it. Are you serious?"

"I've already talked to my travel agent. A month ought to do it. You can get the time off, can't you? In fact, why don't you just quit?"

Quit her job. That was something she didn't want to deal with yet. "I've got vacation time coming out my ears." Something cold and wet touched her arm. "Look who's here." Lucky stood, tail wagging, by the side of the bed, his nose laid on the pillow, eyes begging for attention. She fingered the tags hanging from his red leather collar, stroked his long muzzle. Such a handsome dog, all shiny black except for the white star on his forehead and the white tips on three of his small paws. Ridiculous looking, Tom called them. Labradors were supposed to have big paws, not dainty like Lucky's. Somewhere among his ancestors there lurked a terrier.

Tom rolled out of bed. "Come take a shower with me. Hate to disappoint you but I'm leaving. I want to get home before the roads get too bad."

"Okay." For some reason, she wasn't disappointed at all.

After her shower, she walked into her huge, flower-scented, mirror-lined closet to grab a robe, and paused, as she often did, to admire her beautiful clothes. Hanging neatly on padded hangers were her skirted business suits, Armani's mostly, and a few Albert Nipon's and Tahari's. Long, open shelves held rows of fine leather boots and shoes. Clear plastic covered her cocktail dresses—the burgundy velvet Eileen West, the slinky silver Helene St. Marie.

Her special pride hung on its extra heavy hanger—the full-length ranch mink coat Tom had given her. She stroked the fur, admiring its deep, rich sheen. Funny, she'd never even dreamed of owning a fur, but now that she owned a mink, she loved it.

"I'm leaving!" Tom's voice sounded from downstairs. "Don't forget my housewarming party next Saturday, and we're going out with clients tomorrow night. Be sure to wear your mink."

"I won't forget. Goodnight, darling." She heard the front door close. She was alone and that was fine. She never minded alone time in her beautiful condo. She could have bought closer into the city, but when she saw these luxury townhomes nestling on a heavily wooded hillside off I-70, she couldn't resist, despite the longer commute. She slipped into a comfortable flannel nightgown and fleecy robe, called for the dog to follow and headed for the kitchen, Lucky close behind. *A month in the Caribbean on our own private yacht. Life is wonderful.* She bounced down the carpeted staircase, looking forward to fixing a snack and settling in for the rest of the evening with a good book, or maybe she'd do some planning for the wedding. What color would the bridesmaids' dresses be? She still hadn't decided.

That meant another fun trip to Mrs. Mayo's Wedding World. She'd always been a bridesmaid, never the bride. Now it was her turn to choose the engraved invitations, the thing on the top of the wedding cake, the little cocktail napkins with *Tom & Jillian* and their wedding date printed in gold.

As she entered the kitchen, the telephone rang and she saw it was Karlin. "Hi there, Sis, how's Park City? How's the snow?"

She noticed a slight pause before her sister answered, "The snow's fine. Couldn't be better."

"Is everything okay?"

"Sure. Everything's fine, only I have this little problem."

She tightened her grip on the phone. "What is it?"

"It's this dumb leg of mine, the one that's been bothering me lately? Well, I fell again, and this time it's hurting real bad."

"Then you'd better not ski."

The words came out bravely. "I'm not."

"Oh, Karlin—"

"That's the breaks. There's always next year."

"Are you coming home?"

"Heck no. I'll stay 'til Sunday. I can cheer them on anyway. I'll be home Sunday night, and you can pick me up like we planned. The doctor here thinks I should see my own doctor as soon as possible. Could you come with me? I'll make an appointment with Dr. Collins as soon as I can."

"Of course. We'll make sure you get in right away."

"Good. See you Sunday, Sis. Don't worry, it's got to be just some little thing. I'm sure everything's fine."

Chapter 5

Union Square, San Francisco
Saturday afternoon

The white-haired lady in the full-length beaver coat glanced briefly at the leaflet. When she realized its message, she let it drop to the pavement like a red hot coal. "Shoes is killing, too!" She hurled her parting shot with an angry toss of her head and stalked away.

Terry Woodard stood amidst the crowd, dealing leaflets like cards from a deck. *Horrible woman.* The heat was making her cross. For San Francisco, this winter's day was surprisingly warm, so different from last week's demonstration in Santa Marta where she'd shivered from the cold in front of Linderman's. Her heavy, full-length rabbit suit didn't help. She wished she could rip off the floppy-eared head that was beginning to make her sweat. *I'll smell like a goat and Travis won't want to get near me.* She turned to Krista beside her who was wearing an old fur coat draped over a black body suit painted with luminous white bones. A grotesquely grinning skeleton mask hid her face. "Did you hear that lady in the beaver coat? Was she ever pissed."

"Definitely pissed." Krista continued to pass out the leaflets non-stop.

A short fox holding a STOP THE CRUELTY sign stood nearby. Sparrow's voice came from beneath the grinning head. "Guess we're not too popular with ladies wearing fur coats today."

"At least they're getting our message, whether they like it or not." Not for the first time that afternoon, Terry glanced towards the southeast corner steps of the square that led up to the raised central area. A shaggy brown bear with a long tail stood on the top step, directing WEELA's demonstration against fur coats. As she watched, the bear reached up and pulled off his head, revealing the hot, flushed face of Travis Kerrigan. "Hey, Travis, here's a new one—'Shoes is killing, too.'"

Travis set the bear head on the step beside him. "Another gem. Who said it?"

Terry bounded up the steps to his side and set her leaflets down. "If you can do it, so can I." She pulled off her rabbit head and dropped it to the side of the steps. "What a relief. I was about to melt." She shook out her long, brown hair and pulled at the neck of the costume to let cooler air inside. "Some old lady in a beaver coat said that. Boy, was she mad."

"No wonder. She comes downtown to shop, all dressed up in her fancy fur, and some Union Square kook hands her a leaflet asking how many murdered animals made her fur coat. No wonder she's mad. You ruined her day."

"Whose side are you on? Am I a kook?"

The corners of his mouth lifted, almost imperceptibly, into the sly little grin that always tugged at her heart. "Of course not. What could be more normal than hanging around Union Square in a rabbit suit?" His eyes swept over the crowd. "Look around you. We fit right in."

He had a point. Terry looked out over the Saturday after-noon hubbub of Union Square. Shoppers battling their way towards Macy's, Saks, the elegant shops of Maiden Lane—gawking tourists with their cameras—gays strolling hand-in-hand—purple-haired punkers. Across Geary in front of Macy's, a one-man band with "Jesus Is Coming" on his drum played gospel music. Next to him, an old man with a beard sold San Francisco 49ers baseball caps. A dozen feet away, a teenaged black boy tap-danced to a ghetto blaster on the curb. On nearly every corner, vendors sold bunches of bright flowers from colorful sidewalk stands.

The members of WEELA were scattered around the square. Terry was pleased with the best-yet turnout, fifty people at least, though it was hard to count exactly. Mrs. Bagley was here, such a nice old lady with her red tennis shoes and sweet smile. Terrible Bernadette was here. The sign she carried didn't conform to the theme of the day, but who had the nerve to tell her? Larry, the young veterinarian, was here. He never missed a demo. Sparrow. Krista and Josh from Berkeley—people from everywhere—caring about animals their common bond.

Travis interrupted her thoughts. "Getting back to your mad old lady, what she meant was—"

"Oh, I know what she meant. We all wear shoes. Shoes are made of leather. Leather comes from the animals we kill. That's dumb. I've got my tennies on. They're made of canvas, for Pete's sake." Terry scowled at the spot where the lady had disappeared. "Mean old bitch. She should know we don't wear leather shoes."

Travis slung a friendly paw around her shoulders. "Don't let them get to you. Do I have to remind you we can't change the world in a day?"

"No, but it's just frustrating when the ones with fur coats can't see why we're taking the time and trouble to be here. They think we're a bunch of crazies who ought to be locked up." She was acutely aware of his arm, feeling its light pressure right through the rabbit suit. To him it was only a friendly gesture. To her it was a lover's touch. It mattered not that this was Union Square, teeming with people. Tiny quivers of desire shot through her. *Travis, I love you.* She used to think her love was hopeless, but now she had a plan. It was going to work, and when it did, Travis would be hers forever. "Okay, I'll be patient. Someday, if we work hard enough, that mad old lady will see the light and throw her fur coat into the nearest dumpster."

"Right." Travis gave her an encouraging grin. "Then she'll join WEELA and lead a demonstration at Berkeley."

"And get tossed in the slammer and we won't bail her out."

Travis nodded a solemn agreement. "You're getting meaner every day. Don't be too hard on her. At least we made her think about it, didn't we?"

"That we did." Terry looked out over the square. "Do you think we should go around again?"

"Go for it. Be sure to hit Saks. Macy's, too. Give them a chant this time. Meanwhile...let's see, Channel Two has already been here, and Five. When Four shows up, I'll bring them over.

Some footage of us all parading in front of Bloomingdale's would be great, but be careful. I don't want anyone arrested this time."

"Stop worrying. I didn't mind riding in the paddy wagon. It was sort of fun. I was almost disappointed they didn't handcuff us." Terry paused for a moment and frowned. "Only, I didn't like being charged with obstructing the sidewalk. I mean, that was definitely not fair."

"Of course it wasn't fair. But what concerns me now is the fine. They dropped the charges last year, but this time I hear it's going to cost us one hundred dollars each. Not you, though."

"I'll pay my own fine. I knew what I was doing. You're not responsible, even if I do work for WEELA."

"But you do so much for us. You *are* WEELA. It's not right you should have to pay."

"No. It's almost like...it's hard to put into words, but like I'm proud to pay it. Like, it's an honor because I really believe in helping the animals. If I didn't pay my own fine, I'd be copping out, not putting my money where my mouth is, sort of. Does that make sense? It's time." She turned away, not wanting to hear any more discussion about paying fines. From her vantage point on the steps, she called in a ringing voice, "Come on everyone, let's go around again."

"Wait, Terry, 'til I get a new sign." Krista bent over a stack of posters placed against a wall and began thumbing through. "I don't like MAKE COMPASSION YOUR FASHION. It's too glib."

The fox strolled over. "Why do you want a sign? That crazy costume says it all."

"Sparrow, what's a demonstration without a sign?" Terry came down the steps and joined them, bending over the posters while the crowd milled around. She picked one out of the stack. "How about BOYCOTT THE FUR BUSINESS?"

Terrible Bernadette arrived. A dumpy woman in her forties, she was carrying a huge MEAT IS MURDER sign. "That's an awful sign, Terry." Her brows knit together in a ferocious scowl. "Shows no imagination whatsoever."

"Look who's talking. Your sign's wrong for this demonstration, Bernadette. MEAT IS MURDER belongs to next week. What does it have to do with furs?"

Bernadette sniffed. "I'll carry whatever sign I please."

Terry sighed to herself. Useless to argue with this pigheaded woman. She pulled out another poster and held it up. "Krista, how about HUMAN BEINGS ARE BEAUTIFUL CREATURES WITHOUT FURS?"

"Not enough pizzazz."

"Hmm…oh, here's a good one. FURS ARE WORN BY BEAUTIFUL ANIMALS AND UGLY PEOPLE."

"Perfect." Krista took the sign and held it high. "Let's go, one more time around, then I'd better get back to Berkeley and study. I'll stop at Ananda Fuara first, if anyone's interested."

"I'm game," said Sparrow. "I'm in the mood for a barbequed Tofu burger."

Terry shook her head with regret. "Sorry but I can't. I'm starting my diet today."

Krista reached up and whipped off her skeleton mask, revealing a skeptical expression. She pulled Terry aside so Sparrow couldn't hear. "Not another crash diet so you can win the love of Travis Kerrigan?"

"This time I am not going to fail."

Krista shook her head with friendly disgust. "Oh sure. You've worked for WEELA how long now? Two years? The man hasn't done more than shake your hand. When will you wise up?"

"I know he likes me a lot."

Bernadette had joined them, avidly following their conversation. "You'd better watch out, Terry. I've never seen Travis interested in any woman." She lowered her voice. "I've said it before and I'll say it again. The man is—"

"No, don't say it."

"*Gay*. I'll bet my bottom dollar on it."

"That's not so. Don't forget, he was married once."

"Doesn't mean a thing and you know it. That's probably why he got divorced so he could take up with some gay lover he keeps secret." She backed away, shaking a warning finger. "Mark my words."

Terry turned back to Krista. "Bernadette's crazy. Listen, here's my plan. Today I weigh one hundred forty-five pounds. By April 11th I will weigh one hundred twenty-five, the perfect weight for five-feet-four. That's right, one hundred twenty-five pounds. Don't look at me that way. All I have to do is starve for a month. For him, it's worth it. I know in my heart the only thing standing between Travis and me is these twenty pounds of flab. Bernadette will eat her words. She'll beg my forgiveness for calling him gay."

"You honestly think all you have to do is get thin?"

"I don't think it, I know it."

"In five weeks you're going to lose twenty pounds?"

"Gone by April 11th. That's the night of WEELA's annual banquet. Travis doesn't know it yet, but he's going to take me. I've got it all figured out."

Larry broke in. "Are we going or not?"

"Tell you the rest later, Krista. Better believe I mean it." Terry turned her attention back to the WEELA members in the crowd. "Okay you guys! Come on, Mrs. Bagley. Hey, Sparrow, hey Josh!" She picked up the BOYCOTT THE FUR BUSINESS sign and hoisted it high. "Let's get 'em. Here we go." She plunged into the crowd, a determined white bunny, followed by a ragged line of animal activists, some in animal costumes. "Once around, then on to Saks."

Brandishing signs, proffering leaflets, they circled the square, crossed Post Street to Saks Fifth Avenue. Once there, they paraded, signs held high, back and forth on the sidewalk in front of the store. Terry began the chant. "Don't torture animals, don't wear fur. Don't torture animals, don't wear fur..." Everyone joined in, repeating the phrase over and over, their voices resounding with fervor. Soon a small crowd of shoppers gathered.

Terry marched back and forth, chanting as loudly as she could. *It's going great.* She was working for a cause she believed in with all her heart. So what if not everyone agreed? That was okay too. In fact, it was kind of fun watching the different reactions of the crowd. Some people looked vaguely amused. Others had expressions that ran a gamut from mild curiosity to amazement. Some, mostly the younger people, dropped encouraging words as they watched or passed by.

"Good going!"

"Keep it up."

But there was the other side, too, older ladies, mostly, the ones with the minks and foxes and Persian lambs, who sneered and grew angry. "You eat meat don't you?" Well, she wouldn't bother to defend herself, even though for years she'd been a vegetarian. Too bad it didn't show. Travis was right about not condemning anyone. Only, if they just knew how inhumane trapping was. If they just knew how the animals suffered.

"Here comes Travis," Krista called. "He's got Channel four with him. Let's head for Bloomingdale's."

The voices had died away. "Come on, you guys!" Terry took up the chant with renewed vigor as they marched to Bloomingdale's. "Don't torture animals, don't wear fur. Don't torture animals, don't wear fur. Let's hit it now." Travis was watching her. She raised her sign higher, stood taller, pulled in her stomach, a useless thing to do in the baggy rabbit suit, but she did it anyway.

Krista, waving her sign, leaned towards her as she passed by. "Sure you don't want to go to Ananda Fuara?"

So tempting. She'd eaten no breakfast or lunch today. Just thinking about a vegetable omelet, or maybe a barbecued Tofu burger made her mouth water. She looked over at Travis, busy with Channel Four. How gallant he looked in his baggy old bear suit. He *was* gallant. He'd been a hotshot lawyer once, living in Mill Valley, making tons of money. Now he worked mostly for WEELA for free. She had no idea how much money he made, but she could tell from the casual clothes he wore and the Prius he drove that he didn't care about material things. All he wanted was to work for the animals, fight all the cruelty. She'd do anything to help him. If only she could read his mind! He was always polite and kind, remembered her birthday, gave her rides when her car broke down, but never let her get close. It was like he'd put up an invisible barrier she could never get through.

That was all going to change. Five weeks from now, the night of WEELA's banquet, she would know how much he cared because she was going to look gorgeous. Her face wouldn't be pudgy anymore. Her thighs wouldn't look like slabs of beef and she'd have a waistline. She'd wear a new dress, something slinky in a size twelve, or maybe ten. She'd tell him her Honda broke down again. He would take her to the banquet. Afterwards, when he brought her home, out of politeness she'd ask him up for a drink. Inside her apartment, she'd dim down the lights and pour them a glass of wine. No. Better, champagne. She'd splurge on something French sounding, like Moet or Chandon.

She'd switch on the stereo and put on Bruce Springsteen, who he didn't know she knew was one of his favorites. They would sit on the couch, not close. They'd sip champagne and listen to the music and talk, not about office stuff, no animals either, but maybe he would open up a little and talk about himself. She'd sit and listen, and he'd know from the riveted way she looked into his eyes how truly interested she was, not like those self-centered girls who only talked about themselves. She'd get up to pour them a second glass. This time, when she sat back down, she'd sit closer, just accidentally, and stretch her arm out on the back of the couch. Her dress would stretch tight across her boobs. He'd notice. They would talk some more. When they finished the champagne and set their glasses down, he'd be all relaxed and mellow and then next…

She wasn't sure except somehow he'd reach for her. She'd be in his arms. He'd kiss her a long, long time, start breathing hard, break off and whisper, desperately, *Terry, I want you.* Surprised and very cool she'd answer, *Why, Travis, I never knew you felt like this.* No, that wasn't honest. *Travis, do you know I want you so bad that sometimes my knees get weak and I have to go lie down? Do you know how many times I've driven across town in the middle of the night just so I could drive by your apartment?* (You, my darling, could not even imagine such insanity.) *Travis, will you please come in the bed-*

room and make love to me?

"Terry, are you coming?"

"Sorry, Krista, I'd better just go home and feed my cats. I don't dare get anywhere near a restaurant."

"I think you mean it this time. Good luck."

"Thanks." No Ananda Fuara for her. She'd stop at Safeway on the way home and load up on celery, lettuce, tomatoes and a box of frozen black bean Gardenburgers.

The Channel Four reporter was leaving. "When will we be on?" Travis asked.

"Look at the five o'clock news, maybe the eleven o'clock, though they'll probably pare it down by then."

"Good. Thanks." Travis turned to watch Terry lead the marchers around the square. What a wonder she was. A natural born leader—energetic, tireless, dynamic, the driving force behind the demonstration. What would WEELA (or he, for that matter) do without her? Did she think he didn't know she had a crush on him? The hell of it was that some day, maybe soon, he would have to hurt her, and that would pain him, as well as her. *But it won't work, Terry. I can never love you. Never.*

Denver, Colorado,
Pine Mountain Condominiums

Pressing a button on the dash, Jillian swung her Camaro into her snow-lined driveway. With well-practiced timing, she slowed while the garage door swung up, then pulled inside. Karlin sat beside her. "Uh-oh," she said, "listen to that."

Through the door that led from the garage to the kitchen, came an ecstatic "Arf! Arf!" Jillian shook her head in disbelief. "Lucky knows you're with me, Sis. How, I don't know, but I never get a greeting like that." She climbed from the car, walked to the door, and grasped the knob. "Get ready."

"Like a black bullet, Lucky raced towards Karlin as she got out of the car and with a joyous howl flung himself into her arms. He bounded away. Head down, he charged out the garage door and raced through the foot of snow in the yard, twice around in a big circle, fast as he could go, making a joyous howling sound. With a peal of laughter, Karlin followed him to the front and knelt in the snow. "Do you think he's glad to see me?" Lucky raced by, swung abruptly around, and threw himself at her again. Karlin wrapped her arms around him. "I missed you too, Lucky. Were you a good boy?"

Jillian joined her. "Of course, he was good. Not once did he pee on the carpet."

"Isn't he a super dog? I mean, he's really smart. Did you hear him try to talk? It makes me feel sad because he's really trying to say something and all that comes out are those awful noises." Karlin hugged Lucky again. "But that's okay, baby, I know what you're trying to say." She stood up and winced, reached down and touched her right knee. "Ouch! There it goes again." She shook her head. "I feel so bad. My team lost, all on account of me and this dumb leg of mine."

"Hey, don't you dare load yourself with guilt, Karlin Dahl. It wasn't your fault and nobody blames you. You'll be fine as soon as we get your leg checked out. I'm sure it'll be just some little thing Dr. Collins has a pill for."

Chapter 6

Denver, Colorado,
St. Francis Memorial Hospital

Jillian drove straight from work to the hospital. She caught herself frowning and paused at the door to Karlin's room. With an effort, she forced a smile to her lips and walked in. "This place is beginning to look like a birthday party." Her high heeled boots clicked smartly across the tile floor. Shrugging out of her coat, she looked around the room. "Balloons, flowers, cards and candy. You are so popular!"

Karlin was sitting up in bed, her bandaged knee propped on a pillow, looking more like fourteen than twenty with her pink polka dot bed jacket, hair tied back with a bright pink ribbon. Her cheeks were flushed with a rosy glow that looked healthy, but Jillian knew better. She was running a low-grade fever. "See what just came?" Karlin pointed towards the window. Jillian walked to the wide window ledge. Crowded in among the flowers and cards was the new arrival, a huge bouquet of pink and purple chrysanthemums. A silver Mylar balloon floated above it, decorated with curlicues of blue and yellow ribbon and fancy purple letters that read GET WELL SOON, TIGER. WE LOVE YOU, LAKEWOOD SKI CLUB.

Karlin lifted her hands, palms up, in protest. "I told those guys I was just here for tests, but wasn't that neat of them?"

"It sure was." Jillian sank into a chair at the foot of the bed. She'd been running back and forth between work and the hospital since Monday, the day Dr. Collins had literally taken one look at the leg and popped Karlin right into St. Francis. Since then, a white coated medical army had taken over Karlin's life. Pathologists—radiologists—orthopedic surgeons—Dr. Collins, of course, and a man with a cynical twist to his mouth who was some kind of doctor—they had all barraged her poor sister with X-rays, blood tests, urine tests, a CT scan and God knew what else. As yet nobody was saying anything. When she asked questions, they all, Dr. Collins included, shook their heads and went "Hmm."

"What's new since lunch?" Jillian did her best to sound cheerful.

"Guess what? I got another test."

"Wonderful. Just what you needed."

"This one was called a scintigram. They injected some kind of radioactive stuff into my vein and scanned me with a special camera." Karlin regarded her bandaged knee. "I'm sure getting tired of this. Why all the tests? Why did they have to do that biopsy?"

Biopsy. The word chilled Jillian's heart every time she heard it. Didn't Karlin realize? If she did, she hadn't said. "Well, it shouldn't be much longer." What a stupid cliché. She was full of them tonight, too, tired, too distressed, to think of anything original.

"It had better not be much longer. I've got to get back to school." Karlin's lower lip protruded in a rare pout. "It's just not fair."

"Life is not fair." Jillian leaned down to remove her boots. Still another dumb cliché. It was the kind of thing she had a problem tolerating in others, and here she was doing it herself. She grasped the tab of her boot zipper and began to tug. "Did Dennis bring your homework?"

"He was here earlier. He went around to each of my teachers and got my assignments. Maybe I won't fall too far behind."

The door swung open and Doctor Collins walked briskly into the room. In his early fifties, he looked gray-haired and dignified in his white jacket. He nodded to Jillian, walked to the bed and took Karlin's hand in both of his. "How's Karlin this evening?"

Karlin looked up at him with an impish smile. "Don't you know?"

The doctor chuckled and replaced Karlin's hand gently on

the cover. "Not yet, but we're working on it. Have patience." In another second he was out the door.

Jillian had observed his whirlwind visits each evening. He wasn't going to get away so easily this time. She rose from her chair to follow him. "I'll be right back."

Karlin's face clouded with suspicion. "If this were a movie, this would be the scene where the sister traps the doctor in the hallway and finds out what's really wrong."

"Don't be silly. I want to ask a couple of questions, that's all. He was in and out of here so fast I didn't have the chance. Be right back."

"Don't hurry. I'm not going anywhere."

"Smartass." Jillian stepped into the hallway and caught up with Doctor Collins. "Can't you tell me anything, Doctor? All these tests...you must know something by now."

"I do. Let's go to the waiting room at the end of the hall."

With a resigned sigh, Dr. Collins hunched forward and clasped his hands between his knees. "We were going to tell you tomorrow, but..." he sadly shook his head "...it doesn't look good, Jillian. It's cancer..."

Oh, no, no, no. She stared at the doctor. He was still talking and she wasn't hearing a word he'd said. She must concentrate.

"...it's in her leg, of course. We'll have the final test results tomorrow, but I can tell you now..."

Cancer. It couldn't be true, not Karlin.

"...and the cure rate gets higher every day. Teddy Kennedy, Senator Kennedy's son, had much the same thing and he licked it..."

Teddy Kennedy. A vision flashed through her mind of a young boy skiing down a hill on one leg. "But didn't they..." she could hardly choke the word out "...amputate?"

"Yes, but you must keep in mind that he's alive today and cancer free."

"But what about Karlin?"

"We'll know tomorrow for sure. There's no use telling her before we have to, and we may not have to. You see, her condition is complex. The size and location of the tumor, its involvement with major blood vessels and nerves, the presence of infection, other things. Lately, they've had some success with limb sparing surgery."

She grasped the idea as eagerly as she would a life preserver if she'd been drowning. "Limb sparing?"

Dr. Collins nodded warily. "Yes, sometimes, *sometimes*, mind you, the surgeon can replace the diseased bone with a metal one. Or, in some cases, he can use bone from some other part of the body."

"And you can do this with Karlin?" She blurted the words, waited in an agony of suspense.

It seemed an eternity before the doctor finally answered. He spoke slowly, as if he was weighing each word carefully. "We'll know tomorrow. The doctors will have all the test results and then they'll decide what's to be done. If it makes you feel any better, Karlin's got a highly trained team of specialists working for her. That's why I put her in this hospital. They've got the best there is, right here at St. Francis." He sat back in his chair, looking concerned, yet relieved he'd finished the dreadful business of breaking the news. "Any questions?"

Jillian shook her head. How could she ask questions when she was still too stunned to think?

Dr. Collins stood up and pressed her shoulder with a comforting hand. "Try not to worry, and don't let on to Karlin, not yet. There's still a chance she might not lose her leg."

"What'd he say?" Karlin asked as Jillian walked back into the room.

"He said the test results will be in tomorrow."

"That's all?"

"Guess we'll just have to wait and see." Jillian heard her voice begin to waver. Karlin mustn't see her cry. She walked to the window and peered out, turning her face away from her sister.

"I wish Mom and Dad were here. I sure miss them."

"Me, too." The old, familiar gorge of anger rose in Jillian's throat when she thought of the drunk driver who killed her parents and himself, too. Why did they have to die? They should be here, now, when she needed them. *I want my mother.* Despite the grim moment, she laughed at herself for such a childish wish. And yet, how could she handle this alone? Aside from losing her parents, nothing like this had ever happened to her. No family to help either, other than a cousin or two up in Fort Collins, and they weren't close. She had no one to turn to except Tom, of course, but he was out of town right now, in Dallas. Still, she had Tish and all the rest of her friends, and Karlin's friends, and Dennis.

She stared out the big glass window. Darkness had fallen. In the distance, she could see a steady stream of car lights flashing along the Sixth Avenue Freeway. They weren't going very fast. She checked a street light. Sure enough, white flakes swirled in the bright halo. Oh, great. Snow was just what she needed to make the day complete. It would be hell getting home, one of the prices you paid for living in the foothills of the Rockies.

Tomorrow...oh, no, she'd think about it later. No way could she break down in front of Karlin. She made sure the tears that had nearly surfaced were under control before she turned back to her sister. "What do you know, it's snowing. Guess I'd better get home and feed Lucky."

When Jillian walked into her condo, Lucky was barking, his tail wagging with joy. With a sigh, Jillian pulled off her gloves and slung her purse on the table. For the first time since she'd bought the condo she hated going home. Usually on the nights she knew she'd be alone, she looked forward to popping a Lean Cuisine into the microwave, changing out of her work clothes into a cuddly robe, sitting down to her Oriental Chicken, or whatever, along with a little salad and a diet cola. Then she'd read or watch TV. Tonight was different. After a day like this, she didn't want to be alone. At least Lucky, with his wagging tail and joyous barks, was making it easier. Funny how a dog could raise your spirits. She would change her clothes and call Tish. Maybe Tom would call from Dallas.

"Old boy, I bet you're hungry. I know you want to go outside." She walked through the living room to the rear patio door and opened it. Lucky raced outside, bounding through the drifts. He really did have to go and she should have remembered, first thing. With a pang of guilt she slid the door shut and watched through the glass as he lifted his leg again a tree, sinking clear to his stomach in the deep snow.

The phone rang. The ID screen said it was Trish. Good. A friend was what she needed right now. "Hi, Tish, it's so good to hear your voice."

"Jillian, what is it?"

"It's Karlin..."

She was on the phone for at least five minutes before she remembered Lucky. "Listen, Tish, let me call you back. I'm still in my coat and boots and I've got to get the dog back in. I forgot all about him. He's probably half frozen by now."

She slid open the patio door. "Lucky? Lucky?" No big black dog bounded back into the house. She switched on the patio light and stepped outside, her feet sinking into the deepening snow. Her gaze swept over the entire back yard. Oh, no. Lucky was gone. She should have remembered that when it snows two feet, a six-foot fence becomes a four-foot fence. She floundered through the snow to the back gate, tried to shove it open, but the snow on the other side was too deep and it wouldn't budge. Damn! She turned and ran back through the house, grabbed a flashlight from the kitchen drawer, ran through the front door and around. The wind lashed her face as she aimed the light downward and searched for Lucky's footprints. Already they were covered by the fast falling snow. "Lucky?" Her voice seemed lost in the wind. "Lucky?"

She stood in the bitter cold night, the wild wind cutting through her coat, already chilling her to the bone. Snowflakes knifed her eyes. Hopeless. No way could she go looking for the dog in this blizzard. How long could Lucky last on a terrible night like this?

Oh, God, I've lost Karlin's dog.

Chapter 7

I-70, near Denver

"Breaker, breaker, all you I-70 cowboys. Anybody wants to have a real good time, kick it back to Colorado Cutie."

"Yeah, baby!" Vernon Jerome Huffman, wearing his lucky ten-gallon Stetson, yelled as he guided his thirteen gear Peterbuilt west from Denver, bound for California through the storm. He reached for the microphone on his Cobra 29LXBT. "Get ready for ol' Huff, sweetheart, 'cause tonight you're gonna get it like you never got it before. You'll beg for more. You'll be so grateful, you'll pay me. So how about that, Colorado Cutie?"

He replaced the mike. *Sure, Huff, you're brave as hell when the talk button's not down.* A warm swell of excitement hit the pit of his stomach. He remembered Colorado Cutie from the summer before. Saw her at the Mid-America Truck Stop one day when he was working beneath his tilted up cab and she'd come sashaying down the line. Lots of hookers were around that day, but he remembered her best—the slender one with the shiny blonde hair that bounced on her back when she walked. She wore a red halter top, white pleated miniskirt and boots with swinging tassels. Looked more like a cheerleader than a hooker. What stuck in his mind was when she'd dropped her little purse on the ground. When she bent to pick it up, he caught a glimpse of tanned thighs smooth as the inside of a dog's ear, and white, high cut panties that only half covered her tight little ass. When she got to him, he'd smelled her sweet perfume as he rose up, wrench in hand, and looked down at her. "Hi, little lady."

She put a hand on her thrust-out hip and tilted her head so she could see to the top of his six-feet-two inches. "How're ya doing, handsome?"

Handsome? What a laugh. Tom Cruise he was not. He weighed forty, maybe fifty pounds too much, mostly in the big gut that hung over his tooled leather belt. Not only was he bald-ing on top, but what hair he had left was mostly gray. He was proud of his full, salt-and-pepper beard (it disguised his chip-munk cheeks), but some things couldn't be hid, like his broad pug nose and the lines around his eyes, deep etched by twenty-five years of trucking. Fact was, with his scuffed boots, faded jeans and old plaid shirt, he looked like just about every other trucker on the road, and that sure didn't make him handsome.

"Fine," he'd said in reply to her greeting. He couldn't think what else to say.

"Want to have some fun?" She flashed her dimpled, fake smile.

She sure didn't pussyfoot around, but he guessed time was money to her, too. Now he knew what to say. "No, ma'am," he replied, courteous but firm. For good measure, he reached with his left hand and touched the brim of his Stetson, letting the wide gold band on his finger show, real plain.

She was no fool. She gave him a sassy little tilt of her head, and a "have a nice day" and went on her way to the next truck in line.

What if he'd said yes? What if she'd climbed into his cab on that summer afternoon? What if they'd ducked back into the bunk bed and she'd slipped those little white panties down her thighs? Well, shoot! *Change the subject, ol' buddy.* He had more important things to think about on a night like this. He hunched his broad shoulders forward, peering intently through the windshield at the flakes that swirled, with ever-increasing thickness, in the headlights' beam. The muscles in the back of his neck began to tighten. His hands gripped harder on the wheel. It was getting so bad they might close I-70 up ahead and then he'd never get his reefer to Sacramento on time. He knew when he started this trip would be a killer. He'd made this haul many a time—oranges from Fresno to Denver, backload of meat. He'd always had a co-driver but this time was going it alone, driving straight through, one thousand miles in eighteen hours without any sleep. He had no choice after last month's disaster. Just thinking about it made him shake his head with disgust. Fuel—$4,500. Co-driver and road expenses—$1,500. Two new tires—$600. Christ on a bicycle! He'd grossed over $160,000 last year but paid over seventy thousand just for diesel fuel. Where would it end? When you were an independent, you took your chances. You had to be tough. There was no such thing as an eight-hour day with weekends and holidays off. There was no such thing as a guaranteed profit, either, when you got to the end of the line. But no sense worrying. *Lord, just let me get over the passes.* The rest, somehow, he would handle.

The CB came alive again with a voice that was fast and squeaky. "Hi Guys, this is Eager Beaver callin' from Mid-America. Which of you kings of the road out there is looking for a little action?"

Huff grinned. Again, the microphone button remained untouched as his booming voice filled the cab. "Sorry, Eager Beaver, Colorado Cutie gets me first. But if you don't mind standing in line, I'll be pleased to do you second."

Eager Beaver, what a name. He remembered her, too—a skinny brunette in tight jeans with tiny, fried-egg-sized boobs in a hot pink top. No bra. You could see her nipples poking through. *Enough.* He snapped his head to clear his thoughts. Why were the hookers getting through to him tonight? In all his years of trucking, he never used a prostitute or did drugs except for stay-awake pills and they didn't count. Lord knows, he could have. Nowadays, there were truck stops where you could add sex and drugs to your bill, charge them to "fuel and repairs" right along with the diesel. But he never had, and by golly, he never would. That's what he'd always said. That's what he always just knew.

Yes I would. Now where did that come from? Do it with a prostitute? Not this kid. Not the Vernon Huffman raised in Amarillo Texas, where his Baptist folks made sure he never missed church on Sunday, where drinking, dancing, gambling were sins, and sex was such a sin you never discussed it. Not the Vernon Huffman who was scared shitless of getting Herpes, or worse, far worse, AIDS.

Do it with a prostitute? *Yeah. I'm going to do it.*

When Colorado Cutie called again, he would talk to her for real. If she didn't call, he'd take Eager Beaver, or Peaches, or Peppermint Patty, or Baby Doll, or Butterfly, whichever one of those Mid-America hookers called first. Oh yeah, he was gonna get his ashes hauled tonight. It was like he had no choice, like his brain told him no but his tallywacker said yes.

A mile up the road, he wondered, was he crazy? He'd end up with herpes for sure. And worse. Even if he used a condom, with his luck it would break. He would catch AIDS and be dead in a year. He would die alone. No one would come to his funeral, not even Mom. They'd just put him in a wooden box and drop it in a hole. That settled it. Throughout five years of marriage, he'd never been unfaithful, so why start now? Debbie had nothing to worry about.

He let a few miles go by, concentrating on his driving, before he asked himself, *but would she care?* Lately, something was wrong. The last few times he was home, she'd been cool and distant. He wasn't getting any, that was for sure. Last time, it was her period. Before that, she had a cold. Before that, it was her period again. Always an excuse.

It wasn't like he didn't treat her good. Shoot, she didn't have to work; he gave her a big allowance. And when did he ever forget to bring her a present when he got off a trip? Something nice, like a box of See's Candy, or a bottle of Opium Perfume, or a black lace see-through nightgown like he'd brought last time. So what was wrong? He had no excuse. His friends had warned him when he married her.

"She's too young for you, man. Twenty years difference? You nuts?"

"Face it, bro, she's not the sharpest tool in the shed."

"She's shallow, man, shallow."

"Old buddy, you're gonna be sorry."

Of course he didn't listen. He married Debbie anyway, and with good reason. She might be young, she might be dumb, she might be shallow, but she was dynamite in bed. Besides that, he loved her.

The Peterbilt slithered and started to slip. Black ice. He

applied the air brakes gently...gently...until finally he regained control. Man-oh-man, he'd better pay attention, concentrate on the road ahead and how he'd get eighty-four thousand pounds of truck over the Rocky Mountains while driving through a fine, rip-roaring, Colorado snowstorm.

He was heading up the grade to Idaho Springs, going thirty-five now because of the snow. Pretty soon he'd pass the old mining town of Georgetown and, higher, Silver Plume. Beyond there, the grade turned into a mean 7.5%, and he'd have to slow down, maybe stop if the Colorado State Police were checking for chains or snow tires. When he reached the top, he'd be eleven thousand feet above sea level. That would be the worse spot, right before the Eisenhower Tunnel, where the plows would be losing the battle to keep the snow from piling up, where a bunch of white knuckled drivers would be slipping and sliding and creeping along. Guys in their trucks, like him, would be worrying about staying on schedule. Guys with loaded ski racks atop their cars would be just real concerned they might not get to their fancy condos at Aspen, or Vail, or Keystone in time for the hot tubbing and champagne.

It was going to be a long, long night. He'd have to fake the logbook again, or get another one—carry two sets of logs like a lot of truckers did. He was not going to stop at Mid-America. Wouldn't even think of stopping at Mid-America. *Just haul your ass to Sacramento, and then home to Fresno, to Debbie, and she better not have any excuses this time.*

Only somehow, he knew she would. What would it be? Another cold? A headache? Not her period, she knew he could count. Would she even be there when he got home or out with her wacky mother at the bingo parlor?

"Breaker, breaker! Colorado Cutie's still looking for a party here, guys. Why don't ya come in outa that storm?"

Those little white panties...

Like he was outside his own body, he watched his hand as it reached for the mike and his thumb as it depressed the button on the side so he could talk for real. His mouth dried and his pulse raced as he cleared his throat and took a deep breath.

"Colorado Cutie! This here's the Fresno Flash calling you. Do you read me?"

"Hi there, Fresno Flash."

"I'll be at Mid-America in ten minutes."

"Whatcha driving?"

"A Peterbilt twinstack. Trailer's white, no markings. Tractor's blue with a black pinstripe."

"I'll find you. Flash your lights when you get here, okay?"

"Okay." He hung up the mike, wondering if his heart was going to pound its way right out of his chest. How could a guy feel so excited yet so doomed, all at the same time? In ten minutes Colorado Cutie was going to be right here in his cab. His foot pressed harder on the accelerator until, noticing, he eased off. As for the doomed part, he didn't want to think about that now. It was too complicated, not just the herpes and the AIDS and all the other stuff he might catch, let alone the hundred dollars he shouldn't be spending, but how was he going to feel afterwards and how was he going to look Debbie square in the eye? That was heavy stuff, better left 'til later, after the deed was done. Because he was going to do it and that was that.

After the patio door slid closed, and he'd done his business, the dog spotted a place where the snow had packed high against the fence. Not for a moment did he hesitate. He climbed to the top of the drift and leaped across. Free! With spirits soaring, he raced away, headed downhill towards the highway. All at once, the force of the storm hit with cruel swiftness. Swirling snowflakes stung his eyes; tiny shards of ice formed in the wedges of his paws. The biting wind penetrated his shorthaired coat, chilling him almost instantly to the bone. He began to shiver but kept on, finally finding his path blocked by a metal fence. He followed along until he found an opening, an onramp to Interstate 70 that had just been plowed. He bounded down the ramp to the westbound lanes of the freeway and trotted through the snow along the edge. He kept searching for shelter, but a steep canyon wall paralleled the road, and there was no place to hide. Ice quickly covered his coat. His head and tail drooped. His shivering increased to a near violent shake as cutting gusts of wind forced his gait into a half forward, half-sideways cringe. He struggled forward, knowing instinctively he had to keep going, but he couldn't survive for long. Only a few tortured minutes remained before he must lie down and surrender to the storm.

On the highway, a slow-moving line of traffic moved upwards towards the top of the pass. Frowning motorists stared tensely through their windshields, concentrating on the lane ahead. No one noticed a lost, forlorn, near frozen dog struggling through the snow by the side of the road.

Huff's heart pounded like a sledgehammer. *Relax. Think of something else.* He leaned back on his Cush-N-Air, lit a Tiparillo, and pictured the 2014 Kenworth T680 he would buy some day, the fancy one with the bath and shower and queen-sized bed. There'd be a microwave, refrigerator, raised roofline so he could stand up in the sleeper compartment to get his clothes on. Then Debbie could come with him. That was his goal, the two of them on the road together.

Don't think of Debbie right now. He slipped a Willy Nelson CD into the deck and listened to "On the Road Again" for about the millionth time. He looked at the clock in the dash. Five minutes more to Mid-America. He heard a noise. At first he tried to ignore it, not wanting to acknowledge that he might have to stop. The noise persisted, a thump-thumping coming maybe from a tire. Damn, he'd have to pull over. It wasn't easy in the dark, but he spotted a turnoff ahead, a good spot, cut out of the side of the mountain where he could get clear off the road. He pulled off I-70 and glided, air brakes hissing, to a halt. He pulled on his bulky sheepskin coat, laid his lucky Stetson carefully on the seat, and replaced it with a heavy wool cap that he pulled down low over his ears. The sting of snow near blinded his eyes when he opened the cab door, accompanied by a blast of frigid air that knifed his lungs with his first breath. Lordy, lordy what a night. He swung down from his truck, flashlight in hand. Crouching low, he ran alongside the truck, aiming the beam of the flashlight underneath until he saw the tire with the cap coming off. That was it then, just a loose cap he'd have to get fixed at Mid-America, along with something else he had to get fixed. His hands were turning numb. He headed back to the cab, anxious to get back inside. When he did, he'd call Colorado Cutie and let her know he was running a little late. His foot was on the first step when he saw something staggering towards him from out of the storm. He caught it in his flashlight's beam. *What the...? A dog?*

It was about the most pitiful sight he ever saw—a dog, hard to tell what kind, covered with ice and moving sort of sideways, head and tail down, shivering like crazy from the cold. It stopped when it saw him and stood, just looking at him, waiting to see what he'd do. *No time for dogs. Colorado Cutie. Sacramento. Time is money.* He'd better get out of here right now before he got involved. He went up one more step, and then stopped. If he just drove off and left this dog here, who would know? *I would know. How would I feel if I was covered with ice and freezing like this poor animal? And if I was lost in the middle of a blizzard, how would I like it if the only bastard who could help me got back in his truck and drove away?*

That did it. God had the answer to that one and he knew what it was. He climbed back down to the ground, bent over, and carefully extended a hand. "Tell me, pooch, what are you doing out on a night like this?"

The dog bounded towards him, tail wagging, eyes pleading, and touched his hand with its nose. "Ergggyeowwww." That weird sound it let out touched his heart. The poor animal was trying to talk like a human, only it didn't even come close. "Let's not stand here freezing our tails off." With a powerful swoop, he lifted the dog, tucked it under his arm and swung up into his cab.

There was only one place for a shaking, freezing, soggy wet dog—his neatly made bunk bed. Before he put the animal down, he reached for one of his extra sized bath towels and spread it, one-handed, over the top blanket. He laid the animal on the towel and began to rub it dry. "So you're a male, I see." As he rubbed, the dog lay quietly, still shaking, looking up at him with eyes wide and trusting. "How the heck did you get on the freeway? You can't be a stray. You're too well-fed for that."

"Yeoweeerroooee."

"Hey, you're gonna have to talk plainer than that." He checked one of the tags that hung from the dog's collar. "Hmmm...Mile Hi, 445982, Rabies Registration, 2013. That don't tell me much." He checked the other. "So your name's Lucky? From Lakewood, Colorado, and here's a phone number. Looks to me like you're somebody's dog. I'll call your owner when we get to Mid-America."

When the dog was dry enough, Huff wrapped him tightly in his one extra blanket so that only his head poked out. Dammit, now the bunk was all wet. Melting ice from the dog's fur had soaked right through the towel, into the blankets, sheets, and mattress. He stripped them off and laid the dog on the bare mattress, still wrapped in the blanket. "Okay, Lucky, you stay there now. Don't move 'til you get warm."

He climbed back into his seat, started the engine, and kicked up through five gears as a Kenworth slowed down to let him in. Rolling at thirty-five again, he lit another Tiparillo. What was he going to do now? He glanced backward. Lucky hadn't moved an inch, poor guy, was still bundled up, gazing at him with those big, soulful eyes, lying right smack dab in the spot where he'd planned to sock it to Colorado Cutie. Well, shoot. Would Colorado Cutie want to do it on a wet, bare mattress? Where would he put the dog?

The lights from the big "Mid-America Truck Stop" sign loomed ahead to his right. As he pulled in, he lifted his mike and pressed the button. "Colorado Cutie, are you there? This here's Fresno Flash."

"Yeah, Fresno."

"Listen, something's come up and I can't make our date." He wasn't being fair to her, canceling like that. Maybe he should pay her anyway.

"Think nothing of it, Fresno Flash. Catch me next time."

Bless her heart. Who said they were all bad? "Sure will, and thanks." Hard to figure but he felt relieved. Finding the dog had knocked the lust clean out of his head. Next, the tire and the phone call. He drove under the high canopy and asked for a tire change. Leaving Lucky in the truck, he slogged through the snow to the restaurant, stomped the snow off his boots and pulled out his cell. He would call that number on the tag, talk to the owner and tell him what? That he'd wait 'til the guy got up here? Already he was behind his schedule. No way could he wait. Maybe he could leave Lucky with someone... No, that wouldn't work either. Who would want to keep a strange dog? There was no one he could ask except a few tired looking waitresses. He could guess what their answer would be.

Only one bar on his cell phone, so no use trying to call. Probably the storm had something to do with it. That settled it. There was only one thing to do—take the dog along.

An hour later, the tire was changed and he was back on I-70. He'd bought a bag of dog food and found a pan for water. He still had to get to the Eisenhower Tunnel and down the other side. Then the Vail Pass, and that was no picnic either. He felt good, though, not a mite sorry he canceled with the hooker. In fact, the more he thought about it, the more he thought maybe fate had a hand in putting Lucky at the very spot on I-70 where he pulled over. You never knew about those things. A cold nose nudging his arm. He looked back. The dog had kicked out of the blanket and was standing there, tail wagging like crazy, all warm now, wanting to be friendly. Just looking at Lucky made him glad he'd taken him in. He reached back and patted the dog's head. He would call that number on the tag when he got to Fresno. In a couple of weeks when he had another haul to Denver, he'd bring Lucky back. His owner had nothing to worry about.

"Guess what, pooch, you're going to California." Huff headed his 18-wheeler upwards, towards the top of the pass.

St. Francis Hospital

Karlin has cancer and Lucky's lost. This wasn't happening. Jillian stomped her boots extra hard on the soggy matting inside the entrance. She pulled off her hat and gloves, unzipped her ski jacket. Only a week ago she'd been planning her engagement party and another visit to Mrs. Mayo's Wedding World, and now...

How could Lucky have run off in the midst of a blizzard? What an awful way to die, cold and alone. She stopped in the lobby when she heard her smartphone ring. She pulled it from her purse and saw it was Tish.

"Hi, Jillian." Tish talked softly. No kidding around today.

"Any luck?"

"I looked all over that fancy condominium complex of yours. Nothing. What about you?"

"I drove I-70 clear to Idaho Springs and back. Not a trace. Then I thought I'd better get to the hospital."

"Jesus." Tish heaved a heavy sigh into the phone. "Did you call the animal shelter?"

"For Jefferson County? Three times. They don't have him, but they'll let me know."

"How about—"

"Denver? I called there too. Nobody turned in a black Lab. I even called the State Police, but they couldn't help. I thought maybe if Lucky got on I-70 they might have spotted him. But they didn't..." There was such a weight on her chest it was hard to talk.

"What about Tom? Isn't he back from Dallas today?"

"Yes, I talked to him this morning."

"So is he out looking?"

"Well, no...you know how busy he is. He's got meetings this morning."

"Hmm, I see. So are you at the hospital?"

"I just got here. On top of everything else, now I've got to tell Karlin her dog is gone."

"So you haven't talked to the doctors yet? You don't know if...?"

"They're not going to take her leg, Tish. I refuse to believe it. They'll find a way. I told you what the doctor said about the limb sparing surgery."

"I hope you're right."

"Oh, God, I hope so too. Damn! Why did Lucky have to run away?"

"Well...shit."

"Yeah, you could say that."

Tish let a long moment pass before she spoke again, this time in a brisker tone. "Okay, listen. I've got a couple of things to do here. But right after, I'll cut out and come to the hospital. Don't give up, kiddo. Lucky's got his tags on. Somebody's bound to find him and call. That reminds me. Whose phone number's on the tag?"

"My land line number. Karlin never changed it after she moved. Now I wish I'd put her cell number on the tag, or mine."

"Well, you've done all you can. That dog's out there somewhere. We're going to find him."

"Thanks, Tish. I...I've seen better days than this."

"I know, but for Karlin you can be strong."

Jillian's steps dragged as she walked to the elevator and pressed the button for the third floor. She would rather be on her way to the dentist, or an IRS audit, or anything, anywhere than be on her way to tell Karlin that Lucky was gone. She stepped into the elevator and pressed "3". Maybe she could put it off, not say a word until Lucky was found...if he was found. It sounded fine, not having to tell Karlin today. Tomorrow, maybe, or if Lucky was found quickly, not at all. Good idea. What a relief. But then, since when did she tell lies to her sister? Trash that idea.

The elevator doors slid back. She walked down the antiseptic white corridor and saw Dr. Collins by the third floor nurse's station, talking to the tall, dark-haired doctor she'd seen before, the one with the cynical smile.

"Ah, there you are, Jillian." For once, Dr. Collins' professional smile was missing. She'd never seen him so deadly serious. He nodded at his companion. "This is Dr. Richard De

Leon. He's a specialist in oncology and a top rated surgeon. He'll be in charge of Karlin's case here at St. Francis."

Oncology. What an awful word. Jillian warily stretched out her hand. "Pleased to meet you." *No I'm not.*

Dr. De Leon nodded briefly, returned a perfunctory shake and slipped his hands into the starched white pockets of his lab coat. He stared at Jillian with eyes that were startlingly shrewd, no warmth in them at all. "You're the sister?" Jillian nodded. "We'll have to take the leg off right away."

It was like she'd been hit in the stomach. Standing there, gasping, she fought to understand what she'd just heard. She shut her eyes against the doctor's words, then forced them open. "You can't mean that." Shaking her head, she backed away. "She's only twenty years old. You can't." Her voice sounded strange to her, as if it came from someone else.

"Your sister has a tumor in her leg," Dr. De Leon continued in a voice so critical, so detached. "It's osteogenic sarcoma, a very fast, very deadly kind of bone cancer. You have to understand, her chances of beating this are not good."

Jillian swung a desperate gaze to Dr. Collins. "Didn't you say that maybe we could save her leg? You talked last night about some kind of limb sparing surgery, and I thought—"

"It won't work." Dr. Collins' face appeared strained and worried. With sad finality, he shook his head. "Of course we considered it, but we're more concerned with saving her life than saving the leg. It must go."

"But this is so sudden. Can't we think about it? Can't we—?"

"There's no time to waste." Dr. De Leon appeared almost annoyed. "Sarcomas tend to metastasize to the lungs very quickly. What he means is the cancer cells will break off from that tumor in her leg and get carried to her lungs. We don't want that to happen."

"You mean if you don't take the leg off she'll die?"

"It's a definite possibility."

"And if you take the leg off?"

"Then she's got a chance." Dr. De Leon slanted an impatient glance at his watch. "The surgery's scheduled for tomorrow. If you want second opinions, you can get them, of course, but I suggest you hurry." He turned on his heel and walked away.

Dr. Collins looked apologetic. "He tends to be rather abrupt, but he's a fine doctor. Actually, a team of doctors made this decision. They're the best around."

Jillian hardly heard. A cluster of little memories filled her mind. Karlin skiing—on roller skates—in ballet slippers and pink tutu in the dance recital when she was ten. Oh, what an agony to think... Don't fall apart now. Karlin needs you. She pulled out a wadded tissue from her pocket and wiped the tears welling in her eyes. "Does she know?"

Dr. Collins laid a gentle hand on her shoulder. "I thought I'd wait until you were here with her. Is that all right?"

Jillian drew a deep breath and stood tall. "I'm her sister and I'm all she's got. Of course it's all right."

Karlin looked surprised when she saw Jillian and Dr. Collins come through the door. She was propped in bed reading, surrounded by a clutter of textbooks, papers, pens, and folders. She wore her own nightgown, a flowered blue flannel granny style with a ruffle around the high neck. "Hi Guys. What are you doing here at this time of day? Did you just come from work, Jillian?" Her gaze swept over her sister's hiking boots, ski jacket, jeans and sweater. "But you must not be working today, not in those clothes."

Jillian stepped to the side of Karlin's bed. "Hi, Sis, I took the day off. Any tests this morning?"

"Just some X-rays and they took about a gallon of blood. I'm doing my homework. There's a biology test next week. I figure if I study really hard and get back to school by then, I won't have any trouble."

"Are you feeling all right?"

"Sure. I just want to get out of here." Karlin frowned in speculation. "Is anything wrong?"

Jillian clasped Karlin's right hand in her own, opened her mouth to speak, and found that she could not force the words to her lips. She swallowed again, but a sudden dryness seemed to have stuck the sides of her throat together.

"Sister, what is it? What's wrong?"

"Dr. Collins has something to tell you." She held tight to Karlin's hand.

The doctor stepped forward. "I'm afraid it's bad news. It's cancer."

Karlin's eyes grew wide. "I've got cancer?"

"It's what we call a sarcoma. It started in the connective tissue of your leg, and it's got to do with the way the cells grow. Something went wrong. The cell division...well, you might say it went crazy, out of control. A tumor grew. We've been testing, hoping it was benign. It's not, it's malignant."

"Are you sure?" She'd turned pale.

"Yes, we're sure, but hear me out. These days, medical science has made great strides in treating sarcomas."

Karlin gripped Jillian's hand. "You mean there's a cure?"

"Of course there's a cure. It won't be easy. You'll need some radiology and chemotherapy. But with a little luck, and a lot of treatment, you're going to be fine."

Some of the stark terror left Karlin's face. "Truly?"

"Truly, there's a good chance you can lick this thing, that in five years not a trace of cancer will be left. But there's more bad news, I'm afraid. We're going to have to take your leg. There's no other way."

Karlin gasped, as if she'd been struck. "My leg? They're going to cut my leg off?"

As long as she lived, Jillian would never forget the sound of Karlin's scream or the next five minutes when she'd held her sobbing sister in her arms, trying to convince her with *it's going to be all right* when it wasn't all right and would never be all right again.

A nurse entered the room, hypodermic needle in her hand, and whispered to the doctor. "We're going to give her a shot to help her relax."

Karlin heard. "A happy shot? Good. I'm going to need lots of happy shots." She lay back on the bed, pale and despairing, while the nurse jabbed the needle in her arm. "Jillian, are they sure? Isn't there some other way?"

"Do you think I'd let them do this if there was?"

"When are they going to do it?"

Dr. Collins answered, "Tomorrow." Jillian heard the strain in his voice. He was the doctor who'd brought Karlin into the world. Of course he'd be upset.

"Who's going to do it?"

"Dr. De Leon."

"Oh, him. I don't like him. He's always so cold, like he doesn't have a heart."

"He's an excellent doctor, Karlin, and he cares more than you think." Dr. Collins managed a faint smile. "I'm so sorry, Karlin, but this surgery will save your life, I can almost promise."

"Almost?"

"Twenty years ago...even ten years ago...you'd be in big trouble, but cancer isn't a death sentence anymore. The cure rate's getting higher and higher."

"So I'm not going to die?"

"No, you're not going to die. Well, maybe from old age some day, but not from osteogenic sarcoma."

Some of the horror left Karlin's eyes. "I feel like I just skied over a cliff." A hint of her normal cheerfulness returned. "Don't worry, I'll be brave. And, hey, I'm going to live aren't I?" She squeezed her sister's hand as the shot took hold and her eyelids began to droop. "I've still got you. I can still be a doctor. I've still got Dennis, and Lucky, too. A faint smile crossed her lips as she lifted heavy lids to look into Jillian's eyes. "So how's my dog?"

Chapter 8

Fresno, California

Debbie! She was all Huff could think of as he rolled along Highway 99 towards home. He'd had a one-track mind since Reno. When he reached the outskirts of Fresno, he turned off the freeway and heavy-footed down the sharp curve of the off-ramp. It took the tilted truck sign and Lucky sliding sideways on the passenger seat to make him realize he'd better slow down. Man, don't foul up now. She'd be sitting in front of the TV when he got there, watching—quick glance at the clock—*The Price Is Right*. He'd waste no time. He'd sweep that soft, cuddly body into his arms right off, carry her into the bedroom, and, well, he'd have to shower somewhere in there, maybe they'd shower together and then...

She'd be his old Debbie again. It wouldn't be her period, and she wouldn't have a cold. No sir, no more excuses. And she'd better not be out playing bingo with her wacko mother. *Debbie, be there for me, darlin'! You might be kinda dumb, but you're the best thing that ever happened to me.*

And thank you, God, for not letting me do it with the hooker.

Deborah Sue Huffman was more than "kinda dumb." She was, in fact, a lot dumber than Huff, and nearly everyone, realized. How dumb was she? Debbie's I.Q. was so low she just missed falling, by a mere point or two, into the below-eighty "moron" category. She was doomed to stupidity before she was born. For openers, her mother, Norma Jean, possessed an I.Q. that hovered in the low nineties, thus throwing her daughter a genetic curve before the sperm ever hit the egg. When Norma Jean became pregnant at age seventeen, her unforgiving father tossed her out of the house, showing no mercy after her tearful announcement that she was two months along and had no idea who among three boys (a ballpark figure) was responsible. With no money except what her mother could slip her on the side,

Norma Jean moved into the dumpy apartment of her current boyfriend, a sporadically unemployed busboy who may or may not have been the baby's father. There she spent the next seven months in total ignorance of even the words *prenatal care*. Other than making out with the busboy, she did not exercise and instead, spent her time sitting lump-like in front of the TV. Her diet consisted mainly of beer, pizza, peanut butter, and chocolate bars. She did not drink milk or orange juice. She did not eat fruits and vegetables. She never heard of supplemental vitamins.

Further compounding her assault on the brain of her unborn child, Norma Jean puffed her way through an entire package of cigarettes daily, smoked pot whenever she could afford it, and never saw a doctor until the night she gave birth. Also (although for this last, she could not be blamed) she contacted a light case of mumps during the third month of her gestation, thus firmly sealing the lid on whatever remained of Debbie's chances for normal intelligence.

Except for a low birth weight of four and a half pounds, Debbie appeared at first to be a normal baby. As the months went by, her mild retardation became apparent or would have, had anybody cared enough to notice. Her case was not so severe that she lay dull eyed and lethargic in her crib. Actually, she was a pleasant, bright-eyed baby who cooed and smiled a lot, but the signs were there. Baby Debbie seldom reached for a toy, choosing instead to lie placidly, wherever her mother placed her. She was nine months old before she sat up, nearly two before she took her first step. She was never "into everything" as a normal toddler should be. At eighteen months, she managed "Mama," but no other words escaped her rosebud lips until she was nearly three.

By now, Norma Jean was smoking pot daily and drinking heavily. The grudging care she gave her baby was, at best, indifferent, the kind that bordered but didn't quite cross into the area of neglect. Beyond that, if she noticed Debbie at all, it was only to brag about "the neat kid" she'd produced, a child who grew more adorable looking each day, whose rusty red hair twisted naturally into tight Orphan Annie curls, whose plump, rosy cheeks dimpled whenever she smiled, whose pleasingly placid disposition never altered.

"That little shit don't ever give me problems," was Norma Jean's way of putting it. And that, for all the wrong reasons, was true. When Debbie was four, another disaster befell her. Norma Jean moved in with a bearded, leather jacketed, sweat-band-around-the-head drug dealer named Rocco Capozzi, whose swarthy looks and macho manners had captured her affections. Rocco hated kids, especially one who stole even a miniscule part of Norma Jean's attention away from himself. Debbie's cuteness had no effect on his glacier heart. He soon perceived she was none too bright, and thereafter bullied her constantly.

"Watch out, dimwit, or I'll throw you in the garbage can," he yelled when a glass slipped from her little fingers.

"Shut up, dummy, or I'll flatten you," he threatened when she began to wail.

By the time Debbie entered first grade, Norma Jean had left Rocco, whose parting gift to her was two black eyes and a broken nose. Fortunately, Rocco had confined his physical abuse to Norma Jean, but the mental damage he'd inflicted upon little Debbie was severe. Lacking in spirit, low in self-esteem, she coasted like a zombie through the first four grades of school, a quiet, docile, withdrawn little girl just bright enough to feel the humiliation of being "the dumbest kid in class." Semester after semester, she sat at the back of the room in a near trancelike state, enduring the taunts of her classmates, unable, unwilling, to learn. When she reached fifth grade, there was talk of holding her back, though her teachers were reluctant to do so. Such a sweet, pretty little thing, they said. She's no problem, really.

But the painful truth was that Deborah Sue could not read or write and didn't know her numbers. "Maybe we should test her," some genius of a teacher suggested. "She might just belong with the mentally challenged."

It was then that Debbie's luck finally turned. She was tested, and when the results revealed an I.Q. of sixty-five, was henceforth loaded each day onto the bus which carried the special education students to Mrs. Cunningham's class for the mentally challenged at Pinedale Elementary. Agnes Cunningham, a smart, warmhearted woman in her early fifties, who just may have been the most patient woman in the world, rescued Debbie from the dim, dead-end world of the mentally deficient. In a class where I.Q.'s ranged from the eighties down to the low fifties, Debbie soon discovered she wasn't the only dummy in the world. Thereafter, she began to blossom with Mrs. Cunningham providing lots of attention, and drill, drill, drill. Soon Debbie began to read and write, and when Mrs. Cunningham put her in charge of little Timmy (I.Q. fifty-three) and asked her to help teach him to read, it was the proudest moment of Debbie's life. She was useful. She didn't belong in the garbage can.

Within three years Debbie's I.Q. zoomed to eighty-two. She could print and write. She could read at a sixth grade level. She knew her numbers and could perform simple arithmetic. And if her brain refused, as it often did, to deliver up the proper name of something, she called it, as Mrs. Cunningham taught her, a "gadget." What a fine word that was. "Gadget" was a Special Ed student's lifeline. Armed with "gadget" she could fool the world. Debbie was indeed "educable," as were the other members of her class even those in the lowly fifties. Docile and trusting, wanting only to love and be loved, they would surely never go to college, or even finish high school, but with fourth to sixth grade reading skills, they could pass in the real world. They could be file clerks, yardmen, fast-food cooks, domestics. They could perform any repetitious job where they knew exactly what they were supposed to do. They could read a newspaper and get a driver's license. They could play bingo. *May they not be hurt*, Mrs. Cunningham thought each June when her "sixth graders" were promoted out of her care. The trouble was people never knew how many times they dealt with someone mentally challenged. People would get annoyed because "the boy" didn't get the order right or "the girl" sounded like a robot when she said, "Have a nice day." People didn't understand these kids who looked so normal but were not. They should be commended, not scorned, for their courage in making their own way in the world despite their limited intelligence.

Mrs. Cunningham worried especially about Debbie, so pretty, so vulnerable, so easily led with a mother who wasn't much brighter. That girl could end up in trouble. The teacher kept track of her ex-pupil, felt bad when Debbie dropped out of high school, relieved when she found a job with The Merry Maids Cleaning Service, rejoiced when Deborah Sue Cline married Jerome Vernon Huffman—truck driver, church goer, reliable citizen. Thank heavens. Debbie would be safe now.

Wrong.

The marriage went well the first few years. Debbie quit her Merry Maids job to take care of the small house Huff bought on Weber Avenue in Fresno. Snug and secure in her own small world, she'd never been happier—cooking, cleaning, and watching the game shows and soaps on TV. When Huff was gone on the long hauls, she went to the bingo parlors with her mother. When Huff was home, they spent long, joyful hours in the bedroom making love. That was the best of all. There wasn't a woman in all the world who enjoyed sex more than Debbie Sue Huffman. She was like an animal in bed, totally uninhibited. A smarter woman, in the midst of a passionate embrace, might allow her thoughts to stray to "Is the pot roast burning?" But Debbie's depthless mind had no room for intruding thoughts or hang-ups. Debbie relaxed and enjoyed. She immersed herself in the pleasures of the moment, both hers and her partner's, and let the good times roll. Huff figured that was fine. So what if his wife couldn't discuss nuclear disarmament, play gin rummy, manage their budget? None of that stuff mattered. He'd adored his little Debbie from the day they met in church when she was just sixteen and still a virgin. When they married, he took a vow to love and cherish, and he sure intended to for the rest of his life. She depended on him, loved him. It gave him a good feeling to know that she needed him, that he was the only man she'd ever had.

It would never have happened had not Huff been away on a long haul, had not Debbie and her mother attended Tuesday

Night Bingo at The American Legion Hall, had not Norma Jean, who usually did her drinking at home, decided to stop for "just one little drinkie" at the Longhorn Lounge.

Cal Ryska was sitting at the bar when they came in. In crotch hugging Levis and faded blue T-shirt, he was tall and lean, in his late thirties, with hawk-like eyes set in a narrow, darkly handsome face. Idly sipping his Budweiser, he cast an indifferent glance at the redheaded girl with the creamy white skin who hoisted herself onto the stool beside him, then swiftly looked again. *She's solid as a brick shithouse.* His gaze boldly swept over the curved firmness of her slender figure. When his scrutiny finally reached her face, Debbie casually looked his way. Though her stare was merely vacant, Cal saw *come get me* written in her soft gray eyes. He caught a whiff of her heady perfume. Man he'd like to have him some of that. But what was that on her finger? Just his luck, a wedding ring. The tub of lard on the other side looked like her mother. Well, hell, it wasn't nothing he couldn't handle. The mother was no problem, and if the husband wasn't around, just maybe...

Cal Ryska was a sometime mechanic who worked when he had to and left a trail of unpaid bills behind. A divorced father of two, he bragged he'd never paid a penny in child support. He was also a chronic gambler who'd won, then lost, countless small fortunes on the crap tables of Nevada. Long ago he concluded his luckless life was the fault of others, certainly not his own. As a result, his philosophy of life was *Look out for Number One, and fuck the rest of the world.*

Debbie Sue didn't have a chance, not from the very first night when Cal Ryska told Norma Jean (who had gained in pounds but not in smartness as the years rolled by) she needn't bother taking Debbie home. "I'll be glad to drop her off, Ma'am. It's right on my way."

The slam-bang affair began. Soon, Cal could be found at the little house on Weber Avenue nearly every night Huff was on the road. He made himself right at home, soon discovering half the fun was screwing his unsuspecting host as well as his host's wife. Such a deal. He would drink a couple of Huff's

Coors, screw Huff's wife on Huff's bed. He'd shower, using Huff's soap, towels and Right Guard. Before he moseyed on home, he'd make himself a sandwich from Huff's special pumpernickel and choice bologna. Sometimes, just for the hell of it, he'd wash it all down with another one or two of Huff's beers.

After the first charge of excitement, Debbie Sue grew increasingly unhappy. Cal's lovemaking wasn't gentle like Huff's. He got real rough, and she didn't like that. She was so sore and tired she didn't want Huff anymore. And that, she guessed, made her husband kinda mad the last few times he was home. Why didn't Cal just go away? One night she told him maybe he shouldn't come around anymore. He laughed, and the next night came right back. What was she going to do?

Had Debbie's brain permitted any deep thought, she would have contemplated with horror the mess she was in. She would have considered, with the utmost trepidation, the gamut of dreadful possibilities should Huff discover her infidelity. But since her thought processes rarely projected beyond the next hour or two, she had only an uneasy feeling that if Huff found out about Cal, he wasn't going to like it. Nope, not one teeny-weeny bit.

"Hey Baby, I'm home." Huff entered the living room, Lucky by his side, finding Debbie right where he expected, curled up on the couch in front of the TV watching *The Price Is Right*.

"Hi, Sweetheart." Debbie didn't get up. She was worn out. The night before, she and Cal had done it for four straight hours. He wasn't nice. She had bruises on her arms where he'd been too rough. Her eyes brightened when she saw Lucky. "Oh, gee, where'd you get the dog? Here, doggie." When Lucky, tail wagging, trotted over, Debbie patted him and gave him a hug. "Umm, pretty dog."

Huff stood watching. "Now that you've hugged the dog..."

"What?" She looked up, eyes blankly staring. He held out his arms. "How about a hug for me?"

"Oh, yeah." Slowly got off the couch and went into his arms. He greedily clasped her tight and kissed her hard, bending her back, swaying in a love rhythm, immersing himself in the delight of her smooth skin, sweet scented hair and moist, warm lips. With a passionate gasp, he lifted his mouth from hers. "Baby," he whispered, sending her his message with the growing bulge he pressed against her. "Let's not even talk. Let's go in the bedroom right now." He covered her mouth with his again, reached down and tugged up her skirt. His fingers journeyed slowly up her satin thigh until they found her panties and slid a finger underneath.

Pouting, she backed away. "Don't do that."

"Why not?"

"Because I have a headache, and...and...I'm just not in the mood."

Dammit. He had to leave for L.A. in the morning. But no, don't get mad. With Debbie you had to be patient. "I'll get you some aspirin." He strode to the kitchen, grabbed a bottle of Bayer's from the cupboard and poured three tablets into his hand. He opened the refrigerator and got a bottle of water. Funny, the loaf of pumpernickel he kept in the fridge was almost gone. He'd swear he'd bought a new loaf last time he was home. Also, he'd just bought a twelve pack of Coors. Only two left, but shouldn't there be six? Debbie hated pumpernickel. Since when did she drink beer? Back in the living room, he forgot the bread and the Coors. He handed her the aspirin. "Take these. That should fix your headache."

She hadn't missed the angry glint that flashed through his eyes. As she obediently swallowed the aspirin, she made a decision which for her was amazingly wise. She was worn out and didn't want to do it with Huff or anybody, but maybe she just better had.

It wasn't any good. Huff rolled off her and sat up on the edge of the bed. Why had she just lain there? He'd have gotten more response from a sack of potatoes. But that wasn't fair. Maybe she did have a headache. Maybe he shouldn't be after her all the time like he was, but damn, it was hard to keep his hands off his wife. "Guess you still have the headache."

She yawned. "Yeah, I guess I do."

He heard a quick whine, glanced over, and saw a black nose resting on the side of the bed. "Say, we forgot the dog. That reminds me, I've got to make a phone call." Huff reached for the telephone. "Come here, Lucky. Let's see that phone number on your tag."

Santa Marta, California

Damn it all. Dr. Harvey Linderman, clutching a sheaf of papers, impatiently pulled his wallet from his pocket and held it near the steel sliding door of Corridor "B." Safety doors hadn't been necessary back in the old days, before groups like WEELA threatened to break in. Now he couldn't walk down his own hallway without a fucking plastic card. At least with the Proximity Access System, he didn't have to take the card out of his wallet and jab it into a slot, but still, it was bad enough. "Clarence, are you busy?" Not waiting for a reply, he strode into his colleague's office and threw himself into a chair.

Dr. Clarence Osborne, seated behind his desk, touched fingertips together, leaned back and regarded his visitor with amused eyes. "Don't tell me you've just seen the new directive from the National Institutes of Health, and those…" he nodded at the papers "…are the additional guidelines from the PHS."

"They're out to get us, Clarence. Have you looked at this thing?" With an angry flip, Harvey tossed the Public Health Service's "Guide for the Care and Use of Laboratory Animals" on his associate's desk. "I can't believe this. Now they want us to exercise the dogs, for God's sake, and…and…" he grabbed up the pages and quickly scanned "yes, here—" he jabbed with his finger "—'exercise, defined as socialization and opportunity for motion.' *Dogs*, Clarence, *dogs*. And listen to this. 'The primates must be furnished a physical environment adequate to promote their psychological wellbeing.'" He slammed the papers back on the desk, leaped up and started to pace. "What is that supposed to mean?"

"It means we've got to be nice to the monkeys. Sit down, Harvey. That presents a problem, doesn't it? Costs being what they are."

Harvey continued his pacing. "I'll ignore them. They can't touch me."

"That's what they thought at the University of Pennsylvania before the activists broke into the head trauma lab where they were bashing the baboons. Remember what finally happened? The NIH suspended U.of P.'s grant."

"An outrage."

"And what about City of Hope Medical Center? They broke in, destroyed equipment, made off with some animals. Remember that unpleasantness about those dogs being tested for tobacco carcinogens? Something about 'deficiencies in facilities' and 'veterinary oversight.' As I recall, NIH suspended a million dollars in City of Hope grants. And the center acquiesced to a twelve thousand dollar fine by the Department of Agriculture, all because of a raid by animal activists—"

"Who should have been lined up and shot."

"Beside the point. The University of California at Riverside? Remember the to-do when the Animal Liberation Front broke in and carried off all those research animals? And the fuss about the stump-tailed macaque they rescued? The one whose little eyes had been sewn shut?"

Harvey Linderman snorted. "*Rescued.* What a travesty. They were using that macaque on research for the blind. There's the great injustice. How many experiments were ruined? How many years of work down the tube? These bleeding heart do-gooders will set medical research back a hundred years."

"Whether they're right or wrong, you've got to realize times are changing. We must comply. If we don't, we stand to lose millions in NIH grants. Not only that—" Dr. Osborne clamped his mouth closed, as if he knew he'd better shut up.

"What? Out with it. Say it."

The pleasant expression on the genial doctor's face disappeared, replaced by one of unexpected sadness. His eyes softened and he spoke with a sorrowful shake of his head. "They're right, you know. Unspeakable cruelties go on within these walls. You know it, I know it, only we've seen so much for so long, we've become immune."

Linderman began to sputter. Osborne continued, "Don't get your leg over your head. I'm on your side, just as guilty as you are and just as much aware of the good things we're doing here." He paused, carefully selecting his next words. "While I'm being honest, contrary to what I've told you in the past, I do worry about security."

"Meaning what?"

"I worry about the activists breaking in here."

"But the guards—the Proximity Access Control System—the fence—"

"Worthless as tits on a boar. As good as you can do, I suppose, except for that cheap security guard service you use, but if they want to get in here badly enough, believe me, they will. Let's not get sidetracked. The winds of change are upon us, Harvey. We need to tidy up and become more open. Let a few groups inside to look around."

"Travis Kerrigan and his goddamned WEELA will never get in here."

"Let's hope not, unless it's by invitation. Just don't forget there are people out there who are willing to risk arrest, years in prison, in order to stage a break-in. Those are the ones who've got me scared."

Linderman threw up his hands. "Good God, what do they want from us?"

"Their goal?" Clarence Osborne leaned back thoughtfully, putting his hands behind his head. "Some of your more moderate groups accept the need for animals in research. But face it, my friend, there's a growing wing of the movement—your old-line antivivisectionists as well as your new animal rights groups—who want to do away entirely with using animals in labs. The magic words are *Computer Models*."

Harvey sank wearily back onto the chair. "Computer

models, my ass. Don't those fools realize we need the animals? Don't they want a cure for cancer? Heart disease? What about AIDS, for Christ's sake?" He pulled a handkerchief from his pocket to wipe the sweat from his brow. "You can bet—" he punctuated his words with stabs of the wadded handkerchief "—if Travis Kerrigan, by some lucky miracle, got cancer, he'd be begging for a vaccine along with the rest. Then we'd see how much he cared how many 'screaming in agony' primates we used to do the job."

"That's unkind. You didn't mean that. Let's not wish cancer on anyone, not even Travis Kerrigan."

"They've got us by the short hairs, haven't they?"

"Yes, they do, but we'll make the best of it. We will comply."

"Perhaps."

"Think about what I said." Dr. Osborne brought down his arms and shifted to a comfortable position in his chair. Knowing Harvey, it was time for a change of pace. "So how's your new experiment?"

"Dog heatstroke after reduction of gut flora? It's coming along. We've ordered the dogs."

"From Johnny Valentine?"

"He's got the best prices."

"I suppose, but I dislike dealing with the man."

"Who likes dealing with bunchers?" Calmer now, Harvey got out of the chair and headed towards the door. "I must go. I've got to make a phone call."

"All right. You'd better stop off to visit the macaques on the way back."

"What?" The tall doctor paused, puzzled, at the door.

"To say hello, give them a pat or two. We mustn't forget their psychological well-being."

"That's not funny, Clarence."

The door slammed shut, causing a smiling Dr. Osborne to jump slightly in his chair.

Back in his own spacious office, Harvey Linderman lifted

the telephone, replaced it, and lifted it again. He had not intended to call her tonight. She deserved to sit waiting and wondering by the phone. After his talk with Clarence, though, he would damn well call. He deserved a little relaxation after such a grueling day. Who could provide it better than Gretchen?

"Hello?" Her purring voice triggered a tingling memory of their fantastic weekend in San Francisco wherein he'd fulfilled his wildest fantasies. She, simple little secretary that she was, had been thrilled to be with such a distinguished doctor, excited by the opulence of the hotel, overwhelmed when he gave her those genuine opal earrings. When he invited her to live rent-free in one of his apartment buildings, she shed real tears, so stunned was she by his generosity. If only he hadn't...quickly, he put the depressing memory out of his mind. It happened only the once, doubtless because he was tired. It wouldn't happen again. "Baby," he purred back, "Harvey here."

"...Harvey?"

What the...? "Yes, Harvey." Why the hesitation? How many Harveys did she know? "The man you just spent the weekend in bed with?"

Her bubbling laugh dispelled his annoyance. "Oh, hi. Gee, I'm sorry, you caught me by surprise. I wasn't expecting you to call. You said you weren't going to."

"No? Well, I've changed my plans. I've a yen for Italian tonight. Pardini's for dinner? Sevenish?"

"Oh, doggone it, honey—" her voice oozed regret "—I'm a wreck...and I'm awfully tired...and I planned to wash my hair. We'd better make it another night."

Who did she think she was? He stifled his temper. If he was going to get what he wanted, anger was the wrong approach. "Take a nap, darling. We'll make it eight o'clock. Surely you can wash and dry your hair by then."

"Uh...okay. Sure. I'll be ready, honey, and I'll be wearing my new earrings, too."

"Eight o'clock." He hung up the phone. Why did he feel suddenly depressed? He almost had the feeling...but no, girls were always washing their hair. Why would she lie? She was crazy about him. He had one more phone call to make. Hell, what was the new maid's name? Chiquita? Consuela? He pressed "1" to speed dial his home number and waited, confident someone would answer. Someone always answered, if not the maid, then fuzzy voiced Connie herself. Five rings, then voice mail told him to leave a message. He slammed down the phone. Strange. Where was she? Not that he gave a damn.

Santa Marta, California

The horror began in the middle of *Minute to Win It*.

Not a drop of alcohol had touched Connie's lips for two days. She'd show that awful Dr. Tessler! The trouble was she had terrible nausea, had broken into a sweat and was shaking, and the shaking was getting worse. Hugging herself tight, curled up in the pink velvet armchair, she vowed she wouldn't take a drink—would see this through no matter how bad it got, but then a hairy tarantula spider, the size of a small dog, crawled out from the back of the TV, followed by several more. She stared, transfixed, as they wobbled towards her, and when a hoard of rats poured like a torrent from the very same spot, she leaped up, flinging her glass of just plain water so that it smashed, unheeded, against the wall. She let out her first scream. As she ran for the door, still screaming, the first bat attacked, not touching, but diving from above, out of nowhere, zooming by so close in front of her face that she barely missed when she swiped at it with her hand. The rest of the bats joined in, and she was flailing at them with both arms, staggering in a circle, still trying to get out the door, despite the writhing snakes hanging down from the top of the doorway.

"Senora, Senora! Que pasa?" The maid rushed in, somehow getting past the snakes, and stood there wide-eyed, balling up her apron in her small, brown hands.

Connie crouched on the floor, covered her head with her arms, and screamed and screamed.

"Dejo! Quiero salir de aqui!"

After a time, when Connie dared look up, the awful creatures and the maid had disappeared. She rested her cheek on the carpeting. They were going to come back any minute now. She could not possibly stay in this room, could never face this horror again. She couldn't think what to do, short of slitting her wrists, and maybe she'd have to. She couldn't ask Harvey for help. If anything, he'd laugh and find her predicament amusing. Other than him, who could she turn to? She had not one single friend she could call anymore, so that left no one, except...

That horribly rude Doctor Tessler. He'd offered his help, not that he could, not that anyone could help, but maybe...

She needed him. As she recalled, she'd thrown his card in her purse. It wouldn't hurt to give him a quick call. She tried to get to her feet but could not. Shaking violently, in a cold sweat, she crawled to where her purse lay on the stripped-down bed and pulled it to the floor. She dumped the contents on the carpet and rummaged through, looking for the card she'd so carelessly dropped inside that day in Winslow's office. There it was. She pulled the phone off the nightstand. Lying on her back on the floor, she punched in the number.

"Answering Service." The female voice was cold, impersonal.

"Dr. Tessler?"

"He's not in his office. Is this an emergency?"

"Yes, you could say that."

"What is the nature of your emergency?"

"I'm dying! That's the emergency!"

"Give me your name and number. Hang up and we'll have him call you."

After she hung up, she hauled herself to a sitting position on the floor and waited, head back, eyes closed, death grip on the phone. Finally it rang. She jerked the receiver to her ear. "Doctor Tessler?"

"Mrs. Linderman? I'm glad you called. I've been worried about you."

His concern was more than she could bear. She hardly ever cried, but a sob welled within her. "I...I..."

"You're in trouble, aren't you?"

"Yes."

"I'll be right over."

"You mean you'd make a house call?"

"Hey, no sweat. Hang in there. I'm on my way."

Fort Mason, San Francisco

Eight pounds gone. With a pleased lift of her chin, Terry Woodard turned her Honda right, off busy Marina Boulevard, and swung into the entrance of San Francisco's old Fort Mason. Not once had she gone off her diet. At this rate she'd be thin as a toothpick by April 11th. The little blue car bounced along the wide, paved parking lot, past rows of small sailboats jammed into a snug yacht harbor, their bare masts a tangled forest, swaying gently with each swell of the bay. Her thighs were thinner. She went wide around the old guard house, empty now, and steered towards a cluster of ancient, two-story barracks. Was he here yet? She turned the corner, her heart thump thumping, her gaze quickly sweeping over the row of cars parked in front of Building "C." No Prius. Oh, well. He would definitely be here later. On newsletter day everyone helped. She whipped the Honda neatly into a parking spot, hopped out, and as she shut the door, caught sight of her reflection in the window. For sure, she did look skinnier. She ran a hand over her stomach, pulled it in, turned sideways, and looked again. Wonderful. That one glance was worth every starving hour she'd spent since she started the diet. Of course, it was only eight pounds. She still had a long way to go, but that little bit of weight gone made all the difference. For the first time in ages she felt attractive. She'd dressed just right, too. Travis would love her new, full black skirt that reached nearly to the tops of her black boots, and her oversized green sweatshirt with the whale on the front and "Greenpeace" in darker green letters above. He'd like her hair, too, woven into one long braid down her back and tied with a bit of green ribbon. No makeup, just a round, slightly thinner face, scrubbed and shining. Travis liked things simple. That was part of his charm.

What a great day. What a neat place. She picked up her big canvas bag stamped with "Animal Defense League National Conference, 2012" and swung it in wide arcs as she hurried towards the building, taking a deep breath of the moist, salt air. How she loved working at old Fort Mason. So historical, where soldiers had embarked for faraway places in the Pacific in World War II. The Army was long gone. Now Fort Mason was a cultural center. Groups of caring people sponsored the good things in life like art galleries, museums, actors' workshops, music schools. Environmental Traveling Companions provided access to wilderness and environmental education activities for people of all abilities. She loved Greens Restaurant, operated by the San Francisco Zen Center, where she could get a great gourmet vegetarian lunch. How proud she was to be a part of it all. Nowhere in the world would she rather be than this exciting place, working for the animals, close to Travis.

She bounced up the cracked steps that led to a long, covered dock and strode towards the entrance. WEELA was located in a big room on the second floor of Building "C." At the end of a wide, chopped-up corridor, its entrance was marked by a small sign overhead and flanked on either side by long tables piled high, and not too neatly, with anticruelty pamphlets, bulletins, and papers of all sizes and colors, under hand printed HELP YOURSELF signs tacked to the wall. Another sign announced PLEASE, WE NEED YOUR SIGNATURE, with an arrow pointing downward. A jumbled stack of petitions lay beneath, providing passing-by protesters with a multitude of causes. With a stroke of the pen, an animal lover could petition to keep elephant abuse out of California's Nevada County Fair; tell Washington University in St. Louis to stop hurting cats; tell the Indian Government to enforce their animal protection laws; request Governor Jerry Brown not to rescind the Hayden Law that protected shelter animals from being immediately killed instead of waiting at least four to six days; and on and on...

The disorder continued inside. Floor-to-ceiling shelves, bulging with all kinds of anticruelty literature, lined the side walls. At the back, stacks of books and pamphlets weighted down a faded, flowered chintz couch which stood beneath the room's one window. Pictures of birds and animals covered the walls. A huge, black papier-mâché eagle, slightly drooping and beginning to fade, perched atop a filing cabinet. An old Xerox machine stood in the corner. Two battered desks and a few tables holding computer terminals completed the furnishings. At a computer, Bernadette typed furiously, working on WEELA's monthly newsletter.

Terry burst into the room, her long skirt swirling as she tossed her canvas bag atop a cabinet. "Hi, everybody." Mrs. Bagley sat at the desk, talking on the telephone. The rest were gathering for the weekly meeting: Larry, the veterinarian, Krista, Josh, Sparrow. Bernadette gave Terry a frosty stare over the top of her smudged reading glasses. "I believe we said two o'clock? You're late, and where is Travis?"

"He's been in Sacramento for two days," Terry answered airily (you never gave Bernadette an inch). "I don't know when he'll be back. You know Travis, he does his own thing."

Krista addressed Terry. "So what's in the newsletter this month?"

"The usual stuff—rodeos to picket, another fur protest against Bebe Inc." Terry looked over Bernadette's shoulder at the computer screen. "Our main article is about the thousands of animals killed for profit and how we should protest."

"Like how the San Francisco Animal Liberationists raided Marin Sun Farms?"

Bernadette stopped typing. Her mouth curved into a satisfied smile. "They glued the locks on their new San Francisco meat processing building, slashed all sixteen tires on the four trucks parked out front. Then they went to their butcher shop in Oakland's Market Hall and slathered etching cream on the glass door, all of which damn well served Marin Sun Farms right."

Terry frowned. "Bernadette, you know we don't do that. We want to save the animals, but that's too extreme."

"No it's not. I'd march up Market Street naked if I had to, just like they do at PETA."

"I'm not going to take my clothes off," Mrs. Bagley called from across the room.

Oh my God, Bernadette and Mrs. Bagley with their clothes off? Terry suppressed a smile. "You won't have to, Mrs. Bagley. We're not like PETA and never will be."

Bernadette sniffed her disapproval. "We should be. We should have the guts to break the law if it will save an animal. Otherwise, we're all cowards."

That Bernadette, always so critical, always so sure she's right. "We all do our best." Terry tried to sound like Travis would sound—patient, without malice. If only she could see the good in everybody like Travis did, but she wasn't that noble. No way could she make herself like Bernadette. The woman just wasn't lovable, a dried-up divorcee who lived alone, age forty-five at least, with a dumpy figure, crimpy salt-and-pepper hair, a yucky wardrobe of baggy slacks and fuzz ball sweaters. She hardly ever smiled, went around with a disapproving, pinched look on her face, her mouth all ugly because it always curved down. Travis didn't see her that way. In his eyes, Bernadette was one of their most devoted volunteers. She gave more of her time than anyone except Travis himself. If only she didn't launch into those long harangues, denouncing all the evils done to animals. The woman loved animals, but people were far down on her list.

"Terry, how's the diet going?" Mrs. Bagley asked. "I swear you look thinner."

"I am. I've lost eight pounds since—" Her back was to the door, but she didn't have to look to know he'd arrived. She could tell by the way the others looked up, sat straighter.

"It's about time." Bernadette pounded on the keyboard with extra vigor. "You were supposed to be here at two."

Terry turned, not too fast, to feast her eyes upon Travis Kerrigan. She could never get enough of his lean good looks—the way he carried himself with such grace and confidence. Krista once called him a combination of the best of Ashton Kutcher and Matthew McConaughey. She was right. He walked across the room, dropped his briefcase in the corner, shrugged out of his jacket. He wore a blue cotton shirt and the familiar old Reeboks. His well-cut denim pants revealed how absolutely flat his stomach was. With the unconscious gesture that she loved, he shook his head, ran his fingers through his long, straight hair to smooth it down.

"Hello, everyone." He held up a hand in an easy greeting, ignoring Bernadette's sharp remark as he looked around the room, catching each person's eye and nodding. He noticed Terry's Greenpeace sweatshirt. "I see we're saving the whales today. Ah!" His eyes lit when he saw page one of the monthly newsletter on Bernadette's computer screen. He clapped his hands together. "Way to go."

"Where've you been?" Sparrow asked.

"In Sacramento doing some lobbying."

"On AB 339?"

"It's done. They won't be selling animals at swap meets anymore. I was there mainly for SB 969, the pet grooming act."

"Which one is that?"

"An outrage." Bernadette's eyes sparked. "These supposedly humane pet stores hire groomers off the streets. They've had no training, so as a result a lot of deaths and injuries have resulted. Just the other day, a Yorkie mix named Lucy had five of her nipples shaved off, and her eye and leg permanently injured."

"There's always something, isn't there?" said Josh. "We no sooner get laws passed like banning steel-jawed traps or targeting the veal industry, when we're fighting for something else. When will it end?"

Travis sadly shook his head. "Maybe someday we'll have a perfect world where all animals are treated humanely, but not in our lifetime, I'm afraid."

The slam of the telephone diverted his attention. "We did it," Mrs. Bagley exclaimed in a jubilant voice. "Chalk up another one for Pet Finders."

Terry asked, "Did you find another pet?"

"Yes, and this is a special one. All week long this poor old widow's been calling, trying to find Shauntay, her poodle who got out of her yard somehow. She sounded just heartbroken.

Had him for eleven years, her only companion since her husband died. That call was from a little girl, twelve years old, who lives two blocks away. She found a poodle that's got to be Shauntay. The descriptions match exactly. She didn't want to take him to the pound, so when she saw our ad on Craig's List, thank goodness, she called." Mrs. Bagley reached for the telephone. "I'm going to call that lady right now."

Travis smiled. "Pet Finders scores again, thanks to you."

Bernadette's lip curled. "I don't suppose that little old widow was aware her darling poodle could have ended up being tortured in a research lab."

"Well, of course she wasn't aware." Mrs. Bagley raised her eyebrows indignantly. "Poor old thing, I wasn't about to tell her. Besides, we don't have pound seizure in San Francisco, as you very well know."

Bernadette drew herself up, all body movements pointing to another of her familiar, long harangues. "Oh, sure, our pound doesn't sell its animals like some do. Even so, it's a crime most pet owners don't realize how animals are kidnapped and sold all the time to laboratories where they are subjected to the most horrible—"

"Let's get back to work, shall we?" Terry was in no mood for another Bernadette rant. She looked towards Mrs. Bagley, who beamed as she dialed the phone. "It's moments like this that make it all worthwhile, isn't it, Mrs. Bagley?"

"Another small triumph," Travis added. "I wish we could have more."

"Aw, you've had lots a triumphs, Trav." Sparrow gave him a pat on the back. "Don't forget about dogs in the back of pickup trucks."

"Thanks for reminding me. We had to fight like hell, but we won that one, didn't we?" Travis looked toward Bernadette's computer. "Let's get the newsletter done."

"And then let's all go for lunch at Greens Restaurant," said Krista. "I'm dying for a tomato pizza with grilled onions and fennel. It's just so good."

* * *

Darkness had fallen by the time they finished the newsletter. In the parking lot, Terry asked, "Are you coming with us to eat, Travis?" She held her breath. Usually he joined them.

He shook his head. "Sorry, I've got an appointment. Maybe next time. Goodbye, all." He headed for his car.

Krista gave Terry a knowing glance. "Hmm...did you catch that?"

Terry tried to sound casual despite the sudden ache in her heart. "Sounded like he had a date, didn't it?"

"It sure did. Wonder what her name is? *Bruce?*"

Krista leaped nimbly away just in time, barely avoiding the swift, murderous arc of Terry's canvas bag.

Travis drove up Van Ness in the early evening traffic. Bernadette, Terry, Sparrow, all of them, what would they say if they knew? And why didn't he want them to know? He was doing nothing wrong, not in this day and age, or any day and age, but even so, his private life was none of their business. He hated to see the hurt in Terry's eyes, but wouldn't she be more hurt if she knew? She'd never understand. It was better she didn't know, the lesser of two evils. He stopped at a liquor store and bought a bottle of Mateus Rosé. He drove farther up Van Ness, forcing himself not to speed, and turned onto California. At Hyde he turned again, shifting into low gear at the start of the steep hill. Halfway to the top, he stopped and backed into a parking space in front of an old apartment building, typically San Franciscan with its furbeloved, three-sided windows jutting over the sidewalk. He turned the wheels of the Prius outward and firmly set the hand brake. He picked up the Mateus and a small, wrapped box from the seat of the car.

At the entrance, he pressed the button under "Johansen, 5D." Seconds later, a loud buzzer sounded, allowing him to unlatch the door. In the marble-floored lobby, he entered an ancient elevator, pressed "5," and was borne, with excruciating slowness, to the fifth floor. He got off and walked down the carpeted hallway toward the door marked "D." It swung open. She stood there, waiting. "Good Evening, Miss Johansen, your star pupil is here." He grinned and held out the box and the bottle of wine. "Happy fifty-ninth birthday."

"Travis, do come in." The short, dark-haired woman standing in the doorway awarded him with a welcoming smile that lit the mature, yet nearly unlined, features of her face. Although her figure had settled into matronly curves, she did not look her age. She was slender still, and looked exceedingly attractive in slacks and a yellow, long-sleeved cable sweater. "You rascal!" Her warm brown eyes shone as he came in and she shut the door. "Did you have to remember my exact age? The dining room, dinner's all ready." She examined the bottle. "Ah, Mateus, how nice. We'll have it with the Cornish hen. Well, come sit down and eat. My, you look as if you've lost a little weight. Are you eating right?"

Over the candlelit dinner, he relaxed and unwound, telling her all of it—the fights, the hassles, the never-ending struggle for the animals, until finally, over her empty dessert plate, she raised a protesting hand. "Enough. Let's change the subject. This is my birthday, after all." She held up the gold bracelet on her wrist. "I love it, dear. You always know what I like."

"I'm glad."

"Fifty-nine. Incredible. Travis, how long have we known each other?"

As if she didn't know. His insides glowed from the wine, and he was happy to tell her what she wanted to hear. His smile grew warm, remembering. "I was twenty-one years old when I walked into your English 101 class. Do you remember?"

She cast him a beguiling glance as she picked up her wine glass. "I remember you were having trouble with your tenses."

"So you invited me to your apartment for special tutoring."

"And I've been special tutoring you ever since."

They both laughed, savoring the old joke. He shook his head in disbelief. "My God, how you took my breath away that day."

"I guess I did, didn't I? Shame on me." She did not look sorry.

He could wait no longer. He finished his last drop of wine and laid his napkin on the table. Concealing his eagerness, he said softly, deliberately, "It's time, Florence."

Slowly she shoved her chair back. "Yes, dear, it's time."

"Three hours, Travis. Do you realize we've been at it for three whole hours? That's disgraceful."

"Let's go for another three."

"There was a time..."

Her head rested on his naked shoulder. They lay, spent and exhausted, on a bed that looked as if a tornado had whirled across it. "It's past one in the morning. I must go."

"You can't spend the night?"

"I've got a meeting tomorrow, early."

"Before you go, I have something to tell you."

"You're pregnant? Don't worry, your unborn child will have a name. I'll marry you tomorrow."

"Be serious. I want to retire, and I'm thinking of moving to Mexico. I bought a book the other day that says I could live like a queen in Acapulco or Puerto Vallarta for twelve hundred dollars a month. You know, Travis, my teacher's pension won't stretch all that far in San Francisco."

"Are you sure?"

"It's worth a try. There are a lot of Americans down there, living in little colonies, doing artsy-craftsy things. I could do some writing, try my hand at painting."

"I should miss you."

"*Would* miss you. *Should* implies an obligation, whereas…"

"*Would* miss you, dammit."

"You'd miss the sex."

"That's true. But more, I'd miss you."

"I believe you, but you know we can't keep this up forever. I'm not getting any younger, baby. Gravity is taking its toll. Remember how we used to make love in the daytime, in the bright sunlight? Haven't you noticed? It's always at night now, with the lamp turned low."

"I don't care."

"I do."

"You're beautiful to me. You always will be."

"Thank you for that, Travis, but I'd be doing you a favor."

"How do you figure that?"

"If I left, you'd get on with your life instead of satisfying all your sexual urges with your old college English teacher. You might even get married again."

"Never."

"Was your first marriage that bad? You never told me."

"A nightmare. My own fault, of course. I don't blame Sandra."

"Didn't you love her?"

"I was twenty-four. All my friends were getting married. I was fond of her. My parents were putting the pressure on, expecting me to follow that old American dream—a house in the suburbs, patch of lawn to mow, watching football Sunday afternoon. I tried for a while. We were your typical Marin County couple, the hardworking husband out there hustling, trying to prove himself a man. The unselfish, self-sacrificing little wife, passive as hell. The sex was awful."

"Was it? I wondered. I missed you those years."

"Sandra never liked it. She *did it* for me. Sex was her gift, her token of appreciation for being protected and provided for."

"That's sad."

"What's sad is how we stuck it out for ten long years. I was miserable. Now I know she was, too."

"So what happened?"

"She came to me one day and told me she was sorry but she wasn't happy and wanted to leave to 'find herself' was how she put it. She hoped I wouldn't be too heartbroken."

"And did she?"

"Find herself? Oh, yeah. Sandra's changed. The last time I saw her, a year or so ago, she told me she was happy as a clam because at last she was free to express her horniness. I naturally wished her every success."

"So you became a late bloomer."

"I've just begun. It's sad, but I think a lot of men begin to die when they're in their twenties, when they make that commitment to a fixed life. I escaped that. Thank God, I don't have to live up to any image of what a man is supposed to be in this society. I'm not going to walk that narrow line, ever again. Let them scorn, laugh, call me a crazy misfit, but I'm doing what I want to do. I'll never go back to suburbia and play some phony role."

She raised her head off his shoulder and looked him in the eye. "I'm truly impressed, Travis. Three solid hours of screwing and you make a speech like that. My, my, you are a remarkable man."

He gave her a quick kiss and pulled her head back to his shoulder. "I've only one raging passion, and that's to save the animals. There's so much to do. Do you see now why I'll never marry again? And why I don't want any deep attachment with a woman? Except you, of course."

"You've never really been in love, have you?"

"No. Even back in high school I never had so much as a mild crush on a girl."

"That's what I mean." She pulled her head up again. "You know what I think? At least once in your life you should have a raging passion for a woman. How I'd love to see you smitten— lifted on the wings of love, stumbling, bumbling, weak with longing—"

"Stumbling, bumbling? Sounds like you're going into your Vachel Lindsay routine."

"I'm not quoting poetry. I'm trying to tell you something."

He sat up and swung his legs over the side of the bed. "Florence, you're a true romantic at heart. You're waiting for me to fall madly in love, but don't hold your breath. It's not going to happen."

"Oh, piffle. We shall see, Travis Kerrigan. Mark my words, she's out there. You're bound to meet her."

"So when are you going to Mexico?"

"Not quite yet, but soon."

Chapter 9

Denver, Colorado,
St. Francis Memorial Hospital

Karlin's leg was gone. Jillian had sat by her sister's bed ever since they brought her back from the recovery room, had been there for hours while Karlin drifted in and out, sounding slightly drunk from whatever painkiller they'd loaded into her IV.

Tish had come and gone, along with Tom and Dennis. She didn't know how long she'd been sitting here. It was all a blur. The operation was a success, they said. They'd taken the leg from three inches above the knee. At least there was something there. At least the blankets weren't flat, where a leg ought to be. In his cold, clinical voice, Dr. De Leon had explained. "She was fitted with a plaster cast, right on the operating table. A metal tube is attached, and to that, a molded rubber foot." The cast would keep the swelling down and help her adjust to the idea of a prosthesis.

Prosthesis. She'd have to practice pronouncing it. She'd also have to get used to the idea, stop feeling sick inside whenever she thought about how her lively, pretty, talented sister was suddenly a cripple. The doctors and nurses all seemed so cheerful, so optimistic. Chances of recovery were good, they said.

If only she could find Lucky. Two days now. Short of standing beside I-70 waving a LOST DOG sign, she'd tried everything. Ads in the Denver Post, the Lakewood Sentinel, Craig's List. Calls to the animal shelters. Notices in Safeway and King Soopers, placed there by Tish. Tom was still too busy. So far, nothing.

Her smartphone played its tune. It was Tom. "Hi, darling, is she still sleeping?"

"Yes, she's asleep."

"Listen, about my party tomorrow night—"

"I told you, don't feel guilty. It would be silly to call off the party. Besides, it wouldn't help Karlin a bit." *It wouldn't bring her leg back.*

"Well, it wasn't that. Actually it hadn't crossed my mind to cancel. This is my housewarming that I've planned for months. All my best clients will be there. Besides, my deposit with the caterer is nonrefundable."

"Of course. This is hard on all of us."

"Hmm. Well, you know, there were two reasons for the party, one to show off my new condo, and the other—"

"To show me off?"

He didn't laugh. "I want everyone to meet my new fiancée. You said you'd be late, but I've been thinking it would be nice, darling, if you could come earlier."

"Tom, can't you understand? I'm not in the mood for parties. Karlin needs me here. I'll come, but don't look for me before ten or so, and I won't stay long."

"Hmm…of course I understand. Just don't leave me spinning in the wind, is all. See you tomorrow." Abruptly, he rang off.

Uh-oh. Along with everything else, now Tom was ticked. There were a lot of things he didn't understand.

Karlin opened her eyes. They looked clearer now. "Hi, Sis, I'm back again. I keep drifting in and out, don't I?"

"So? Don't worry about it."

"Anything new on Lucky?"

"Don't I wish."

Tears formed in Karlin's eyes and splashed down over her cheeks. "I'm thinking about him out in that awful storm, lost and freezing."

"It didn't happen that way. Somebody found him. They'll be calling us soon."

"I love that dog. I didn't know how much until now. He's friendly and smart, and never bit anyone."

Please stop, this is killing me. "He was never mean."

"The world's greatest dog, we used to say that, didn't we? I wish…"

Jillian patted her hand. "Don't you dare give up hope. I'm

going to keep looking for Lucky. I'll go anywhere, do anything, whatever it takes to get him back." She pulled out her smartphone and dialed. "I'm calling home right now—see if I got any messages." She listened. Her face lit. "Oh, my God, there's a message." She grabbed pen and paper, wrote down a number. She dialed again.

"Hello?" The voice was male.

"I'm Jillian Dahl. You left a message about my dog?"

"Yes, ma'am, Lucky. I've got him." He had a Texas drawl.

Karlin's eyes went wide. "Is it Lucky? Have they found him?"

Jillian gleefully nodded her head. She leaped the rest of the way from her chair. "Wonderful." She covered the phone. "This man says he's got him." She spoke into the phone again. "Where are you?"

"Well, this might surprise you, ma'am, but I'm in a place called Fresno, California."

"That's a thousand miles from here. What's Lucky doing there?"

"Well, it's a long story..." Huff told Jillian about finding Lucky on I-70 and why he had to take him to California. "But don't worry, Lucky's fine. I'm due for a haul to Denver in two or three weeks. I can bring him back then."

"Two or three weeks?" Jillian watched Karlin's face fall. "Just a minute." She covered the phone again. "He's a trucker. He says he'll be back this way in two or three weeks and he can bring Lucky then."

"Oh, Jillian, must I wait that long? I want Lucky back now, so I'll know he's safe."

She didn't have to think about it. Only one thing to do. She spoke into the phone. "I'll come get him."

"Say, ma'am, you don't have to go to all that trouble. Don't you worry, we'll take good care of your dog."

"Oh, I'm sure you would, Mister...?"

"Huffman, I'm Vernon Huffman, but call me Huff. Like I say, I'll be coming back through Denver soon."

"Thanks, Huff, but the problem is Lucky's owner, that's

my sister Karlin, is in the hospital, and she...she isn't feeling well, and I'd really like to get Lucky back now. I'll just come out and get him. Can you give me your address?" She grabbed the pen.

"Sure. It's 1409 Weber, Fresno, California. I'm taking a load to L.A. tomorrow. I'll be gone a few days, but my wife, Debbie, will be here. Come by any time."

What a nice man. She could tell, just by the warmth in his voice. "Wonderful. I can't thank you enough."

"Hey, think nothing of it. My pleasure. Glad I found you."

"I'm glad you found Lucky. I'll be there...let's see, I'll have to check the flights. Where is Fresno, anyway? Do I go through San Francisco or L.A.?"

He laughed. "Fresno's right smack dab in the center of California. We're not the boonies. There are direct flights from Denver."

"Okay then. I'll be there sometime this weekend, depending on when I can get reservations. I'll let you know."

When Jillian hung up the phone, Karlin was glowing. "I am so relieved! You can go tomorrow, can't you?"

"Are you sure? I hate to leave you here, just after—"

"I'll be fine. Dennis and Tish will be here and all my friends. I won't get lonely."

"Well then, why not? Tomorrow it is. With luck, I could be back tomorrow night, in time to see you. Oh yes, and go to Tom's party."

Karlin frowned. "I've caused you lots of problems, haven't I?"

"Don't be dumb. Hmm...Denver to Fresno. I'll get a direct flight. As I recall, most airlines have those dog carriers."

"Lucky won't like flying baggage class. He'll make you buy him a first class ticket."

Karlin joking, that's good. "Thank God that man called. Just think, Karlin, if all goes well, I'll be home with Lucky by tomorrow night."

Fresno, California

Driving a dented '99 Chevy, Cal Ryska cruised slowly down the fourteen hundred block of Weber Avenue towards the vacant lot on the corner where Huff always parked his truck. A smirk crossed his thin lips. Nothing like screwing a broad whose husband was a truck driver. Not only was the dumb sucker gone a lot, but when he was home, he might as well hang a WATCH OUT, CAL, I'M HERE sign in the window as park that Peterbilt down at the corner. His face lit up when he got to the end of the block. His luck was holding today. Not only had his income tax refund finally arrived, but the lot was empty. Debbie's husband was off on another haul. He hadn't expected that. The jerk only got home yesterday. *Tahoe, here I come with seven hundred dollars in my pocket and the hottest tail in Fresno to keep me company.*

"But I just don't think I should, Cal." Debbie's lower lip stuck out in a pout. Her forehead furrowed in a troubled frown.

"Why not, baby?" It was all he could do to keep his temper. He had her down on the couch, kissing her hard, feeling her up, but was having a hell of a time talking her into it. "You want to miss good times in Tahoe? Hey, that's not like my sweet baby."

She kept turning her head away from his kisses. "But what if Huff comes home?"

Cal began nibbling on her ear. "How long's that husband of yours gonna be gone?"

"He said five days but—"

"Five days? You little dingbat. We're only gonna be gone one night. We'll be home way before that old husband of yours gets back."

"Yeah, but what about the dog?"

He raised his head. "What dog?"

"The one that's in our back yard..." She told him what happened. "And like, you know, Huff said to be here when this lady comes to get her dog. I'm not supposed to go anyplace, and I know he'd be mad if I left the dog alone."

"When's she coming?"

"Huff said maybe today. I've got to be here."

Sometimes it was hard to be patient. "Leave him with your Mom. You can put a note on the door."

"I can't. They won't let her have any pets in that little apartment, not even to visit."

He worked on her ear some more. "Then we'll take the dog with us."

"But Cal..." The good feelings started right from the ear where he was nibbling to all over. It felt so good. "You think it will be okay?"

He paused his nibbling. "Okay? Sure, honey baby. Don't you worry, we'll take good care of that dog. If she's so anxious to get it, she can wait 'til we get back."

Denver, Colorado
Pine Mountain Condominiums

Jillian opened her closet door. "So, Tish, what would you wear on a one day whirlwind trip to Fresno, California?"

"I'd wear my jeans and Adidas, but knowing you, you'll be wearing your five-hundred dollar Bruno Magli's and a God-knows-who designer outfit. You'd better take an overnight bag."

"Why? I told you I'd be back the same day."

"Take it. You never know what's going to happen. A girl should never get caught without a toothbrush, a change of underwear and a month's supply of birth control pills. Too bad you'll miss Tom's party."

"I won't miss it, I'll just be late. He can't understand why I'd go all the way to California just for a dog."

"The man's all heart."

"Oh come on...he just doesn't understand, that's all."

"Sure."

"Look outside. It's snowing."

"The sun's probably shining like crazy in California."

"It's still winter. Guess I'll have to take a coat."

"So wear your mink. That'll impress the hell out of Fresno."

San Pedro Harbor, California

It was a gray, soggy feathered seagull skimming low over the murky waters of the harbor that caused THE TRUTH to trigger in Huff's until-that-moment unsuspecting brain.

He'd waited extra long while a slow-moving crew unloaded the cartons from his truck. He didn't mind. The dock was a busy place with lots to watch, like the cranes swinging giant cargo containers aboard a big freighter tied alongside. He leaned against a railing in the sunshine, thumbs hooked on pockets, hat pushed back, one boot idly toeing a loose plank. Where was that ship going? Who would end up eating the oranges and kiwi fruit he'd just hauled in from the San Joaquin Valley? Someone far across the sea, for sure. Japan? Tahiti? Australia? Who knew?

Some day he and Debbie might take a ship to some of those faraway places. By golly, not might, would. She'd like that. He sniffed the salt air and watched the sea gulls, real pretty as they dipped and soared, picking up pieces of the garbage that bobbed on the water near the pier. Pretty soon he'd check and see if his truck was unloaded. Then he'd pick up the load of frozen TV dinners and hit I-10 for Arizona.

The gull flew by, a big chunk of dark bread clenched in its beak. Bread...*pumpernickel.* The question that had lain dormant in the back of his brain popped into Huff's consciousness. How come his loaf of pumpernickel, the one he'd just bought and hardly touched, was nearly gone? Strange. Debbie hated the stuff. So who ate it? Except for her wacky mother, she never had company, and Norma Jean liked white bread.

Who's been eating my pumpernickel?

What about his beer? That was strange, too. He'd bought a twelve pack of Coors last time he was home and drank maybe six bottles total. Now there were only two bottles left. Debbie didn't like beer and her mom drank wine.

Who's been drinking my beer?

It all came back to him, all the little pieces of the puzzle that had bugged him and he didn't know why. All those excuses Debbie had been making. She was tired—it was her period—she didn't feel good. And what were those bruises on her arms he hadn't asked about? Only one explanation...

Who's been screwing my wife?

Debbie's mother, Norma Jean, loved to watch old Shirley Temple movies. The one she was watching now was pretty good, so when the phone first rang, right in the part where Shirley's mother is hit by the bus and the birthday cake gets squashed, Norma Jean didn't move from her easy chair. It wasn't only the movie. Just hauling herself up was a big pain in the butt these days, now that she'd put on a little weight. The phone wouldn't quit. With a disgusted grunt, Norma Jean hoisted herself up and waddled to the kitchen. She hoped it was Debbie calling to say she'd changed her mind about going to Lake Tahoe with that Cal Ryska. As she reached for the phone, she shook her head and tsk-tsked. Cal Ryska was nothing but trouble, and if Huff ever found out...

"Hello? Huff?" *Uh-oh*. She could tell from his voice he was mad. "Yeah, I know she's not home. Nope, she's not here. How should I know?" Oh boy, he was real mad. "You're what? Well, listen, Huff, she's probably just gone to a movie or something. Maybe she went to play bingo. Four hours?" *Oh, Jesus*. "Yeah, okay, Huff, see ya."

Norma Jean hung up the phone and swung open a cupboard door. She grabbed a full bag of Fritos, ripped it open, and crammed a handful of chips into her mouth. From the fridge, she pulled her four-liter jug of Chianti and poured herself another. Clutching bag and wine glass, she plodded back to her chair. As she sank back into its soft depths, she shrewdly observed to herself that in four hours, when Huff got back to Fresno, it was all going to hit the fan.

Meanwhile, little Shirley was in a hell of a mess.

Chapter 10

Lake Tahoe, Nevada

Hot damn, he felt lucky. Cal Ryska's hopes rose with the altitude as he steered up the winding highway, rolling with the usual pack of gamblers, hell-bent for Tahoe at eighty miles an hour. By the time he reached the South Shore, and turned into the parking lot behind The Silver Palace, a solid feel of optimism tingled through his veins, running deep into his gut. Sure, his luck had been rotten lately. He wouldn't be surprised if he got fired at Jerry's Jiffy Lube just because he took a couple of days off. He didn't have a choice, though. Bill collectors were hot on his tail. The old Chevy was falling apart. There were holes in his shoes. He'd made trip after trip to Reno and Tahoe, and for what? Those robbers took his last nickel every time. But that was over and done, another part of his past he'd just as soon forget. Now, courtesy of the IRS, seven one-hundred-dollar bills, tucked deep in his wallet were sending him a message. *Go for it, Cal baby. Tonight you're a winner.* He swerved the car into an empty spot and jerked to a stop.

"Geez, Cal." Debbie braced her arms against the dashboard. She looked into the back seat at Lucky who was scrambling on the floor. "Look what you did to the dog."

"Piss on the dog." Cal was already out of the car. He hitched up his jeans, tucked in his T-shirt. "Come on."

Debbie climbed out slowly. "Shouldn't we get our room first?"

"Later. Come on, move it."

Debbie shut the door, smoothed her slacks and pink sweater, sniffed the air and looked around. "Umm, I love that pine smell. Look, Cal, at all the rocks and pinecones." She gazed towards the sky. "Just look at the pretty sunset, and those trees. Gee, they're so tall..."

Cal spun around and started towards the glittering entrance of the casino. "So stay with the fucking dog then."

Debbie ran after him and tugged on his sleeve. "The doggie needs some air, Cal. Maybe we should roll a window down." He kept going, not slowing his long, purposeful stride. She stopped and called after him in a pleading voice, "Cal...?"

"Christ!" Scarcely looking, he flung the keys back at her. They landed at her feet. "So roll one down then, but just a crack. Meet me inside."

Debbie picked up the keys, walked back to the Chevy, and opened the door. Lucky was right there, frantically wagging his tail, wanting to get out. "No, doggie, you stay." Debbie rolled the window down an inch. Gee, maybe she should let the dog out for a minute, get it some water, but she'd better hurry and get inside. New places were scary. She didn't want to lose sight of Cal, not when she'd never been in a casino before. "You just stay there." She pushed Lucky back from the door. "Be good now, and we'll be back pretty soon."

With an eager pull, Cal opened one of the big double doors of the Silver Palace, Tahoe's grandest, gaudiest casino. Inside, he paused, blinking, his pulse quickening as he adjusted his eyes to the vast, windowless interior with its lavish, fake western decor. Sweet, familiar sounds caressed his ears. Merry tunes came from the slot machines. A soft, female voice called out names for the next poker game. In the distance, beyond the banks of slots, far into the acre of roulette, twenty-one and crap tables, he heard the lusty hoot of an excited winner. Reaching for his wallet, Cal threaded his way through the crowd to a cashier's booth. He tossed one of his hundreds on the counter. ."Gimme twenty five dollar chips."

Debbie touched his arm. "I'm back, Cal."

He didn't need some ding-a-ling broad hanging around, not when he had important things to do. "Got some money?" He nodded towards her big straw purse.

"Huff gave me three twenties for my grocery money."

"Get out a twenty. Go play the nickel slots and stay out of my hair."

She looked up at him with a bewildered expression. "Can't

I stay with you? I don't know how—"

"You slide the twenty into the slot. You press the button. If you win, it'll tell you. If you lose, you try again. Got that, dummy?" He grasped her shoulders, turned her around, and aimed her at the nickel machines. "Now go." With a headshake of disgust, he watched as she clutched her twenty and disappeared, with uncertain steps, into the crowd. Another winner's delighted shout made him forget about Debbie. He set off for the crap tables, chips in hand.

It was the kind of game he liked—plenty of action from a crowd that pressed around the table, yelling at each throw of the dice. There was a guy in a dark suit waving hundred dollar bills, *East Coast high roller* written all over him. An old guy in a cowboy hat who had to be from Texas hooted "Yeee Haw!" when he won. A plump grandmother played her tiny hoard of dollar chips like they were gold, one at a time. A rich-bitch broad, diamonds dripping from her fingers, showed off her sagging cleavage when she leaned over the table sprinkling hundred dollar chips around.

Four employees ran the game. Two dealers, both tough looking birds, who paid and collected the bets—the stickman, a young kid with a shock of blond hair, who called out the numbers and raked the dice—the sharp-eyed box man, sitting in the middle, not missing a thing. Cal shouldered a place for himself between the high roller and the grandmother. Texas held the dice, ready to roll. Cal's hand hovered briefly over the table. Pass? Don't Pass? *Go with the shooter.* He dropped a chip on the pass line just as the dice skidded across the table.

"Seven, a winner."

Right on! As Texas hooted his *Yee Haw*, the dealer paid Cal's bet. Let it ride? You betcha.

"Seven, a winner."

Yeah. He wasn't even surprised. The dealer slid his winning chips across. Let it ride? *No, the old fart's going to lose this time.* Cal stacked his chips and set them on the don't pass line a second before the dice flew again.

"Nine. Your point is nine, shooter. A field roll."

Cal sniffed. Man, they always were after you to play the field, a sucker bet if ever there was one. The old gal next to him placed one of her precious chips on top of the twelve. But then... *Go for it, Cal Baby. Yeah, the field.* He slid four chips next to Grandma's.

"Hardway four. Pay the field."

Granny squealed. Cal picked up his winnings and put them on the come line. Two rolls later, Texas, still trying for his nine, rolled a seven, and that was just fine because Cal had him faded, so he won there, and won off the come line too. He hadn't lost yet.

The stickman offered him the bowl of dice. "You rolling?"

Was the Pope Catholic? Did the sun rise in the east? Cal nodded. Chips, bills, and silver dollars flooded the table as the stickman dumped five dice in front of him. He picked his two and shoved twenty chips onto the pass line. One hundred dollars on one roll. Was he crazy? As his fingers curled around the dice, he felt the scrutiny of the snooty broad who stood on the other side of Grandma. He shot her a glance. She was staring at the front of his shirt. As he watched, her nose twitched and pinched in, like she was smelling a dirty sock. Her lips pursed. A flicker of distaste flashed through her eyes. He looked down. Oh, yeah, that T-shirt, the one with a big globe on the front and The World Sucks underneath. *Don't like my T-shirt, lady? Hang it on your nose.*

She glared right at him, gave him the fisheye while she dropped two hundred dollar chips on the Don't Pass line, then carefully aligned them with her fancy red nails. *You're gonna lose, lady.* He drew a deep breath—no sense getting tense—and with a lightening right hand, sent the dice hurtling to the far end of the table.

"Eleven, the winner."

That was the start of the luckiest streak he ever had. He couldn't lose. He kept playing the pass line, winning the percentages like any smart money player would, but he won on the dumb stuff too. When he laid one hundred dollars on the Big Six, a bet designed exclusively for little old ladies from Dubuque, his next roll came up six. When he played the field, where he could win only sixteen ways against the house's twenty, the dice came up four, a winner, then nine, a winner, then two, which paid double, then twelve, and that paid double too. When he put two hundred dollars on a hardway eight—and only genuine, bonafide idiots ever played the hard ways—the dice came up four-four on the very next roll. He won eighteen hundred dollars on that one, plus a flinty stare from the snooty rich bitch who'd bet against him every time. She was about to pee her pants, she was that mad.

Man, he was hot. He still had the dice. He was betting two hundred dollars on the pass line now, the house limit, plus the two hundred dollar limit on the other stuff. A row of hundred dollar chips lay in the slot on the ledge in front of him. No time to count, but there had to be at least two, three thousand there. His point was eight. He rolled again.

"Seven the loser."

Shit, that was the end of it, but look what he'd done. A small fortune lay in front of him. Grandma got the dice as he counted his chips...and counted...and counted, and it wasn't two or three thousand, it was four thousand, plus the six bills still in his pocket. Enough to get the collection agencies off his back— to fix the Chevy, or better yet, make a down payment on a new one—to buy a new pair of shoes. That is, if he cashed in now. *Pick up your chips. Leave.* This time he'd know when enough was enough. For once in his life he'd walk away from the table with money in his pocket.

He gathered up his chips, ready to cash in, just as Grandma crapped out, her last chip gone. The dealer shoved the dice to the snooty bitch. She picked them up, flicking him a look that said *what's the matter, asshole, can't stand the heat?* Well, hell, he wasn't going to stand for that. He'd leave in a minute, soon as he showed that broad what craps was all about. He laid five hundred dollar chips on the "Don't Pass" line, slow, so she couldn't miss it.

She noticed all right. He was the recipient of a dagger-eyed glance, right before her diamonds flashed and she fired the dice to the far board.

"Seven, a winner."

She didn't have to look at him. The tiny smirk on her face said it all. She stacked her chips on the pass line and let it ride. Who the hell did she think she was? He dropped another five hundred on Don't Pass.

"Eleven, and the lady wins again."

He'd swear the young, blond-haired stickman hid a smile. Whose side was he on anyway? Even the box man was trying to keep his face straight. They were all against him. They always were. Okay, that was it. Walk away. That smartass broad was laughing at him. It was like his feet were set in cement. No woman was going to get the best of Cal Ryska. He had no choice but to try again. Besides, three passes in a row? No way she'd make a fourth. He stacked another five hundred on the Don't Pass line and because he knew he'd win this time, stacked chips on the dumb bets, all over the board.

She rolled. Another seven.

It couldn't last, but it did. She rolled three more sevens. He kept on betting, and losing, even the six bills he'd kept safe in his pocket, until finally he was down to…he counted and his heart sank…five hundred left. She had chips coming out her ass. Six straight passes in a row. So okay, he'd had a bad streak there, but one thing he knew—six successive passes meant the odds on a seventh were one hundred twenty-seven to one. Therefore, laying his last five hundred on the Don't Pass line was a mere formality. How could he lose?

The diamonds flashed, the dice rolled, the blond kid grinned. "Seven, the winner."

The dealer executed a lightning fast swipe, and the last of his money vanished. *Gone, all gone.* Stony-faced (mustn't let her know), he turned away from the table. Damn the snooty bitch, and damn his father who'd deserted him when he was five, and his mother who beat him until he ran away from home, and the teachers who hadn't cared, and the bosses who'd fired him. Damn Debbie too, for no reason he could think of except she was here.

Damn the whole goddamned fucking world.

There'd be no hotel room now. No screwing around with Debbie, not that he was in the mood for it anyway. They'd have to drive back to Fresno tonight, if there was enough gas in the car, and if there wasn't, then what would he do? Where was she? He strode down a row of slot machines. *Debbie's money.* Hadn't she said she had three twenties? Yeah. She'd have forty left. So he wasn't dead in the water after all. Now if he could just find her...

A bell rang, not one of the ordinary jackpot bells that you ignored, it was a loud bell and then "We're in the Money" started to play. From somewhere in the banks of slot machines he heard excited voices.

"A giant jackpot! Some redheaded girl..."

Screw it, all he wanted was to find Debbie, get the money, and get back to that crap table... *Redheaded girl? Oh, my God.* Cal raced towards the little crowd gathered in front of one of the progressive dollar machines. He saw a flash of pink. There she was, standing by the machine, eyes wide and frightened, looking like she'd just committed some crime. She saw him, rushed over, and grabbed his hands. "Oh, Cal, I'm sorry. I know you told me to play nickels but I used them all. And then this lady said I should try dollars, so I put one of the twenties into this...this...gadget." Debbie pointed at the machine. "Then I pressed the button and got those silver stars, all the way across, and then the bell rang." She looked up at him, eyes pleading. "You're not mad at me, are you?"

Jesus Christ on a high roll. The machine was going crazy— lights flashing, bell ringing. Up on top a flashing arrow pointed to the progressive jackpot total and...his heart lurched...*thirty-three thousand, nine hundred eight-one dollars.* He gulped. His knees went weak. He put on a smile and gave her a hug. "No, baby, I'm not mad at you. You did just fine, sugar, just fine."

A bald guy in a tux, with "Manager" on his badge, came scurrying up. He poked a key into the machine and turned off the lights and all the noise. "Well, well, looks like we've got a big winner here." He shook Debbie's hand. "Congratulations.

You'll have to come into the office and fill out some forms. IRS rules, you know."

They followed the manager into the casino office. By the time they got there, Cal knew he deserved the money way more than Debbie and had every right to take it. After all, if he hadn't brought her to Tahoe, she wouldn't have won. Besides, what could she do if he took it, tell her husband? The jackpot was his. He wouldn't have to work for a year, maybe more. Hell, if he went down to Mexico, he'd make that thirty-three thousand last forever.

In the office, Cal sat quietly while Debbie filled out the form, tried not to sneer when she couldn't remember her Social Security number and had to look in her wallet. Hey! He would get the money tax-free. Old Huff would get nailed for the taxes. Let her explain *that* when the IRS knocked at their door.

When Debbie had finished filling out the IRS form and shown her ID, the manager asked, "Cash or check?"

Cal spoke up. "We'll take cash."

The manager looked at Debbie. She cast a fearful glance at Cal, then nodded.

"Very well, cash it is."

They walked out of the manager's office. Thank God, Debbie's purse was a big one. Now it bulged with thirty-three thousand, nine hundred eighty-one dollars, all cash. He steered her toward the front desk. "Hey, babe, let's check in."

"That's fine, Cal, but we've got to go back to the car and see the doggie."

He started to snap at her, and caught himself. Better ease up while she still had the dough. "Okay, sweets. We'll go see the dog and then we'll check in."

The driver's seat was soggy. The air stank of urine. Ashamed and humiliated, Lucky waited for Cal and Debbie to return. He was desperate for water. His tongue hung out. He was panting hard. In abject misery, he cringed on the back seat, as far away from the wetness as he could get. He heard foot-steps. They were coming. With a fearful heart, he waited, knowing he had done a bad thing.

Cal opened the door. "God damn, it stinks in here. The fucking dog peed all over the seat."

"Oh, Cal, he didn't mean—"

"Let me at him." Cal charged around to the other side of the car and yanked open the back door. "I'll teach you to fuck up my car." He unfastened his leather belt and slid it out from the loops of his jeans. He wrapped one end twice around his right hand. With his left, he reached for Lucky's collar, grasped it tight, and hauled him out of the car. "God damned mutt." He raised his arm high, slashed the belt downward, cutting across Lucky's rear flank. The dog squealed in pain, turned his head and sunk his teeth deep into the hand that gripped his collar. Cal yelled and let go.

Lucky leaped away and started to run, but Debbie grabbed him. "You let the doggie alone, Cal!" He raised his arm again, but Debbie pulled Lucky close. "Don't you dare."

She meant it, he could tell, but what did he care? He'd be gone shortly, anyway. This was no time to get mad. Besides, his hand hurt like hell and he'd better take care of it. "Okay, okay." He lowered his arm, unwound the belt and threaded it through the loops in his pants. "So what're you going to do with him? The hotel don't allow dogs."

Debbie jutted her chin out. "Then we'll just sneak him into the room."

"What about my car seat?"

"We'll put some towels over it. Can you think of anything better?"

He couldn't. It didn't matter. He'd be getting rid of that pile of junk tomorrow. "You wait here. I'll go check us in."

Room 107 was located in the casino annex on the first floor, overlooking the parking lot. Cal dropped their overnight bags on the baggage rack and examined his throbbing hand. *Jesus.* The bleeding had stopped, but it was red, swollen and hurt like hell. He'd be lucky if he didn't get rabies, but he'd worry about that later. First, get the money away from Debbie and haul ass out of here. Shouldn't be hard but one small problem. Debbie was pissed. Walked right by him without speaking. After she filled a glass with water and set it on the floor for the dog, she plunked herself on the side of the bed. Now there she sat, arms folded, lower lip pouting, gazing down at her shoes. "What's the matter, honey?" No answer. He sat down beside her and tried to put his arm around her shoulders.

She pulled away. "Don't touch me."

"Heyyyy." He cupped her chin in his hand and tried to turn her head towards him.

She resisted, jerking her head away. "Leave me alone, Cal. I'm mad at you."

"But what did I do, sugar?"

She glared at him. "You were mean to the dog."

"So is that all you're sore about? You'd be mad, too, if the dog peed on your seat."

"You didn't have to hit him."

"Okay, so I lost my temper. Look what he did to me." He held up his wounded hand. "But he's all right isn't he? I didn't really hurt him, did I?"

Debbie's pout began to recede. "I guess not."

Cal's hand crept around her shoulders. This time she didn't resist. "Of course not. Now give us a kiss." He kissed her hard. She began to kiss him back. He pulled her down on the bed and started massaging her body, rubbing and kissing her until she was breathing hard. "Know what we should do?"

"What, Cal?" Her eyes were closed.

"We should hide that money. What if a thief broke in while we were sleeping? The first place he'd look would be your purse."

"Okay, Cal, will you go hide it? And hurry back."

Cal got off the bed, pulled the money from Debbie's purse, and laid it on the dresser. It made a sizable pile. He looked around. Where could he hide it? The beat-up canvas gym bag he used for a suitcase was pretty small. It'd be hard, cramming all those packages of bills in there. He'd better find another place, somewhere where he could grab the money in a hurry when he sneaked out. He spotted a wastebasket by the bathroom door. Perfect. He sneaked a peak at Debbie. She wasn't even looking. He walked to the wastebasket, the piles of neatly bound hundred dollar bills stacked in his arms. He could drop them into the plastic liner of the basket; tuck the plastic around them to conceal them from view. But then…maybe the gym bag would be better after all. Where was he going to hide the money?

It was done. With a smug smile, Cal pulled off his clothes, tossed them to the floor, and climbed into bed with Debbie. His plans were set. He'd get one last screw with the dummy, sleep a couple of hours, sneak out long before she woke up. Drive back to Fresno, pick up his stuff, clear out of his miserable one-room apartment, and hit the road to…?

Hot damn, he could go anyplace he wanted. For thirty-three thousand dollars the world was his. He'd head south, hit Las Vegas, Palm Springs, then on to Acapulco. As for Debbie, no sense being cheap. He'd leave fifty dollars on the bureau. She could take the Greyhound home.

Chapter 11

Fresno, California

"Here's 1409 Weber Street." The taxi driver pulled over and stopped behind a big truck parked at the curb.

"I'll only be a minute." Jillian slid out of the taxi, leaving her overnight bag and fur coat on the back seat. She touched her hair and smoothed the straight skirt of her Adolfo suit, glad she'd ignored Tish's advice to wear jeans and a sweater. The black and off-white plaid silk jacquard jacket fit beautifully. As they promised at Neiman Marcus, it *traveled well.*

The house, a boxy white bungalow, sat behind an expanse of green lawn clipped and neatly mowed. Well-trimmed shrubs grew under the shuttered windows. Green in March, definitely California.

She hurried up the walkway that divided the lawn in two. She could hardly wait to see Lucky again. Out of all the despair of the past few days, something good was going to happen. She glanced at her watch. So far, she was on schedule. Time would be tight, but she had it all planned. Hug Lucky, thank Huff, take the taxi back to the airport, and fly back to Denver. She'd be too late to visit the hospital, but in time to catch the end of Tom's party. That should make him happy.

Tomorrow Karlin would have her dog again. She pushed the doorbell and heard a faint "ding-dong" inside. Maybe she should offer Mr. Huffman a reward. A hundred dollars would be good. He deserved it for all his trouble. He'd sounded so nice on the phone. Maybe he'd be insulted if she offered him money, but if she was tactful enough he might accept.

The sound of pounding footsteps interrupted her thoughts. The door burst open. She leaped back, nearly falling off the porch as a bearded giant of a man wearing cowboy clothes tore through. He charged down the sidewalk like a raging bull towards the big truck at the curb. He hadn't even noticed her, but if this was Huff and he was leaving, she'd better speak up fast. "Oh, wait!" She stretched out her hand. He didn't stop. "Wait!"

He spun around. He was holding a gun. "WHO ARE YOU? WHAT DO YOU WANT?"

Her eyes locked on the gun dangling from his hand, pointed not at her but downwards at the ground. She had never seen a man so angry. Maybe in movies or TV, but not for real. Certainly not one with a gun. "I...I..."

"WELL?" He waited a second longer, turned and made a beeline for the truck.

He couldn't leave, not yet. "Just a minute!" She ran down the walk after him. She had to know about Lucky, crazy man or no. She touched his arm, the one without the gun. "Are you Huff? I talked to you on the phone, remember? I came to get the dog."

He turned and regarded her through eyes glazed with rage. "The dog?"

"Lucky. You picked him up on I-70."

A light dawned. "Oh, yeah, you're the little lady from Denver."

"That's right. And you're Huff—"

"I'm Huff. I found your dog, but I can't talk now."

"Well, I'm so delighted to meet you." She extended her hand, giving him the benefit of her most charming pleased-to-meet-you smile.

He ignored her hand. "Lady, I've got to go."

"Could you at least tell me where my dog is?"

Her question kindled his rage. Beneath his big Stetson, his face puffed up like a bullfrog. His beard quivered. His eyebrows peaked into arches of wrath. "Where's your dog? He's in Lake Tahoe with my wife and a no-good bastard named Cal Ryska."

So Lucky wasn't here. Now it all came clear. The wife and some boyfriend had taken Lucky to Lake Tahoe. Now what? She was almost afraid to ask, but she'd better. "So what do you intend to do?"

"Ma'am, what do you think I'm going to do? I'm going to

drive up to Tahoe and kill the sonofabitch, that's what I'm going to do."

Jillian opened her mouth to speak, but for a long, shocked moment, nothing coherent came out. "Are you serious?"

"Serious? I'm mad as hell, in case you hadn't noticed."

She pointed to the gun. "You're going to use that?"

He regarded her as if she'd just asked the world's dumbest question. "Yes, ma'am, that." He raised the gun and slapped it into his palm. She didn't know much about guns except it was awfully big. "It's called a 357 magnum, and it'll do the job just fine. Excuse me, I've got to go." He started off towards his truck again.

Jillian followed him to the curb. "Mr. Huffman, what about my dog?"

Without stopping, he hollered, "Lady, isn't it plain I can't be bothered with somebody's dog right now?" He circled around the front of the truck, scaled the side steps, and climbed into the cab.

Jillian looked back at the taxi, where the driver sat stony-faced, uninterested in the scene. So what was she supposed to do now, fly back to Denver without Lucky? No, by God, she hadn't flown clear to California for nothing. She stepped off the curb, stood directly in front of the truck, and placed balled-up fists defiantly on her hips. "I want my dog."

From six feet above, Huff poked his head out the window and glared down at her. "You heard me. I've got no time for dogs." He pulled in his head. Seconds later, came the grinding noise of a starter. The roar of the truck's engine blasted into her ears. "GET OUT OF THE WAY."

"No!" She didn't move. He wouldn't dare mow her down…she didn't think. Or was he just crazy enough that he might? No, he wouldn't. Mad though he was, this man wouldn't do such a thing. She stood her ground. He revved up the engine again. She glared up at him with a thrust out chin.

He dropped the engine to idle. She kept her fists on her hips. "Take me with you."

He stuck his head out the window again. "Have you ever

been in a truck before?"

"No."

"Then take my word, a nice lady like you doesn't want to ride in a noisy old truck like this all the way to Lake Tahoe, Nevada."

"Try me."

"You're not going to like it."

"It doesn't matter whether I like it or not. I want my dog back."

"Don't say I didn't warn you. This ain't a fun ride. I'm heading hell-for-leather for Tahoe with no stops in-between." He frowned down at her. "Changed your mind?"

For a moment, she hesitated. What had she let herself in for? Drive to Lake Tahoe in a truck with a mad man? She peered around at the tiny, vertical steps on the passenger side. She'd never be able to climb up there in her spike-heeled Bruno Magli pumps and the tight skirt of her Adolpho. Tish was right. She should have worn her jeans.

Huff scowled down at her. His hand slammed the side of the truck. "If you're coming, hurry up. I want that bastard dead by midnight."

Maybe she shouldn't. She would miss her flight and Tom's party. He'd counted on her being there. But on the other hand...

"Make up your mind right now, lady. Either piss or get off the pot."

Karlin, leg gone, waiting in Denver for her dog. "Wait while I get my things. Don't leave without me, I'm coming with you." She jumped back up on the curb and sprinted, as best she could in the Bruno Maglies, toward the taxi.

Madera—Merced—Modesto—Stockton. Jillian sat in the passenger seat as Huff sped north through the night on Highway 99. Would he ever speak? Heedless of speed signs, of the ever-lurking California Highway Patrol, he'd driven at a steady, illegal eighty-miles-per-hour, mile after tense mile, crouching silently over the steering wheel, gripping it with a white-knuckled grasp, staring steady and unblinking at the road ahead.

Actually, this wasn't half-bad, almost like an adventure, rolling up the highway in an 18-wheeler, like Queen-of-the-Road in her lofty seat, peering into the lowly passenger cars below. If only the huge man beside her would speak to her, but so far he sat silent, brooding, murder in his heart.

Out of Lodi, she wondered if he would stay like this the whole trip, not saying a word.

"DAMN." Huff slammed his palm on the steering wheel.

"Want to talk about it?"

He hesitated but not for long. Like a dam bursting, he opened up, told her how he'd loved and trusted his Debbie Sue, how he figured out the truth on the pier in San Pedro. How he'd driven like a crazy man back to Fresno, praying it wasn't so. Five angry, shouting minutes with Debbie's wacko mother was all it took to learn that for weeks now, weeks, some god-damned grease monkey named Cal Ryska had been screwing his own wife in his own home. He'd only stopped off at his place to get his gun. "DAMN." He clenched his fist, hammered at the steering wheel.

Jillian cast a measured glance to the floor, directly beneath his legs, where he had laid the 357 Magnum. "You're not really planning to use that thing are you?"

"You bet I am. You just don't know..." His voice choked. He could not go on.

"What about Debbie? Will you shoot her too?"

"Kill Debbie? Are you crazy? This isn't her fault. She's too dumb to know what she's doing."

"So you still love her?"

"It's only that grease monkey I'm after." He set his jaw. "Cal Ryska's gotta go."

"I can't help wondering, who's going to take care of Debbie after you get sent to prison for shooting Cal Ryska?"

"She's got her mother."

"But didn't you tell me—?"

"Well, yeah, Norma Jean's only got one oar in the water herself. But hell, I can't be worried about that." He threw her a crafty glance. "I know what you're trying to do and it won't work. You can't talk me out of it."

Jillian sighed and gave up. Maybe she'd at least planted a seed of uncertainty in that emotion-charged brain of his.

By the time they reached Sacramento, she'd related the story of Karlin, and why she wanted the dog back so desperately. Huff forgot his own troubles for a while. "She lost her leg? Why that's terrible, just terrible. Don't you worry, we'll get that poor little lady her dog back."

How could a man that compassionate turn right around and kill someone?

They rolled through Sacramento and headed east on Highway 50. Thank goodness, she had plenty of cash with her, and credit cards, too. She glanced at her watch. Twelve o'clock in Denver. Tom's party must be going full blast. Just about now he'd be realizing she wasn't going to show. She could call, but the noise in the truck was deafening. She'd call when they got to Tahoe, no matter how late.

Still going eighty, sometimes more, they reached the mountains and began to climb. Near the top, they passed a sign, LAKE TAHOE 15 MILES. The truck sped faster as they came around a sharp curve and started down from the summit. Ahead, the glow from Lake Tahoe lit the sky. To her right, faint lights shone far below. The road must border a steep cliff, hidden by the inky blackness. Without thinking, she gripped the armrest.

Huff noticed. "Relax. It's a narrow road and a long drop, but I've been driving trucks for twenty-five years now, and I'm not about to go over the edge. I know what I'm doing."

"You do?"

He didn't answer.

"I'll bet you don't even know where they are."

"They're at The Silver Palace. Her mom told me."

"You don't know what room they're in."

He threw her a look of disgust. "You think I don't know how to ask at the desk? I know how to get things done."

"I didn't mean—"

"And another thing. When we get there, don't follow me.

You can wait at the bar."

"I can't—?"

"No. They're probably in their room by now. I don't want you coming with me, and that's final." He shot a warning glance her way, looking for confirmation. "I'll get you your dog, soon's I can, but this is something I've got to do alone."

"Okay, that's fine with me, but promise me one thing."

"Yeah?"

"Aim carefully when you shoot Cal Ryska. Whatever you do, don't hit the dog."

Although Room 107 was on a quiet corridor, Cal couldn't sleep. Even after he'd set his wristwatch alarm for four A.M. and told himself to get some shuteye, he tossed and turned. What if Debbie woke up while he was sneaking out? What if she told Huff about the money? What if the alarm on his Cassio didn't go off? Jesus! He was crazy to worry like this. Debbie snored gently beside him. She was a sound sleeper. No way would she wake up when he left. She'd better not tell her husband. She'd be a fool if she did, but then, she was a fool. Why couldn't he get to sleep? Even the dog, curled up in the corner, was sawing logs. He glanced at the luminous dial on his watch. A little past one a.m. He'd give it a few more minutes. If he couldn't get to sleep, he'd light out of here right now, even though he needed the rest. He punched his pillow, rolled to his other side, and began to drift off.

KNOCK KNOCK KNOCK. He sat up like a jack-in-the-box. From the corner, he heard the dog spring up and growl. Debbie, waking quickly, grabbed his arm. "What is it, Cal?"

"Shit, how should I know?" Cal's heart began to pound as he fumbled with the lamp switch and turned it on, just as the knocking began again—a firm, insistent kind of a knock, not the kind that was going to stop and go away. *Oh, no. Oh, no.* He leaped naked from the bed, grabbed the jockey shorts he'd tossed in the corner, thrust one leg through.

"Gee, who do you suppose it is?" Dressed in a pink baby

doll nightgown, Debbie slipped from beneath the covers and started towards the door, Lucky trailing close behind.

One leg in, one leg out of his shorts, Cal hopped around, trying to keep his balance. "DEBBIE DON'T OPEN THAT DOOR."

She turned the deadbolt and swung the door open. A huge bearded man dressed like a cowboy with a Stetson on his head stood in the entrance, fire in his eye, a gun in his hand. *Oh, Jesus, the husband.* Where could he go? Cal staggered and stumbled mindlessly around the room, still trying to get into the other leg of his shorts as he searched for a way to escape. The guy just stood there looking at him, a cold rage in his eyes.

Huff stepped silently into the room. Debbie began to cry. "Honey, please don't be mad. I didn't mean to—"

"Get over there, baby, I'm not going to hurt you." Huff's voice was deadly calm. He waved his gun towards the far corner of the room. She gulped and did as she was told, going to huddle in the corner, wiping at her eyes with her hand as she watched his every move. Huff looked back at Cal. "Stop running around like a damn fool."

Cal stopped abruptly, poised on one leg, still not into the jockey shorts. Caught off balance, he fell to the floor and lay there, staring with round-eyed horror at the 357 Magnum Huff was pointing directly at his balls. "You ate my pumpernickel." Huff accompanied his words with a loud and menacing click. He'd let the safety off.

Cal began to shake. "Jesus, God...please—"

"You drank my beer."

Holding up the palm of his hand, as if it could ward off a bullet, Cal begged, "Now, wait, just wait...I can explain..."

Huff took careful aim, this time at Cal's heart. "YOU SCREWED MY WIFE."

He was a goner for sure, about to die. "No, please no." Cal scooted backward on his bare bottom until his back hit the wall. Trapped, he waited, staring into the face of death as Huff kept the gun pointed at him, first his balls, then his heart...his balls...his heart...then a miracle! The huge man lowered the gun.

"Know why I'm not going to kill you?"

Wordlessly, Cal shook his head.

"I'm not afraid to shoot you. I'd be doing the world a favor if I did, but someone's got to take care of Debbie Sue. I can't afford to get thrown in jail the rest of my life for doing away with scum like you." With a quick swipe of his palm, he put the safety back on the gun. "Grab your pants and get out of here. If ever I catch you within a thousand miles of my wife, you're a dead man."

"Yes, sir." Cal half rose to his feet and scrambled like a crab to where his jeans lay crumpled on the floor. *I'm not going to die. Let me out of here before he changes his mind.* He thrust his other leg into his shorts, pulled them up, and grabbed his jeans and gym bag. He started towards the opposite corner where he'd tossed his shoes.

"Haul ass. Now!"

Before the next second ended, Cal had streaked out the door. As if a thousand demons were after him, he shot down the hallway to the exit, out into the parking lot, running like an Olympic sprinter until he found his car. The keys. How could he get away without the keys? He remembered and thrust his hand into the rear pocket of his jeans. Thank god, they were there. With fumbling fingers he unlocked the door, threw his jeans and bag in the back, and leaped in. "SHEEEEiiiiiit."

As he sank into the seat, a cold, clammy wetness squished around him, instantly soaking his shorts. He was sitting in dog pee. His stomach churned in revolt as the urine smell hit his nostrils. Nothing he could do about it now. He had other things to worry about, like getting his ass out of town fast.

The old Chevy burnt rubber as he tore out of the parking lot and headed for the highway. Shit, he'd left his shoes behind, along with his wallet, left lying on the dresser. *And the thirty-three thousand dollars.* His howl of frustration filled the night. Why had he taken the money out of the suitcase and stashed it in the wastebasket? Now here he was, barefoot, broke, and—he checked the gas gauge—*aw, nuts.*

Without a doubt, this was the shittiest day of his shitty life.

Huff was going to get the money after all. But would he? How would he even know it was there? Far as Debbie knew, he'd put the money in his gym bag. She hadn't seen him bury the bills deep in the basket, wrapped in the plastic liner. *He'll never find it.* Hot damn! He wouldn't get the money but neither would Huff.

In an agony of suspense and indecision, Jillian waited in the casino as long as she could, wondering if she should call the police, yet not truly believing that Huff, angry though he was, could actually kill a man. She had not called. Instead, she sat on a bar stool for fifteen anxious minutes before she finally left the bustle of the casino and found the quiet, deep-carpeted corridor that led to Room 107. Now, with a fist poised to knock, she stood outside the door. Inside, she heard a man's deep, angry voice, and a woman crying. This was no time to intrude but she could wait no longer. She'd just reclaim Lucky and get out of their way fast. Quietly, she knocked.

Huff swung open the door. He looked surprised, as if he'd forgotten all about her. "Oh, it's you. Come on in." He stepped aside and let her come in.

Sitting on the edge of the bed, a pretty, redheaded girl in a pink nightie looked up at her. "Hullo." She dabbed at her tearstained cheeks with a crumpled tissue.

"Hi, you're Debbie?" The girl nodded. "Sorry to bother you, but I wonder if I could get my dog?"

Tears started rolling anew down Debbie's face. "Aw, gee, I'm sorry." The tissue disintegrated. She jumped off the bed and ran into the bathroom. Jillian turned questioning eyes to Huff, who held a gun in his hand. "What's happened?" She looked around the room. No dead bodies littered the floor. No dog either, that she could see. "Where's Lucky?"

Huff shook his head back and forth in disgust. "I'm sorry as hell, ma'am, the dog's gone."

Debbie came out of the bathroom with a fresh supply of tissues clutched in her hand. "He ran out of the room when my husband—"

"When I was ushering out a friend of hers." Huff laid the

gun lay on the dresser. "The door was open and in all the excitement, Lucky must have run right out."

"He's gone? Again?"

Huff confirmed with a sad nod of his head. "Gone again."

"This is too much." Jillian sank into a chair, letting the keen disappointment soak in. She'd been so near.

"Maybe he didn't run far." Debbie cast an apologetic look at her husband. "Maybe he's just out in the parking lot or something."

"She's right," Huff said. "We'd best go look. Like as not, we'll find him."

It was worth a try. Jillian hauled herself from the chair. As days went, this one had gone from bad to worse. Her tailored suit was no longer *traveling well*. She needed a shower. Her feet throbbed and burned after too many hours in her spike-heeled shoes. At least, thanks to Tish, she'd brought an overnight bag, but why hadn't she thought to toss in a pair of flats? "I'll go look in the parking lot."

"We'll both go." Huff looked at Debbie with a half-stern, half-forgiving expression on his face. "Stay here, babe. Don't you open that door to anybody."

2:00 a.m.

Two figures, calling "Here Lucky" in muted voices, toured the parking lot and the area around the hotel. No dog. A few minutes later, back in the room, Jillian slumped in the chair again and kicked off the torturous shoes. "No sense searching anymore tonight. I'll get a room and start looking again in the morning."

Huff tossed his hat on the dresser and sat down on the bed, shaking his head with exasperation. "And you came all this way...that's terrible." He glanced towards the bathroom where Debbie was taking a shower. "I feel awful, like I'm to blame for what she did."

"Oh, please." Jillian held up her hand. "Blame is a useless emotion. It happened, that's all. I'll find Lucky in the morning,

I'm sure."

Huff leaned forward, resting his arms on his knees, clasping his hands together. "If you want us to stay and help, we will, but I'd sure like to get on home."

"Now? Tonight? After all the driving you've done today, you want to drive five hours more?"

"Yep." He gave her an emphatic nod.

"That's too much."

"You're talking to a truck driver, remember? Five hours on the road is like a quick pee in the ocean, if you'll pardon the expression. You can stay right here. No sense you getting another room when you can have this one." He nodded towards the bathroom. "I want to get her home, that's all. *Home.*"

In all her concern over Lucky, she'd given hardly a thought to the fate of Debbie's lover. "Whatever happened to—?"

"Gone."

"I take it you didn't...?"

"He's alive and kicking." She detected a faint gleam of amusement in Huff's eye as he nodded towards a shabby wallet lying on the dresser. "Funny how he went off and left his wallet behind." He looked towards the corner. "And his shoes." He shook his head. "Can you beat that? He sure was a forgetful sonofabitch."

Jillian smiled. "I'm sure glad you didn't..." How to put it? "He got off better than he deserved."

Huff's grin quickly faded. "Yeah, only it's my fault, too."

"How could you think that?"

"Debbie ought to be on the road with me. I should never have left her alone like I did, with nobody but her mother to keep an eye on her. Like I told you, old Norma Jean's two-thirds out to lunch herself."

"Then why don't you take Debbie with you?"

An old, ongoing frustration revealed itself in the deepening lines of his face. "Because I can't afford it. That old truck of mine isn't near nice enough for her. What I want is a Peterbilt Conventional with a 450 cat engine and a walk-in sleeper, but

I'd need thirty thousand down. I don't have near that, and I won't, either, at the rate I'm going, for a long, long time."

Debbie, her skin pink from the shower, came out of the bathroom, dressed in slacks and pink sweater. Hearing Huff's last sentence, her face lit up. "Guess what? I won a bunch of money."

"Yeah, babe? How much you win?"

"There were five silver stars, all the way across, and I won thirty-three thousand dollars plus some more in this giant jackpot. I forgot to tell you."

Huff stifled a tired yawn and ran a weary hand over his eyes. "Sure, Debbie, sure. What say, we all go for coffee before you and I head on back?"

"I'll show you." Debbie walked across the room, grabbed her big straw purse off the dresser, and looked inside. A look of bewilderment crossed her face. Then she bit her lower lip with disappointment. "Oh, yeah, he took it out. He said he was going to put it in his gym bag."

"Put what in his gym bag?"

"I told you, the thirty-three thousand dollars I won."

"Debbie! Cut that out. This ain't no time for jokes."

"But I mean it, Huff. Here, look—" Debbie reached into her purse and pulled out her copy of the IRS form. She handed it to Huff. "The man made me sign this. He said it had something to do with the IRS."

The door clicked shut. They were gone. Jillian kicked off her shoes and removed her jacket. How good to be alone, especially after the unpleasantness of the last few minutes, after Huff found out about the money. After he realized Cal Ryska had made off with Debbie's jackpot, it took a while to get him calmed down. Mostly he'd blamed himself, raging around the room hollering, "WHY'D I LET HIM TAKE THAT BAG?" And then, when he realized the implications of the IRS paper— that he'd be liable for the taxes—he turned pale and looked downright ill. Life was not fair. Why did bad things happen to good people? Why couldn't Huff have the money so he could buy a new truck? That awful Cal Ryska didn't deserve it. He was probably halfway back to Sacramento by now. They'd never catch him.

She dug into her overnight bag and pulled out her toothbrush, toothpaste, and the nylon pajamas she'd, thank heaven, packed because Tish insisted. The phone call to Tom would have to wait. All she wanted was to take a quick shower and crawl into bed. Besides, it was four a.m. in Denver. He'd be sound asleep by now. Tomorrow she'd make amends. She'd have to call Karlin, too, and tell her...*no, don't even think about it. I'll find Lucky in the morning.*

In the bathroom, she bent over the basin and began brushing her teeth. Just sickening, that lowlife Cal running off with Debbie's jackpot. He made Debbie get cash instead of a check, which meant he planned to steal it right from the start. Thirty-three thousand dollars in packages of hundred dollar bills would be pretty bulky. Debbie had to cram it into that oversized straw purse of hers. Could Cal fit all the bills into his bag? What if he couldn't? Did Debbie say she'd seen Cal put the money in his gym bag or had she just assumed he had? *What if he hid the money in the room?* Her mouth still full of toothpaste, the brush clutched in her hand, she straightened up abruptly. It was a crazy idea, but...

She rinsed out the toothpaste, threw down the brush, walked back into the room and slowly looked around. Where would he have put it? Under the bed? She knelt and looked. No, not there. Under the mattress? She lifted it and found nothing. Did he put it in a drawer? One by one, she pulled open the drawers of the long, low combination desk/dresser. Nothing but stationery, a Gideon Bible, and a lucky buck coupon book for the casino. Too bad, no place left to look.

She returned to the bathroom and picked up her toothbrush. As she did so, her gaze fell to the wastebasket. It certainly wouldn't be there, but that plastic liner...maybe inside? No way, but she'd take a look just to make sure.

At the rear of the casino parking lot, Huff sat in seething

silence, letting the truck warm up. Finally, he shoved into gear, allowing the big rig to roll slowly towards the exit. On the seat beside him, Debbie clutched a handful of tissues, steadily sniffing as she cast a series of woebegone glances in his direction. "I'm sorry, honey."

"Stop saying that. What good's it do to be sorry?" What more could go wrong? *Thirty-three thousand dollars.* He could have gotten out of debt, bought a new truck, taken Debbie on the road instead of leaving her behind.

"I won't do it anymore." Debbie looked at him imploringly, tears streaming down her cheeks.

"Yeah, sure. Not until the next time I'm on the road and some slick dude wants in your pants."

"Oh, Huff, you sound so mean. You never talked to me like that before."

Huff slammed up into the next gear. So he sounded mean, did he? She was right. He'd never talked to her like that before, but then, she'd never done anything like this before and she damn well deserved it. It'd be a long time, if ever, before he'd forget.

Through the darkness of the dimly lit parking lot, he saw the figure of a woman running towards him. Now who's that? The Denver lady? She was running barefoot and hell-bent-for-Texas, directly towards him. He braked the truck. As she approached, he could see she was carrying a big plastic bag. He rolled down the window and stuck out his head. "What is it?"

Breathless, Jillian held up the bag. "Guess what?"

He opened the door and swung down from the truck, not quite yet comprehending. She handed him the bag. He opened it. "Oh my God!" There it was, thirty-three thousand dollars and some odd, tied up in neat little bundles. "Yippee, you found it!" He grabbed Jillian, lifted her off the ground, and swung her around. "You have surely made my day, ma'am." He set her down with a big grin on his face. "Where was it?"

"Would you believe the wastebasket? Wonder why he hid it there."

He'd never know and it didn't matter. All he knew was

that life was worth living again. He looked up at Debbie, who had poked her head out the window. "Hey, babe, looky here. We got the money after all." He turned back to Jillian. "Say, how can I thank you?"

She grinned and shook her head. "You can't, so don't try. I'm just glad I found it. It looks like you'll get your new truck after all. Go home. Be happy. Now if I can just find Lucky…"

Chapter 12

Aboard the Fun on Wheels Tour Bus
Rolling east towards Lake Tahoe on Highway 50

"Are we having FUN?"

Joe "Mr. Melody" Cartwright hung on a pole at the front of the swaying bus, his other hand clutching a microphone. A short, roly-poly man with shiny false teeth, he was wearing his tour-host grin. He waited expectantly, and with supreme confidence, for his answer.

"YES," came thirty-nine voices, accompanied by stomps, whistles and cheers.

From her seat at the back of the bus, the fortieth passenger looked bleakly over the sea of heads, most of them gray, some white, the rest bald. A small, slim woman with short, neatly combed brown hair, Martha Trimmer frowned with annoyance. *This bus is full of old people. What am I doing here?*

Mr. Melody's deep baritone voice blasted through the bus again. "Want to hear another?" More shouts and whistles. "Okeydokey! Folks, here's my special version of 'On Top of Old Smokey.'" With a gleeful twinkle in his eye, he started to sing again, accompanied on the harmonica by an ancient, bent stick of a man hunched in the front seat.

> *On top of spaghetteeee*
> *All covered with cheese*
> *I lost my poor meatball*
> *When somebody sneezed*
> *It rolled in the garrrrden*
> *Under a bush*
> *By then my poor meatball*
> *Was nothing but moosh...*

What have I done? Martha picked up the "Fun on Wheels Tahoe/Reno Combo" timetable she'd glanced at when she got on board.

8:15 AM Depart Fresno. "Lake Tahoe or Bust!!!"
10:07 AM Continental Breakfast served at Highway 99 rest stop near Turlock
2:00 PM Arrive in Tahoe for your one night's lodging at The Lucky Buck Inn.
4:00 PM The Silver Palace! Wait on bus until they come on board to give us our coupon books good for $20 CASH!!!! And $5 for FOOD
8:30 PM Depart back to The Lucky Buck for those who wish to go back at this time. If you don't, you're on your own! And don't forget your "Fun on Wheels" Courtesy Continental Breakfast in the morning!!

And that was only the first day. The next two were even worse. On the bus, off the bus, a FUN ON WHEELS prisoner, doomed for three whole days to do as she was told, completely at the mercy of Mr. Melody. She let the paper drop, hunched forward and turned her face towards the window. Tall trees flashed by. "Look there, a patch of snow!" Mr. Melody announced. "That's Apachee snow, folks. A patchee here, a patchee there."

Oh, please, oh God.

She hadn't been in the mountains for ages. There were times these past few years when she'd been tempted to simply hop in the car and head east towards the Sierras and when she got there, stand beneath the tall trees breathing in the lovely pine smell that always brought back memories of when she was a little girl. The picnics at Yosemite with her grandparents and getting wet from the mist of the falls—the trip to the Giant Sequoias where Daddy once drove the Ford smack dab through the middle of a big redwood tree—the time they camped along the isolated shores of Lake Tahoe and she swam in the cold, crystal water.

Well, here she was, up in the mountains at last, trapped on a bus with thirty-nine senior citizens and an old coot who thought he could sing. She didn't belong here. It was all Pamela's fault. "Mom, you have got to get out more. Start enjoying yourself. Dad's been gone nearly six months now, and all you do is mope around the house and watch TV."

"Enjoy myself? How?"

"Loads of ways. Heck, you're only sixty-five. These days that's young. You've still got your figure. Your face isn't all wrinkled like some women's. You don't have grey hair."

"Thanks to Miss Clairol."

"The point I'm making is you've got to get a life."

"So what should I do? Take disco lessons?"

"*Mother*. Nobody discos anymore."

"Sign up for basket weaving?"

"You need to get out of town. I've got an idea. Why don't you take one of those gambling busses to Reno? Or Tahoe? I just happen to have..."

That's when she whipped the FUN ON WHEELS brochure out of her purse, trying to act like she hadn't planned the whole thing. "Look at this." She spread it out on the kitchen table. On the cover a busload of smiling passengers looked like they were having the time of their lives. "See, there's all kinds of tour buses to Reno and Tahoe. You'd have a fabulous time. You'd meet some people your own age. Who knows? Maybe find a boyfriend."

"But I don't have anyone to go with."

"So what? Go alone. You'll make a bunch of friends the first day."

Ha! What a laugh. There was practically nobody on this bus but old married couples and groups of white haired ladies sticking together like glue. You could tell from the way they talked they'd been on these tours dozens of times. They all knew each other, and Mr. Melody was a dear old friend. Naturally, they couldn't be bothered with a stranger, an outsider. There were two single men on the bus, too, both so feeble they could drop dead any second. Who needed another sick old man? She'd done her best the whole time Martin was sick—all those years it took him to die because when you have Parkinson's disease, you don't die right away. To the very end she took care of him. Bathed and fed him, watched his every step so he wouldn't fall, hauled him up when he did. Saw him fade away inch by inch. Saw a fine, hardworking man turn into a vegetable.

The kids wanted to put him in a nursing home. Not Pamela, of course, but the others, especially Richard and Heather, that fancy wife of his. Poor, poor Heather. How she'd cringed toward the end, whenever she had to be around Daddy Trimmer. Such an embarrassment, the way he staggered around like a drunkard, trying to talk, only it all came out wrong, so garbled that nobody except his wife could understand. He tried so hard...

Here came the tears again. She wiped them away and stared out the window. What did Heather care? Had she ever wondered what kind of justice was it that a man could work hard for forty years—supporting his family—being a good person—and then, two months after he retired, get diagnosed with Parkinson's? Had she ever thought *what rotten luck?*

And they said there was a merciful God? Forget it.

She never put Martin in a home. He wouldn't have done that to her, and she didn't do that to him. But still, there were times she felt just as trapped by that awful disease as Martin had been. In moments of weakness, hadn't she yearned to be free? To run from that sick old man who really wasn't Martin anymore? Well, she hadn't run. She'd stuck with him to the bitter end. Now Martin rested in his grave, and here she was at last, footloose and fancy free. So who cared? What good was it?

Year after empty year stretched ahead. Oh, yes, she was as healthy as a horse, would probably live to be a hundred. Martin gone, kids grown, she had no one to care for now. Oh sure, she could babysit the grandkids. How many times lately had Heather called with her *I know you won't mind, Mother Trimmer* routine? "We're glad it takes your mind off your grief." Ha!

Could it be she was just like the other people on this bus? Old, retired, with nothing better to do than take gambling tours like this, play the slot machines, listen to this awful man singing his corny songs. *Am I really any different?* She never thought of herself as old, but if oldness meant that snip of a waitress at Chicken Delight the other day, charging her the senior citizen price when she hadn't even asked, then she was old. Pamela was wrong. She really was old, her beauty faded and gone. Gray and wrinkled—sagging in places she'd never sagged before. Too old to work, too old to have fun. Excess baggage. Useless, with nothing left in life but watching the soaps on TV—taking dreary, stupid tours like this—laughing at Mr. Melody while she waited her turn to die.

"Ready for another one, folks? How about an oldie but a goodie?"

Oh no. Would he never quit? She braced herself. Only this time...

The song wasn't silly and the harmonica didn't wheeze. She listened, and the old fool made her want to cry, just remembering Mel Carter singing hers and Martin's special song...

Hold me, hold me
Never let me go
Until you've told me, told me
What I want to know
And then just hold me, hold me...

Nineteen sixty-five. Hot summer nights in Fresno. Dancing with Martin, him holding her close. He, about to leave for Viet Nam, so handsome in his army uniform...so tall and slender...so gently smiling...so very young...

How foolish she'd been back then. Wanted to be an actress. Even after she married Martin, in the back of her mind lurked the thought she would be a star some day. After all, she could act. She'd never forget that glorious moment in high school when Mr. Reese, the drama teacher, gave her the part of Nora in *A Doll's House*. Because she could do the part justice, he said, because no other girl in school could do it half as well as she. The audiences loved her. She'd played opposite Garth Robbins, the heartthrob of half the girls in school. How thrilled she'd been. Popular, good-looking Garth, with the dancing blue eyes and the marvelous deep voice that was perfect for an actor. Oh, the crush she'd had on him. Before she met Martin, of course.

Garth could very well be dead by now. Lots of her friends were already dead, just like her movie star dreams were dead. "Martha, you've got talent," Mr. Reese told her. "Keep at it, and who knows? You could go far."

Well, she hadn't. Somewhere along the way, the dreams disappeared forever, maybe when little Bobby was screaming with his earaches night after night and she lost so much sleep she was staggering. Or when Martin was in that terrible auto accident and the doctors said he might not live. Or when the house burned down and Martin lost his job, all in the same week. Or maybe when Pamela, her strength now, went through her wild phase and got pregnant when she was sixteen. Martin never knew about that horrible day she took Pamela to Planned Parenthood and an ugly crowd jeered as they walked in. Pamela was Daddy's girl. It would have broken his heart...

Tiny Bubbles…in the wine...

"Okay, folks, EVERYBODY SING."

Old goat, would he never shut up? Why did he have to sound so happy? Didn't he know what a rotten world this was? One thing for sure, she should never have come on this trip. She was going to have a terrible time.

The Silver Palace Casino

What had the world come to? Why couldn't everything just stay the same? What were they doing on "Survivors" tonight?" If only she were home watching TV in the comfortable dullness of her own living room, instead of here in this gaudy, noisy place.

She hadn't been in a casino for twenty-five, maybe thirty years. The memory was dim, but she clearly recalled her excitement when she and Martin, just passing through Lake Tahoe, won an astonishing two dollars and thirty cents on the nickel slot machines. They weren't nearly as fancy back then. You dropped in your nickel, or your quarter if you felt daring. You pulled the handle, and the machine either paid off or it didn't, and there wasn't any fuss.

Now the machines were all electronic. *Sex and the City, Wheel of Fortune, Cleopatra*—all big glitzy affairs with flashing lights and voices that talked to you. When you won, they serenaded you with a little tune and gave you a ticket, no coins anymore. Even the crowd was different. In the olden days, people dressed up in their good clothes, everyone neat with their hair combed. Now it was anything goes, the weirder the better. The women wore crazy things like tight jeans with high-heeled sandals, low-cut blouses, big earrings dangling from their ears, too much makeup and their brassiere straps showing like it was stylish. Until now she hadn't realized how different she looked in her tweed skirt with the prim white blouse, boxy jacket and sensible, mid-heel brown shoes.

Well, who cared what she looked like? She turned away from the machines. She'd had enough. These electronic marvels had just devoured the last of the ten-dollar bill she'd slid into the slot.

She threaded her way through the crowd, trying to find the exit. Martin was never a big earner. She spent a lifetime on a budget, yet here she'd just thrown ten whole dollars away. Was this the same Martha Trimmer who never bought a dress that wasn't on sale? Who never in her life bought a lottery ticket? Who spent extra minutes in the grocery store agonizing over which can of peas was cheaper? No, this was the Martha Trimmer who'd decided she was Kim Kardashian, the way she was throwing her money around.

Well, that was the end of it, as of this very minute. Where's the door? All she wanted was to get to bed and to sleep, so when she woke up in the morning she'd be one day closer to going home. She craned her head looking for a way out. There, in a far corner, was a small stage with people dancing on it. Young men and women dressed in harem outfits, dancing to a beat that sounded like "Begin the Beguine." She moved closer. My, they were good. Professionals, obviously. (How many years had their mothers sent them to dancing school?) The three young men were bare-chested, in harem pants, easily lifting their partners and swinging them around. The three girls were all beautiful in their scanty costumes, their eyes made up slanty, long hair—wigs for sure—swinging down their backs. How lithe and graceful they were. She'd taken dancing lessons when she was little—tap, ballet and toe "for grace and poise" her mother said. Grace and poise were big items back then. The tap dancing was the best part. She could put on her black patent shoes with the big bows that tied on top and in a twinkling become Debbie Reynolds in *Singin in the Rain*. Or her pink ballet slippers and be Cyd Charise or Leslie Caron, dancing her way into the hearts of millions while the cameras turned. She drew closer to the dancers. There was a long bar in front of the stage. You could sit right there, have a drink, and see the show for free. She spotted a vacant stool between a young man with a bright blue shirt and a white-haired gentleman. She hoisted herself onto the tall stool just as "Begin the Beguine" ended and the curtain closed. "Oh, no, it's over," she whispered.

The white-haired man turned towards her. Tall and lean, he had a clipped mustache and kind blue eyes deep set under bushy white brows. Nicely pressed gray wool slacks—gold pullover sweater with a wide-collared gray silk shirt underneath. "Only for a few minutes," he told her. With a pleasant smile, he nodded towards a sign resting on an easel at the side of the stage. "See the sign? It gives performance times. The next show starts in—" he looked at his watch "—ten minutes."

What a lovely voice he had, so deep and resonant, an actor's kind of voice. "Why, thank you. In that case, I believe I'll wait." She jammed her big purse into her lap, clasped her hands and rested them on the bar. Well, for heaven's sake, a video poker machine was built flush into the bar in front of her with buttons you pushed instead of a handle. You could have a drink, watch the show and gamble, all at the same time. Clever, those casino owners. They didn't miss a trick. *If only*...the grief, always so close to the surface, suddenly, unexpectedly, pinched her heart. If only Martin could be here to enjoy this, too, but he wasn't and she WASN'T, WASN'T, WASN'T going to cry.

The bartender, a young man with a butch haircut—buzz cut they called it now—came to get her order. He wore black pants and a snappy short red jacket. With a practiced flourish he wiped the bar and slapped a tiny napkin next to the machine. "What'll it be?"

Oh, my. What could she order? She didn't know what to ask for. When was the last time she'd ordered a drink at a bar? Had to be before she met Martin because Martin didn't drink at all. Oh, dear. The bartender was standing there waiting. She was holding him up and he was thinking what a silly old lady she was that she didn't know what to order. Her mind was blank, but she'd quick have to think of something. "I'll have a..." From long ago, she remembered her mother in the summertime mixing up a batch of... "A Gin Rickey, please."

"A gin what?"

Oh, dear. "A Gin Rickey? My mother used to—"

"Never heard of it." The bartender's expression told her if he didn't know what it was, then it wasn't worth knowing.

"That's all right then...I'll just order something else."

Next to her, the man with the beautiful voice looked up from his drink. "Never heard of a Gin Rickey? One and a half ounces of gin, carbonated water, half a lime. Put it in an eight ounce highball glass and leave the lime."

"Gotcha." The bartender turned away.

She turned towards the man to her left. "Why, thank you. I was beginning to feel embarrassed."

He was leaving, climbing off the stool. He smiled back. "No problem. He should have known. Have fun, enjoy the show and good luck." He walked away.

Good luck. That was sure the right thing to say around here. Her gaze dropped to the built-in video poker machine. How did you play this thing? There were a few quarters in her change purse and she might as well...She pulled out her quarters and fumbled with the slot. Something was wrong.

"Want to play it?" The young man to her right, in the blue shirt, asked politely.

"Why, yes, I thought I'd...uh...give it a try."

"That's a dollar machine. You have to feed it dollars."

Oh dear. How many times had she felt like a fool this evening? "In that case, I guess I'll skip it." The bartender arrived with her drink.

"I'll get it," the young man said, cool as you please. He slapped five dollars on the bar and added, "Keep it," as the bartender swept it up.

He paid for her drink! "Why, thank you. I...that's very kind of you." She fought back tears. Somebody was actually being kind to her. Somebody cared enough to buy her a drink. What a nice, kind young man.

"Not at all. You're welcome." He was good-looking, with a dimple in his chin that emerged when he smiled back at her. "I'll bet you don't come here very often."

"How can you tell?"

"From the way you tried to put quarters in the dollar slot machine."

They both laughed at his little joke and she suddenly felt better. "Do you know I haven't been in a casino for twenty-five years? Maybe thirty."

"You've got to be kidding. Where've you been?"

She picked up her glass and sipped. My, that was tasty. She could feel the gin as it slid down into her stomach, warming its path the whole way. For the first time, she leaned against the back of the stool and started to relax. "Where have I been? Oh, you know, the usual thing, like being a housewife and a mother raising the kids and things like that." She stopped. She could go on and on about her family, but she didn't want to be a bore.

"How many kids?" He wasn't asking out of politeness but as if he really cared.

"Three. Two boys and a girl. They're grown now. I have three grandchildren, too."

"You don't look like a grandmother."

She glowed. "Well, I am."

What does your husband do?"

"I'm a widow. My husband died six months ago. He had Parkinson's."

"Aw say, that's tough."

"Yes. It was awful. We were married forty-two years, and when he died...well of course I knew that he was going to...but when he did, I…"

The young man's gaze had been fastened on her but suddenly his eyes shifted, as if he'd caught a glimpse of someone he knew. "Hey Nicole," he yelled sharply, looking beyond her at someone down the bar. "Over here!"

"You come down here."

Martha turned her head in time to see a pretty young girl with long blonde hair seat herself at the far end of the bar. Too bad she'd lost her new friend so soon, but that was the way it went. She turned back. "It was nice talking to you. I—"

The young man waved to the girl, picked up his drink, slid off the stool and left.

Martha sat with her mouth open, the incomplete sentence still waiting to be said. He never even said goodbye. Not, "Nice to have met you," or "Well, I've got to run along now," or anything, he just left. Because why bother? Because she wasn't even worth saying goodbye to. She finished the rest of her drink, grabbed her purse, slid off the stool and headed for the exit. Why had she ever come on this awful trip? Tears blurred her eyes as she rushed through the exit, head down so no one could see her face. When she got to the curbing in front of the hotel, she stumbled and would have fallen had not a firm hand grabbed her arm and held her up.

"Watch it! You almost took a nasty spill."

The man with the beautiful voice. She pulled her arm away from his grasp and looked up at him. "Thank you. I'm fine now." She backed away.

"Wait! Are you all right?"

"I'm just fine, thank you."

He took a step towards her. "Look, don't I know you from somewhere? You seem so familiar. I'd like to talk to you."

All she wanted was to get back to the motel. In her tiny room she could be alone, away from all the hurt in the world. "No, I don't know you. Now, if you don't mind..." She spun around and started up again.

"What's your name?" he called after her.

It was none of his business what her name was. She kept on going, up the street towards the Lucky Buck Inn. Funny, though, he did seem familiar. Where had she heard that voice before? Maybe she did know him from someplace, but it didn't matter now. She'd never see him again.

Chapter 13

Lake Tahoe, Nevada

"Hello, Tish? You'd never guess where I am."

"Jillian! So why don't you tell me?"

"The Silver Palace Casino in Lake Tahoe, Nevada."

"You missed Tom's party."

"That's the least of my worries. Lucky's gone again..." Jillian told Tish what happened and why she was in Lake Tahoe. "I'll start looking for Lucky as soon as I have breakfast and make a couple more phone calls. He's probably running around loose somewhere, but first I'll check with the animal shelter, and if that doesn't work, I'll start walking the streets. It's not going to be easy in these spike heels."

"I told you—"

"I know, I should have listened. Tish, I've just got to find Karlin's dog."

"You will. Karlin's fine, by the way. I dropped by the hospital before I went to Tom's party."

"She's still cheerful?"

"Yes, the reason being she thinks you're bringing Lucky back."

"Damn! That's like twisting the knife."

"Sorry."

"How was Tom's party?"

"The party was fine. Very elegant. Tom was not fine."

"Pissed?"

"Highly pissed. You didn't call."

"I had a good reason. Listen, I'm not coming into work tomorrow. I've already called in."

"So are you going to call Tom?"

"Guess I'd better."

"I guess you'd better, too, if you want to save your big romance. Last night at the party, he said, and I quote, 'Jillian and I are not singing off the same song sheet these days.' If that doesn't strike fear into your heart, what will?"

"All I care about right now is finding Lucky."

"Listen, if there's anything I can do at this end, you tell me."

"Just keep an eye on Karlin for me. I'm not going to call her right now. If I did, I'd have to tell her—"

"Yeah. I understand. Hang in there."

"You too. You're a good friend, Tish."

"Sure. At least you and I are singing off the same song sheet."

Martha Trimmer awakened early after a miserable, toss-and-turn night. She might as well get up, go for a walk, and take a look at the lake that she hadn't even seen yet because of all the buildings blocking the view. Somewhere along the way, she'd figure out what to do. She knew what she wanted to do—go home. She could catch the Greyhound back to Fresno, easy. But if she did, then Pamela's feelings would be hurt because Pamela wanted her to have a wonderful time on this trip. She'd be so disappointed.

Martha dressed in slacks and an oversized red sweater and went downstairs. She thought she'd be the first one up, but most of the bus crowd was already there, helping themselves to coffee and donuts from the "Fun on Wheels Courtesy Continental Breakfast," laid out in the lobby. She should have remembered how old people liked to get up early. They didn't want to waste what time they had left.

Nobody said hello, but that was all right because by now she didn't expect anyone to speak to her, didn't want anybody to speak to her. She wrapped two donuts in a paper napkin, poured herself a Styrofoam cup full of coffee and fitted a plastic lid over the top. She bought a copy of the Reno Gazette and left the motel. In the crispness of the early mountain morning, with the pungent scent of pine trees in her nostrils, she walked down the two blocks of winding road from the Lucky Buck Inn to the lake. She intended finding a place along the shore, but a high chain link fence at the end of the street blocked her way.

She looked along the fence for an open gate, but there wasn't one. You couldn't go down to the water's edge anymore. It was all private—some kind of yacht club with a strip of sand and PRIVATE PROPERTY, MEMBERS ONLY signs all over the place.

What had happened to Lake Tahoe? Where were the lonely, deserted shores where you could camp at the water's edge and imagine you were a thousand miles from civilization? Look at it now. Built solid, block after block, motels all jammed together, service stations, fancy restaurants, and towering glass hotels. She should have known. Things never stayed the same, they got worse. She spotted a little park across the road with a strip of grass, a few shrubs and a bench to sit on. At least she'd have a view of the lake, even if it was through a chain link fence. She crossed the road and sat on the bench, set the coffee and donuts beside her, and opened her newspaper. Not much going on. She skimmed the pages, finding nothing of interest until her eye caught the headline of a back page article.

GOLDEN GATE BRIDGE HOLDS WORLD RECORD FOR SUICIDES.

Span Claims More Lives than Eiffel Tower, Japanese Volcano

SAN FRANCISCO – *The woman in the blue coat was determined, ignoring the pleading of horrified tourists who tried in vain to dissuade her from leaping off the world's most famous bridge. But the woman, who became the bridge's one thousand thirty-fourth confirmed suicide victim, climbed over the railing, leaned out over empty space and plunged some 420 feet into the chilly waters of San Francisco Bay. "She looked at us and then stepped off," said Winifred Flowers of Kansas City, Kansas. "It took such a long time for her to reach the water..."*

Martha let the paper drop to her lap. That poor woman who jumped off the Bridge—such a terrible thing to do, yet she could understand why. When your life stretched before you with nothing but emptiness ahead, why go on? She reached for her coffee, pulled off the lid, and took a sip. If she jumped off the bridge, who would come to her funeral? Ha! There was a laugh for you. Her friends had drifted away during those long years when all she did was take care of Martin. At least the family would be there. Pamela and Dick. Bobby, who would jet in from Seattle and no doubt jet himself back the same day. Richard, of course, and that spoiled, whiney Heather. You could bet your bottom dollar she wouldn't miss dear Mother Trimmer's funeral for the world. She would hardly be able to control herself during the service, she'd be so anxious to get over to the house and start poking around. Pamela had better keep an eye on her. Like as not she'd head straight for her jewelry, then grab off the silver tea service she'd had her eye on for years and the crystal vase she made such a big fuss of admiring every time she came over. Then there was Grandma Graham's French Haviland china that was worth a small fortune and didn't Heather know it. She'd be carting stuff out in a wheelbarrow.

No way. Martha sat up straight on the bench, her lips compressing with anger. Pamela was to get the French Haviland china, silver and everything, even if she had to haul it all over to Pamela's house before she jumped off the bridge.

She reached for her donut and started with surprise. A dog's black nose was poking through the slats, from back of the bench, inches away from her breakfast. "No, you don't." She snatched up the donuts. She'd looked forward to eating them, the glazed one first, then the chocolate with the tiny colored sprinkles.

The dog cringed and backed away. Oh, dear, he was hungry. "I'm sorry, pooch, come here." She leaned forward, snapping her fingers, and the dog came around the bench, its tail wagging hard. She got a tug in her heart when she saw it was a big black Labrador retriever, male, just like Trigger, the dog they owned for years. Trigger was Martin's dog. He adored Martin, followed him around wherever he went. He was fourteen when he died. Martin said he'd get another, but he never did.

Martha looked around for the dog's owner, but no one was in sight. "So what are you doing here? Are you lost?" The dog's whole body wiggled with friendliness. He had a red leather collar around his neck and two dangling tags. "Here, let me see...so your name's Lucky, is it? And...my, my, so you're a Colorado dog. Tell me, do you ski?" She sniffed a tiny laugh at her bit of humor, then noticed the pleading look in Lucky's eyes as they returned again and again to the donuts. "Hungry, are you? Well, here, I'll give you one, but that's all. I'm hungry, too."

She extended the glazed donut, careful of her fingers. In two lightning-fast gulps, it disappeared. The poor animal was really hungry. "Uh-oh. Looks like you'd better have the chocolate, too." The dog swiftly devoured the second and looked expectantly for more. "Hey!" She held her hands palms up, "That's all. You ate my whole breakfast. What more do you want?"

As Lucky stood watching her expectantly, Martha caught sight of a man strolling down the winding road towards the lake. Oh my lord! It was the man with the beautiful voice who'd seen her make a fool of herself last night, the last person on earth she wanted to see this morning. Maybe if she sat perfectly still, he wouldn't notice her. In fact, it appeared he was going to turn the other way when he got to the fence and, yes, he was turning and heading the opposite direction, away from her. Thank goodness, he hadn't seen her sitting here.

With a bark and a joyful bound, the dog leaped away and raced toward the retreating figure of the man. "No, Lucky, no, come back!"

Too late. Lucky approached the man, prancing and wagging his tail. The man bent to pat him. He raised his head and looked around. "Is he yours?" he called.

"No, not really." Now there was a dumb answer if ever there was one. He started walking towards her, the dog close behind. *Go away, will you please just go away?* He kept coming. What a fine-looking man. Had to be in his sixties somewhere, but hadn't let himself go like some men did. Not an ounce of extra flab, and he carried himself tall and proud. Early though it was, he was dressed as elegantly as last night. Sharply creased slacks, deep brown corduroy jacket, and blue shirt. He couldn't possibly be somebody ordinary, like a mailman or auto mechanic. He looked...she searched for the right word...theatrical, like one of those old movie stars who had aged so gracefully. Gregory Peck, maybe, or Burt Lancaster. *But whoever you are, will you just please go away?*

"Good morning. Fine morning, isn't it? This isn't your dog?"

She guessed she'd have to answer him. "Good morning. No, he's not mine."

"What a beautiful black Lab. Wonder who owns him? He must be lost because I don't think —" His eyes widened. "Why, it's you."

She felt herself blushing, the redness starting from her forehead on down. She tried to smile, but the corners of her mouth refused to lift. "It's me, the crazy lady."

He stood looking down at her. "You shouldn't have run off so quickly last night. I wanted to—"

"I was just fine."

"Then I'm glad."

That full, deep, resonant voice—where had she heard it before? "Yes, well, I was just tired." She injected what she hoped was a carefree lilt into her voice. "You know Tahoe. Fun, fun, fun! My goodness, you wear yourself out here before you know it." It didn't work. She'd ended with a laugh that sounded phony as a two-dollar bill.

His eyebrows rose inquisitively. "May I sit down? There's something I want to talk to you about."

"If you like." She picked up her coffee cup and the napkin. This was a free public bench. He could sit where he pleased, but she didn't owe him anything, didn't have to talk if she didn't want to. Just the same, she was curious. What did he want to talk to her about?

When he sat on the bench and settled back, the dog flopped down in front of him and he asked, "Do you know who owns him?"

"No."

"He's surely not a stray. Look at those tags."

"I don't know where he belongs." She stared straight

ahead at the lake. Out of the corner of her eye, she could see him staring at her.

"Are you sure you're all right? You look so sad."

She heard the genuine concern in his voice. He was trying to be nice. She ought to at least be polite. "I'm sad because my husband just passed away. I'm not myself these days. Sometimes it gets the best of me and…" Shoot! Here came the lump in her throat again. She turned away and lifted her chin, gulping hard to fight back tears. "People don't understand, and they don't want to hear about it."

"I lost my wife not long ago."

The tears spilled over. She reached for a tissue in her purse. "Then you know. It's so hard—" she dabbed at her eyes "—we were married forty-two years."

"Ah, yes. We've been fighting the same demons, haven't we? That paralyzing grief, it's what we all go through at first, no way around it. At least you've come to Tahoe." His voice lightened. "Shows you're trying, getting on with your life. You're with a tour?"

"Fun on Wheels."

"Good. So you—"

"I hate it."

"But have you given it a chance?"

"This was my daughter's idea, not mine. I just want to go home."

"And sit and cry?"

She bit her lip and nodded. "And sit and cry."

He leaned forward and silently petted the dog, looked up to watch a squawking blue jay fly by. "Ella Jean and I had forty years together. One day she went to the doctor for nothing special, just a regular physical. He found knots in her stomach, so they opened her up, and—the classic case—took one look and closed her up again. Cancer. It had already spread. He gave her three months. He was exactly right."

"Oh, I'm sorry." *Ella Jean?* That rang a bell. It wasn't that common a name. She'd known an Ella Jean in high school, Ella Jean Johnson, a pretty, popular girl who wore the fullest of full skirts and was a cheerleader. But this would have to be another Ella Jean. "How long ago did she…?"

"She died a month ago."

"One month? That's all? And you're here, in Tahoe, having fun?" She couldn't keep the astonishment from her voice.

He nodded.

You must not have loved her.

He sensed what she was thinking, and it seemed to amuse him. "Yes, I know. His wife's not cold in her grave and there he is, the calloused monster, carousing in the casinos at Lake Tahoe. That's what you're thinking, right?"

"I'm not thinking anything."

"I loved Ella Jean, as much as a man can love a woman. If tears could bring her back, I'd cry an ocean full. But they won't, so I don't cry. Instead, I've come to terms with my grief. It's there, but I've tucked it away, into a special place. In the dark of the night, it comes to visit me, but I absolutely will not allow it to interfere with my life."

"For me it's been six months. I miss my husband so much it's all I can do to face each day."

"Of course, we must each work through those dark moments in our own way. For now, both of us are learning to live with loss. In time we will, and will pick up the threads of our lives again. So you must never lose your hope and your courage. You must wipe the tears away and try. Know what works for me? When I find myself falling into—if you'll forgive my hyperbole—the black pit of despair, I think back to a geology class I had in college where we studied the ancient eras of the earth. The Cenozoic, sixty-five million years. The Mesozoic, two hundred million years. The Paleozoic, five hundred seventy million years, and so on. Just the thought of those millions and millions of years boggles the mind. I cannot begin to imagine even one million years, and that makes me realize how fleeting, how infinitesimal is a human being's stay on this earth, a visit so brief it's like a drop of water in the ocean, like—"

"A grain of sand in the Sahara?"

"Exactly. For the time we have left, what a waste it is to

grieve. Each day is precious." He swept his arm in a wide arc. "Look around you. Sparkling lake, tall green trees, blue sky, beautiful birds singing, the sun just now rising to warm you and brighten your day. Look! Feel! Enjoy each moment. You don't have time for gloom."

"I know what you're trying to say, and thanks for the pep talk. But that doesn't work for me. My life is over. What years I've got left, if I chose to live them, are empty and meaningless, and that's that." What was it Martin liked to say? Oh, yes. "Case closed."

He looked at her with astonishment. "Empty and meaningless? Case closed? How old are you?"

"I'm sixty-five."

"Only sixty-five? You've got twenty years left, maybe more. That's a sizeable chunk of your life. You've got time to do the things you've always wanted to do."

"Like what?"

"Surely there must be...well, let me ask you first, what have you done with your life? To now?"

"I've been a housewife and a mother. I'm a good cook and I crochet a lot."

"Fine. Now tell me, isn't there something in your heart of hearts you always wanted to do and never did? Paint? Write a novel? Play the guitar?"

For a long moment she pondered. "You'll think this is silly."

"No, indeed I won't."

"I always wanted to be a movie star. I was an actress back in high school. I starred in the senior play, played the lead in *A Doll's House*. They said I was good and I was, even if I do say so."

His eyebrows rose with startled suddenness. "You played Nora?" She nodded. An incredulous look spread over his face. "Are you from Fresno, California?"

"Why, yes."

He grasped her shoulders and turned her towards him, his eyes examining her face. "By God, I knew I knew you. You're

Martha Lou Turpin. You went to Fresno High School, graduated in nineteen sixty-six."

He knew her? She couldn't think what to say.

"Look at me. Don't you know me?"

Of course, that voice. "Garth Robbins! But I thought you were dead."

"With a huge grin, he caught her hands, gripping them tight. "I can't believe this. Martha Lou Turpin! I had a crush on you in high school."

"You did? But I had a crush on you."

"Weren't you dating one of the guys on the football team? What chance did I have?"

"You were so handsome half the girls in school were after you, so how could you possibly know I was alive?"

He tilted his head back and broke into laughter. For the first time since Martin died—no, really since long before—the dark cloud hanging over her lifted a little and she started laughing, too. When she was able, she gasped, "But where have you been all these years? What have you been doing?"

"Went to college, married Ella Jean Johnson, remember her? Moved to San Francisco, and got into advertising."

"Are you retired now?"

He shook his head firmly. "Heavens no. I'll retire the day they bury me. I own an advertising agency there, which is why I…" He dug into his jacket pocket, brought out a card, pointing to a name as he handed it to her. "Here, that's who I am."

Nationally Recognized
Garth Robbins Agency
Advertising – Marketing - Public Relations
Full Service Producers for Television,
Newspaper, Radio

She looked up from the card. "Why, Garth, this is wonderful. Your own agency and television? What do you do?"

"TV commercials, mostly local, but some national. We're geared to do anything."

"How exciting."

"I love every minute of it. You should see our sound stage on shooting day. It's organized chaos with sometimes as many as twenty people on the set, all going in different directions, doing different things." He grinned and shook his head incredulously. "And that reminds me, can you believe, that's why I wanted to talk to you?"

"I don't understand."

"Last night, when I first saw you at the bar, it didn't click. But when I got outside, it hit me—there's the grandmother type who can drive a truck."

"What?"

"We're doing a commercial for Style Rent-A-Truck. I've been looking high and low for just the right type. We're going to Arizona for this one. Picture a big truck with a STYLE RENT-A-TRUCK sign on the side, roaring across the desert on I-40, past sand and cactus. And who's driving it? Grandma sticks her head out the window. Now, she's obviously a grandma, but she's a good-looking, can-do grandma driving this big truck all by herself. 'I move it with Style,' she calls, 'you gotta have Style.' Then big smile, jaunty wave, and off she goes into the sunset. What do you think? Will you do the part?"

Martha leaned back on the bench and put her hand over her heart. "Me? Acting in a commercial? That's crazy."

"No it's not. I remember you well, Martha Lou Turpin. You were a marvelous actress, one of the special ones—attractive, but that alone doesn't cut it. No, it was more than that. When you played Nora, you showed a force of talent and personality that electrified the audience."

"I did?"

"You did." He raised a hand. "But I'm coming on too fast, aren't I? Don't give me an answer now. Have you had breakfast?"

"The dog ate my breakfast."

He stood up, bent over, and extended his arm. "Then we're off to the Silver Palace. I suspect we have some reminiscing to do plus a few odds and ends of things we must get caught up on."

"Forty years' worth of odds and ends." She stood up and touched his arm lightly. "Oh, but…" She looked down at Lucky.

"The dog?"

"We can't just leave him here. He's lost, and he's still hungry."

"Not to worry. First, we'll get him some proper dog food, some water, and I'll tie him to my van while we have breakfast and you think over my offer."

Think it over? Ha! She already knew what she was going to do.

"Hello, Pamela? This is your mother calling."

"Mom! How's the trip? How's Fun-on-Wheels?"

"Everything's fine. How are things there?"

"We're all fine here. So what's happening?"

"Oh, not much. I slightly changed my plans, though."

"You did?"

"I'm not with the tour anymore."

"You're kidding."

"They went on without me this morning. I decided to take a little jaunt over to San Francisco instead."

"Mother! What's his name?"

"Whose name?"

"Look, I know you. You wouldn't suddenly decide to take a jaunt to San Francisco all by yourself. You've met a man."

"I didn't exactly just meet him. We were friends in high school, so it isn't like I'm going off with some stranger."

"Of course, Mom. We all know you're not picking them up off the streets."

"Well, I should think not. Anyway, his name is Garth Robbins. He owns this advertising agency, and he's hired me to do a television commercial."

"Slow down. My mother, Mrs. Martha Trimmer, is going to be in a television commercial?"

"That's right, Pammy. I called because I wanted to let you

know where I'd be. Also, I want you to give Heather a message for me."

"I'm stunned, but go ahead."

"Tell her I'm awfully sorry but I won't be able to babysit this Saturday night."

"You won't be back by then?"

"I'll be on location. We're cutting this spot in Arizona."

Martha looked around the lobby. Garth wasn't down yet, so she'd make one more call. She glanced at the piece of paper where she'd written the Colorado number. She punched the numbers on her cell and waited.

Hi, this is Jillian Dahl. Sorry I can't answer the phone right now, but if you'll leave a message at the beep I'll get back to you as soon as possible.

She waited for the beep. "Hello? This is Martha Trimmer. I'm calling you from Lake Tahoe, Nevada, because I found your dog, Lucky. Now I...uh...uh...oh, dear...I guess we'll take him with us because we're going to San Francisco and we don't want to leave him in the animal shelter because you know what happens there. Anyway, call me. My cell number is area code 559-555-9152. Goodbye."

She dropped her cell in her purse and sat down to wait for Garth. A pretty young woman dressed in a tailored suit walked through the entrance. My, but wasn't she attractive. So tall and slender, with all that gorgeous hair. She didn't look happy, had a tired, strained look on her face. Not happy at all. She was limping a little too, like maybe her shoes were hurting her feet.

Why did those young girls insist on wearing those spike heels? To be fair, she used to wear those ridiculous four-inchers, too, back when she was young and thought she was hot stuff. Vanity, that's what it was, sheer vanity.

On throbbing feet, Jillian limped through the lobby and headed to her room. What an awful morning. Lucky was gone, just gone. There was no place left to look and nobody else to ask. Only one ray of hope remained. She would pick up her messages from her voice mail. Maybe someone found Lucky and called the number on the tag. The day had been a bummer from the very beginning, starting with the smartass assistant manager of the Silver Palace who looked down his nose when she inquired about Lucky. "Pets are not allowed in the rooms, so I'm afraid I can't help you."

She maintained her cool, wasting no time arguing with his stupid logic. Instead, she'd asked him for directions to the nearest animal shelter. She rented a car and drove to the South Lake Tahoe Animal Shelter, but it was a useless trip. She filled out a "lost dog" form and drove back to town. There, as a last resort, she walked the streets around the hotel, methodically trudging up one street and down another, questioning motel clerks, children playing, casual strollers, everyone she met. "Excuse me, but have you seen a big, black Labrador retriever? Male, very friendly, with a red collar and two tags."

"No, honey, sure haven't, sorry."

"No, not today."

"No."

Nothing but "no's" and she'd been so close. Her chances of finding Lucky were fading fast. That wasn't all that was wrong. She hadn't yet called Tom because she knew he'd be mad. The longer she waited, the madder he'd be. Better call him this minute, after she checked her messages.

She pulled out her smartphone along with her leatherbound notebook and gold Cross pen and dialed her own number.

Beep. "Dr. Whalen's office calling. Time for your six-month checkup and you'll need your teeth cleaned, too. Call for your appointment."

Beep. "Hi there, Jillian recorded. This is Judy not recorded. Lunch tomorrow? Gimme a call."

Beep. "Hello? This is Martha Trimmer, and I'm calling you from Lake Tahoe, Nevada, because I found your dog, Lucky..."

Oh, my God! Swiftly she jotted down the name and number. When the final beep sounded, she said, "Thank you very much, Martha Trimmer Recorded," not caring in the least she was talking to herself. She spun around, wanting to jump up and down, clap her hands and hug—her gaze swept the lobby—whom? Strangers, all of them. No one who cared was there to share her elation. There must be someone she could call…ah, yes, of course…

"Hello, Tom? It's me."

"Jillian? Good to hear from you at last. Where are you?"

He was ticked. She could tell from the not-quite-totally suppressed annoyance in his voice. She told him she was in Lake Tahoe, and why. "I'm sorry I missed your party. Tish told me it was great. But what I called for—"

"I don't understand why you had to hear about it from Tish. You could have called me."

Oh, yes, definitely ticked, and with good reason. "I should have called, but…" She tried to explain, but every excuse she gave sounded so lame.

"Jillian, I've got a home phone, office phone, and a smartphone. The bills are paid right on time every month. You've got all my numbers, so there's no excuse."

The words of apology stuck in her throat. She had better get them out, though, or Tom would be history. "It won't happen again, darling. You know how awful things have been lately. Will you forgive me?"

Long pause before he answered. "Sure. What more can I say? The ball's in your court. It's your serve."

"I still don't have Lucky."

"After all that you still don't have the dog?"

"He got lost again, but I know where he is. I've got to go to San Francisco." She filled him in on what had happened.

"San Francisco, huh? I guess this means you won't be home tomorrow."

"Who knows? I've already rented a car. I'll spend one more night here in Tahoe and leave for San Francisco first thing in the morning. If all goes well, I could be back by tomorrow night." Oh, yes, she'd definitely be back by tomorrow night but not because of him.

"Good." His voice lightened. "Let me know what time,

and I'll pick you up at the airport. We'll have dinner at my place before I take you home. I got my new bed, darling. The damn thing cost over two thousand dollars. Dynasty Mattress with memory foam—upper and lower body massage and wave massage—adjustable, hundreds of positions. Can't wait 'til we try it."

Sex? He wanted sex at a time like this? "I'll let you know."

"I sure miss you." He sounded happy again.

She'd deal with his fancy new bed later. After she talked to Tom, she called the San Francisco number but got no answer. Next she called Karlin.

"Hi, baby sister, how are you doing?"

"Jillian? Where have you been? I've been waiting to hear."

"Well, I had some problems getting Lucky back." She told Karlin what happened. "…but mainly I wanted you to know Lucky's all right. I'm going to San Francisco to pick him up."

"You think he's okay?"

"I'm sure of it. Martha Trimmer isn't answering yet, but I'll keep calling."

"Just get back as soon as you can."

"How are you feeling?"

"Hey, okay. They're taking me down to physical therapy tomorrow so I can learn how to use my new leg."

"Not wasting a moment are they?"

"Heck no. And guess what else?"

"What?"

"They're starting the chemotherapy right away. Guess it won't be too much fun. It's supposed to be pretty gruesome. I'll throw up a lot and feel awful, and I'm going to lose my hair. We'll have to go shopping for hats and maybe a wig, but don't you worry, I'm fine, just fine."

"Whatever comes, we'll handle it. You hang in there, baby. Lucky and I will be home as soon as we can."

San Francisco

San Francisco, as in I left my heart in...as in Baghdad by the

Bay…as in a wonderful place to visit, but I wouldn't want to live there.

Jillian guided the rented blue Impala west across the Bay Bridge. She'd been here twice for computer conferences but hadn't yet had a chance to explore the city. She wouldn't this time, either. Driving along 4th Street, she looked for a place where she could pull over and try Martha Trimmer again.

What a gray, dreary morning, and not very warm, either. Trish was right when she said to bring her fur coat along. Thanks to Tish, she'd packed an extra dress that, luckily, was warm. She was wearing it now, a simple sky-blue knit that showed off all her curves and had a skirt so short it was almost a miniskirt. If only she'd brought extra shoes. She would buy a pair today, after she picked up Lucky. Never would she travel without flats again. She spotted a drug store parking lot, pulled in and got out her cell phone. *Please, Martha Trimmer, please, answer this time.*

"Hello?" A woman's voice.

"Hello, is this Martha Trimmer? My name's Jillian Dahl. I'm calling about my lost dog."

She waited for a reply, but all that came over the phone was a long, heavy sigh.

"Is something the matter?"

"Oh dear, yes, this is Martha Trimmer and I'm afraid I've got bad news."

"What happened?"

"We lost him. I am just so sorry. This morning, my friend and I were driving along Market Street, right in front of the Westfield Center. He was showing me the sights, you see, because it had been years...but that's another story. Anyway, I had the window on my side down, and without any warning, Lucky jumped right through the window."

"Oh, no."

"At least we were going slowly, but by the time I was able to get out of the van and go after him, he was gone, disappeared into the crowd. Oh, dear, I'm so sorry. We're going to call the pound right now, or the animal shelter or whatever it's called here. I can't imagine what made him jump out like that, unless he thought he saw someone he knew. Do you think that's possible? Has he ever done that before?"

The poor woman sounded downright distraught. "I've heard of dogs doing that, but Lucky never has. Don't feel bad. These things happen."

"Well, I know they do, but even so, I feel terrible. He was such a nice animal, so intelligent and friendly. I found him wandering down by the lake. I didn't want to take him to the pound, and now look what's happened."

"It's not your fault. Tell you what, since I'm actually here in San Francisco, I'll take over and check the animal shelter, and wherever else I can."

"All right, but you will let us know, won't you?"

"Of course I will."

By the end of her conversation with Martha Trimmer, a heaviness had centered in Jillian's chest. Lucky lost again—Karlin losing her hair—the awful chemotherapy. This day was turning into a nightmare. Don't think of it now. She checked her smartphone for the address of San Francisco's SPCA. She squared her shoulders and hurried to the car. *Okay, Jillian Dahl, so you've had a little setback, but everything's going to be fine. Karlin's going to be okay. Lucky's waiting for you at the SPCA.*

No, he wasn't. Jillian stepped outside the entrance to the SPCA, her mood matching the dreary fog that still hung over the city. The attendant at the counter had been kind. "We don't have a matching description, but feel free to look through." She had done just that, walked up one aisle and down another checking each cage, trying to avoid all those sad eyes pleading for a home.

"Keep checking back," the attendant said. Great. Meanwhile, she couldn't just stand here on the sidewalk trying to decide what to do. Maybe she should find a restaurant, considering she hadn't yet eaten today. No, she'd never choke a bite down. She would get back to the car, call the newspapers and place ads, of course, but there must be something more.

She'd parked the Impala by the side of the building near the ground level garage where the Society's trucks were housed.

Walking back, as she reached the entrance to the garage, a truck marked with the SPCA emblem turned in front of her and parked just inside. It was a longshot, but worth a try. She stepped into the garage just as a slim, gum chewing young man sprang out of the truck and saw her standing there. "Hi, looking for your pet?"

"A black Lab. I've just been inside and he's not there. I was wondering…." She looked toward the truck.

"It's empty, sorry. Of course, not all lost pets turn up here. You should try Pet Finders. They're pretty good, I hear. They're down at Fort Mason run by that WEELA bunch. You know the ones I mean. They're headed by that guy who keeps getting arrested all the time…uh…what's his name? Oh yeah, Travis Kerrigan."

Chapter 14

Fort Mason, San Francisco

In the Fort Mason office of WEELA, Travis Kerrigan stood at the Xerox machine watching copies of the latest fund-raising letter fill the tray. Idly he watched the others in the room. Cheery Mrs. Bagley working the Pet Finders phone—indispensable Terry stuffing envelopes—terrible Bernadette at the computer. What a pain in the butt she was, a woman for whom the word serenity had no meaning. Each day brought the dawn of a new battle for Bernadette. She didn't so much live through the day as she fought her way through, marching to an angry drumbeat only she could hear.

Nearly noon. He must leave soon to meet Sparrow, then head for U.C Berkeley to do some leafletting. After that...*Florence.* He wanted to see her tonight, not really for the sex (or was he kidding himself?) but when he felt the need to talk, where else could he go? The world saw him as a solitary man, basically a loner, cool and unflappable; but inside where it didn't show, he harbored such a passionate, consuming, boiling rage at the cruelties inflicted upon animals that Bernadette and her outbursts paled by comparison. Unlike Bernadette, however, he kept a tight rein on his emotions. Only Florence Johansen ever penetrated his cool facade. She was the only person who ever would.

Damn. Why does she want to move to Mexico?

Terry's voice interrupted his thoughts. "Say, Bernadette, how's your article on trapping coming along?"

Bernadette was groomed in her usual fashion, frizzled hair sticking out in all directions, no makeup, wrinkled slacks and a faded, baggy, pea green sweater. She looked up from her keyboard with a fearsome scowl. "Taking shape quite nicely, thank you."

Terry looked over at Travis. "We're going to feature her article in the next newsletter."

With a burst of speed, Bernadette forced her keyboard into a fierce clatter, and then stopped abruptly. "Thinking about it is bad enough, but writing it, seeing it on paper, I tell you, Travis, I seethe with rage."

"I can see that."

Bernadette focused on her computer screen. "Listen to this. Tell me what you think of what I've got so far. 'Martyred Victims Of The Steel Jaw Traps.' That's the title." She looked up expectantly.

"Excellent."

"That's what I think. Here's the rest. 'Every year tens of millions of animals are trapped, about 16 million in the United States alone, including beavers, lynx, squirrels, wolves, arctic foxes, red foxes, muskrats and raccoons. Struggling for days and nights, sometimes for weeks in the well-hidden steel jaw traps, they suffer unimaginable anguish, thirst, hunger, freezing cold and exhaustion. In their desperate efforts to free their trapped leg, they only succeed in most cases in tearing the flesh, breaking the bone, or breaking their teeth against the hard steel of the trap.'" Bernadette took a breath and looked up. "How's that so far?"

"Great. Very powerful."

"That's nice, dear," Mrs. Bagley called from across the room.

"Only the beginning." Bernadette's eyes blazed with malice. "I wish every woman who ever owned a fur coat could get caught in one of those horrible traps just to see what it's like. Then maybe they'd think twice before they strutted around in furs."

Travis's brows rose quizzically. "That's a tad on the harsh side, don't you think?"

"No, not when you consider…" Bernadette looked toward the door. She drew in a shocked breath. Her eyes grew wide.

Following her gaze, Travis saw a tall, slender, beautiful woman standing in the doorway. Slim legged and elegant, she had a clear smooth skin, a fine, straight nose and a lot of honey blonde hair that fell in bouncy curls to her shoulders, blending in with the…oh Jesus!…*her mink coat.*

He glanced back at Bernadette. She was gripping her computer desk with both hands and staring, transfixed, at the young woman in the doorway.

With a tentative look on her face, the visitor looked directly at him and smiled. "Hi, is this We Especially Love Animals?" Her voice was cultured, soft, and melodious.

She had beautiful eyes—not just an ordinary brown, but clear, velvety brown. The lashes were exceptionally long, though they didn't appear to be false. He nodded. "Yes, this is WEELA. What can we do for you?"

"I'm looking for Pet Finders."

Terry spoke up quickly. "This is Pet Finders. Did you lose a pet?" She glanced uneasily at Bernadette, who still stared silently, appearing almost to be stunned.

The visitor took a few steps into the room. "Yes I did, a black Lab named Lucky. I hope you can help me. He jumped out of a van on Market Street and—"

"I don't believe it." Bernadette spoke in a whispered hiss as she rose from her chair.

Terry murmured, "Uh-oh."

Travis warned, "Let's be calm now."

"I DON'T BELIEVE IT."

"Bernadette!" Travis spoke sharply, trying to stop her. Not that he could. He'd have as much luck trying to control an erupting volcano.

Trembling with righteous wrath, Bernadette drew herself up to full height and pointed an accusing finger at the woman in the fur coat. "How dare you come into WEELA's office wearing *that?*"

A bewildered expression spread across the beautiful visitor's face. "What?"

"Do you know how many innocent little animals died in excruciating pain in *traps* so you could flaunt yourself in that mink coat?"

The woman took a startled step backward. "No, I—"

"Do you know how they suffer? For hours? Sometimes days? And you...you…" Bernadette tried to find words, wagging her finger for emphasis. "Furs are worn by beautiful animals and ugly people like you!"

Terry cried, "Bernadette, no."

Travis yelled, "Bernadette, for God's sake."

The visitor turned pale. She backed away, began to turn. As if to steady herself, she grabbed the back of a chair. Her face turned white. Travis started towards her.

"Oh…oh…" She looked directly at him. A sudden, frightened expression crossed her face. Her eyes went out of focus. "I don't think I...I...uh..."

She started to crumple. Travis raced the last few steps, arriving just in time to catch her as she pitched forward into his arms. "Clear that junk off the couch!" He lifted her limp form. Despite her dead weight, and the weight of the mink, he had an impression of lightness as he carried her across the room, all the while smelling the fragrance of her sweet perfume, and laid her on the couch. Everyone except Bernadette hovered around.

"Like as not she just fainted," said Mrs. Bagley. She took a closer look at the unconscious figure. "My, she's as pretty as a fairy tale princess, isn't she, Terry?"

"Maybe a little." Terry studied Jillian's limp form. Oh, to have that beautiful face, those cascading locks of hair. The mink coat had fallen back, revealing the woman's long, long legs, teeny waist, and big breasts outlined clearly by that gorgeous blue knit dress. A princess, all right, ruby lips and all. Sleeping Beauty, waiting for her prince to come and wake her up. And there was Travis, Prince Charming himself, kneeling attentively by the beautiful princess's side

Why couldn't I have been the one who fainted into Travis's arms and got carried like a feather to the couch? Oh, how unfair.

When she opened her eyes, Jillian didn't know where she was or what had happened. Her first clear view was of the back of an old chintz couch, then of a strange man kneeling next to her, and a pretty young woman and a sweet looking little old lady standing by with anxious faces. From atop a filing cabinet, a bedraggled, papier-mâché eagle regarded her with beady, hostile eyes. "Where am I?"

"You're in the office of WEELA," the man answered. "You fainted."

"I did? But I've never fainted before." Only weak, fragile females with fluttering hankies ever fainted, so how could she be lying flat on her back on a strange couch, with no memory of what happened. "How long was I out?"

"Only a minute." He took her hand in his, voice full of concern. "Are you all right?"

She remembered him then, the man who'd been standing by the Xerox machine, the one with the long straight hair, whose eyes had examined her so intently when she entered. She remembered him yelling, too, at—suddenly it came back—that woman, the one who screamed at her. Was she still here? She struggled to sit up.

"Stay still." Gently the man pressed her shoulder back on the couch. "Don't worry, she's gone."

The grey-haired lady bent over and patted her arm. "Bernadette is gone, dear. Travis sent her packing."

"Would you like some water?" the man named Travis asked.

Jillian stirred and pulled her hand away. "Please...I'm fine. I want to sit up."

"Are you sure?"

She ignored his question and started to rise. Seeing she was determined, he helped her to a sitting position. She pushed her hair away from her face, leaned back weakly, and looked with dismay at the scattered books and papers, hastily swept to the floor, all because of her. She thought of that woman, Bernadette, "sent packing" because of her. They were all staring. She shut her eyes. "I'm fine now. Please...leave me alone for a minute, okay?"

They all backed away except Travis. "It seems I've created quite a stir," she said.

"It's not our usual morning. Not many women walk into

our office and faint dead away."

She bit her lip. "I am so embarrassed."

"Don't be. It wasn't your fault."

"I don't feel guilty, but I'm mad at myself for fainting like some southern belle in a hoop skirt. I hate that." She looked down at her coat. "This is a ranch mink. The little minks weren't trapped for this coat, they were raised for it. Doesn't that make a difference?"

Slowly he shook his head.

"No?"

"I can hear Bernadette now. 'Wild animals forced to spend their entire lives in tiny cages. Innocent little minks murdered with strychnine or tortured to death by primitive electrocution,' and so on. No, you wouldn't get Bernadette's approval of ranch mink either."

"She's a gutsy old gal, I'll say that for her."

"Yes, she is, and not shy about letting you know what she's thinking."

"For sure." A faint smile finally found its way to Jillian's lips. "Wearing a fur coat into the office of WEELA—not the smartest thing I ever did."

"You didn't know."

"I never gave it a thought, but you better believe I'll never do it again." *And I'll never come here again, either.* All she wanted now was to get out of here, to escape to some quiet spot where she could be alone to think and get her act together. What an awful day. Losing Lucky again and now this horrible embarrassment. "I'm leaving."

She tried to rise but gasped as a sudden dizziness overtook her. He gripped her shoulders and helped her sit back down.

"In a minute, that is."

"What's your name?"

"Jillian Dahl. What's yours?"

"Travis Kerrigan."

Travis Kerrigan. She remembered what the SPCA man said. "I've heard of you. You're the one who…"

"The one who what?"

Too late now. "The one who gets arrested all the time."

His mouth twisted into a wry smile. He dipped his head in agreement and thoughtfully scratched an eyebrow. "What can I say? My reputation has preceded me." For a few moments he regarded her silently. "Don't be in such a rush, Jillian Dahl. I don't want you walking out of here until I'm sure you're okay. Don't forget your lost dog. You must fill out a card for Pet Finders with Mrs. Bagley over there."

He had a remarkable voice. On the soft side, but steely firm. Funny how he appeared so easygoing, but when he opened his mouth to speak, he displayed such strength and authority she didn't feel up to defying him, not at the moment anyway. He seemed truly concerned, not like Tom who'd been nothing but selfish and unthinking. "Okay, I'll stay long enough to fill out a card, for whatever good it will do." She heaved a sigh. "On a scale of one to ten, this day has been a minus twenty."

Travis nodded with sympathy. "Losing a pet can be a real heartache."

"Actually, Lucky isn't my dog, he's my sister's dog." She was tempted to tell the whole story. This man would listen, and care. But no, she would not. Why take the time? She just wanted to get out of here.

"Where else have you been?"

"This morning I looked at every animal in the SPCA"

"Not easy."

"No, and then I came here."

He looked apologetic. "We must do something about Bernadette, but I honestly don't know what."

"Hey, it wasn't her fault." Maybe she could get the poor woman off the hook. "I haven't eaten anything today. That's why I fainted, not because of her."

"Then I'm taking you to lunch."

His answer surprised her. "Really there's no need—"

"I'm taking you to lunch."

"Travis," the young woman called. She was stuffing envelopes but listening to their every word. "Don't forget you're

169

meeting Sparrow. You don't have time for lunch."

Travis frowned. "She's right." For a moment he looked troubled, then brightened. "No problem. I'll make a phone call. We're still going to lunch."

She didn't feel like arguing. She had to eat somewhere and it might as well be with him. "Okay, let's have lunch."

The young woman named Terry went back to stuffing envelopes but not before Jillian saw a look of dismay cross her face, a look that Travis didn't see.

The fog still hung over the city. As Travis steered the Prius past the sailboat harbor and out the Fort Mason parking lot, Jillian wrapped the fur coat tightly around her and thrust her hands up the opposite sleeves. After that big scene, she'd hated to keep wearing it, but she was cold. He turned on the car heater. Driving up Marina, she began to feel cozy and warm. She glanced at Travis. Hmm...nice broad shoulders. His profile wasn't bad at all, straight nose and a firm chin. His hair was what she liked on a man—defiantly long, not the short, straight-from-the barbershop style Tom wore. A stubble of beard covered his face. Funny, how on some men it looked raunchy but on others, sexy. On Travis it was definitely sexy. He was dressed casually, jeans and jacket, plain cotton shirt, old Reeboks; but even so, she sensed the elemental power hidden behind his soft voice, wit, and wry smile. An interesting man, certainly not your average, run-of-the-mill guy. Where was he taking her?

He seemed to sense what she was thinking. Keeping his eyes on the heavy traffic ahead, he said, "In case you're wondering, we're heading for the South Korean Consulate on Clay Street. You're not from San Francisco, are you?"

"Denver. What are you going to do there?"

"Just drop off some leaflets to a couple of our members. It's a protest against dog cruelty."

"What do the Koreans do?"

"You fainted once today. You don't want to know."

"Tell me."

"Dogs are treated horribly in South Korea. They're literally tortured to death because they believe the more the dog suffers during its death the more virility a man will receive when he eats their meat."

"My God, that's unbelievable."

"According to folklore, when a man tortures the dog before killing it, the increase in adrenaline and other hormones from the animal will go into the meat and then into him when he eats it—and increase his stamina and virility." He turned onto Marina Boulevard. "We plan to do some picketing—hand out leaflets."

"Is it legal, what you're doing?"

A touch of irony edged his answering laugh. "Sometimes yes, sometimes no. Not long ago, we held a major demonstration. Seventeen of us got cited because we 'caused a minor traffic jam.' A ridiculous charge, but we were trying to get in, so they had to do something. They took us to the nearest police station where we were 'cited out,' meaning you're not booked, fingerprinted or thrown into jail. It's just a misdemeanor." He drove for a block in silence. "What do you do?"

"I'm the programming manager for Alpha Oil in Denver." She expected some sign of disbelief, what she usually got from a man when he learned she had a good career going, not some low paying, female-type job.

Busy with traffic, he finally asked, "Like what you're doing?"

"I love my job, even though it's a battle all the way. I'm trying to fight my way beyond middle management right now. Being a woman, I have to be better than best."

"It's not easy is it? Maybe it's not quite the total man's world it used to be, but women have yet to reach total equality."

How perceptive. Most men wouldn't know enough to make that comment. "It's very hard. Want to know the secret of my success? Never put yourself down and never apologize. Men never do. I never call myself dumb or admit I was wrong. I never act silly or get feminine. At work I'm tough as nails. On a scale of one to ten—"

"What scale is this now?" He cast a teasing glance. "We've had your bad day scale. Is this your toughness scale?"

She had to laugh. "You could say that. On the toughness scale, I'm a ten." *And inside a one.* She considered telling him about Karlin, but no, she wasn't about to unload her problems on a man she hardly knew. She was stronger than that, didn't need a man to lean on.

They arrived at the Korean Consulate where Travis got out and gave a pack of leaflets to two young men who looked like college students. Back in the car, he turned to her. "I've got a demonstration at Union Square, but I'd better take you to lunch first."

"Then you'd be rushing. I can wait. All I need is a snack."

"No problem." He opened the glove compartment and pulled out a box of granola bars. "Help yourself. Union Square first. Another demonstration against furs. Then I'll take you to a restaurant I know you'll like."

At Union Square, Travis parked in the underground garage. "Wait in the car if you like. This won't take long."

"I'm coming with you." At least the Granola bar had dulled her hunger pains. She stepped out of the car and slipped off the mink coat. "I guess I'd better not wear this."

A slight smile curved his mouth. "A wise decision." He pulled off his denim jacket and held it up. "Wear this."

She started to protest but suddenly shivered. "All right, but what about you?"

"Don't worry, I'll survive."

She slipped into his jacket, grateful to feel warm again. She must look awfully silly in an oversized jacket hanging over her short blue dress, her long legs sticking out below. At least she was wearing her classy, opaque pantyhose, the smoky gray ones that made her legs look sleek and shiny.

They walked up to the Square where they soon found a short, chubby young man whose teeth made her think of a chipmunk. His hands were full of leaflets. "Trav, it's about time."

"Hey Sparrow, looks like you're doing fine without me.

Meet Jillian, a friend of mine. Jillian, this is Sparrow, my right-hand man." He slung a friendly arm around Sparrow's shoulders. "He's a photographer in his spare time when he isn't fighting the good fight."

Sparrow's plain face lit with a big smile. "Hi, Jillian, did you come to help us?"

"Hi, Sparrow...well...yes, I guess I did. But first, I've got to ask you why do they call you Sparrow? Is that really your name?"

The young man blushed. "Heck, no. My real name's Virgil, but nobody calls me that. When I was a kid I used to find birds with broken wings 'n' stuff, and I'd bring them home and fix them up. They were mostly sparrows, so people started calling me that." He shrugged and looked embarrassed.

"It's a good name. I like it and it suits you." Jillian looked towards the BOYCOTT THE FUR BUSINESS leaflets in his hand. "So what do I do?"

Sparrow gave her some of his leaflets. "Just give one of these to whoever goes by."

"What if they don't want one?"

"Then don't give them one." Sparrow looked delighted with his own logic. "But most people take them."

What was she getting into? She, Jillian Dahl, Alpha Oil's executive programming manager, handing out anti-fur leaflets in the teeming heart of San Francisco? But she'd said she would. No way would she back down now.

Pedestrians walked by in a nearly steady stream. Jillian handed her first leaflet to a woman with a pink sweater over a white waitress uniform who took it, smiled, and said, "Thanks."

Not bad for starters. A man in a business suit was next. Without slowing down, he grabbed a leaflet from her hand as he wordlessly loped by. Easy, nothing to this. If Tish could see her now! An older man in a sports coat came striding along. She guessed retired military from the erect way he carried himself. She extended a leaflet. He took it, glanced at its contents, and threw it to the sidewalk. "Crap." He strode off.

"Well!" She stood nonplussed, gripping her leaflets.

Travis joined her, laughing because he'd heard. "Not everyone likes us."

"I can see that."

Travis began distributing leaflets. "I should say, we're disliked by some, but appreciated by others. A lot of people don't want to think, don't want to know. But many people—will you read this, sir? Have a nice day—are deeply concerned."

"So what are you doing besides this?"

"As much as we can."

A dented old Chevy approached and suddenly slowed. The driver, a middle-aged male, poked his sneering face out the window and glared straight at Jillian. "Go back to the Kremlin!" He gunned his engine, and with a screech of tires shot forward and disappeared.

Jillian turned to Travis. "Who was that?"

"Definitely not one of our supporters."

"But what has the Kremlin got to do with anything?"

Sparrow joined them. "Aw, you get stuff like that all the time. Some guy in a pickup just flipped me the bird, but you can't let it bother you."

Two well-dressed women approached. Jillian handed them each a leaflet. "Hi, would you read this please? Have a nice day."

They both smiled and said thank you. "Keep it up," one called.

"Well done," Travis said. "You're a born leafletter."

She felt herself glowing, just like Sparrow, under Travis's praise. There was something stimulating about him, something warm and vital and electric, something…this was ridiculous. She shrugged and tried to look indifferent. "I'll have 'Born to Leaflet' tattooed on my arm." What time was it? So far, the day had not gone at all as she had planned.

"Did you enjoy the meal?" Travis laid a credit card atop the bill.

"It was great. You definitely don't get this view in Denver."

His choice of restaurants came as a complete surprise. She expected a Pizza Hut or Denny's. Instead, here she sat in Sinbads, an elegant seafood restaurant on Pier 2, Embarcadero, at the foot of Mission Street. Tom himself couldn't have chosen a classier place. The table sat next to a big window overlooking the bay. The view could only be called spectacular. Throughout lunch, Jillian watched pelicans perching on the nearby pilings, salty tugs chugging by. Farther out on the bay, a cruise liner headed majestically out to sea. Travis did most of the talking, regaling her with stories about WEELA, on the lighter side, making her laugh with his description of Bernadette, armed with her MEAT IS MURDER sign, marching like an avenging angel in front of Wendy's. "They may not quit making hamburgers, but they won't forget Bernadette."

The liner was a mere dot on the horizon when she settled back comfortably in her chair and smiled across the table. "I feel much better. That was a treat. I wasn't planning on fine wine and charbroiled swordfish for lunch."

"Expecting MacDonald's, weren't you?"

"That came out wrong. What I meant was I'd probably have bought myself a hot dog and a Coke if you hadn't invited me to lunch."

"Then I'm glad I invited you. This used to be one of my favorite spots, but I don't get here much anymore."

"What do you do? I mean, besides working for WEELA?" Damn, that was nosey. The words had just popped out.

"You mean, how do I make my living?"

"That was rude. You don't have to answer."

"I'm a lawyer. I used to work hard at it, back when I was married and lived in Mill Valley."

"Successful?"

"I made piles of money. That's success, isn't it?"

"Oh, no you don't." She gave him a good-natured up-tilt of her chin. "If you're fishing for where my values lie, forget it. I won't fall into your little trap."

He looked pleased. "Good." Thoughtfully, he picked up a fork and began tracing lines on the linen cloth. "I don't make *piles* anymore, just enough to get by on. Well, maybe a tad more. Now WEELA is all I really care about and will be until the day they put me in a box and throw dirt on top."

"But why? Aside from the South Korea dogs, and the trapping, what more is there to do? Aren't the whales saved? Didn't they decide not to hunt the mountain lions? Don't the SPCA and the Humane Society take care of all the rest?"

For the fleetest of moments, before his face became unreadable again, his perceptive blue-gray eyes regarded her intently. Such a mixture of compassion, frustration, and embedded rage sparked in their depths that she realized the shallowness of her question and instantly regretted it.

He put down the fork and spoke again. "I wish that were true, but it's not. Animals are not things. They're individuals who feel pain and fear just as we do. They're entitled to enjoy life and stay alive, just as we are, yet every year millions of dogs, cats, monkeys, rabbits, doves, turtles, lambs, and other gentle creatures die slow, agonizingly painful deaths in research laboratories and elsewhere."

"Millions? How awful. I had no idea, but don't we need the research? Aren't there laws?"

"Sure, there are plenty of federal regulations to protect lab animals, but too many times they're not carried out. One problem is we activists fight among ourselves. There are some who want to do away with all animal research immediately. That's not going to happen, at least not in my lifetime. Politically and socially, it's unfeasible, so there are some who believe that if we can improve the actual protection that laboratory animals are supposed to receive under the law, then that's a sufficient end in itself, at least for now. Unfortunately not all activists feel that way."

"But why should there be any cruelty to animals, ever?"

"We could debate all afternoon. Lord knows, few areas touch more nerves than animal research. But that's not all. Lab animals are only a small part of the problem. Are you aware of the farming of animals? What goes on boggles the mind. At least the public has a glimmer of what goes on. Back in 2008

California passed a law outlawing veal cages. It doesn't take effect until 2015, which means as of this moment countless calves are chained their entire lives in dark wooden boxes, forced to lie until they die in their own filth. And chickens. Have you ever been through a chicken processing plant? Chicken slaughterhouse is more like it. And pigs. We're back to the labs here. Do you know how smart a pig is? Its intelligence is rated higher than a dog's. But pigs aren't lovable, right? Who cares what happens to a pig? Now they're breeding them for use in labs, mainly because they don't evoke emotional protest, which is, of course, the researchers' first concern.

"And then there's fish. Who but a nerd would ever defend a fish, right? But did you ever think how incongruous and horrifying it is that millions of adults, who supposedly love nature, happily engage in stressing, mutilating, killing these defenseless animals? Yes, they are animals. They think and they feel. Hooking is extremely painful. Sport fishing is cruel. Deep sea fishing is an abomination, perhaps the cruelest sport of all—playing the fish on a low weight line, putting it through hours of stress and struggle and torture to break down its resistance."

Jillian suppressed a fleeting thought of Tom and his passion for deep-sea fishing. "But here we sit in a seafood restaurant...ah! So that's why you ordered the eggplant parmesan. You're a vegetarian."

He nodded. "I'm throwing you mixed signals, aren't I? I could have taken you to a vegetarian restaurant, but would you have settled for a soy cheese sandwich with tofu mayonnaise? You can see how I'm trying to impress you."

"Go on. There's got to be more."

"Yes, much, much more. I could go on all afternoon. Hunting...well, I'll not even get into hunting. The whales are not saved, okay? The mountain lions are still under siege. The wild horses are in a desperate battle. In Alaska they shoot wolves from airplanes for fun. The snow leopards are about to disappear forever, as are the walruses, orangutans, sea otters, to name a few—all victims of Man and his greed and cruelty. That's enough. I don't what to ruin our lunch."

"You haven't so far."

"But I could. In Australia, they slaughter their kangaroos by the millions. In the Philippines, they hogtie dogs, bind their jaws and let them lie without food, water or shade in the searing heat of the markets...for hours, until they're finally killed and barbecued."

"Barbecued? How awful. That's barbaric."

"Are we any better? Have you heard of the infamous Draize test? The cosmetic companies are responsible for this one. Millions of rabbits, every year, are immobilized in wooden restraints so that their eyes can be smeared with eye makeup, hair spray, nail polish remover...etcetera. Have you ever heard a rabbit cry? They do, you know. Need I tell you—?"

"NO. Please don't."

"I've said too much. Sorry."

"It's okay, I won't faint again. But that makes me feel bad when I think of all the cosmetics I use."

"There are companies that don't use animals. I'll get you a list." He picked up his cup. "There's more, but I've said enough." He took a sip of coffee, relaxed in his chair, and looked at her with inquisitive eyes. "Are you married?"

Again, he had caught her off guard. At least they were back to familiar ground. "No, I'm not married."

He gazed at the big diamond on her finger. "Engaged?"

"Yes, to a wonderful man." Why had she said that? Tom was definitely not wonderful today, not after that phone conversation.

"Do you love him?"

"Why else would I marry him?"

"Tell me about him."

"Tom? He's...well...a really great guy, very attractive, in his forties. He's wealthy, owns his own business, plays racquetball and skis, and I mean, skis really well and...uh..."

"Loves animals and is kind to his mother?"

He was trying to be funny, but she wasn't laughing. "Something like that." Defending Tom wasn't high on her list of priorities right now. Time to change the subject. "So what do you do for fun?"

"Is that all you have to say about your wonderful fiancé?"

He sounded downright jealous, but that couldn't be. She tossed back her hair. "That's all I have to say. Now are you going to answer my question, or what?"

"What do I do for fun?" He looked at her strangely. "Define fun."

"Well, I mean fun, you know, as in having a good time, as in parties, dancing, Caribbean cruises, gambling trips to Las Vegas."

"I don't gamble in Las Vegas or anywhere else."

"Tennis? Skiing? Scuba diving?"

"None of the above."

"River rafting?"

"Never."

"How about movies?"

"I can't remember when I saw the last...maybe a couple of years ago."

"Not even movies? That's terrible."

"Save your sympathy. I'm doing what I want to do. That's my idea of fun. On a scale of one to ten—"

"And what scale is this now?"

"The enjoying life scale. On a scale of one to ten, I—"

"Don't tell me ten. I won't believe it."

"Nine and a half?"

"One, at the most."

"Oh, come on. What kind of a frivolous female are you?"

"I'm not talking frivolous, I'm talking a good, balanced life. Work hard, play hard. Doesn't that make sense? Now, Tom and I—"

"Let's get back to you."

"Now who's changing the subject? There's not that much more to tell about me. You know the main things, my job, my fiancé, and let's see...I have a nice condo in the mountains near Denver and a sister named Karlin who..." *who could be dying of cancer.*

"And Lucky's her dog?"

"Yes." She didn't want to banter anymore.

He sensed her change in mood. "Finished?"

"Yes. I'd better get back to my car."

As they left the restaurant, he walked behind, looking down. "You're limping."

"I only brought this one pair of shoes with me. Don't tell me it was a mistake, I already know. I've been meaning to stop somewhere and buy some low-heeled shoes, but I probably won't bother now."

"But your feet are hurting. We'll get you some comfortable shoes right away."

"Oh, no, you don't have to."

At the door he took her arm and turned her towards him. "I know I don't have to. Trust me, okay? First, we'll get the shoes, and then we're going for a ride."

"But I must—"

"Don't worry, we'll stop off at the SPCA again. Also, Mrs. Bagley's putting an ad in the paper, just for you."

"I thought you had to go to Berkeley."

"This once they can do without me. I'm going to drive you on the scenic route around the city. Maybe we'll stop at the Cliff House and watch the seals. You'd like that."

On the way, he turned on the radio. Avril Lavigne was singing, *Gotta let it go, just let it go…I've said goodbye…Set it all on fire…Gotta let it go, just let it go….*"

Gotta let it go. Yes, that's what she'd have to do with Travis. She'd only known him a few hours but somehow she knew putting him out of her mind was going to be a hard thing to do.

She loved her new shoes, bright pink tennies with Velcro fastenings, cushy soft inside. Now, as she climbed out of the Prius back in the parking lot of Building "C," she took another admiring look. They didn't go with her dress, let alone the mink, but she didn't care. Her feet hadn't felt this good since she'd left Denver. After all, she didn't have to be glamorous all the time, though Tish accused her of trying. But how selfish and thoughtless could she get? Driving around the city after the wonderful lunch—talking, laughing, joking, with a man she'd scarcely met. How could she have so thoroughly enjoyed herself these past few hours while Lucky was lost and Karlin was going through all kinds of hell. The desperate urgency clutched at her again. *Find Lucky. Get back home.* With darkness falling, it was definitely time to go. Travis came around the car with her coat. She took off his jacket and handed it back. "Thanks for everything, the lunch, and especially the shoes. You really didn't have to."

"I wanted to. Here, get your coat on before you catch cold. Must you go?" No mistaking the regret in his voice.

"Yes, I must." He helped her slip into the mink. "I've got to keep looking. I've got to find Lucky and get back to Denver soon as I can."

"Let's take a walk, shall we? Only a short one, then I promise I won't keep you."

He'd been so kind. What mattered a few minutes more? "Sure." He took her hand in his as they strolled slowly towards a long pier. She let it stay, feeling the warmth and closeness that was there. More fog was settling in, enveloping the old buildings of the fort and obscuring the view of the bay. A foghorn blared—such a mournful, lonely sound.

They reached a low concrete wall overlooking a deserted dock where huge, rusted stanchions stood like faithful sentinels from a time long ago. White gulls bobbed in the murky water. Haloed lights from the bridge glowed in the distance. Straight ahead, Alcatraz Island lay grim, barely visible in the growing darkness and thickening fog. A large ship, painted navy gray and tied to the dock, towered over them.

Travis pointed. "That's the Jeremiah O'Brien. It's an old liberty ship from World War II, the last of its kind in commission. It's open to the public. Someday we'll go on board and look around."

Some day? What did he mean? This was it. They would never meet again. "I'd love to if I'm ever in San Francisco again." He was so close—too close. They shouldn't be holding hands, either, but she didn't feel like breaking away. "I wish I had time to see the whole city. Thanks for lunch and the tour. It was fun. And thank you for catching me when I fainted."

"You're welcome. Catching you was a pleasure." He looked her up and down. "I want you to know, it's been an honor to be seen with such a snappy dresser as you."

"What? You like my outfit?" Playfully she bounced away and pirouetted around. She held the mink out like a model and struck a pose, daintily pointing a toe. "Well, you should feel honored. It's the latest fashion—mink and pink tennis shoes. Only a klutz would fail to appreciate it."

"You are a vain creature, aren't you?"

She flung back her hair and grinned impishly. "Me vain? Hey, nobody's perfect, not even you."

"I don't believe it. What's wrong with me?"

"For openers, you take life too seriously."

"Perhaps. What else?"

"Mmm..." She tilted her head and thought a moment. "You don't ski."

"Agreed, a fatal flaw."

At that, they couldn't hold back their laughter, and when he put one hand on her shoulder and with the other touched her hair, it seemed a natural thing to do. His eyes softened. "Jillian Dahl from Denver. You're so unexpected. God, how you've brightened my day."

"Thanks, I needed that. My day has been extremely shitty, except for you."

"How beautifully put." His arms slowly wrapped around her. Now, this instant, she should push him away. But she didn't, and instead allowed her arms to creep around his neck as she rested her cheek against his. Tight together, they swayed until somehow, she didn't know exactly how, his hands were beneath her coat, softly caressing her waist, and she heard his hard, swift breathing as the warmth of his fingers penetrated the blue knit dress, almost as if it weren't there. "Jillian," he whispered with a shaking intake of breath. "Jillian?"

She tilted her head back and wasn't surprised when he kissed her, his strong arms pulling her closer, if that was possible, so that she felt totally captured by the press of his body against her and the firmness of his lips on hers.

The kiss went on and on. As she knew would happen, because it always did, she felt the tip of his tongue pushing softly against her mouth. She hated French kissing, only this time, as it had never, ever happened before, she found her breath coming as rapidly as his as she melted against him, loving the touch of his hands, letting his tongue explore her mouth and wanting it to go in even deeper. But this had to end. Catching her breath, she broke away. "What are we doing?"

"Kissing, I thought." He reached for her again. She threw up her hands and pushed against his chest. "I can't."

"Didn't you—?"

"You know I did, but this isn't such a hot idea."

He backed away, stuck his hands in his pockets, and brought his breathing under control. "Tell me why then. Kindly spare me any *I'm engaged* excuses. I know you better than that already."

"It's because..." Because what? She was an expert at making excuses. She'd made them countless times on countless dates. This wasn't even a date, yet this man was drawing her like a magnet with his warmth and charm and caring. His kiss stirred her as no man's ever had, but how could she think of love and sex at a time like this? Lucky lost, Karlin maybe dying.

"Something's wrong. It's not just the dog, is it? What is it? Tell me."

She nodded, grateful he asked. The words came pouring out. "Karlin, my sister, has cancer. Three days ago they amputated her leg. Now she's starting chemotherapy. She's twenty years old. *Twenty.*" Her voice quavered, but she gulped and went on. "I was supposed to be looking after Lucky while she was in the hospital. Instead, he ran away in a blizzard, and it was all my fault. Can you see why I'm so desperate to find him? Karlin wants her dog back, and I'll do anything, anything…"

"That's terrible. How awful you must feel." Again, he put his arms around her and drew her close. This time there was only compassion in his touch.

Silently she nodded, feeling the solid strength of his enfolding arms. Finally, knowing she had to, she backed off again. She mustn't forget Tom, but she would if she stayed in this man's arms much longer.

Travis questioned her silently with his eyes.

How could she explain? "My life's too complicated right now. There's no room for anything but my sister…and Tom." Tom sounded like an afterthought. Maybe he was. "Can you understand?"

He looked almost angry. "No, I don't understand. You're the first woman in years I—come on, I'll walk you to your car."

What more could she say? She was doing the right thing, but if that was so, then why did she want him to kiss her again? How perverse could she be? Well, she would play no games with Travis Kerrigan. He was not a man to be trifled with.

At her car, she extended her hand. "Goodbye, and thanks for everything."

"Try not to worry about Lucky. If Pet Finders can't find him, nobody can. We'll put ads in the papers and Craig's List, check the SPCA, and whatever else we can think of, I promise you."

"Then I'll head for the airport. I want to get back to Karlin now, tonight."

"Yes, go home, your sister needs you." He took her hand and briefly held it tight. "You're a beautiful woman, Jillian Dahl. Goodbye. Drive carefully in the fog."

She climbed into the Impala. "Goodbye, I will. You, too."

With brisk steps, hands in pockets, Travis walked away. He stopped, turned and called, "What kind of car does he drive?"

"Who?"

"Tom, your wonderful fiancé."

"A Mercedes."

He shrugged and jammed his hands farther into the pockets of the denim jacket. "That figures."

She watched as he disappeared into the fog.

"Hello, Tish?"

"Jillian! Did you find—?"

"No. he's lost again."

"What rotten luck."

"Yeah. Listen, I've got to get out of here. I'm coming home tonight."

"And where is *here?*"

"San Francisco. I'm at the airport. I got a seat on Delta's last flight out. It gets into Denver around eleven. Can you pick me up?"

"What about Tom? Wasn't he supposed to—?"

"I don't want Tom. You come and get me, okay?"

"Gotcha. See you in a little bit."

"Thanks, Tish. You're an angel. Bye for now."

Chapter 15

San Francisco

He sat in a doorway on Howard Street near Sixth, a thin, stoop shouldered man with a three-day stubble of beard on his chin and a shapeless gray hat on his head. Of medium height, he wore spotted khaki pants, a faded blue shirt and a frayed denim jacket two sizes too large. His face retained the vestiges of pleasant, even features, now obscured by the ruin of his left eye, its sightless pupil staring forever askance from amidst an opaque milky whiteness, half covered by a drooping lid. His feet were stretched out in front of him, shapeless stumps in linty wool socks and cheap, open toed sandals. A faint smile curled his lips. This was the life! Bill held up his head and breathed deeply, savoring the faint tang of salt air in his nostrils. What could be finer than a spring morning in San Francisco? Maybe it was chilly, and foggy too, but early morning was the best time of all before the Howard Street traffic got heavy and polluted the air with its noise and fumes. It would be a perfect day if only his feet, what was left of them, didn't ache so much.

Ah, well...how many times had he told himself, forget feet? What was gone was gone.

The harsh screeching of a sea gull flying overhead—a sniff of the fresh salt air—made him think of the summer he was sixteen, a skinny kid living with his family in Marin County. He had found a great summer job, working as a copy boy for The San Francisco *Clarion*. Each morning he commuted by bus across the Golden Gate Bridge, his eager eyes capturing the beauty of the sparkling bay and the pristine silhouette of the city etched against the morning sky. From the Greyhound Bus Depot he walked to the newspaper offices on Mission Street. Winos were everywhere—miserable looking bums slumped in doorways or lying dead drunk on the sidewalk. Passersby walked around them, or stepped over them, acting like they weren't there. So did he, ignoring them like everyone else. But he never forgot.

He was going to be a journalist back then, maybe a foreign correspondent, wearing a trench coat, dangling a cigarette out of the corner of his mouth, reporting from dangerous places but never getting hurt. It never happened, like a lot of things never happened.

Enough. Dump that memory, too. Nothing was going to spoil his day. He felt clean and rested after a night at Jesus Saves where he'd had a good shower and slept in a soft bed. So what if they turned him out at 6 a.m.? He didn't care. This spot, the sheltered entrance to a boarded-up hotel, was his favorite. The urine smell wasn't too bad here. He'd even cleared a clean space by shoving the trash back underneath the rusted-out shopping cart that occupied the rear of the entryway. The one step was the perfect height, recessed so his legs didn't stretch across the sidewalk. He could lean back on his bedroll, watch the world pass by, and not have to worry about someone bumping his feet. Altogether this doorway was a fine place to spend the day. Best of all, the brown paper bag pressing against his leg held his unopened bottle of T-bird. He reached down and patted it. He didn't want a drink yet. At the moment, it was enough to know it was there.

First, a cigarette. He reached into his shirt pocket for the pack and lit one as he squinted out at the world with his one good eye. The view wasn't much. Trash-strewn street, alley filled with garbage, dilapidated row of mostly boarded-up buildings lining the entire block. At least George's Bar on the corner was open, run by a raghead who couldn't speak English too well and whose name sure as hell wasn't George. But who cared? George opened up at six A.M. If you came in shaking at that hour, he gave you a drink for free.

A pain stabbed through the stump of his left foot. He groaned, flipped his cigarette into the gutter and shifted his feet into a different position. Better. Thank God, he wouldn't have to take many steps today. He'd go to St. Anthony's for lunch and that was only a block away. And for dinner? Always a big decision. The food at St. Anthony's was only so-so, but the sermon was short. At Jesus Saves, the food tasted great and the beds were soft, but your ass turned numb on the bare wooden chair by the time they finished pounding Jesus into your brain. He endured it last night, but two nights in a row? *Jesus.*

Dinner was too far away even to worry about. Tonight he might just drink his dinner and maybe sleep outside. No problem either way. He shifted his feet again and settled back perfectly content. Most people didn't realize the next best thing to being very, very rich was being very, very poor. He was living proof. There was no place he had to go, nothing he had to do. He had enough food and enough clothes. He had shelter when he wanted it and plenty of booze. What more could a man want?

A well-groomed young man dressed in a gray suit, swinging a briefcase, strode by. They were always in a hurry, the well-dressed ones, looking neither right nor left as they fast-stepped through the wretched neighborhood towards the shelter of their offices. Only when they got to their destination would they look warily around as they punched their security number into a control box, waiting impatiently for automatic locks to open.

Bill watched the retreating figure. Once he, too, played the game. Wore a suit and tie, carried a genuine alligator briefcase, had his own office and secretary. That was back when he worked for a public relations firm in Houston, when his career was on the upswing, when they said he was going places. That's when it started, the three-martini lunches that led to the five-and-six-martini lunches that led to the vodka bottle stashed in his desk. Patrick, his boss and good friend, ex-friend now, wouldn't talk to him anymore. Back then he'd been full of advice. *Damn it, Bill, you've got to stop. I can't keep covering for you much longer. You keep drinking and you're going to hit bottom. You're about to lose your job. Next it'll be your family. Mark my words, you'll end up sleeping under a bridge with nothing but a bottle of Thunderbird for company. You'll be a Skid Row bum, Bill. Think of it, SKID ROW.*

A little smile played across Bill's lips. Old Patrick was right. He lost his job. He lost his family. He was on skid row. Only the joke was on Patrick because Skid Row wasn't so bad after all. In fact, it was a great place to be. A man could make a lot of friends here. There was always something going on. If he felt like a party, no problem. There were bottle parties going on all the time in the hotels, some lasting for days. If his disability check ran out, so what? Somebody would always stand him a drink, or he could sell his blood for plasma. If he needed clothes, he could get whatever he needed at Jesus Saves or the flea market. Shabby maybe, but who cared? And food? You'd have to be a fool to starve around here, what with the missions begging to feed you so they could save your soul.

Some day he would leave, take up his old life where he left off. When the time came, he would know. Meanwhile, Skid Row suited him just fine. He lit another cigarette and looked around. Up the street came a lone, staggering figure. Old Perry. Jesus, the guy was a disaster, a walking corpse. Like a sailboat tacking against the wind, Perry zigzagged his course across the sidewalk, at each turn coming close to smacking into a wall or falling off the curb. As he drew near, Bill could see his frayed plaid shirt with all the buttons missing, filthy undershirt beneath, stained pants unzipped halfway, faded black knitted cap atop his head. His feet were bare.

"Hey, Perry, where's your shoes?"

"Huh?" Perry stopped abruptly, staggered, and looked in Bill's direction, blinking his rheumy, red-rimmed eyes. Deep, grime-filled creases lined the old drunk's face. Saliva dribbled from his chin. Bill's nose crinkled at the stench of urine and sweat. He shook his head in sad commiseration. Even by this neighborhood's standards, the guy was a basket case. They said Skid Row was the last step before the grave? Well, Perry tottered on the brink.

"Your shoes are gone, Perry."

He staggered closer. "Somebody took 'em. I was sleeping in some weeds down the street and when I woke up they was gone." He shook his head, as if not quite understanding what had happened. "I was just going to Christian Missions to get me some shoes."

Bill reached for the brown paper bag. "That's a good idea. You'd better have a drink first."

Perry nodded solemnly. "No problem, I got my own." He held up a brown bag. Switching direction, he aimed for the doorway, staggered to the step and sank down. He unscrewed the cap of the bottle, not taking it from the bag, and raised it to his lips, tilting his head back as the cheap wine slid down his throat. He wiped his lips with the back of his hand. "Ahhh..."

Bill looked over at the bottle. "Night Train?" Perry nodded. "I'm a T-bird man myself. Or sometimes Cisco."

Perry handed him his bottle. "Have some."

Bill took the bag, pulled the bottle partway out and read the red and black label aloud. "Night Train Express. Serve very cold." He handed it back without drinking. "It's not chilled, Perry."

"Huh?"

"Never mind." Bill sighed. Out of politeness, he asked, "Want some T-bird?"

"Nope, don't need it. Most times I keep a point-three-zero, that's what they tell me at Detox. It don't take much to keep me on a high."

Bill shifted his legs and gazed into space for a moment. There was something he wanted to tell. Usually he didn't because it sounded like bragging. Even so, he felt like telling old Perry. He dropped his bombshell in a quiet voice. "I had a point-five-eight once."

A spark of interest flashed through Perry's bleary eyes. "Point-five-eight? The hell you say. Nobody can have a point-five-eight and be alive."

Bill cast his eyes upward, beseeching an unseen deity to forgive yet another disbelieving fool. He reached into his back pocket and pulled out a well-creased paper. With slow, deliberate motions he opened it and spread it on his knee. "Read it." He thumped the middle of the page with his finger.

"You better read it." Perry looked suddenly sheepish, like maybe he didn't know how to read.

Bill brought the paper closer to his one good eye. "You

want to hear the part about my feet, too? And my eye?"

Perry looked at the stumps that were Bill's feet. "Yeah, I wondered."

"This is called a 'Statement in Support of Petition.' This was in Kansas City. They're giving their reasons why they're going to commit me, okay?" Perry nodded. "'On or about December 10th, 2002, the Respondent was brought to the emergency room of Lutheran Hospital. All his toes were frostbitten. The toes, along with approximately half his left foot, became gangrenous and were later amputated.

"'In March, 2003, the Respondent was again brought to the emergency room of Lutheran Hospital with a severe concussion. While drunk he had fallen out the back of his camper. Later it was discovered that he had struck his left eye on the doorknob of his camper and subsequently lost the sight of that eye.

"'During the summer of 2003, the Respondent was taken by the Kansas City Police Department to the Kansas City Detox Center where it was found his blood alcohol level was a verified point-five-eight.'"

"Jesus God. Who'd a thought?"

With a modest shrug, Bill folded the paper and put it back in his pocket. "Point-five-eight. They didn't believe it, either. Thought the machine was broken, but it wasn't."

"You remember it?"

"Sort of, but I don't remember when they called an ambulance and had me hauled off to the hospital. I was blacked out then, you understand."

Perry nodded in sympathy. He sat for a while, soaking in the sunshine. "How'd you get your feet frostbit?"

Bill was always happy to tell the story. "I had a three-quarter-ton pickup with a camper. Lived in it after my wife kicked me out. So I head up to Kansas City from Houston, you know, to get a change of scenery. I'm camping in parking lots all over town. Walmart, Smith's, wherever the mood strikes me. They always chase me away after a few days, but who cares? I just keep moving around. This one night, I'm camped in the parking lot of the Foremost Liquor Store when this blizzard starts. You've got to know, the Foremost Liquor Store is one of those huge stores, big as a supermarket, filled with every kind of liquor you could possibly want. I'm stuck in the snow there and can't go any place, but that's okay because where else would I want to be? It's a handy spot. Late that first night, right before closing time, I go in to buy a bottle of vodka. I get back to the camper, have to wade through some snowdrifts to get there, and can't get the key in the lock. I'd been drinking some, you see. That's all I remember. Maybe I slipped and fell, I don't know. Next thing I know, I wake up in the emergency room. They tell me some guy who was passing by found me next morning, lying by my camper, covered with snow. I'd been there all night."

"Geez, you could of froze to death."

"Yeah, almost did."

Bill tipped back his head and shut his eyes. The weeks in Lutheran Hospital—nurses coming in every hour day and night to treat his blackened toes—the doctor shaking his head. "Sorry, Bill, the toes have got to go and maybe some of your foot, too. We'll know more when we get in there."

She coming to see him, clear from Houston. Clucking and headshaking over his bandaged stumps, so full of pity it's sickening. She can't keep her mouth shut. "Now do you see what your drinking has led to, Bill?"

He would always savor the moment when he gazed solemnly into her eyes and replied, "Guess I'd better go back to social drinking."

He could still see the shocked look that jolted across her face, followed by those silent seconds while she struggled to accept this final defeat. Sadness filled her eyes. "Social drinking." That's all she said. She knew there was nothing more to say.

"Gotta go." Perry picked up his brown bag and tried to push himself to his feet. Halfway up, he lost his balance and sat down hard. "Jeeze, I got dizzy."

"Wait a minute." Bill stood, wincing at the pain from his

feet. He got a firm grasp on Perry's arms and hauled him up. "There you go, old buddy."

"A-yuh." Perry weaved for a moment, then started off, resuming his zigzag course towards Christian Missions.

"Take it easy!" Bill settled back into his doorway. It was time. He unscrewed the cap on his T-bird, lifted it to his lips, and poured the warm wine down his throat. Ahhh...he might just have another little swallow. Old Perry was a real loser. How could a man let himself sink that low? He raised the bottle to his lips again.

With a joyful yip, Lucky had leaped from the window of the van, hit the street running, and dashed after the woman who looked like Karlin. Up close, the woman didn't look like her or smell like her either. To make sure, Lucky sniffed her leg.

The woman who resembled Karlin jumped back. "Look, it's a dog! He's going to bite me," she cried to her leather-jacketed companion who wore cowboy boots with pointed toes.

"Get away there, you mutt." The man pulled his foot back. With brute force he kicked Lucky in his ribs, knocking him across the sidewalk where, with a frightened howl, he landed in the gutter. For a moment he laid there, eyes wide with fear, then leaped up and ran. At Sixth, he turned and made his escape into the heart of Skid Row.

Darkness fell. A thickening fog chilled the air and dampened the sidewalk. As Lucky limped down Sixth Street, the adrenalin that had masked the pain subsided. Waves of torment shot along his ribs where the man had kicked him. He walked slower and slower as each step he took became an increasing agony. Where was water? With his head hung low, tail drooping, he dragged himself down the street. He passed a group of men lounging on the sidewalk in front of a pawnshop. Some were squatting, some leaning against the parked cars at the curb. Half cringing against the wall of the building, he tried to hurry by, but one of the men spied him. "Hey, pooch, how 'bout a little Wild Irish Rose!" He waved a half-empty bottle, lunged and tried to grab Lucky's tail. Lucky snarled, lip curled, and snapped at his hand. His sharp teeth just missed. The man jerked his hand away. Lucky kept snarling and backing as the man stood uncertainly, not wanting to seem a coward in front of his companions but afraid to reach towards the dog again.

The men all laughed.

"Don't your new friend like you, Hank?"

"He's mad at you, Hank. He don't love you no more!"

The man decided not to tangle further with an angry fifty-pound dog. He backed away. "Shit." He took a swig from his bottle. Lucky saw his chance and bolted. Loud laughter, humiliating laughter, rang in his ears as he ran farther down Sixth Street towards Mission. No one came after him. A new wave of pain radiated from the injury. At the corner, he paused as a big truck rumbled by. Tail between his legs, he dragged himself across Mission and started along another block of sleazy stores. By the time he reached the end of the block, he was shaking and could barely walk. At the next corner, he blindly turned onto Howard Street, but after only a few steps, his legs wouldn't carry him. He cringed against the wall, eyes pools of torment. He could go no farther and collapsed, legs buckling beneath him. An agony of loneliness welled in his heart as he lay on the cold, wet sidewalk. He whimpered in despair.

Bill sat in his doorway, feeling no pain, pleased with the way his day had gone. Lunch at St. Anthony's was a cut above ordinary—the usual baloney sandwiches, a good potato salad, white cake for dessert with peaches and ice cream. He was happy with his decision not to go back to Jesus Saves for dinner, or anywhere. He wasn't hungry. The bottle of T-bird, only his fourth of the day, was all he really wanted. Soon he'd polish it off. Then he'd get into his bedroll and sleep right here in the doorway. Risky. You never knew when you'd get ripped off in your sleep, but hell, what could they steal? He started to reach for his bedroll and heard a noise, a whimper. He ignored it, but there it came again. He leaned out his doorway to take a look. A black shape was pressed up against the wall just a few feet away.

He moved closer. A dog! "Hey there, what's the matter?" A low growl started deep in the dog's throat. "Say, you don't want to growl at me. I'm your friend." Bill knelt down and slowly extended his hand. When it was a few inches away from the animal, he said, "Don't you bite. I'm not going to hurt you. Are you a male?" He took a quick look. "Yep." The dog whimpered, looking up at him with pain filled eyes. "Are you hurt? Let's see" In the dim street light, Bill ran his fingers over the dog, touching lightly here and there. When he got to the left side, the animal winced. So that's where he was hurt. No blood, maybe just a bad bruise. "What happened, bud? Did you get hit by a car? Did somebody kick you?" The dog licked his hand. "Hey! Cut that out!" He kept stroking, puzzling what to do next. He could just leave him here on the street, but if he did, the dog might not make it 'til morning. Animals did not fare too well in this neighborhood. He'd seen some cruel things. "So what do I do with you?"

He stood up, rocked back and forth on his sore feet, and frowned. This dog was hurt, probably hungry and thirsty, too. His old dog, Hot Shot, was a black Labrador retriever, just like this one. A lot like this one. He would never have deserted Hot Shot and he couldn't desert this dog, either. He'd better get him off the street. He was a big one, fifty pounds at least. Hell, he could manage. He bent down, carefully slipped his arms underneath the dog's belly and lifted him, grunting as the extra weight pained his feet. He carried him to the doorway and laid him down gently, as far back in the entrance as he could. The animal whimpered once, then lay quietly looking up at him. Now what? It was dark and he was pretty well sauced. He hadn't planned on going anywhere tonight, but the dog needed food and water. He'd have to go. "Now you stay here. I'm going to the deli, but I'll be back. Understand?"

He stashed the near-empty bottle of T-bird in the trash beneath the shopping cart, picked up his bedroll and slung it by its frayed rope over his shoulder. No way could he leave that behind. He started up the street towards the deli-liquor store three blocks away. He'd never paid attention to anything beyond the rack of cheap wines by the cash register, so he wasn't sure if they even had any dog food. Even if they did, maybe the extra walking and money he spent would all be for nothing. The dog would be gone by the time he got back, but what the hell. He pointed at the step. "Stay here."

At the deli, he bought a large bottle of Arrowhead Mountain Spring Water and four cans of dog food with pull-tab tops. There went some of his wine money for tomorrow, all for a dog who'd probably run off by now. He didn't have much left, but ah, well. He could always sell some blood to the plasma center and pick up a fast thirty bucks.

He trudged the three blocks back to his doorway and peered into the darkness. By golly, there he was, looking at him with those soft brown eyes, whimpering a greeting and even thumping his tail.

"Hi, buddy, so you decided to stay." He patted the top of the dog's head, found an old Styrofoam cup in the trash and filled it with the Arrowhead water. The dog lapped it up in nothing flat so he gave him some more. He opened one of the cans of dog food, dumped the contents on a newspaper and set it on the step. A few garfs and it was gone. "Hey, I guess you were hungry." He gave him another can. Gone in a flash. The dog must have had enough, though, because he lay down beside him, nose tucked between his front paws.

Bill found the bottle he'd hidden in the trash. He half raised it to his lips, and then put it down. No, by God, he didn't want any more right now. He'd save it for morning. "Let's get some sleep." He unrolled the bedroll, wrapped the two blankets around himself, and lay next to the dog. He pulled the animal close, put his arm around him and a piece of his blanket. Drifting off to sleep, he recalled all the dogs he'd ever owned. Butch, the little white terrier. Prince, the feisty Pomeranian. Rusty, the cocker spaniel and the last, Hot Shot. He'd had him the longest, nearly eleven years. When Jennifer threw him out, he had to leave Hot Shot behind. Last Christmas he telephoned Houston collect, not to talk to her but to ask about his dog. She refused the call. Hot Shot was old, probably dead by now. Damn, mostly nothing mattered anymore, but he sure did miss that dog.

A thick fog hung over Howard Street when Bill awoke in the morning. The dog still lay beside him, hadn't even moved. He sat up and yawned, relieved no one stole his blankets during the night. Or his shoes. "Good morning, pal." Spying the red collar around the dog's neck, he reached for the tags. "So your name is Lucky. From Lakewood, Colorado, I see. Look here, a phone number. Guess we'd better make a call."

Lucky thumped his tail, stood, and shook himself, managing a lick on Bill's face before Bill gently pushed him away. He limped to a patch of ground not too far from the doorway, sniffed around and relieved himself. When he came back, Bill patted him and he winced. "It hurts to walk, doesn't it?" That injury needed attention. Jesus Saves might help, but how to get there? He couldn't walk all that distance with a heavy dog in his arms. He needed to get to Jesus Saves anyway, to eat and clean up, but he wasn't about to leave Lucky behind. He scratched his head. If he couldn't take the dog, and couldn't leave him, what was he going to do? He opened another can of dog food, put the contents on a newspaper and watched Lucky gobble it down. When he looked up, he saw Perry coming down the sidewalk. Jesus, look at him now. Yesterday he was barefoot. Today he wore a pair of dazzling orange tennis shoes with blue laces, each side decorated with a bright blue scroll. They were way too big, size twelve or maybe thirteen, and looked funny as hell, those huge, orange shoes, sticking out from beneath Perry's too short pant legs, but he didn't laugh.

"Hey Perry, you've got some new shoes."

Perry staggered over. "Niki's. Nearly brand new. Had to stuff paper in the toes, though." He noticed the dog. "What have you got there?"

Bill put an arm around Lucky. "I found him on the street last night."

"A-yuh?" Perry blinked and rocked back and forth on his heels. "Will you keep him?"

Bill sighed and shook his head. "Don't know if I can. His

tag says his name is Lucky. It's got a phone number on it. Pretty soon I'll call if I can call collect. He's hurt. Looks like somebody kicked him. He should have a vet look at him, but I don't know how I'd find one. I'd take him to Jesus Saves, but he can't walk that far and I can't carry him."

Old Perry really surprised him then. He showed some sense. He peered into the doorway at the old shopping cart. "Why don't you put him in that? Then you could just push him over to Jesus Saves."

Now there was a good idea. Should have thought of it himself. The cart was rusted, dirty and filled with trash, but the wheels looked all right. "Good thinking, Perry."

He dumped the trash from the cart and hauled it to the sidewalk where he wheeled it back and forth, testing it out. The wheels squeaked but worked fine. He got his bedroll from the doorway and put it in the cart, laying the blankets in the bottom. "Help me lift him, Perry."

"Will he bite?"

"Nah, he's a good dog."

They lifted Lucky into the cart. He didn't seem to mind, just looked curious. At first he tried to stretch out but found he was too big to fit. As Bill, assisted by Perry, started to push the cart up the sidewalk towards the Fifth Street Jesus Saves Mission, Lucky sat up straight, ears pointed and nose held high.

They stopped at a pay phone where Bill placed a collect call to the phone number on Lucky's tag. When the call went to voice mail, the operator told him sorry, but nobody was there to accept the call. Too bad he couldn't leave a message, but he'd try again later. He almost wished nobody would answer because then he could keep the dog.

John Turner, the bald, potbellied director of the Fifth Street Jesus Saves Mission, had been a kind man once, but thirty-odd years of dealing with the dregs of humanity had taught him many harsh lessons. As a result, whatever compassion he may have felt for his fellow man had long since withered and died, replaced by the sad and bitter knowledge that Skid Row inhabitants could not be trusted; that given the chance, Skid Row inhabitants would lie, cheat and steal; that even though a man leaped up in evening meeting to claim he was saved and off the booze forever, you could safely bet by morning he'd be swilling his Night Train or T-bird as usual.

At the beginning, John was not beyond bending a rule or two, but no more. Out of necessity, he got tough. Compassion was for those who obeyed the rules, no exceptions. Anyone who didn't could hit the street and had better, not ever, come back.

This morning, he stood at the front door of the mission, looking down the steps where the shabby line of men and a few derelict women waited patiently for their morning feed. They were all in their usual shabby state, but as long as they were quiet, and not obviously drunk, he said nothing. But what was this? Crippled Bill with a dog? "Bill! What are you doing?"

Bill took the dog from the basket, cradled him in his arms, and came up the steps. "Good morning, Mr. Turner. Mind if I bring my dog in? I don't want to leave him on the street."

"No dogs. That's the rule."

Bill paused, one foot on the next step, and halfway rested Lucky on his knee. "I didn't know that. I found him last night, and I thought—"

"No exceptions."

"He's hurt. Maybe someone here could help."

"Hurt? Then the SPCA should have him."

"If I can't find his owner, I want to keep him myself."

John Turner sighed. Would these people never learn? "Where do you live, Bill?"

Bill gulped and looked away. "Nowhere."

"There you are. See what I mean? How you gonna keep a dog? I'm calling Animal Control."

"But they'll put him to sleep."

"No they won't. The SPCA runs the shelter. They hang onto those animals as long as they can. They'll try to find the owner, but if they can't, like as not, they'll find a home for him." John Turner gave Bill a piercing look. "It's the only way. You can't keep a dog when you live on the street."

Bill nodded, agreeing because he had to. Mr. Turner was right. He couldn't keep the dog. It was just that Lucky reminded him of old Hot Shot, but if the SPCA could find the owner, then fine. He waited while the director went in his office and made the phone call. He returned with a confident look on his face. "It's all settled. They'll be here in a few minutes. We have to keep him tied up until they get here."

"Sure, no problem." Carrying Lucky, Bill felt the warmth of the dog's body against him as he walked down the steps and put him back in the cart. "The SPCA's coming to get him," he said to Perry. "It's the only way."

Perry shook his head like he knew how bad Bill was feeling. "Go get breakfast. I'll stay here and watch the dog."

Who said you couldn't have a friend in Skid Row? "Okay, I'll make it fast." He went inside, cleaned up, and ate some hot cereal at a Formica topped table with a dozen silent men. He couldn't get much down, though. Back outside, he saw Perry had moved the cart up the street, away from the doorway. Sitting on the fog-wet sidewalk, his back against the wall, Perry was well into his bottle of Night Train, the first of the day. Lucky still sat in the cart, safe and sound.

Bill remembered he'd left the remains of his T-bird in the trash back at his doorway. Dumb! How could he have forgotten? He'd spent the last of his money, too, except for the change in his pocket. For sure, he'd have to head for the plasma center, but later, after the SPCA came. He squatted on the sidewalk next to Perry. They sat in front of Jesus Saves for he figured nearly two hours before a van with the SPCA emblem on the side pulled up in front. A young man got out. Bill stood up and hobbled over, with Perry close behind. "Good morning. Did you come for a dog?"

"Good morning." The young man consulted a piece of paper. "Is this the Fifth Street Jesus Saves Mission?"

"Yes. Tell me..." Bill groped for the right words. "What happens to the dogs you pick up?"

"We wait five days for an owner to show. It helps if the

dog has a chip, of course. Then we put them up for adoption."

"And then how many days?"

"We're a no-kill shelter."

"But what happens if, say, the dog is hurt?"

"If it's bad enough, they put the animal to sleep, but it's painless. I've got to be honest. When they've got too many…well, there's only so much room, so even if an animal isn't too bad off…" The SPCA man looked around. "Where's the dog?"

Perry started to point to the rusted shopping cart, but Bill gave him a warning glance. "Inside. You're supposed to check inside."

"Thanks." The SPCA man sprang up the steps and disappeared.

Perry's eyebrows shot up. "What's that all about?"

"Come on, Perry, we're getting out of here." Bill headed for the grocery cart, swung it around, and started up Fifth Street towards Market fast as he could go.

Perry fell in beside him. "Are you crazy?"

"Probably."

"But the guy said—"

"I don't care what he said. Sure, maybe they'll find his owner. Then again, maybe they won't. You can't trust them, Perry. That's why we're getting out of here. They're not going to get my dog."

Tyler Todd Cameron, young scion of the prominent pre-1906 earthquake Camerons, worked hard at perfecting his cosmopolitan, man-about-town image. Blond and handsome, with carefully styled hair, correctly trimmed mustache and well-cut, vested pinstripe suit, he looked every inch the young and successful stockbroker. At the moment, Tyler was experiencing a tiny twinge of guilt. He should be sitting in his mahogany-paneled office at the Montgomery Street brokerage firm of Sutton, Dursten & Pfisser. Instead he'd left early for lunch, intimating to his secretary he had certain important errands, vaguely unspecified, he must run. Untrue, of course. All he really wanted to do was drive around town for a while in his brand new, fifty-seven thousand dollar Corvette Stingray.

Now, as he made a right turn onto Market Street from Montgomery, heads turned in his direction. Oh, yeah, these wheels would make him the center of attention wherever he went. With the twinge of guilt fading fast, he headed up Market, hands fondly gripping the leather-wrapped steering wheel. For a brief instant, his gaze flicked over the hood to admire the shining Laguna blue metallic tintcoat, then swept lovingly over the dash shaped like a cockpit inspired by a fighter jet. Breaking for a red light, he reached to turn on his SiriusXM satellite radio. Sinking back into the contoured leather elegance of the bucket seat, he listened to soft rock from his premium ten-speaker deluxe audio system. He glanced at the console, wherein rested his cell phone. If they needed him at the office, they could damn well call.

How he loved this car! At sixteen, he'd been thrilled when Dad gave him the Mustang. At twenty-five, he bought the BMW with his own money. Nothing compared to a Stingray, though. If he wanted, he could get from zero to sixty miles per hour in four seconds. If he so desired, he could wind this baby up to one hundred ninety-nine miles an hour, or so they claimed. Nothing he'd care to try on Market Street. Maybe later he'd nip over to the 101 and let it out—that is, if the CHP weren't around. Right now he was content to drive, ever so cautiously, through the tangle of San Francisco midmorning traffic.

He remembered the suit he'd left for alterations at the tailor's on Third Street. A genuine errand, after all. He'd make a quick stop and pick up his suit. Humming along with the music on his deluxe stereo, he headed towards Third.

A grating squeak came from the wheels of the old shopping cart. "Jesus God, where are we going?" Old Perry was panting as they hurried up Sixth Street, pushing the cart ahead of them. Lucky was getting a rough ride, but he was taking it well, sitting straight up, eyes alert and ears back. They were almost to Market Street, nearly out of Skid Row—back in the real world where the old Golden Gate Theater, well remembered from Bill's childhood, sat directly across the street.

"I don't know where we're going, just away from there. I'm damned if they're going to kill this dog." Bill's feet were beginning to hurt really bad, but he wasn't about to stop, not yet. It had been a long time since he'd cared this much about anything. At the corner of Sixth and Market, he turned right, not knowing why. No plan had formed yet in his mind. So far, he just wanted to get as far away as possible from the Fifth Street Jesus Saves Mission and the SPCA.

At first, as they headed down Market, no one in the teeming, motley crowd paid them the slightest attention. As they approached the financial district, the nature of the street changed. The sidewalk was cleaner, the stores more elegant. Heads began to turn as well-dressed pedestrians gazed with surprise, curiosity, or undisguised disgust at the two ragged bums pushing a dog down the sidewalk in a squeaking grocery cart. At Third and Market, they paused.

"I got to rest." Perry hung over the cart handle, winded and sweating hard.

"Okay, let's get off Market. Then we'll slow down."

Turning right again, they headed towards Mission. They passed a tailor shop, and then a fancy hotel where a tall, skinny, black doorman in gray tuxedo and top hat loaded luggage into an airport van while a group of men in business suits stood around. They crossed the street and kept going on Third.

Tyler Todd Cameron swung into the parking lot on Third Street. Although he hated to leave his car anywhere, he knew this lot was safe because the parking attendant always removed the keys and kept them in a steel cabinet inside his small shack. Tyler pulled up in front of the attendant's shack and got out, leaving the keys in the ignition and the engine running.

Manuel Gomez, the slender young attendant, poked his head out. "Yes sir?"

"I'll only be gone a few minutes." Tyler noted a slight

smudge marring the gleaming perfection of the Laguna blue finish on his left fender. He whipped out his handkerchief. With tender care, he wiped the spot away and stepped back to admire his car once more. Nodding a silent approval, Tyler turned and with a crisp, jaunty step, headed towards the tailor shop.

Later, Manuel Gomez told his boss and the police that such a circumstance had never happened before and probably would never happen again. At the very instant that Manuel, having come out of the shack to park Tyler's car, was about to slide under the wheel, he heard a noise at the back of the lot. Looking around, he saw two boys, crouched and running. They were carrying chrome wire wheel covers, obviously newly stolen, one of which had just dropped to the pavement, thus making the noise. "Hey!" He instantly gave chase, heading down Mission after the boys. Later he recalled seeing two poorly dressed white males, age uncertain, with a shopping cart, cutting across the lot. He thought maybe there was a black dog in the cart but he wasn't sure.

Perry's new dazzling orange tennis shoes were dragging. As they started to cut through the parking lot on the corner he protested, "I ain't used to this. I can't go no more."

Bill gladly slowed his steps. Though he wasn't as much out of shape as Perry, his feet were throbbing clumps of pain. He couldn't go much farther, either, and yearned for the security of his doorway. *Oh, my God, look at that.*

The blue Corvette Stingray sat in the middle of the lot— empty, engine running, open door beckoning. Of course! The perfect solution. "Stop!" Bill grabbed Perry's arm and looked around. No one in sight. "We're going to borrow this car."

"Huh?"

"You heard me." Bill pushed the basket over to the Stingray. He hauled Lucky out. The car only had two seats so he laid Lucky in the open trunk behind. While Perry stood staring, Bill pulled his bedroll and Perry's bottle out of the basket and tossed them in the rear with the dog. He slid into the seat, leaned across, and opened the passenger door. "Hop in, Perry, we're going for a ride."

Perry swayed and stared. "Where?"

"How the hell do I know? Just get in."

Perry shrugged, went around the car and climbed in. After he closed his door, he reached into the back and retrieved his bottle. "Let's go."

This was crazy. This was breaking the law. Bill lifted his hands in front of him and spread out his fingers. His hands shook a little but not much. He hadn't had a drink since last night, before he found the dog, so he was sober, or better to say, more sober than usual what with his high blood alcohol level. He knew what he was doing, and what he was doing was illegal. It wasn't too late. All they had to do was get out of the car right now. No one would be the wiser, but then....

Almost of their own volition, his fingers curled around the fine leather steering wheel. Jesus that felt good, just to be in the driver's seat again. He hadn't driven an automobile for at least three years, maybe four. Why was this car just sitting here, keys in, engine running? It had to be a sign, like God was telling him something, like maybe it was time to leave Skid Row. Even if he did get caught, could jail be so bad? There were men in Skid Row who begged to be thrown in jail, just so they'd have three squares a day and a place to sleep. Come to think of it, either way he didn't have a hell of a lot to lose.

"Fuck it!"

He threw the gearshift into drive, tromped on the accelerator, and burned rubber as he drove Tyler Todd Cameron's new Stingray off the lot and into the Third Street traffic. Quickly he covered the short block. At the corner, because it was easiest, he turned right on Market Street, into the wide, frightening, obstacle course of cars, buses, streetcars, traffic islands, fog-wet tracks, and crazy pedestrians.

"Jesus God, watch out!" Perry flinched as Bill swerved to miss an old lady with a shopping bag who stepped off a traffic island.

"Relax, I know what I'm doing." What a lie. He hadn't

remembered how tricky driving could be with just one eye. His heart pounded wildly. His body broke into a sweat. He wished he hadn't taken the car but too late now. Or was it? He stopped for a red light. Maybe he should leap out right now and abandon car, friend and dog to their fate. No, he wasn't a quitter, he'd hang in there. He reached the Ferry Building at the bottom of Market and turned left because the car ahead turned left. Now he was on the Embarcadero, the historic thoroughfare that borders San Francisco Bay. He guided the Stingray northward, following the shoreline. When he was ten or so, he drove with his parents along this very road, had gazed in awe at the white-capped bay, the sea gulls dipping and soaring, the giant ocean-going vessels tied up at their deep-water piers. Somehow the old memories eased his heart, and it ceased to pound. He leaned back, loosening his desperate clutch of the wheel. Not so much traffic now. Maybe...maybe...

Perry took a swig from his Night Train. "Where are we going?"

"I don't know yet. Let me think."

The wide thoroughfare curved gently westward. They passed Pier 39, the shoppers' delight; passed the three-masted Balclutha, last of the Cape Horn fleet; passed Fisherman's Wharf and beyond. "Look, Perry, the bridge." Bill pointed to the Golden Gate Bridge in the distance. "That's where we're going."

"A-yuh?"

"Yes, the bridge." It felt right. A good decision. They had no choice but to leave San Francisco. What better way than to take off north over the Golden Gate? He pressed the accelerator. "Perry, have you got any money?"

"Just got my disability."

Bill glanced at the gas gauge. Full, by God! He picked up Highway 101, curved through the beautiful green grounds of the Presidio, rolled onto the approach of the bridge. At the moment they sped past the NO STOPPING NORTH-BOUND signs at the tollgates, the sun broke through the morning fog, bathing the giant orange towers with sunshine, casting a diamond sparkle on the waters far below. A warm body pressed his shoulder. The dog stood directly behind, pushing against him. "Want the window down, Lucky?" He pressed the button that opened the window, and the dog poked his nose out, far as it would go, eyes half-closed, blissful expression on his face. Who said dogs didn't smile?

"Jesus God, we're on the bridge." Perry clutched his bottle in his arms, eyes wide with amazement.

"This is SiriusXM radio." A woman's voice, smooth and seductive. The music started and Neil Diamond was singing *I've been gone for a long time...Comin' home...comin' home...*

Free, out of Skid Row! And here he was, rolling across the Golden Gate Bridge in a Corvette Stingray with his friend, his dog, the sun shining and Neil Diamond singing *Comin' Home.* Bill lifted his head and let out a joyous, "Whooooeee!"

It was going to be a good day.

Chapter 16

Halfway across the bridge, Bill heard a melodious warbling sound coming from somewhere in the car. "What's that?"

Perry looked around until his eyes fastened on the console between the seats. "It's a telephone."

"Then answer it, Perry. I'm busy."

Perry reached for the phone and put it to his ear. "Hullo?" He listened, gravely nodding every few seconds. "A-yuh, a-yuh." He listened some more. "Say, that's not friendly."

Bill gave Perry a quick glance. "What was that all about?"

"That's the guy who owns the car. He was mad." With a regretful shrug, Perry lifted his bottle and took a generous swig. "Real mad."

"What'd he say?"

Perry wiped his mouth with the back of his hand. "Said he wants his fucking Stingray back. Said if he don't get it back he's going to rip my balls off and stuff 'em down my throat. And that's for openers."

Bill shook his head. The guy didn't have to be so rude. "Open the window, Perry. Throw it out." Perry shrugged and tossed the phone out the window. Good. One less thing to worry about.

He'd forgotten the call by the time he got to the Marin side of the bridge. In fact, the last of his tension had disappeared. He felt fine, really fine, for the first time since...he couldn't remember when. A sign just beyond the bridge said VISTA POINT. He took the off ramp and entered the large, circular parking lot on the cliff that overlooked the bay. "Got to stop a minute, Perry. Got to figure out what we're going to do."

"Yeah, you'd better." Perry didn't sound too concerned.

Bill pulled into a parking spot and shut off the engine. He reached back and patted the dog. "How're you doing, boy? See, I said they weren't going to get you." Lucky thumped his tail and gazed at him with grateful brown eyes. Bill turned back, draped his arms over the steering wheel and focused on the view beyond the windshield. The huge towers of the bridge loomed directly in front of him. The City of San Francisco lay in all its sparkling glory beyond. In the far distance, he could see the cities that ringed the bay—Berkeley bathed in sunshine— the University of California where he'd gone to school, back when he hiked uphill past the Campanile with a spring in his step, discovering the world through two good eyes.

Up close, tourists thronged along the stone wall of Vista Point. A young mother lifted her small son to the top of the wall. A well dressed, little Japanese guy adjusted his Camcorder. An overweight, gray-haired good old American couple fussed around their motor home. On a terrace, a pair of young lovers strolled arm in arm, regarding the seven-foot tall, bronze statue of the Lone Sailor who stood forever gazing at the bridge. *Where have I been? Why have I wallowed in the grime of Skid Row so long?* No more! He would never return to Howard Street. It wasn't too late to start his life anew. He could still have a Sting-ray of his own, and a 3-D flat screen, and camcorder, and 4.0 surround sound, all the best stuff. He'd find a good job, find a good woman to warm his bed at night. Oh yes, he'd get it back, all of it. He slammed his fist on the steering wheel. "By God, Perry, we're through with the old life."

"A-yuh?"

"Damn right. We've had our last drink."

"We have?"

"You better believe we have. For a while, anyway, until things get settled."

He gestured towards the world beyond the windshield. "Look at the people out there. They're having fun, enjoying their lives. That's where we should be."

Perry lifted his nearly empty bottle. "Got to get some more."

"Forget wine. That's it, man, we are done." Bill grabbed the bottle out of Perry's hands. He swung open the car door, got out, and resolutely dropped the bottle into the nearest trash bin.

When he slid back into the driver's seat, Perry gave him a

reproachful stare. "You shouldn't of done that."

"We've got more important things to think about. I'm telling you, Perry, today's the day we turn over a new leaf."

"Jesus God." Perry slumped into his seat.

Bill reached for the key and turned on the engine. "We're going to Portland, Oregon. My Grandmother lives there and I've got an uncle in the carpet business. We've as good as got jobs right now." He backed out of the parking spot and circled around until he found the exit. He revved up the engine, shot into the heavy traffic on Highway 101 and in five seconds accelerated to seventy miles an hour. Hot damn, this Stingray was smooth. He felt more at ease with it now, almost like it was his own. His foot grew heavy on the accelerator. He weaved in and out of the four lanes of northbound traffic, passing cars going seventy as if they were standing still. He passed a speed sign. Oops, still forty-five, but what the hell, nobody was doing forty-five.

"Jesus God." Perry, wide-eyed, was looking at the speedometer. Bill looked, too. *Ninety-five.* Maybe he'd better slow down a little. He braked and joined the slow movers in the outside lane, settling into the comfort of the bucket seat. What a waste of a fine automobile, but he'd better cool it for a while, go slow and look at the scenery.

He used to live in Marin County where yacht harbors filled with leisure sailboats dotted the shore, luxury condominiums crowded the hills, lush green shrubbery and tall eucalyptus trees lined the road. The names of the Marin County towns on the highway signs brought a nostalgic ache in his heart. Mill Valley, Fairfax, San Anselmo, all well remembered from his boyhood days.

He kept north, past San Rafael, and was heading towards Novato when he passed a black and white car just pulling onto the highway, on its side, the star emblem of the California Highway Patrol. Come to think of it, the guy who owned the Stingray would have called the police by now. "Perry, we've got to get off this freeway. We'd better take the back roads."

His palms grew sweaty and his tension returned as he

swung off 101 at the next turnoff onto Highway 37, a freeway that took him northeast. A few minutes later, he came to a stop sign. A two-lane road led north. He looked left and saw the road sign. HIGHWAY 121 TO SONOMA AND NAPA. Great, just what he wanted. He turned the wheel left. "Hey Perry, we're headed for the wine country."

Perry, who had closed his eyes, opened them wide. "A-yuh?"

"Some of your finest wineries are up this way—Mondavi, Sabbatini, Buena Vista, Sterling."

"Is that where we're going?"

"We're going right past them, old buddy. What we'll do is, we'll head north through the small towns, like Napa and St. Helena and Calistoga. With luck, no one will spot us."

"When are we stopping?"

"Not for a while. I told you we're not going to drink."

Lucky had pressed himself against his shoulder again and poked his nose through the open window. Bill reached with one hand and stroked his chin. "Feels good, doesn't it, bud, all that good fresh air in your face. Better than the stink in Skid Row." How had he stood it for so long?

Perry and the dog fell asleep as Bill guided the Stingray over the narrow country road. He'd get a job in Portland, anything at first, and then further along, he might go back to public relations. Also he'd do some traveling, get one of those big motor homes and tour the country. Hell, he knew he could do it. He might have to stay away from the booze for a while, but it would all work out.

They were getting deeper into the wine country, passing mile after mile of lush green vineyards with branches weighted down by ripening wine grapes. Tall Eucalyptus trees and pink oleanders dotted the roadside. Red rose bushes and yellow buttercups grew against low stone walls. A sign loomed ahead on the right.

SABBATINI BROTHERS CELLARS
Award Winning Wines

Zinfandel—Chenin Blanc—Johannesberg Riesling—
Chardonnay—Cabernet Sauvignon
Tasting 11 to 5 Daily Turn right 2 miles

Cabernet Sauvignon! Jennifer! A candlelight dinner on a stormy night...

Oh, Jesus, the Houston days. The big house by the bayou, children at Grandma's, sparkling crystal on the table set by the fire. They would dine and sip the wine he chose from their cellar. In those days he knew a lot about wine, a real connoisseur. He kept a respectable selection of his own. Elegant Chardonnays, robust Zinfandels, Petit Sirahs, Penot Jolies, an occasional Gewurztraminer. All delightful, but the Cabernet Savignons were best, not the ones from France but the California varieties. They were the finest, truly superior.

Looking into Jen's eyes across the table...touching his wine glass to hers...savoring the delicate bouquet of Cabernet Sauvignon while he looked forward to the rest of the evening, knowing the best was yet to come. After dinner, they would head for the bedroom where they'd make love by the hour. God, it was good. He never grew tired of his beautiful Jen.

Then it all fell apart. How many gallons of vodka did he drink? A good belt first thing in the morning to chase away the shakes—sneaky gulps during the day from the bottle in his desk—martini lunches. By night, el blotto, el stinko. Man, he just couldn't stop. One day Jen decided she'd had enough, packed his bags and threw him out.

Two miles along, he saw the sign.

SABBATINI BROTHERS CELLARS 3 MILES

A narrow road led off to the right. Too bad he was on the wagon. How he'd love to roll a little Cabernet Sauvignon across his palate. He could almost taste that exquisite dry red wine right now. A real shame. But then, on the other hand...how many times in his life would he pass a winery in Sonoma County, California, where they made the best Cabernet Sauvignon in the world? How could he not stop and taste it? If he let this golden opportunity pass by, wouldn't he regret it to his dying day?

Besides, this really wasn't a good day to stop drinking, what with all the excitement.

He'd go on the wagon tomorrow.

He spun the steering wheel right. Perry woke with a start. "Where are we going?"

"We're going to do a little wine tasting, my friend."

"I thought you said—"

"Never mind what I said. This is social drinking. It's not the same thing at all."

Cody Harper, white cloth in hand, stood alert at his station at the long mahogany bar. A tall, blond young man with a red apron tied over his white shirt, he wore a faint look of surprise that for the moment there was a lull in the crowd. Was his nametag straight? A quick downward glance assured him it was. Good. The old goat would say something nasty if it wasn't. Cody lifted a wine glass, gave it a quick polish and heaved a sigh. Another boring day in the tasting room at Sabbatini Cellars. But then, he shouldn't complain. He was lucky. Not only was he earning straight A's at California State University at Fresno, but for a summer job, this was the best he could ever have. His major was Agriculture, his specialized field, Enology, the science of wine and wine making. In three years he'd worked his way through courses in harvesting, scheduling, crushing, and fermentation. He'd learned winery practice and critical evaluation of selected wines. He'd done wine microbiology, cellar operation and more. This was a great opportunity, working the summer months at one of the most prestigious wineries in California.

Only one thing was wrong with his job. If only Sereno Sabbatini would drop dead. What a pain in the ass the old guy was. He had to be at least seventy-five, maybe eighty, the last living son of the original Sabbatini Brothers. Big deal. Why didn't the old fart retire, or at least stay out of the tasting room?

But no such luck. Hardly the day went by that the arrogant old bugger didn't poke his nose in, just so he could play up to the tourists. They were always thrilled to see him. Thought he was a big celebrity because they recognized him from the TV commercial, the one where he stood in the middle of a vineyard, wine glass in hand, and announced in his snooty voice, "When you serve Sabbatini's, you serve the very best."

Oh, yeah. The old guy loved to go into his high and mighty winegrower routine for the fawning crowd, rattling off names of exotic wines, impressing the hell out of a bunch of tourists who didn't know a Riesling from a Zinfandel. They didn't see what happened after they closed and the old miser went into his tirade.

"I keep telling you, only a splash! Those dumbass tourists are getting it for free! You fill a glass too full, you're fired!"

Of course, he had to admit Sabbatini knew his stuff. No one in the world knew more about wines than that old man. The winery itself was a great place to work. Sabbatini's was one of the oldest operations in California, and one of the most beautiful. The classic stone chateau was built over a century ago, situated in the rolling Sonoma Hills in a wooded nook overlooking a green valley. The oak casks in the aging caverns had been made in Europe and shipped around Cape Horn over a century ago. The wines themselves, some of the best in the world, had won hundreds of awards. Tourists came here by the thousands each year.

Cody ran the cloth over the rich dark wood of the bar. It was a good thing he liked people because the job wasn't at all like he expected. He thought it would be a great place to meet girls. Was he ever wrong. "Don't look for young people," old Sereno warned him on his first day. "Young people don't go for the fine wines. Young people are intimidated by places like this. They stick with their beer and wine coolers."

Man, you could say that again. Cody started uncorking bottles and setting out wine glasses. Tourist wine tasters were dignified, middle aged to elderly people with maybe a sprinkling of young marrieds. Tourist wine tasters pretended they knew

one wine from another which, of course, they did not. Tourist
wine tasters often arrived in groups called "Golden Age Gala-
vanters" or "Senior Citizens on the Go."

But still...there were enough exceptions to make it all
worthwhile. He liked meeting Americans from all parts of the
country. The scattering of foreigners always brightened the day,
like the polite Japanese who bowed and wanted to give him a
present in return, like the twinkle eyed Frenchmen who insisted
the driest of Sabbatini's wines was not nearly dry enough. Yes,
indeed, next to working in the Sabbatini Laboratories, he enjoyed working in the cavernous dark tasting room with the cool
stone floor. Such an inviting place with soft symphony music
playing in the background and tasteful displays of goods for
sale, not cheap souvenirs, but quality stuff like crystal wine
glasses, brandy decanters, etchings of the Sabbatini Chateau and
vineyards, and wicker picnic baskets with special pockets for
wine and glasses. All very nice. And just occasionally, he'd meet
someone who did know a little something about wines, and that
was nice, too.

A big bus roared into the parking lot. Through the arched
stone entryway, he could see the sign on the side. SAN JOSE
SENIOR CITIZENS' FUN CLUB. Cody sighed. The lull was
over.

Bill gestured at the acres of vines they were passing as the
road rose gradually into the Sonoma hills. "Look at the vineyards, Perry. I'd guess Chardonnay and pinot noir."

Perry sat straight. "There's wine up here?"

"That's right, and it's free."

"You don't say?"

"The tasting's free. If we buy a bottle, that's going to
cost."

After three miles, the road ended in a large parking lot
down the hill from a beautiful stone chateau. Bill found a parking space between two tour buses. He and Perry climbed from
the car. Bill opened the hatchback to let Lucky out. "Come on,
old buddy. I'll let you run a minute before I tie you up."

Lucky climbed slowly out of the car, stretched, and limped to the trees that grew at the edge of the lot. Bill found a trash can. He rummaged around inside until he came up with a KFC carton. He found a faucet near a flowerbed, filled the carton with water and set it under a nearby tree. Returning to the car, he reached in the back for the rope from his bedroll and tied it around the dog's neck. He led him to the tree where it was shady, and tied the rope around the trunk. "Okay?" Lucky gazed at him with a questioning look in his eyes. "We're just going to do some wine tasting. Don't worry, we're not going to leave you." Bill reached down and ran his hand over Lucky's back. The dog lay down but kept his nose up, seeming to believe him because his eyes held no sign of worry.

"He'll be okay. Come on, Perry, let's go taste some wine."

Early afternoon at Sabbatini's tasting room was generally busy, and today was no exception. For Cody, the last hour had been a blur of glasses held in outstretched hands, of eager tourists jostling for position at the long bar. Right now, he was pouring Sabbatini's White Gamay for a group of white-haired Iowa ladies and answering their questions at the same time. "Yes, Ma'am, this is a varietal. That means the grape it's made from makes up 76% of the content of the wine."

"How interesting." The lady tasted the Gamay and wrinkled up her nose. "Gracious, I don't like that one."

"A bit too dry? Let's try something richer." Cody reached under the counter for a Gewurztraminer.

"Well, I..." She put her hand over her heart and nodded towards the back archway. "Oh, look, isn't that Mr. Sabbatini himself?

Cody looked up. Shit! "Yes, Ma'am, that's our Mr. Sabbatini in person." He watched Sabbatini, gray-haired and pinch nosed, with beady, darting eyes, make his standard grand entrance. Hands clasped behind his back, he smiled and nodded to the admiring tourist crowd, kind of like a king being gracious to the peasants. The old bastard even dressed the part. Maroon velvet jacket with shiny brass buttons, crisp white shirt with a fluted edging on the cuffs and down the front, perky black bow tie. Gray pinstriped trousers—pointy toed black shoes. Real old country glitz, although he was born and raised right here in Sonoma County.

Here he came, strutting like an old peacock. "Good afternoon, ladies." Sereno cast a lordly smile at the Iowa ladies as he stepped behind the bar. He put his left arm around Cody's shoulders. "Is our young man treating you well?"

"Oh, my yes..."

"You're even handsomer than on TV."

Amidst delighted tee-hee's and giggles, Sereno puffed out his chest. With his right arm he made a grand, sweeping gesture of the tasting room. "Here, in these very cellars, you'll find the finest wines in the world, my dears." He cleared his throat. Cody braced himself. Here it came for the thousandth time. "When you serve Sabbatini's, you serve the very best."

Barf!

The old man continued spouting off while Cody continued to pour the wine without spilling a drop. Just another day at Sabbatini's Winery until one of the ladies looked towards the front entryway and slammed her hand to her chest. "My stars, what is that?" Cody stopped in mid-pour. Two men came through the door, one tall, one of medium height, and they were the worst looking, most decrepit, shabbiest bums he had ever seen in his life. The two stood for a moment looking around, adjusting their eyes to the dimness of the tasting room. When they saw the bar, they started towards it, not walking straight like most people, but rather, kind of shambling across the floor. The tall one in the orange Niki's seemed to be shaking. The shorter one with the shapeless gray hat could best be called a walking disaster with his frayed, faded clothes, awkward limp, and face with a horrible eye. Poor guys, what the heck were they doing here? These bums had to be right out of Skid Row.

The loud hum of voices quickly stilled. Only the muted sound of a Beethoven Concerto filled the air as the two bums approached the bar. People in the way cleared a path for the shabby pair. A lady made a face as the tall one passed by, like she smelled something bad. At the bar, the Iowa ladies backed hastily away. Cody sensed, rather than saw, Sabbatini bristle with indignation. How dare this riff-raff invade his beloved tasting room!

The idea came to Cody in a flash of brilliance. Here was a once-in-a-lifetime opportunity to annoy the shit out of the old man and not be blamed. He picked up his white cloth, made a wide swipe across the mahogany, and flashed the two newcomers his best, most gracious smile. "Good afternoon, gentlemen, and welcome to Sabbatini's. I'm Cody. How may I help you?"

The shorter one nodded and replied pleasantly, "Good afternoon. My name's Bill and this is my friend, Perry. We'd like to taste some wine."

"Of course." Cody flipped up two clean glasses and placed them on the counter. The usual procedure would do nicely: first the whites, then the rosés, then into the dry reds and finally, the sweet. He reached for a bottle. Out of the corner of his eye, he caught old Sereno's incredulous expression. He forced down his laughter—he was about to burst—and put on his most serious face. "Shall we start with a French Columbard?"

"Why not?" Bill, the shorter one, leaned both arms expectantly on the counter and clasped his hands together. Perry, the tall one, grabbed and hung onto the bar with both hands. His mouth hung slightly open. A thin trickle of drool ran down his chin. With Sereno watching every move he made, Cody poured a splash of the driest of the white wines, the French Columbard, into each glass. Perry grabbed his. In one gulp, it was gone. Bill picked up his glass, swirled its contents, and gave it a delicate sniff. He lifted it to his lips, sipped, and swished it around his mouth. He swallowed. For a long moment, he looked up at the ceiling, then back at Cody. Finally he spoke. "Adequate."

Sereno found his voice. "Adequate? Sabbatini's 1985 French Columbard is *adequate?*"

Bill looked regretful and hastened to explain. "It's crisp enough, of course. Not bad, truly. But simply your average dry white wine that doesn't call attention to itself." A brief look of amusement gleamed in his one good eye. "One of the 'work horses of the wine world, you might say."

A long silence followed as Cody and Old Sabbatini exchanged stunned glances. The old man started to sputter. Hastily Cody broke in and spoke to Bill. "May I present Mr. Sereno Sabbatini, head of Sabbatini wineries?" Bill nodded briefly, not impressed. "Well then, shall we move along to the Johannesburg Riesling? The Gewurztraminer? Or better yet—" Cody cast a guarded glance at Sereno "—the Pinot Chardonnay?"

"By all means, the Pinot Chardonnay." Bill glanced at his companion. "How about you, Perry?"

"By all means." Perry wiped the drool away with his sleeve. He pushed his glass across the counter. "Fill it up this time."

Cody reached in the refrigerator for a bottle of 1984 Pinot Chardonnay, a prizewinner, one of the old man's pride and joys. Better believe they never served this one to the commonplace tourists. He poured a jot into Bill's glass. With reckless abandon, without looking in the old man's direction, he filled Perry's glass to the brim. The season wasn't over yet. Hopefully, they'd hire him over at Buena Vista or maybe Sebastiani. Funny, but the old man didn't even notice. Nostrils quivering, his eyes were glued on the bum with one eye.

Again, Bill picked up his glass and took a sip. He rolled the Pinot Chardonnay across his palate, swallowed, and regarded the ceiling. This time when he looked back, his gaze fastened on Sereno. "Respectable enough."

The old man's face puffed up and turned red. "Our Pinot Chardonnay has been a dazzling success, sir. And you call it respectable enough?"

"I grant you, your Chardonnays were at the perfect degree of ripeness when you picked."

Sereno acceded with the briefest of nods. "And?"

"And quite obviously you aged this batch in Limousin oak."

"So?"

"So, sir, that's fine for some, in fact, most people, I'm sure. But for me, it's a tad too much on the oaky side. Oak is like garlic. You need some, but if that's all you taste, it's too much."

The old man's eyebrows shot up. His lips quivered. "This wine won a gold medal at The Orange County Fair."

"I can't help that. It's too oaky."

While Sereno stood speechless, Cody bent low, finding an immediate need to search for something beneath the counter. His shoulders shook with suppressed laughter until finally he pulled himself together and rose up in time to see Perry polish off his wine in two gulps and hold out his glass. "More."

Sereno Sabbatini, his eyes hardly leaving Bill's face, picked up the bottle of 1984 Pinot Chardonnay and filled Perry's glass to the brim, spilling a bit on the counter as he did so. He banged the bottle down and turned back to Bill. "Obviously you don't find anything to your liking at Sabbatini Cellars."

Bill raised a hand in mild protest. "But that's not so. Allow me to try your Cabernet Sauvignon."

Sereno look at him warily. "Any particular year?"

"Come to think of it, no. In recent years, I...whatever year you like."

"Cody, bring me the Estate Bottled 1978."

"Did you say the—?"

"You heard me."

"Yes sir."

Cody left the counter and headed far back into the cellars for the '78. Better believe the tourist wine tasters never got a shot at this one. It was one of the finest, if not the finest, wines in the entire cellar. He found a bottle and returned to the bar. He reached for two fresh glasses. Under the icy stare of the old man, he poured an inch into each glass.

Bill lifted his glass. He sniffed, sipped, and finally swallowed. He gazed upwards, then at Sereno. His good eye lit up. "This is fantastic, the best I've ever tasted. Just the right touch of subtle rounded oak overtones." He held up the glass and gazed with delight at the liquid with his one good eye. "Such a marvelous deep ruby color."

A look of triumph spread over the old man's face. He leaned across the counter in a confidential manner. "Don't let anyone tell you otherwise—our Cabernet Sauvignon is the finest wine made in America."

"True. I thoroughly agree, although you will admit that in the past, many sins have been committed in the name of Cabernet Sauvignon."

"Quite so. Awful wines were produced, and regrettably some from this very area. Dirty, tanky, flabby wines."

"But this one..." Bill held up his glass "...superb!"

The old man looked like he was going to pee his pants. "Painstakingly handmade. We used the finest techniques, from crushing to fermentation to ageing. We used high-priced European presses, the most modern fermenters. Hundreds of expensive oak barrels went into our production."

Perry pointed at his empty glass. "More." Cody filled it to the brim with the Pinot Chardonnay.

The old man didn't even notice and continued speaking directly to Bill. "Of course, the real secret is our vines grow in a special, snug little corner of the Carneros not far from San Pablo Bay. Some might think it's too cool, but that area...sir, your friend... "

Perry was sinking slowly from sight. Bill quickly set his glass down and grabbed Perry by the back of his collar. "Perry, stand up."

With an effort, Perry pulled himself straight and looked inquiringly at Sereno Sabbatini. "Have you got any Night Train?"

Amidst the long, stunned silence that followed, Perry sank slowly to the cool stone floor, Bill easing the fall. He lay on his back, mouth open wide, the orange Nikis pointing up at the oak beamed ceiling.

Bill was the first to recover. "We must be going." He made an attempt to lift his fallen friend, putting one of Perry's arms across his shoulders. Cody came quickly around the counter and grabbed the other arm. He put it behind his neck so that Perry was in the middle, knees sagging, he and Bill on each side.

They hauled Perry across the stone floor of the tasting room, shoes dragging, past all the gaping tourists, outside to the parking lot. They paused in the sunshine. "Which car?" Cody asked.

"Over there, the Corvette Stingray."

Cody took a look. "I won't ask."

The corners of Bill's mouth lifted into the tiniest of smiles. "Don't."

They hauled Perry to the car. Bill unlocked it, and they eased the unconscious man into the passenger seat. Bill went to the tree, untied Lucky, and put him in the back. Just as he was about to thank Cody, he heard a voice calling and looked back towards the chateau.

"Wait!" Sereno Sabbatini, walking with the measured steps of an elderly man, came towards them. "Here, sir, this is for you." In his hand was an unopened bottle of 1978 Estate Bottled Cabernet Sauvignon. He handed it to Bill.

Bill just stood there. "I don't know what to say."

"Say nothing. I want you to have this because...damn it, just take it."

The old man spun around and headed back towards the chateau. Not turning, he lifted a hand and waved.

Bill climbed into the Stingray and laid the bottle in his lap. He looked up at Cody who stood beside the window. "Well, thanks."

Cody reached through the window and clasped his hand. "Good luck, bro."

"Yeah, I'm going to need it."

Bill drove out of the parking lot, not burning rubber this time. Halfway down the narrow winding road, heading back to Highway 121, he remembered his grandmother in Portland died four years ago. The uncle with the carpet business had retired and wasn't speaking to him anyway. Well, hell, it rained too much in Oregon anyway. He'd just as soon go south instead. He thought a minute. Los Angeles was the place to go. All those beaches, and the weather was great.

At the crossroads, he saw a small grocery store on the corner with a liquor sign in the window. It was certainly a lucky thing he had postponed going on the wagon until tomorrow. Tasting that wine had got him started again, just for the day, of course. Right now he really needed a drink. He could break open the Cabernet Sauvignon, but no, he'd save it for a special occasion. T-bird would do fine. Maybe they carried Night Train. He pulled into the parking lot and shook Perry awake. "Hey, Perry, I need some money. Guess what? We're going to L.A."

Officer Stan Galvin, of the California Highway Patrol, had just finished writing a speeding ticket and was returning to his Crown Victoria Police Interceptor parked on the shoulder of Highway 99, ten miles north of Fresno. An eighteen-year veteran of the force, the tall officer cut an imposing figure with his Polaroid dark glasses and khaki uniform with the smart blue stripe down the sides of his crisply creased pants. As he settled into the seat, he heard the dispatcher on his radio. "BOL (be on the lookout) for a possible ten-eight-fifty-one. Stolen from the San Francisco area. A blue 2-door Corvette Stingray, California license, TYLER C. Possible suspects are two white males, age unknown. May be accompanied by a large, black dog."

At that moment, Officer Galvin saw from the corner of his eye a streak of blue flash by. Looking south down the highway, he caught a glimpse of a speeding blue car right before it cut sharply in front of a Bekins van and was lost from view. Holy Mother! That clown was going flat out. In less than three seconds, Officer Galvin rolled his Crown Victoria onto Highway 99, red and blue light bar flashing, pulsating headlights beaming, siren screaming. As he accelerated, he reached for the microphone. "Am in pursuit of a high speed vehicle headed south on 99 near the Kerman exit. Vehicle is a blue Corvette Stingray. Approximate speed…" Officer Galvin checked his own speedometer "…over one hundred."

Far ahead, the blue car cut back and forth between the two southbound lanes, dodging passenger cars, motor homes, pickups hauling boats, huge eighteen-wheelers. Galvin floored the Crown Victoria, but the gap didn't close. Again he reached for the microphone. "We'll need some help on this one. Notify Fresno P. D. You'd better get the helicopter. This guy's not going to stop."

"How's your Night Train holding out, Perry?"
Perry held up a half-full bottle. "Okay."
"Yeah, well, it's time to stop anyway. We've been driving for over three hours." Not that Bill was tired. In fact, he felt fine. The bottle he bought after leaving the winery was nearly gone. Most people would be wiped out by that much alcohol but not him. He might be a little sauced, but he could handle it. He was perfectly relaxed now, enjoying driving this fine automobile which flew past every damn thing on the road. There was a time when he paid attention to the speed limit, but not now. Today he was unconquerable—nothing and nobody could hurt him today. He yawned and pushed halfway up in his seat. "We'll stop off here in Fresno and gas up. I need to stretch, and I'll bet the dog does, too."

The Stingray sped past a sign marked VENTURA BOULEVARD, KINGS CANYON ROAD 1/2 MILE. Just as he spied the turnoff, he caught a glimpse of red and blue flashing lights in his rearview mirror. "Looks like the cops are after someone." He started to brake the car, continued braking as he headed down the off-ramp, following its curved route into the City of Fresno. By the time he rolled onto the heavy traffic on Ventura Boulevard, he was driving at a sedate speed. A small cross street marked "E" lay dead ahead. "We'll just get off the main drag. Got to find a good place to let the dog run."

He turned right onto "E" Street into a neighborhood of older homes, not far from the downtown skyline. Turning aimlessly left and right, he passed several blocks of houses, increasingly rundown with ragged lawns. Here and there he noticed shabby looking men sitting on curbs or standing on trash-strewn corners, paper bags in their hands. *Just like home.* He turned into a dead-end street and spied a small parking lot, overgrown with weeds, beside a vacant, boarded up store. He pulled in. "This looks like a good spot. Let's get out and stretch."

Officer Galvin shook his head in disbelief. The Stingray had disappeared, but not to worry. The guy might outrun a patrol car, but he wouldn't escape the all-seeing eye of the CHP helicopter. The dispatcher broke into his thoughts. "Have notified Fresno PD, but suspects have not yet been apprehended. Forget the helicopter, it's out of town on a rescue mission."

That Stingray was a horrific accident about to happen. Officer Galvin cast a pleading look to the sky. *Please Lord, for the sake of every soul on the road today, don't let it get away.*

Bill formed his new plan while leaning on the fender of the Stingray, still parked by the boarded-up store. To the east lay the Sierra Nevada Mountains in all their spender. When he was an Explorer Scout, he spent a lot of time there, scaling up rock cliffs and rappelling down, panning for gold in icy streams, riding horseback into wilderness country.

Oh, yeah, he knew the Sierras well. The giant sequoias stood almost directly east. He had to bend his head way back to look at trees that were two hundred seventy feet tall, thirty feet thick and thirty-five hundred years old. It would sure be nice to see them again. He had always loved the mountains, always wanted to live there...but of course! What was so great about going to Southern California? If he stayed on 99, sooner or later the CHP would catch him. Not only that, Los Angeles wasn't all that great, what with the high prices and all that traffic. "Change in plan, Perry."

"Where now?"

"This is the best plan yet. There's a better place for us than L.A."

"A-yuh?"

"We're going camping in the high Sierras.

"Geeze, I dunno."

"We're going to do it, Perry, you, me and the dog. There won't be any cops or dog catchers where we're going."

Perry lifted his bottle, squinting at the one inch of liquid remaining. "But—"

"Don't worry, we'll have plenty to drink."

The sun cast late afternoon shadows as Bill guided the Stingray back to Ventura Boulevard. He spied a Good Will store where they bought two warm jackets for three dollars each. Back in the car, he turned east and drove out of the city. A few miles from town they found a Minimart where they bought food for themselves and the dog and some paper goods. They stopped at an ARCO for a tankful of gas and fed the dog.

From the ARCO, the Stingray began its smooth climb into the foothills, past peach, apricot and orange groves, past stunted palm trees fighting for life at the beginning of the western slope. In the back, Lucky went to sleep, stretched out, his nose occasionally twitching. In the passenger seat, Perry half dozed, his empty bottles rolling on the floor. Behind the wheel, Bill sat relaxed, his newly purchased bottle of T-bird anchored securely between his thighs. Only occasionally did he raise it to his mouth, allowing just a trickle to slide down his throat. No fool he. This was no fancy four lane divided highway. This road was two-lane, with plenty of dangerous curves. He would need his wits about him to negotiate it safely. *Keep it at fifty. Drink just enough to maintain your glow.* No sense going fast, especially with such a scenic drive.

In his scouting days he learned a lot about the Sierra forests. Even now he recognized most of the trees and remembered where they grew. At three hundred feet you had the white oaks, blue oaks, California sycamores and willows. At two thousand feet you could spot black cottonwoods, digger pines, ponderosa pines, California laurels and Oregon ash. The incense cedars began at four thousand feet, along with white alders and dogwoods, all crowding in with the pines. He recognized the manzanitas, too, and the mountain alders, California junipers, bayberries with their slender leafs. How grand to behold the wild green beauty of these mountains again. He'd missed a lot, there in the depths of Skid Row. That was all behind him now. It was over.

The deep blue shadows of the June twilight settled over

the mountainside just as Bill reached a small booth in the middle of the road, marking the entrance to Sequoia National Park. His heart quickened its beat at the sight of a stop sign. From the booth, the admiring gaze of a Forest Ranger swept over the car. Bill slid his bottle to the floor and stopped the car as far as possible from the booth. Maybe the guy wouldn't notice his boozy breath.

The Ranger nodded. "Nice car you've got there."

"Yes, isn't it?"

"Twenty dollars to enter the park, sir."

There went the last of Perry's money, but what could he do? The Ranger collected the twenty-dollar bill from Bill's extended hand. He handed Bill a copy of the Sequoia/Kings Canyon Map and Guide. "Thanks, have a nice day."

"Thanks, you too." Bill waved and drove away. Made it, by God. He drove a few miles down the road to the Grant Grove, into the deserted parking lot enshrouded in fast descending darkness. Too bad it wasn't lighter, but they could still see a little. "Hey Perry, open your eyes. These are the biggest trees in the world." Perry's head lolled on the back of the seat. His mouth hung wide open. Bill shook him by the shoulder. No use. He looked back. "How about you, buddy? Let's go take a look."

Lucky jumped from the car. He sniffed the crispy pine scented mountain air, looking happy and wagging his tail. He seemed to be moving easier now. Maybe he was just bruised, after all. Tall sentinels towered silently above them in the soft dim quiet of the grove. Bill, with Lucky at his heels, followed the path to the General Sherman tree, so immense it was hard to perceive how big it really was. He stood, head back, and stared. "Just look at that, old buddy. That first big limb is so high it would stretch out over a twelve story building." Suddenly dizzy, he staggered backwards. Catching himself, he knelt on one knee and put his arm around the dog. "Just think, this tree was here when the Egyptians built the pyramids, when Christ was born, when they signed the Magna Carta, when Columbus discovered America." He had to smile. "When Jen threw me out."

He went silent, the little smile gone. Two tears slid down his cheeks. For a while he crouched silently, stroking the soft fur on Lucky's back. The dog gave him a quick lick on the face. Bill flinched back. "Fine thing, a tree made me cry. Can you believe that?" He stood up, staggered and caught himself. "Let's go. We're almost to the end."

Back at the car, he started to get in and then paused. About time to get another bottle of T-bird from the back. He would save the Cabernet Sauvignon for a special occasion, but then, why not? Wasn't escaping Skid Row a special occasion?

He retrieved Sereno Sabbatini's gift from the back, opened it, and climbed into the Stingray.

Perry was beginning to wake up. Lucky watched, nose resting on the seat back, as Bill unfolded the Sequoia/Kings Canyon Map and Guide and studied it under the dome light. "Okay, we're going to take 180 down to Cedar Grove. Too bad it's dark because it's a beautiful drive. We wind down the mountain, past Boyden Cave. Then we drive right next to the Kings River for a while until we get to Cedar Grove, and that's the end of the road."

The southern fork of the Kings River is a beautiful, awesome, deadly stream. Beginning high in the Sierras, the swift, frigid water smashes and crashes its violent path downward, roaring over rocks and huge boulders, surging through deep-cut canyons until, still running fast, cold, and only partially tamed, it speeds onto the plains of the San Joaquin Valley. Signs posted along the upper river read:

WARNING
The Kings River is swift, cold and turbulent at all times.
Do not wade in or attempt to cross.
Keep children under control at all times.

Swimming and kayaking are forbidden on the south fork of the Kings River, but the river claims its victims all the same.

Fishermen wade in too far. Careless picture-taking tourists slip off the rocks. Motorists, for one reason or another, skid off the highway that borders the river and smash into the raging stream. Because of the high runoff in spring, the southern fork of the Kings River is particularly dangerous.

The headlights of the Stingray cut through inky blackness as they started down the mountain on the tightly curving road. Thank God there wasn't much traffic. Bill enjoyed the solitude. It was good just to let his thoughts run free. The bottle of Cabernet Sauvignon rested between his thighs, clasped tightly in his left hand. As he raised it to his lips, he laughed. A good thing the old man in the winery couldn't see him swilling his precious 1978 right out of the bottle.

He felt a nudge on his shoulder. "You want the window open, do you?" He pressed the button for the window. Lucky stuck his head far out, eager to feel the wind across his muzzle. Bill, too, enjoyed a deep whiff of the pine-scented fresh air. What a day. Was it only this morning he was sitting in a doorway on Howard Street? Eating breakfast with all those losers at Jesus Saves? Now here he was, high in the mountains, free as a bird. He had no idea what the future held, but he wasn't afraid.

Though he couldn't see it, he knew the Kings River ran right by the roadside. He passed Boyden Cave, closed now. He would take Perry to see it soon. Time to maintain the glow. He reached for the bottle and tilted it to his lips.

It was a combination of things: the dark night, the distraction of tilting the bottle, the lack of depth because of his blind eye, the curve in the road, and, too, the point-three-five blood alcohol level in his body.

He missed the turn. The car shot out into space, plunged thirty feet, bounced once and overturned.

Tyler Todd Cameron's brand new Corvette Stingray came to rest upside-down, amidst huge boulders, in the middle of the South Fork of the King's River. Only the wheels were visible.

* * *

From the Fresno *Bee*

CAR REMAINS IN RIVER

SEQUOIA NATIONAL FOREST – A car has plunged into the runoff-swollen Kings River. It remains in the water, upside down, the fate of its occupants unknown. National Park Service rangers who tried to reach the car shortly after the accident which occurred about 70 miles east of Fresno said the water was too swift and cold to allow searchers near the vehicle. Ron Davies, a California Highway Patrol spokesman, said the agency was aware of the accident and was monitoring the water levels. He said a full search would be made when water conditions permitted. A plan to use a large crane to reach the car has been discarded because the force of the water might topple the crane. The car, which was traveling on state Highway 180, a half mile east of Boyden Cavern, went into the river two days ago, officers said. None of the agencies involved has identified the driver, car, or where it comes from. Of the agencies involved, none has reports of any overdue travelers.

The accident is at the same location where a small car went off the road in the spring of 2003, killing two Bakersfield men. One body was never recovered.

Chapter 17

The Coffee Room,
Santa Marta Hospital Detox Unit

"No more spiders?" Doctor Tessler set his coffee on the table and sat across from his patient.

Despite the haze she'd been in since her DT's, Connie noticed how handsome he looked today, like Dr. Mark Sloan in *Grey's Anatomy* in his wrinkled green surgical cottons with his cap pushed back on his head. "No more spiders, Doctor. Not here anyway. They're home, hiding back of my TV." With steady hands, Connie lifted a plastic coffee cup to her lips, managing a half smile along with her little attempt at humor. It wasn't easy. Nothing much was funny when you'd been in a detox center for a week and you were sick, weak and very, very sober. "I must look a fright." She set down the cup and made a halfhearted stab at her hair.

"You look fine to me."

"I can just imagine." She knew how she looked with no makeup, wearing the faded blue hospital gown and robe with those dreadful throwaway paper slippers on her feet. She'd called Harvey and asked him to bring her some clothes, but he hadn't come by. "When do I get out of here?"

"A few more days."

"I want to go home."

"Do you?"

She pulled herself up straight in the plastic lunchroom chair. "Well, of course. Where else?"

"Not a good idea." He waited for an answer, swirling his stir stick around and around the cup. When she didn't speak, he continued, "I don't want you to go home. I want to see you in a rehab center for a least a couple of months, probably longer."

"I'm sober now. I don't need it. Believe you me, from now on I'll control my drinking."

"Don't give me that, lady." He gave her the skeptical, eyebrows-up look she'd seen before.

How annoying, this young, still-wet-behind-the-ears doctor. Yet he'd been so kind. He didn't understand, though, about Harvey. "My husband would never allow me."

"You're right. Your husband wants you home."

"You've talked to him?" She knew Harvey had been called the night she entered the hospital, but he hadn't come to see her, or even phoned in the entire week she'd been here.

"Sure, I talked to him."

"And?"

"He wasn't overly cooperative. In fact, you could say he wasn't too thrilled you were here."

She nodded. "That's Harvey."

"When I told him you should go to a rehab center where you can be properly treated, he—"

"Blew his stack?"

"Yeah."

"You see?" She flopped out her hands. "Even if I wanted to, I couldn't. Harvey controls the money."

"And you."

"That's not so. Harvey doesn't control me."

He tipped his head to one side, gazed at her long and hard. "You've got another addiction besides Valium and alcohol. You're addicted to your husband."

An unconvincing laugh was all she could manage. "That's a ridiculous statement if ever I heard one." Really, she should be very angry if only she had the strength. "What do you mean?"

"I mean I've seen a lot of women like you, so dependent on their husbands they've lost their own identity. They live all their lives in the shadow of a man, addicted, hooked, thinking they can't do without him. The sad part is they can't, unless by some miracle they manage to break away."

Frozen, she stared at him. "Go on," she whispered.

"Connie, break away. If you go home, you're going to start drinking again."

"That's not so!"

"He wants you to. Can't you see that? Ask yourself, in all

the years you've been drinking, has he ever once tried to stop you or has he been shoving glasses of vodka in your hand? You know the answer to that better than I. Now, I'm not saying you should divorce him. What I'm saying is you need to dry out before you decide what to do with the rest of your life." He gulped his coffee and stood up. "Look, there's a place you can go. I can arrange it. It's a home for alcoholic women here in Santa Marta. It won't cost you a penny."

"What about Harvey?"

Doctor Tessler took a deep breath, as if he was trying to quell his anger before he spoke again. "You're an adult. You don't need to ask your husband's permission. Think for yourself."

"Thank you very much. You're very kind, but I just want to go home."

His eyes turned hard. "Life's full of hard choices, Mrs. Linderman. Which do you want? To dive into the bottle again or gain back your self-respect?"

"That's not fair."

"What is?" Without so much as a backward glance, he strode out the door.

By the South Fork of the Upper Kings River

"Daddy, tell Jason to close his mouth. It's full of Oreos and it's totally gross."

"Let's be quiet back there! Can't you see I'm driving? Tell him yourself."

Madame Dracula swung around in her seat and pasted on her angel smile. "Tiffany, darling, you don't hassle your father when he's driving a big RV along a winding mountain road."

"But—"

"Really, if you can't get along with one small nine-year-old-boy, then you'd better go back to Torrance." With a delicate sniff, she turned back around.

Tiffany Clair's adolescence had just begun. She was a shade over five feet tall, her jean-clad hips slender as a boy's.

Her breasts were growing but not yet visible beneath the over-sized cotton T-shirt with Mickey Mouse on the front. Her face was round and pretty, her complexion peaches and cream. Her brown hair hung long and curly, just like Taylor Swift's. It would have been blonde like Taylor's, too, but Rosalind said she was too young to bleach it. Now she was glowering at the stepbrother who sat beside her, lips sealed, cheeks full. "You are the prince of grossness, but really you are."

Jason attacked again, thrusting his face close and opening his mouth wide as he could. A big glob of Oreos sat on his tongue.

"Oh, totally disgusting! Gag me with a spoon." Tiffany turned her back on her stepbrother and stared out the window. Pine trees and boulders flashed by. The awesome river tumbled down the mountain, right alongside the road. Some river. What good was it? You couldn't swim in it, you couldn't wade in it. It wasn't a fun river at all, like death was waiting there to grab you if you stuck in your toe. Nothing was fun. This whole trip was awful. She'd wanted Daddy to herself, maybe go fishing, or go on a hike, but SHE wouldn't let him out of her sight. And SHE kept nagging at Daddy and her, while darling Jason could do no wrong.

Tiffany had only herself to blame. Coming to live with Daddy in his big house in Encino had been her own idea. All last summer she'd begged Mom to let her go. She had tons of good reasons, like she'd have a room of her own, like she'd have the really neat pool with cabanas and a wet bar where she would throw fabulous parties for her friends. She wouldn't miss Mom at all, or her bratty sister, or Princess, her cocker spaniel because she would visit them on weekends. It would all be wonderful. No more tacky little house in Torrance and the tiny bedroom she had to share.

Mom finally gave in. Tiffany got her way, but the trouble was it wasn't like what she expected. She hardly ever got to Torrance because nobody had time to drive her. And how could you throw a party before you'd made any friends? Worst of all, she'd dreamed of spending time with Daddy, only he never got away from HER. Tiffany stared daggers at the back of her stepmother's head. Mom said she should try to like her because she meant well. Mom's advice sucked because she'd never met Rosalind. Maybe Daddy thought she was wonderful with her swan neck and creamy skin, her simpering smile and high lispy voice, but Tiffany knew better. Her stepmother hated her. Nobody would believe it, but it was true. Rosalind didn't want to share Daddy. She only pretended to love her stepdaughter so she could shaft her whenever she could.

"Tiffany's in one of her pouts again, Clifford. I hated to tell her she couldn't wear all that makeup and that pink hair, but what else could I do? And those earrings! Hanging down to her shoulders like some tramp on a street corner. Certainly not suitable for a thirteen-year-old girl."

"Tiffany's been playing her stereo too loud again, Clifford..."

"Tiffany's room is a mess, Clifford. I've asked and I've asked..."

Daddy always sided with HER. *"Pick up your room, Tiffany. If your stepmother says it's messy, then you pick it up. IS THAT CLEAR?"*

A total bummer, but she wouldn't give up. Go back to Torrance? Never. How could she admit she'd made a mistake? The trouble was, she missed Mom more than she thought she would and her dumb sister, and Princess, too. It was Rosalind who'd made her leave her dog behind.

"No, you may not bring Princess, Tiffany. Now, that's where I draw the line. Jason has Attila. One dog in the family is enough."

Now Princess was dead, struck and killed by a car. It wouldn't have happened if she'd been home. That wasn't all that was wrong. She had no one to talk to in Encino, no easy conversations like when she used to pour her heart out and Mom would understand. There was nothing to read in Encino, no messy piles of books, stacks of magazines, fun trips to the library like she and Mom used to make. Daddy and Rosalind watched TV and never, never read. There wasn't one book in the house.

"I wanna stop!" Jason held up his camera. "I wanna take some pictures, Ma."

"We're not stopping." Daddy's bearded jaw tightened. His

broad shoulders hunched over the wheel. He looked at the clock in the dash. "I'm an hour behind schedule already." He steered the RV around a curve and came upon two Sheriff's cars and a big crane by the side of the road. "Look at that." He nodded towards the river. "There's a car out there in the water, upside down. Some poor guy's bought it, for sure. Probably wasn't watching the road." He shook his head in commiseration and passed right by, not slowing down.

Jason slammed himself back in his seat. "Jeez, Ma, why won't he stop?"

"Clifford, darling…?"

Tiffany curled her lip with scorn. When Rosalind went into her act, Daddy never had a chance.

"Clifford, won't you please stop?" Rosalind had turned on her sickening baby doll voice. "Attila needs to run, and you know how Jason loves to take pictures. Please, pretty please?"

Yuk, a thousand yuks.

"All right, but five minutes, that's all."

You're a wimp, Daddy.

After Daddy found a narrow space where he could pull off the road, Tiffany and Jason scrambled down the rocks to the roaring river's edge. Attila, Jason's huge Rottweiler, came with them, bounding clumsily around in circles, barking into the wind. "Attila, shut up," she called. He was not an easy dog to love. He drank out of the toilet with loud, disgusting slurps. He licked his balls in the middle of the living room, even when company was there. His breath was horrible and his nose usually dirt encrusted from burying his bones in the yard. He was an animal, though, so she loved him, only not as much as she'd loved Princess.

Her stepmother's sugar sweet voice sounded over the roar of the water. "Be careful, children. Don't fall in."

You could bet that warning was meant for Jason, not for her. Rosalind would love to see her stepdaughter fall in the river and get dashed and smashed away, never to be seen again. Then she'd have Daddy all to herself… What was that? A black shape lay by the water's edge, nearly hidden by an outcropping of rock above. It was…a dog! A big black dog, a Lab, she guessed, as far as she could tell. "Jason, look." She quickly scrambled down the rest of the way. The dog lay stretched on its side, all muddy, wet and shivering, right by the edge of the water.

"Tiffany!" Madame Dracula's voice. "What are you doing down there? Is that a dog? You stay away from that dog. It could bite, you hear me? Stay away! Jason, don't you dare."

Tiffany spaced out her stepmother's voice, squatted beside the dog and gently reached out her hand. The dog looked up at her with fright in its soft brown eyes, eyes just like Princess had. "Hello, are you hurt?" She edged her hand forward. The dog wagged its tail. She laid her hand lightly on its back. "Nice dog. You're not going to bite me, are you?"

Jason knelt beside her, camera forgotten. "Gee, what's a dog doing here?"

"I don't know what it's doing here. Look how muddy it is, like it's been in the river, you can tell."

"Hey, look, it has a collar on, and tags." Jason reached for the collar and unbuckled it, ignoring Rosalind, who still screeched from above. Holding up the collar he read, "Lucky, Lakewood Colorado, Area code 303 555-9381."

"Lucky, that's a nice name." Tiffany patted the dog again. As if in response to her touch, the dog stood up and shook. A shower of water caught them both.

Jason backed away, laughed, and dropped the collar. "Hey, all right! Look, it's a boy. He looks okay to me."

"Me too. Let's get him up the bank. "We can take him with us."

"Are you kidding? Do you think my mother would let this dirty old dog in the RV?"

"She'd better. We're not leaving him here."

"You wanna bet?"

"TIFFANY NICOLE CLAIR!" Daddy's voice thundered down the bank. "YOU GET AWAY FROM THAT DOG AND GET YOURSELF UP HERE. RIGHT NOW!"

"I'm bringing the dog up, Daddy."

"NO! YOU LEAVE THAT MUTT ALONE AND

GET UP HERE."

"No!"

Jason frowned. "Dad's really steamed, Tiff. We'd better go."

The dog was standing, wagging his tail. He looked dirty, bedraggled and hungry, but his eyes were bright, and now, as they looked directly into Tiffany's, they wrung her heart because clearly they were saying, *help me please*. Tiffany looked up the bank. There they stood, her big, bearded daddy and mean Madame Dracula, both of them so mad they were about to explode.

Jason warned, "You getter get up there, Tiff."

From above, Madame Dracula pointed a warning finger at her stepdaughter. "We'll give you one minute to get up here, or you're grounded for a month, no, two months."

She meant it, Tiffany could tell. Even so, sometimes you did what you had to do. She glared up and tossed her head. "No!"

Jason stared in amazement. "Oh, man, you're in shit city now."

"I don't care."

"You better care because here he comes."

A shower of tiny pebbles rolled by as her father half plunged, half skidded, down the bank. When he got there, he stood over her, all puffed and enraged. "DIDN'T YOU HEAR ME?"

She wrapped her arms tight around Lucky and gazed up at him. "Yes, Daddy, I heard you."

"WELL THEN?"

"He's cold and shivering." She couldn't stop the tears filling her eyes. "We can't just leave him here."

Daddy's expression softened. "This isn't your dog, Tiffany. The thing is, I know how you love animals, but we can't help them all, now can we?"

"But maybe he's hurt. I'll die if I have to leave him behind. Please, Daddy, I promise I'll keep my room clean. I'll do my homework every night. I'll do anything you want, please, please?"

She held her breath waiting for Daddy to answer. He stayed silent, frowning in thought, until finally he took a quick, rueful glance up the hill, like he knew SHE wasn't going to like it. "All right, but mind you, if we don't find the owner right away, off he goes to the animal shelter."

Clifford Clair lifted Lucky in his arms. The strident voice from above grew louder and angrier as he carried the wet, muddy dog up the bank to the RV.

When they got back to Encino, Tiffany and Jason took Lucky to the back yard to hose him off. It was then she remembered. "Where's his collar, Jason? What did you do with it when you took it off?"

Jason shrugged. "How should I...? Oh, gee, I guess I dropped it there."

"Well then, stupid, how can we call the owner if we don't have the tag?"

"Stupid yourself, that's easy."

"Oh, yeah?"

"Yeah, that's because I remember the number. It's area code 303-555-9381."

"How do I know that's right?"

"You don't." Jason made a face and ducked away.

After she'd dried Lucky, she went to her room and dialed the number Jason gave her. After four rings, she heard *This is Jillian Dahl recorded...*

Tiffany listened to the message and waited for the beep. "Hi, my name is Tiffany Clair and like, I live in Encino and I've got your dog, Lucky. Call me at area code 818-711-5950."

Had Jason remembered the number right? Maybe so, maybe not. If she heard from Jillian Dahl, fine, if not...there wasn't much sense in trying that number again, like because her stupid brother probably got it wrong.

St. Francis Hospital

"Jillian, you've been here all day. For Pete's sake, go home.

You flew in so late last night, you must be exhausted."

"Don't be silly, I'm fine."

"Oh sure. I've never seen you so mopey. I keep telling you, we're going to get Lucky back, I just know we will."

Sitting up in bed, perky smile on her face, Karlin nodded confidently, as if she were privy to some source of information no one else had. She looked unbelievably well, had been up and about on her walker most of the day visiting patients up and down the hall, chattering about her plans to return to school, actually cheerful, and it wasn't pretending. She was going to be okay. Jillian forced a frown. "If I'd known you were going to feel all this great, I wouldn't have rushed back from San Francisco like I did."

"I'm not feeling all that good. Shall I fall back on my pillow and look pale and sad?"

"No need for that. But I'm sure glad you're not weeping over Lucky. I keep feeling so damn—"

"Say guilty again, and I'll have the nurse throw you out. I know we'll find him. Now go home. My friends from school will be here soon. Tish, too. She's come by every night."

"What about Dennis?"

A fleeting shadow crossed Karlin's face. "He didn't come by last night, but he's been really busy with school, so I understand, I guess. Anyway, go home, Sis. Get some rest."

"Hi, everyone!" Tish came in. She walked to the bed and took Karlin's hand. "You look better every day."

"Can you believe this girl?" Jillian asked. "Had her leg amputated last Friday, and in less than a week she's walking on a new one."

Karlin shrugged. "At least on the parallel bars."

"Even so, that's super," Tish said.

"I'm going to ski again too. There are lots of one-legged skiers. They've got poles with little short skis—outriggers—on them to balance." Karlin held her head high. "But not for me. One good leg is all I need."

Tish clapped her hands. "Way to go! So when do you get out of here?"

240

"Soon. I've got to hang around for the chemotherapy for a while, and the radiology, too. It's not nearly as bad as it used to be, though I guess...well, I'll probably lose my hair and maybe not feel so hot." Some of the sparkle left Karlin's eyes. "I won't like losing my hair, but a small price to pay, right, guys?"

"A small price." Jillian forced herself to sound cheerful. Not easy this evening, trying to keep it light.

Karlin regarded her with a worried frown. "Now if we can just do something about my dreary sister. Look at how's she's drooping. Tish, will you please tell her to go home?"

Tish turned to Jillian. "You heard her. She's right. You look beat. Have you seen Tom yet?"

"Not yet. He doesn't know I'm back."

"Oh, jeeze, can you believe this?" Tish looked inquiringly at Karlin. "Her fiancé, the love of her life, the man she's going to marry, and she hasn't—?"

"But I'm going to, as soon as I get home."

"There's only one explanation—that man in San Francisco."

"Tish, you've hit it," Karlin said. "It's that animal activist guy she keeps talking about."

"On the way home from the airport, she mentioned him several times."

"She's talked about him all day."

"He's the one who took her to the fancy fish restaurant for lunch."

"And had her handing out leaflets on the street."

"And bought her those wild pink tennis shoes."

"He's the one who caught her when she fainted." Karlin clasped her hands to her heart. "How terribly romantic."

"Okay, guys, knock it off." Jillian tried not to sound annoyed. "He's just a man I met. He means nothing to me. He..." She was sounding way too defensive.

Karlin quickly caught her sister's mood. "We're just kidding, although I do worry about you and Tom. I wouldn't want to think that it was because of me—"

"Never. You haven't broken up my romance with Tom.

Everything's cool. I've just had a lot on my mind, and he can be—"

"An idiot?" Tish asked with a straight face.

Sometimes Tish went too far. Let it go. With a rueful smile Jillian stood up and pulled on her jacket. "Guess I'm not up to fun and games today. I'm going home."

She said her goodbyes and walked out the door. Down the corridor, she spotted Doctor De Leon standing at the nurses' station, wearing his usual frown. "Hi, Doctor De Leon. Karlin's doing great, isn't she?"

The doctor's frown deepened. "She's young and she's strong."

What kind of evasive answer was that? Why couldn't he just agree? He'd skirted the question, and somehow that was ominous. "But don't you think—?"

"I think she's got a good chance. The X-rays don't show any spread of the disease, but be aware that in many cases metastases that are too small to be detected may have already entered the bloodstream."

A chill crossed her heart. "But in Karlin's case?"

"We're starting Karlin on high doses of methotrexate, followed immediately by a drug called citrovorum. It's an antidote that helps to control the side effects of the methotrexate."

"How bad are the side effects?"

"Hair loss, nausea and vomiting, inflammation of the lining of the mouth."

"This too? After all she's been through?"

"That's where we're at. I believe in telling it like it is, okay? Goodnight, Jillian." He started away and then turned. "Too bad you couldn't find her dog."

"I'm still trying, doing everything I can—"

"I know you are." His eyes filled with a genuine compassion and something even deeper. "Find Lucky. Karlin needs a break right now. She's...very special."

Jillian bit her lip as she watched the solemn-faced doctor disappear down the corridor. Very special? What did he mean by that? Did the lofty doctor have a heart after all? As for the rest of what he said, maybe she should start worrying.

By the time Jillian was cruising along the Sixth Avenue Freeway, halfway home, her fears had all but vanished. Doctor De Leon was full of it, just trying to scare her. She switched on her radio. It was Avril Lavigne singing, *Gotta let it go, just let it go...I've said goodbye...Set it all on fire...Gotta let it go, just let it go...."*

Travis Kerrigan. Despite Karlin, Tom, Lucky, everything— she hadn't stopped thinking about him, not one single minute. It was like she was possessed, replaying that night once again, for at least the thousandth time. San Francisco in the fog—the seawall where they'd stood—the lights from the bridge—grim Alcatraz barely visible through the mist—Travis kissing her, there in the falling darkness, to the haunting sound of a fog-horn. Her body went weak with longing as she remembered his arms around her and the warmth of his lips on hers. She couldn't help it, she had feelings for him. It was as if he'd left his footprint on her heart.

How everyone would laugh if they knew nitpicky, up-to-now stonehearted Jillian Dahl had fallen in love, really in love. Never had she felt about a man like this before, but how stupid could she get wanting a man who lived a thousand miles away, a man she'd never see again?

When she got home, she saw she had voice mail. Tom, no doubt. He'd already called her cell and she hadn't answered. She was tempted not to check her messages, but then, someone could be calling about Lucky. It was Tom. "Jillian? Are you there? If you are, then call, right now." Click! End of message. How exasperating. He sounded like he owned her. She slammed down the phone. Wait, hadn't there been two messages? She'd better check again. The phone rang. The ID said Tom. She stared at the phone, sorely tempted to let it go to voice mail, but no, that wouldn't be fair. With a sigh, she picked up the phone and said hello.

"Jillian?"

"Hi, how are you?"

"When did you get back?" His voice was stiff.

No sense lying. "Last night."

"And you didn't call me?"

"I was tired, and quite frankly, I didn't want to deal with your fancy new bed last night."

"And me?"

"And you. That's why I had Tish pick me up."

"I'm coming over. We've got to talk."

"You'd better not. The roads are terrible." The roads were not terrible.

"Tomorrow night, then." He hung up the phone.

Damn, she didn't want to see Tom tomorrow night either, but what was she thinking of? What about Mrs. Mayo's Wedding World—the yacht in the Caribbean—the big diamond ring on her finger? How could she blow all that away? Wasn't that what she really wanted? And Tom, too, of course.

Before she went to bed, she remembered about the voice mail message. Had she missed one? No, she hadn't. She was sure she'd heard them all.

Chapter 18

TANG'S BODY CLEANSING CONTROL CENTER

MADAME ESTHER PALMISTRY

JOSE'S VIDEO & ANTIQUES (SE HABLA ESPAÑOL)

With each passing sign, Connie Linderman's level of dismay shot higher. By the time Doctor Tessler pulled his Lexus to the curb, she was positive she'd made a terrible mistake.

"We're here, Connie. That's it, the Santa Marta Women's Rehabilitation Center."

What a dreadful neighborhood. Near downtown, it had once been the city's finest, the streets lined with sycamore trees and stately mansions. Some of Santa Marta's best families once lived here but not anymore. Now it was all seedy yards, trash-filled gutters and rundown homes turned into businesses, all in need of paint and repairs. "It's not quite what I expected."

Dr. Tessler stepped from his car, opened the trunk and pulled out her suitcase. He opened Connie's door. "They don't have a large operating budget. The Betty Ford Center it's not."

"I can see that." Connie climbed from the Lexus and examined the two-story colonial style house that must have been built at least back in the 1920's and probably before. Peeling white paint—scraggly lawn—shrubbery growing wild and untrimmed. At least it didn't have a sign in front announcing a bunch of women alcoholics lived inside, but that didn't mean she was going to stay. Just amazing, how she'd let Dr. Tessler talk her into this. She'd come close to changing her mind when he swung by her house so she could pick up some things. She'd been sorely tempted to stay, send him and his Lexus packing. Instead, because he was waiting and she didn't want a scene, she dutifully packed a bag and changed to the black Chanel suit she'd treasured through the years (thank God, her stomach wasn't swollen anymore), and the high heeled Ferragamos that went with everything. Was it the correct attire for entering a rehabilitation center? She had no idea. "Are you coming in with me?"

Dr. Tessler shook his head. "I've got to get back to the hospital. They're expecting you. Just go up and ring the bell." He picked up her suitcase and carried it to the big front porch. When he returned, he got back in his car. "You're going to make it, Connie. Good luck."

She watched as he waved and drove away. *Good luck, my eye. I don't have to stay here, Doctor Smartass, and I probably won't.*

"Grab your suitcase, Connie, and follow me. I'll show you to your room." The director of the Santa Marta Women's Rehab Center led the way upstairs. In her forties, she was no great beauty in her Wal-Mart slacks and top, no makeup, and straight brown hair that looked like she cut it herself. "Call me Virginia. We don't bother with last names here. So how long were you in the hospital?"

"A week." *Seven rotten, horrible days and now this.*

"Good! So you're detoxed. We don't allow anyone in who hasn't been drug and alcohol free for at least seventy-two hours. You do know you can only have visitors on Sunday from two to four?"

"I'm not expecting any." And she wasn't. Harvey had never come to see her in the hospital, not one single time. She called him finally. He sounded distant and curt and hadn't asked how she was, only how soon she'd be home. When she told him she was going to enter a treatment program, he exploded, venting his most obscene oaths and then hanging up on her. Not that she cared whether he visited or not. Dr. Tessler was wrong when he said she was addicted to her husband. She'd never heard of anything so silly. She didn't need Harvey. The very fact she was here proved that. Even so, she'd made a ghastly mistake coming to this awful, rundown place. She didn't have to stay here and undoubtedly would not.

Virginia talked nonstop as she trudged ahead of her up the stairs. "...lists of rules are posted downstairs. You will be expected to be up and dressed by 6:30 each morning, including Sundays. You'll be expected to stay here at least three months, during which time you must stay free of drugs and alcohol and submit to periodic room searches, as well as Breathalyzer and urine tests each time you're allowed out on pass. You will help with the cooking and cleaning. I warn you, you'll be scrubbing toilets at first, but don't worry, you'll work your way up. There are restrictions on outside visits and telephone calls. All medications, including aspirin, are locked away—you can't cure pill addiction with more pills—and you will be required to attend Alcoholics Anonymous meetings, family counseling, and chapel. You will volunteer four hours of community service a week. You will be given extensive one-on-one counseling, plus several hours of daily group sessions, lectures, and role-playing. You will jog at least a mile a day."

Jog? That settled it, she was definitely not staying. It was hardly worth going upstairs to see her room because she wouldn't be here that long. No way in the world would she put up with this woman's rules and regulations. Only, where could she go? Not back to Harvey and his sneers. Not back to the spiders. *Oh God, where can I go?*

"…most of them are watching a film right now, but you'll meet them at dinner. A really terrific bunch of women. You'll make a lot of new friends here."

Don't be ridiculous.

"Just give yourself a few days to fit in. It's hard at first, but you get used to it. You'll end up not wanting to leave."

I need a drink.

"…and your roommate's just super."

"Roommate?" Connie stopped abruptly, foot poised on the last step. "I don't get my own private room?"

The director smiled indulgently. "We don't have any private rooms, Connie. Everyone shares. But don't worry, you're going to love Latonia. Everyone does."

Latonia? That sounded like…but no, it couldn't. They wouldn't.

"Here we are." Virginia opened the door of a fair-sized

room. One side contained a stripped down narrow bed, cigarette-scarred chest of drawers with a small mirror hanging above, one straight back chair, a bare hardwood floor and starkly white walls. The other side, although identically furnished, was cozy and cheerfully bright. Pictures of animals, cats mostly, decorated the walls. A collection of stuffed teddy bears lined the wide, old-fashioned baseboards. Ruffled yellow curtains hung over the window. Braided, multicolored rugs lay scattered on the floor. A Sunbonnet Babies patchwork quilt, done in bright hues of blue, green and yellow, covered the bed. Atop the quilt, a woman lay stretched on her back, hands behind her head.

"Oh, there you are, Latonia. Meet Connie. You two get acquainted. I must run." The director left, closing the door behind her.

"Hi," said her new roommate. She waved a laconic greeting with a hand that was very, very black.

Connie stood stiffly in the center of the room. Positively, absolutely, unequivocally she was not going to stay in this horrible place. "How do you do. I'm delighted to meet you."

"Yeah, honey, I can see that." Latonia swung her legs off the bed and stood up, revealing her lanky, beanpole figure. She was six feet tall at least with straight black hair and skin that was as black as black could ever be. She was fairly young, somewhere in her early thirties, although you never could tell with those people, they held their age so well.

Latonia tucked a bright red Stanford University T-shirt into her jeans, and walked to the mirror. She picked up a lipstick from the dresser and started to apply it. "Not what you were expecting am I?"

Connie drew herself up. "I don't know what you mean."

The corners of Latonia's mouth twitched upward. "Sure. Well, don't just stand there." She pointed to the bureau on the bare side of the room. "That one's yours. You might as well unpack. There's time before dinner."

"I'm not sure I'm staying. In fact, I'm definitely not staying." Connie picked up her suitcase and started backing toward the door. "There's been a mistake. I don't belong here."

Latonia returned to her bed, plumped a pillow, and sat back against it, drawing up her knees to beneath her chin. For a long moment, she looked piercingly at Connie before she asked, "You've suddenly got some important appointment to rush off to? Don't go. Sit down, let's talk a little."

"Well..."

"Sit!" Latonia nodded towards the other bed.

"Oh, very well. I guess I can, for a little while." Connie set the suitcase precisely down, walked stiffly to the bed, and perched on the edge like a nervous bird on a rooftop, ready for instant flight.

"Hey, loosen up little. I won't bite. How come you don't want to stay? The truth now. If it's me because I'm black, say so."

How she hated this sort of thing. Connie shifted her gaze towards the door, out the window, down at the floor. She'd been brought up to avoid scenes at all costs and had no idea what to say. Lying wouldn't do, but on the other hand, she didn't want to hurt the feelings of this woman who couldn't, after all, help being the color she was. How to say it politely? She peered directly into Latonia's wise-looking eyes and knew no half-truth would be acceptable. Even so, the honesty of her next words surprised her. "It is you. Partly because you're black and partly because I expected my own room. I'm not used to sharing."

Latonia remained unperturbed. "You're not married?"

"I am, but we each have our own bedroom."

"I see. So aside from me, is there anything else that makes you want to leave?"

Pent-up words burst from her. "Everything! How can you stand it here? All those rules and regulations—scrubbing toilets—jogging, for heaven sakes."

Latonia drew her legs up even tighter, wrapped her arms around them and thoughtfully rested her chin on her knees. "You ask how can I stand it here? I've lived here for two years."

"Two years!"

"You've got it right, honey. Hard to believe but true. At

first, it was awful. I didn't know what to expect and I was terrified. Back then, I was taking twelve antidepressant pills a day.
It's a wonder I hadn't killed myself, combining them with alcohol like I was, and of course they were taken away. I bawled my
eyes out for a week. I was so resentful—angry—afraid. It's a
miracle I didn't pack up and leave."

"Why didn't you?"

"Because I was your basic, desperate drunk. I'd lost everything including my last shred of self-respect. You talk about
down, baby, well I'd really hit bottom." Latonia plucked at the
front of her T-shirt. "This isn't a joke. I am a Stanford grad."
She caught Connie's startled expression. "Yeah, surprise, surprise. Class of '97. Graduated with a degree in Art History with
a minor in French. Had a few good years as an artist, that's my
first love, and actually sold some of my paintings. I designed
clothes, too, owned my own boutique for a while and
then...well it's a long, sad story you wouldn't want to hear. Suc-
cinctly put, I'd been drinking since I was in my teens, and booze
finally brought me down. One day, after I'd lost my money, my
shop, and all my friends, and I couldn't paint anymore, I looked
in the mirror and told myself with the way I was drinking I had
three choices: I could go insane, I could die, or I could get sober." Latonia spread her hands and performed a dramatic half
bow. "So here I am."

Connie sat back more comfortably on the bed, her spine
beginning to lose some of its rigidity. "But two years? Whatever
do you do here? Don't you hate it?"

"*Au contraire.* I'm what you call a graduate in residence. I
have more freedom than you'll have. I do some counseling, and
I've got a couple of things going on the outside. One has to do
with animals. She gestured towards the animal pictures and
posters that covered her walls. "I love animals. Too bad there's
a rule against pets. When I get out, I'm going to own a dozen
cats, at least." With a mischievous grin, Latonia fastened her
eyes on Connie's suit. "I adore your Chanel. It is an original,
isn't it? Not a Karl Lagerfeld?"

Connie's mind did an astonished double take at Latonia's

recognition of her suit. "What? Oh, my suit. You're right, it's a classic designed by Coco Chanel."

"Marvelous. How you must treasure it. Every woman should own a little black suit. Just one suggestion, if you don't mind, your skirt's too long."

Connie answered with the authority of a woman who knew her fashion. "Certainly not. A real Chanel suit always ended at the top of the calf, never higher, never longer."

Latonia appeared not to hear. "If you stay, we'll take it up, at least halfway to your ass. Then you'll be in style."

Tamper with tradition? "Never!" She couldn't suppress a faint smile, envisioning herself in a miniskirt by Chanel.

Latonia erupted into husky laughter. "Good, you smiled. I made a bet with myself you would. Now listen, I'm not going to tell you what to do, but as long as you're here, and it's late in the day, why not stay for dinner?"

"Well, I..."

"Stay the night, anyway. There's plenty of time tomorrow to decide. Besides, there's home-baked carrot cake for dessert tonight. How does that grab you?"

"Well, I guess...all right, I'll stay but just for tonight." She'd definitely leave tomorrow.

When she followed Latonia down the stairs to dinner, she decided she could at least be polite. "So what else do you do?"

Latonia looked back over her shoulder. "I've got a new job, starting Monday. I'm going to be an animal attendant at the Linderman Research Laboratory. Ever hear of it?"

"No, I don't believe so." Just like the little black suit, the little white lie would never go out of style.

Why was she still here? Connie sat down in a chair placed in a circle of chairs for, God forbid, this ridiculous group therapy. She had stayed the night as Latonia suggested, had dinner with this group of strange women, most of them definitely lower class, using the most awful language she'd ever heard. It was all a mistake, anyway. Doctor Tessler was wrong. She shouldn't be here, didn't need this, and would leave shortly, probably right after this group therapy thing. Cautiously, she glanced around. Look at them, what a sad bunch. Ten women sat in the circle, three blacks; two Orientals of some kind, no telling what; three Mexicans and two whites. All dressed atrociously, mostly in jeans, sloppy T-shirts and tennis shoes or flip-flops. Across sat a big black woman wearing a tight pink tank top and bad-fitting jeans. Rolls of fat bulged all over her body. Had she never heard of Jenny Craig? NutriSystems?

A young woman with a springy step entered the room. Blonde and slim, in her middle thirties, she wore oversized glasses on her small, pretty face. She wasn't much better dressed than the inmates of this place, with slacks, flats, and a loose gray sweater. "Hi, everybody." She spotted Connie. "I see we have someone new. Hi, my name is Anne. We'll go around the room and introduce ourselves, then get down to business."

"...so you say you've had a tragedy in your life, Connie? Why don't you tell us about it?"

For the past hour, Connie grew more and more appalled as she listened to some of the most shocking stories she'd ever heard. Some of these women were prostitutes. Three were lesbians. She'd never even met a lesbian before, not that she knew of, anyway. She'd just found out there were lots of alcoholic lesbians. Good grief, she never realized…

"We're waiting, Connie."

She hated being in the limelight, but then, if they really wanted to know... "Yes, a terrible tragedy," she answered in her sad-and-wistful voice, the one she always used when she talked about Christie. "I lost my little girl in an accident. I've never been the same since that day."

"Tell us about it."

"It's so hard, talking about it."

"Try."

Connie took a deep breath. "It happened one morning when my little girl was two. I had an appointment at the beauty salon and was running late. I kissed her goodbye…" a tear started sliding down her cheek, as she knew it would "…not dreaming it was the last time, and told the nanny I'd be back in a couple of hours. Then I went out to the garage and got in the car." She paused, trying to get past the raw ache that invariably formed in her throat whenever she thought about it. "I started backing down the driveway...please forgive me, I can't go on."

Anne nodded with sympathy. "Take your time, we'll wait. Hand her a Kleenex, Justine."

She was all right again after she blew her nose. "So then I felt this bump. I couldn't imagine...not until I got out of the car did I see it was Christie. She'd gotten out of the house without the nanny knowing, and was tottering down the driveway looking for her Mommy. I didn't know she was there and I...I...ran over her. I killed my little girl. Now do you see why I drink?" The tears rolled unchecked down her cheeks. Justine handed her another Kleenex. She dabbed at her eyes. Perhaps she shouldn't have told the story. All she ever did was upset herself, and everybody else, too. Now they'd all express their sympathy which she certainly didn't want from his scroungy bunch.

She sat back and waited for someone to speak. At first, the group didn't react. Finally the fat one in the pink tank top who sat across started shaking her head and making "tsk tsk" noises. Her name was Ida Mae. She was slumped, practically lying in her chair with her legs stretched out and apart in a most unladylike manner. Her hands were clasped together, resting on her big, flabby stomach. Evidently she'd never heard of good posture.

Ida Mae did a few more rolls of her head and tsk-tsks. "That is sure a sad, sad story. Tell me, mama, when did all this happen?"

"Sixteen years ago. Christie would be eighteen now, if she had lived."

"It be SIXTEEN years ago? You're shittin' me."

"I beg your pardon?"

Shaking her head in disbelief, Ida Mae laboriously pulled herself up straight on the chair. "What I mean is that's the biggest pile of crap I ever did hear. What you mean bullshittin' us with that piece of garbage?"

***

Back in her room, choking back sobs, Connie flung herself on her bed and curled into the fetal position. She couldn't imagine how could those cold-blooded women just sat there and let that awful Ida Mae say those terrible things. Instead, they'd all been against her, having the nerve to say she was using Christie's death as an excuse for her drinking. Even Anne, who she'd thought had some semblance of culture and education, hadn't come to her defense. Well, she didn't have to take this abuse, she was leaving. It was beyond her comprehension what she was doing here in the first place, in this wretched old house on the wrong side of town. The bed sagged. Someone was sitting next to her. A warm hand patted her arm. "Kind of rough in there?"

"Oh, Latonia, they were all against me. That woman—"

"Ida Mae? Oh, yeah. She's a real pisser when she gets going."

"I'm going home."

"Oh? Back to that guy who won't sleep in the same room with you? Back to your bottle? Are you sure that's a wise choice?"

Connie groaned and pulled herself into an even tighter ball. "What does it matter? My spirit is dead. The world is dead. I'm dead, dead, dead."

"Well, at least we've got a starting point, haven't we? Listen, if you're going to leave, do it tomorrow. You can't leave now. There's peach cobbler for dessert tonight."

Chapter 19

Santa Marta

"Sweetie, if you can't, you can't. Don't worry about it. I'm kind of tired, anyway."

He distinctly heard her yawn. "I'm not through yet."

In the darkness of Gretchen's bedroom, on her king-sized bed, Dr. Harvey Linderman gritted his teeth and tried again. Astride her, he pushed harder, squeezing his eyes tight shut while he reviewed his best erotic fantasies, but nothing worked. With an oath, he rolled off her.

She giggled. "Don't feel bad, sugar. You're not the only old guy who can't get it up. Have you tried Viagra?"

The remains of his ego shriveled up and died. He burned with shame, all because of a twenty-two year old blonde airhead who wasn't fit to wipe his boots. Yes, Winslow had prescribed Viagra, but it hadn't worked. "Sometimes it doesn't," Winslow told him. "We might try a vacuum. You know, pump up your penis."

Rot in hell, Winslow. But wait, this wasn't Gretchen's fault, or Winslow's either. This was all Connie's fault.. No wonder he couldn't get it up. Her selfish behavior had caused this final humiliation. If she were home where she was supposed to be, he would not be having this problem.

First thing tomorrow he would get the name and address of that rehab center. Time he let her know who was in charge. Time he brought his wife home where she belonged.

Santa Marta Home for Alcoholic Women

"Hey, slowpoke, look at me!"

In the brisk morning air, Connie Linderman, dressed in running shorts and gray sweatshirt, put on a burst of speed and passed Latonia by. At the corner, she stopped and bent forward, resting her hands on her knees. "Not two weeks yet and my running's improving. I'm getting farther every day. Have you noticed?"

Latonia loped up with steady-paced speed. Breathing effortlessly, she jogged in place. "You're poetry in motion, my dear. Another Tiki Galana."

"Who's she?"

"She won the 2012 Women's Olympic Marathon. Where have you been?"

"Drunk for sixteen years." Connie stood straight and puffed out her chest. "I'm really feeling good, Latonia."

"Great, now let's get back. I must get to work." Latonia bent into an exaggerated bow and swept her arm in the general direction of home. "Shall we jog?"

"Let's go! I'll beat you back." She would beat Latonia only if her friend let her, but that was okay. Everything was okay today. She was beginning to feel like a genuine, normal human being again, and maybe, just maybe, life was worth living after all.

When they got back, Virginia was waiting. "Connie, you have a visitor. It's not our visiting hours, but he absolutely insisted."

"I can't believe you're living in this slum. How could you lower yourself like this?"

Connie sat, hands clasped in her lap, looking up at her husband. He was from another world, standing in the middle of the shabby visitor's room in his Gucci shoes and custom-made silk suit, his lips pursed in disgust. "I hated to leave my car at the curb. When I get back, it'll be a miracle if my mag wheels aren't stolen." He scowled. "They weren't even going to let me see you. Are you in prison? What is this place?"

"It's the Santa Marta Women's Rehabilitation Center, Harvey. You knew that. There are rules we have to follow."

"What the hell are you doing here?"

"I'm an alcoholic. You knew that, too. We just never got around to discussing it all those years."

"That's bull. So you drink a little, so what? That doesn't

make you one of them."

Connie held out her hands. "Look at them, Harvey, see? They're not shaking any more. I'm doing well here. I'm even jogging."

His head jerked back. "You? Jogging?"

"I gave up smoking, too."

"When?"

"Five days ago."

"That's nothing." His lip curled in a sneer. "You'll never quit. You're fooling no one but yourself."

"I'm going to group therapy twice a day, getting a lot of things sorted out that I'd buried deep inside me and couldn't get out."

"Like what?"

"Like..." She was about to venture into the forbidden subject they never talked about. He wouldn't like it, but high time they did. "Like Christie's death and the guilt I felt. You didn't help, Harvey. That awful day, remember? I can still hear you yelling, *you killed my little girl!* Yelling it over and over again."

He backed a step away. "I won't discuss it."

"You don't want to talk about anything. That's the problem. We've never communicated."

"If you think you're going to bullshit me with a lot of crackpot psychological gibberish, you can forget it." He folded his arms and glared down at her. "Pack your things. I'm taking you home."

"I don't want to go home. I'm just getting started here. It's not easy, you know. They make me scrub toilets. They rip me to shreds in the sessions. I've gone to so many AA meetings they're all a blur. But, Harvey, I'm getting there."

"By God, I should have divorced your ass years ago. Either you come with me now or I'll drive straight from here to the lawyer's. I'll get a divorce so quick it'll make your head spin."

"But—"

"I'll take everything, you know I can. Look at you. Who'd want you now? Without me, you'll end up old, broke and alone.

Is that what you want?"

"You're not being fair. I—"

"You want fairness? I'll give you fair. You've got until five o'clock to decide. If you don't get home by five, forget it. Don't call, don't write. I never want to see you again." He yanked out his wallet, removed a hundred dollar bill and tossed it on her lap. "When you make up your mind, you can take a taxi home." He turned and strode out the door.

Connie sank back on the frayed couch and covered her face with her hands. *Addicted*, that's what Doctor Tessler said and he was right. She was addicted to her husband. He might be arrogant, selfish, faithless and profane, but how could she live without him? She'd given up her other addictions. No more alcohol, cigarettes, or Valium, but if she gave up her husband, too, she'd end up like he said—old, broke and alone.

No, she couldn't do it. Who needed this place anyway? Of course, she would miss Latonia. Amazing, how she'd actually made friends with a black person. But she wouldn't be sorry to get away from those scruffy, heartless women who kept humiliating her in the sessions, stripping her bare of all her little defenses, forcing her to see herself for what she really was. Maybe, once or twice these past few days, she'd dished it out, too. Maybe, once or twice, they'd almost made her believe she could turn her life around, make a new start, be happy again. Such a foolish fantasy. Harvey just said it all. How could she have thought she could make her own way in the world? What could she accomplish? What was she good for?

Nothing.

Only one thing could make life bearable now. Home—the pink velvet chair—the glass full of vodka in her hand. She was going to drink again. Here, in this wretched, rundown house they kept telling her she should never touch alcohol the whole rest of her life. Fools, what did they know? She knew better. The spiders? No problem, they'd stay put. A little nip of vodka now and then wouldn't bring them out as long as she drank in moderation. That's what she'd do from now on, and this time she knew she could handle it.

Santa Marta, California
The Linderman Research Laboratories

It's not going to work! We'll never get in here.

Dressed in jeans and a blue cotton work smock, Latonia made her way through the labyrinth of corridors to the laboratory where she'd been assigned. A heavy glass and metal door guarded each corridor. For the third time in a minute, she held her plastic key card next to a sensor to make a door slide open. This place was a fortress. The Navy Seals couldn't break in, what with the high fences, guard at the front gate, badges and card keys. Even the most trusted employees couldn't go where they pleased. Only Linderman and his assistant, Osborne, had access to it all.

She reached Laboratory "B." "Hey man, what's coming down?" She walked in and slung herself onto a table in the center of the room and sat, swinging her feet, waiting for an answer.

"Hi, Latonia." Bobby Joe Smith was lifting a rabbit into a tiny cage. A skinny, round-shouldered young man in his twenties, he had a shock of red hair that hung over his pimply forehead. He wore a white cotton lab coat. "They assigned you to me."

"My cup runneth over." Latonia looked around the large room lined with cages in various sizes, stacked from the floor up to above her head. The small cages contained rabbits and mice. The larger ones contained beagles. In one corner—her feet stopped swinging—a large chimpanzee was strapped into a metal chair so tightly it couldn't move. Even his head was held in a vice. There was nothing he could do but stare straight ahead, silently, as if for eternity. "What…?"

"That's Charlie. Doesn't say much, does he?"

"How long has he been there?"

"Aw…a few months, I guess. They keep some of them like that for years. This one, they're doing some laser beam stuff on his eyes." Bobby Joe slammed a cage door shut. "Wait 'til you hear what we're gonna do. Linderman's got a new experiment going. We've gotta shave forty dogs."

She forgot the chimp. "Shave forty dogs? You're kidding! Why?"

Bobby Joe picked a clipboard off a desk and began to read. "'Purpose: to determine if the existence of certain bacteria in the digestive tract contributes to the development of heatstroke in man.' Heck, I know this one." He tossed the board back on the desk. "When I was working at a lab in Texas, they did this one. They did a lot of stuff with sunstrokes. I never saw so many cooked dogs in my life."

"Then why are they doing it again?"

"Why?" He gave an elaborate shrug. "What do they care? These hotshot scientists do the same stuff over and over again, mostly so they can write a paper and get it published. That's all those stuck-up scientists want is to see their name in print."

She glanced at the caged beagles. "So we're using them?"

"They're gonna use trash dogs for this one."

"What do you mean, trash dogs?"

"Strays, people's pets 'n stuff—dogs they get from the pound or they buy from farms, like Linderman mostly buys his animals from Johnny Valentine."

"*Johnny Valentine*, I've heard the name."

"In the newspaper, I'll bet. He's in trouble with the law a lot. He owns this farm where he keeps all these animals. There's a lot of people trying to close him down."

"Why?"

"A bunch of stuff, like he let some horses starve to death a while back, and then the latest thing, they claim he shoots dogs for fun. The place is supposed to be real dirty, too. I mean like filthy, and he doesn't give them food or water. He's still in business, though. Go figure."

"Nice guy."

"Yeah, well, that's the least of our worries. You'll be helping me set up for this experiment."

"So what do we do exactly?"

"We take forty mongrel dogs, I guess it don't matter if

they're male or female. We shave them, and then we, like they say, *induce heatstroke*, which means we put them between two circulating water blankets that we fill with hot tap water. Then we heat them up until their temperature reaches one hundred nine degrees."

"One hundred nine!"

"Yeah, baked dog, you might say." Bobby Joe smiled at his little joke. "Don't feel bad. It's for science, so it's all worthwhile. Before they start heating them up, they pretreat some of the dogs with antibiotics and cathartics and enemas and stuff. Afterwards, they'll wait around for eighteen hours or so to see which ones last the longest after they get baked. Of course, a lot of them will be dead before then."

"Do any of them live?"

"Yes and no. Those that live for eighteen hours get zapped anyway."

"That's horrible!"

Billie Joe raised his hands. "Hey, I just work here. I do as I'm told."

She had to fight the nausea gathering in the pit of her stomach. "So when are we supposed to start?"

"In the next few days. Soon's we get a new shipment from Johnny Valentine."

Santa Marta Home for Alcoholic Women

She was going home to Harvey, back where she belonged. Connie pulled her suitcase from the closet and opened it out on the bed. Packing wouldn't take long. Then she'd call a taxi. She removed her scanty accumulation of clothes from the dresser drawers and laid them beside the suitcase. She would no longer need the borrowed sweatshirt and jogging shorts, so she set them aside.

Latonia walked in just as she finished packing. "Don't tell me." She sat wearily on her bed and pulled off her shoes. Her gaze fastened on Connie's open suitcase. "You're leaving." Connie nodded. Without another word, Latonia doubled up her pillow and lay back, staring at the ceiling, hands tucked beneath her head.

That was all? Latonia wasn't going to try and persuade her to stay? Somehow Connie had expected her to get upset, argue, give her a dozen reasons why she shouldn't go. "You don't want to know why I'm leaving?"

Latonia still gazed at the ceiling. "I know why. I've seen it happen before. The scenario reads, you can't hack it, so you run home to her husband and start drinking again. I don't know who you are or where you come from, but I'll make an educated guess you heard from your husband. He wants you home, and you've decided that's a real peachy keen idea. If you leave here, you can drink again. You won't have to scrub toilets or jog at the crack of dawn. You can start smoking again. A drink in one hand, cigarette in the other. They go together, don't they?"

How did Latonia know? How could she be so accurate, so damnably right? Why was she so unconcerned? Connie sank to the edge of her bed. "I thought you'd care."

Latonia turned her head towards Connie and gave her a long, hard stare. "Your mind's made up, isn't it? You're going to do what you're going to do, so why should I waste my breath?" Her gaze returned to the ceiling. "Look, I don't even want to talk right now. I've had a bad day. There's a lot on my mind."

"Your job?"

"Yeah, my wonderful job."

No mistaking the sarcasm in Latonia's voice. "I thought you liked working at Linderman Labs."

"Are you kidding? Let me tell you something." Latonia swung her legs to the floor, stood up, and began angrily to pace, her six foot tall frame taut with anger. "I've never spoken about it because I've got my reasons. The truth is Linderman Laboratories is a house of horrors. The callousness and brutality that go on in there is absolutely unbelievable unless you see it for yourself, which, God help me, I do every day."

Connie had never heard anything bad about Harvey's precious laboratories. "But Linderman's is one of the country's finest research institutes in the country…that is, judging from what little I know about it."

Latonia continued her pacing. "The place is a hell hole for those poor animals. I've seen dogs standing in their own urine on bare cement floors. I've seen cats, and you know how clean cats are, in cages with no litter pans, the shit piled high around their water bowls. I've seen animals who died, neglected, alone, in excruciating pain. There's a chimpanzee there named Charlie. They've had him strapped to a metal chair for months. I've seen animals used in the most cruel and horrible ways, and why? For the glorification of its great leader, that's why."

"But Linderman Laboratories has done all kinds of good work. I've heard Dr. Harvey Linderman is the most—"

"Dr. Harvey Linderman!" Latonia spat out the words with such contempt that Connie flinched. "The man's a monster. He's the absolute worst example of the 'publish or perish' syndrome. You know what I found out today? He's going to literally roast 40 dogs, no doubt so he can write another of his ego building papers, get himself published again. And the experiment's been done before. That sick bastard. You know what I'd like to do to him? I'd like to put him into one of those tiny, dirty cages where he keeps his monkeys. Keep him there, day after day, month after month, year after year just like he does his monkeys. Never let him out, no exercise, no sunshine, no love and affection, just cold steel bars and a bare cement floor, and knowing he had to stay there without hope, with nothing to live for until the day he died."

Connie felt the blood rushing from her head. "I had no idea."

"It's true." Latonia stopped pacing and sat down hard on her bed. "It makes me sick. If you could see what I see every day you couldn't bear it."

"Then why do you work there?"

"Why?" Latonia paused briefly, as if making a careful choice of words. "There's lots I haven't told you, okay? But since you're leaving and I'll probably never see you again—"

"That's not true. I plan to visit you, and you can come and visit me, and—" What was she thinking? Not likely this intelligent, impassioned woman would want Mrs. Harvey Linderman for a friend.

Latonia continued, "You asked me once before what I was doing at Linderman's. It did seem strange, didn't it? Why would a fashion designer who once owned a boutique be doing grunt work in a research laboratory? I'm not what I seem."

"Then what are you?"

Latonia walked to the open door, leaned into the hallway and peered carefully in both directions. She shut the door, returned to the bed and sat down again and began speaking softly. "Connie, you're my friend and I trust you. This goes no further, okay?" She waited for Connie's nod. "Did you ever hear of a group called WEELA?"

Ha! The laugh of the day. How could she forget Harvey's constant rage because of WEELA? "They're one of those animal activists groups, aren't they? Haven't they demonstrated a few times outside of Linderman Labs?"

"That's not all. They want to break in the place, and that's where I come in. I went to work for Linderman's just so I could find a way to get in."

Connie was hard put to keep her mouth from dropping open. "You plan to raid Linderman Labs?"

"Yes, only it's no use."

Connie remembered Harvey's endless ranting about WEELA, his fear of a break-in, the elaborate security precautions he took to keep them out. "I suppose, what with security and all, it would be difficult."

"You've got that right, honey. Far as I can tell, the place is a fortress. There are so many security devices you'd think it was Fort Knox. The great Dr. Linderman's thought of everything."

"What would you do if you got inside, just destroy everything?"

"That's what Animal Rescue does but not WEELA. We'd rescue as many animals as we could. I'd sell my soul to rescue Charlie, that poor chimpanzee. We'd get some great publicity, let the public know the atrocities being committed in the name of science. People are indifferent but only because they don't know."

"But that's breaking the law. Aren't you afraid of getting arrested?"

"The thought crossed my mind once or twice. Are you acquainted with the writings of Thoreau?"

"I studied him in school, but I've mostly forgotten."

Latonia leaned back against the wall and drew her legs comfortably beneath her. "Old Thoreau really nailed it in his Civil Disobedience back in 1848. I've got it memorized. It's three reasons why we ought to use justice rather than legality as a standard to govern our actions. One, there is a higher law than the law of the land. Two, one has a duty to obey the higher law and deliberately violate the law of the land on the occasions when the two conflict. Three, going to jail is not necessarily negative. It could help to repeal an evil law by drawing the attention of men of good will, or it could make the evil law unenforceable if enough people are jailed." Latonia grinned. "In other words, if I get thrown in the slammer, it's for a worthy cause."

Connie burst into laughter. "Oh, Latonia you're so...so...unexpected. I've never known anyone like you. I really admire you."

"Oh yeah?" Latonia's eyebrows arched. "Then why don't you stick around if you admire me so much? Why must you leave?"

Connie's laughter faded. She leaned forward, elbows on her knees, resting her chin on her upraised fingers and staring out the window for a long, silent moment. If there was one thing she'd learned in this place, it was to be honest and speak the truth, to "let it all hang out" as they loved to say. Latonia wanted an honest answer and she'd get one. "I'm leaving because I'm afraid. I've never, in my whole life been alone, and I don't think I can cut it. That's why I'm running home to my husband, to the only safety I know."

"But, Connie, you're doing so well. You were a basket case when you got here, remember? There was only one way to go and that was up. Now look at you. You've made friends. You're jogging farther every day, and hey! I hear you're beginning to dish it out in the sessions, instead of looking like a scared rabbit all the time. I hate to see you throw it all away." Latonia waited for an answer, but Connie sat silent, eyes averted from her friend. "Okay then, I won't argue." She reached into her nightstand drawer and pulled out a pen and address book. "We'll definitely keep in touch, okay? I want your address and your phone number. I don't even know your last name." Pen poised over the address book, she asked, "You're Connie who?"

She would rather die a thousand deaths than give Latonia her last name. "Was I really? Doing good, I mean?"

"Would I lie? You know me better than that by now."

"No, you wouldn't lie." Connie hardly knew what she was saying, so shocked was she by Latonia's angry outburst. Harvey a monster? Never in all the years they'd been married had she heard anything but the highest praise for her husband. Harvey was always the wonderful one, the great humanitarian, the winner of fine awards, whereas she was the lush, the disgrace of the family. Harvey a monster? Memories she'd always suppressed came flooding back. Harvey sneering—ridiculing—bullying—pouring her a drink when he damn well knew she was a hard core alcoholic. She'd always assumed she loved him, but if what Latonia said was only halfway true, how could she even tolerate such a sick bastard? One thing for sure, she needed time to think. "What's for dessert tonight?"

"Apple pie a la mode."

"In that case, I'll stay, at least one more night." She began to unpack her suitcase. "So you can put your pen away. You don't need my last name."

Encino, California

"Go get it, Lucky!"

On the grass by the pool back of her father's spacious home, Tiffany threw the ball. With a joyful yelp, Lucky bounded after it and brought it back. Tiffany knelt and threw her arms around him. "I love you the best. They've just got to let me keep you."

Nearly two weeks had passed since she'd called Jillian Dahl and not got an answer. No sense calling again. Stupid Jason must have got the phone number wrong. Secretly she was glad. She loved this black Lab. He was the smartest, best natured, most loving dog she ever had. Much as she'd loved Princess, she loved Lucky more and desperately wanted to keep him. Daddy hadn't said anything more about sending Lucky to the animal shelter. Maybe he forgot, but fat chance Rosalind would. Her stepmother knew when to keep her prissy little mouth shut, but you could bet it wouldn't last. She always got her way.

Popping his gum, Jason slid the patio door open and came outside. "Lucky's history."

"What do you mean?"

"I mean he's leaving, dummy. Mom's getting rid of him."

Tiffany jumped to her feet. "Where is she?"

"In her bedroom, but don't waste your breath. You know Ma."

Jason was right, of course. Tiffany instantly knew when Rosalind went into her oh-so-sorry act. "Now you know what I told you, honey. Jason has Attila, and one dog is quite enough in this house. Even though it breaks my heart, Lucky just has to go."

I will not beg. "You're sending him to the pound, aren't you?"

Her stepmother's sweet smile and baby voice made Tiffany want to puke. "Well, my goodness, you don't think I'd send him just anywhere, do you?" Rosalind reached for the newspaper and turned to the classified section. "See?" She pointed to an ad under *Pets for Sale* and read, "Dog wanted for Grandson. Live on farm. Loving care guaranteed. Call Lolly Birdsong, 408-555-7786." She looked up triumphantly. "Now does that sound like the pound to you?"

"No, but—"

"I'm just sorry that woman didn't get here sooner. She was

supposed to come while you were still in school. I knew how bad you'd feel, honey, and I wanted to spare you." The ring of the doorbell interrupted. "That's probably her now. Say goodbye to the dog, Tiffany. It's time for him to go."

Tiffany followed her stepmother downstairs and watched while she opened the door and greeted a plump, white-haired woman dressed in a long, crocheted sweater over a shapeless cotton print dress. Seventy at least, she had snowy white hair, twinkly eyes and apple red cheeks. Rosalind asked, "You're Lolly Birdsong?"

"Yes, I am, dear." The woman stepped inside and caught sight of Lucky. "This is the dog? How handsome he is. Timmy's going to love him."

"Timmy is your grandson?"

"That's right, dear. He came to live with me when my daughter was unable to care for him." Her voice sank to a confidential level. "Drugs, you know."

"Oh, I see."

"I've tried everything, but once they're addicted, what can you do?" After a sad shake of her head, Lolly brightened. "Timmy loves it on the farm. There's cows and chickens and a little brook running through. That's why we call it Sunnybrook. There's horses, too." She bent down and petted Lucky. "He's going to love it there. There's acres and acres of green grass for him to run on. A dog heaven, you might say."

Rosalind nodded eagerly. "It certainly sounds it."

"Well then, is it settled? May I take your dog?"

"But of course. Take him with our blessing. I know you'll give him a good home. You'll never find a sweeter dog than Lucky." Rosalind beamed at her stepdaughter. "Isn't that right, Tiffany?"

Tiffany didn't answer. She was watching Lolly Birdsong pull a rope from her large, scuffed purse. "We'll just use this for a leash." The old lady bent to tie it around Lucky's neck.

A low, guttural *grrr* came from deep in Lucky's throat.

"Mercy!" Lolly Birdsong quickly backed away.

Rosalind threw up her hands. "Well, for heaven's sake,

he's never done this before. Tiffany, do something."

"Like what? Can't you see he doesn't want to go?"

Grrr. Lucky's laid his ears back. He bared his teeth.

Rosalind bit her lip in exasperation. "Well, he's going. Help Mrs. Birdsong, Tiffany. Get that dog out to her car, now!"

Something was wrong, really wrong, but Tiffany didn't quite know what. All she knew was, she didn't like Lolly Birdsong, although she wasn't sure why. Not that it mattered. Nothing would ever stop Madame Dracula from having her way. "He doesn't want to go, Rosalind."

"Well, for heaven sakes." Rosalind's eyes flashed with anger. She took the rope from the old lady's hands, tied it around Lucky's neck and practically dragged him to the car, everyone following. Lucky stopped growling but hung back on the rope all the way. Near the car, he sat down and wouldn't move. "Jason, help me lift him."

Tiffany watched her stepmother and brother lift Lucky onto the blanket-covered back seat of Lolly Birdsong's shiny new Acura sedan. *Something's not right. It's just not right.*

After the old lady slid under the wheel, Tiffany walked around the car and peered through the open window on the driver's side. "Where's Sunnybrook Farm?"

Lolly Birdsong hesitated before her lips curved into a genial smile. "Why, it's down near San Diego, honey. Down where the weather's so nice. He'll love it there." She started the engine.

"But where exactly? Maybe I could visit."

"Bye, bye!" The window rolled up as Lolly Birdsong, with a friendly wiggle of her fingers, merry smile in place, pulled away from the curb. The car picked up speed as it rounded the corner.

Rosalind went back inside. Tiffany and Jason stood and watched the car disappear. Jason reached awkwardly and patted his stepsister on her shoulder. "He'll be okay, Tiff. You heard what the lady said. He'll be on a farm with cows and chickens and a little brook running through, and horses and stuff."

"I don't care. I didn't like that lady."

Jason popped his gum reflectively. "Know what's funny?"

"No, what?"

"Well, she said she came from San Diego, so how come the license plate frame on her car says *Morris Acura, Santa Marta?* Isn't that up north?"

"It's half way to San Francisco."

"Then see what I mean? If she lives in San Diego, how come she's buying a new car in Santa Marta? You know what else? In the ad, her area code is 408. That's north, not south. I'll bet that old lady told a lie."

"I don't know, Jason, I just don't know." Even if she did, there was nothing she could do about it now. Tiffany wiped away her tears with the palm of her hand. Mom would never do such an awful thing. Mom would give her a hug and let her keep the dog. Home didn't seem like a bad idea right now, even if she had to share a room with her bratty sister.

A few blocks away, in the back parking lot of a shopping center, a 2014 Acura Legend sedan pulled in and parked behind a dirty white van. The door of the van swung open, and a tall, skinny man stepped out. Around fifty, he had dark, greasy hair and a thin, deep lined, battered face that had seen rough times. The eyes were hard; the chin receded; the bulbous nose appeared to be out of alignment, as if smashed by a fist in a fight long ago. He wore faded jeans, a plaid wool shirt, and dirty cowboy boots so old they seemed molded to his feet. With an angry stride, he walked back to the Acura. "What the hell took you so long, Lolly?"

"Fuck you, Johnny Valentine."

Lolly Birdsong, a cigarette dangling from her lips, slowly climbed out of the car. The merry laugh, the twinkly eyes, were gone and in their place, a sneering face with eyes as cold as shards of ice. "Is it my fault I've got to go through the whole dog and pony show each time?" Her voice took on a mocking tone. "The cows, the chickens, the little brook running through. If I have to say that one more time, I'll puke." She took a final drag off her cigarette and flipped it to the pavement. She drew a finger across her throat. "I've had it up to here."

Ignoring her, the man peered into her car. "What did you get?"

"One Lab. Smart dog. He knew."

The man opened the back door and grabbed the rope still tied around the dog's neck. He pulled the animal from the car and started to drag him toward the van. The sounds of terrified barking came from inside. The dog's eyes grew wide. He pulled back on the rope, trying to dig his claws into the pavement.

"Goddamn mutt. Lolly, get your ass in gear. Open them van doors and mind you don't let any of them out." The man jerked hard on the rope, nearly pulling Lucky off the ground. With a cry of pain from the rough jerk on his neck, Lucky allowed the man to pull him to the van. Lolly opened the doors. Lucky cringed. Inside, at least a dozen dogs of all sizes and descriptions were crammed together in several cages, howling. There was no food, no water. "Get in there!" Lucky whimpered and backed away. The man charged towards him, drew back his sharp-toed boot and kicked out, barely missing his flank as he dodged away. Cringing and shaking, he allowed the man to pull him close to the door. "Jump!"

Lucky leaped into the horror.

At a stop light, motorists peered curiously at a big white van from which a cacophony of barking came from within. It was headed for the I-5 North entrance of the freeway. On the side of the van was a sign.

SUNNYBROOK FARMS
SANTA MARTA, CALIFORNIA
JOHNNY VALENTINE, OWNER

Chapter 20

Fort Mason, San Francisco

"Damn and double damn!" Bernadette slammed the phone down. "That was Latonia, and guess what?"

Travis, along with Terry, Mrs. Bagley and Sparrow, had been planning the next demonstration at Union Square. "What?" Judging from the disgust in Bernadette's voice, he could already guess.

"Latonia says it can't be done."

"You mean…?"

"I mean breaking into Linderman's. She says there's no way we can get in."

Mrs. Bagley looked relieved. "Then that settles it, doesn't it? I'm glad. I always thought it was too risky."

Bernadette ignored Mrs. Bagley. "Travis, you said we could get in."

"I said we could possibly get in, but I warned you this might happen. Look, I've no problems with breaking the law. Lord knows, I've been hauled off to jail often enough. But this breaking and entering is a dangerous business. The Linderman Laboratories are too well guarded—all that electronic wizardry, and worse, an armed guard. Do we really want to mess with guns? I think not. I'm not saying we'll never do it. I hope someday we will, but for the time being, let's leave the breaking and entering and destruction of property to PETA and the Animal Liberation Front. They're more geared for it than we."

Terry looked surprised. "Why are you giving up so easily? That doesn't sound like you at all."

Sparrow chimed in. "Yeah, Trav, where's the old spark? We've been planning this raid for a long time, and all of a sudden you've got cold feet."

"He's right, Travis," Bernadette said. "You've been off in the clouds lately, like you've got something on your mind."

Travis heartily wished they'd get off the subject. "Come

on, guys, we were planning our next Union Square demo, re-member? Let's get back to it."

Mrs. Bagley darted a wise little smile at the others. "I'll bet I know what's happened. From the day that pretty girl with the fur coat came in here and fainted, he hasn't been the same."

"Back to the demo, everyone. NOW."

At the door, when the meeting was over, Travis helped Terry with her coat. His gaze swept over her figure. "Lost a little weight, haven't you?"

"A little like fourteen pounds." Terry blushed under his scrutiny, or rather, he reflected guiltily, she glowed. She still had a crush on him, still kept gazing at him with those adoring eyes. Another problem he should deal with, although at the moment he couldn't think how.

"Oh, by the way," Terry asked as they headed down the stairs, "are you going to WEELA's banquet next Thursday?"

"I rather think so. Since I'm president, I'm thinking of showing up."

She ignored his attempt at humor. With a strange tightness in her voice, she asked, "Then do you mind if I hitch a ride? My Honda's going to be in the shop."

Uh-oh. Terry had mentioned the WEELA banquet several times. What was she planning? "Sure, be glad to. I'll swing by about seven and pick you up."

Suddenly elated, she bounced down the stairs ahead of him and called back, "Are you going to Ananda Fuara with us?"

"Not tonight. I have a meeting."

"Darling, that was marvelous as always."

"I'm glad." In the darkness, Travis lay in Florence's bed, his arms around her. "It was good for me, too." Of course it was. He'd never lie, but just now, at the peak of things, it wasn't Florence beneath him but a tall, lithe, slim-ankled woman with glorious breasts, creamy-smooth skin, hair spread over the pil-low like gleaming strands of gold. Jillian, JILLIAN.

"Travis, I swear, lately you've seemed a million miles

away."

Only a thousand, but it might as well be a million. *You dumb bastard! Put her out of your mind. You'll never see Jillian Dahl again.*

Denver, Colorado,
Larimer Towers

"How do you like my new bed, darling?"

"Super." Jillian silently sighed. Tom had a cozy fire glowing in the corner fireplace, seductive music pouring from his stereo, but tonight nothing he did was going to work. She wrapped her arms around him, shut her eyes, and imagined herself in the arms of a man with soft, blue-gray eyes, whose deceptively gentle smile turned mocking whenever she tried to fool him. Travis TRAVIS.

When it was over, the grim reality of Karlin, the hospital, and the awful, gnawing fear returned. Quickly, she slid from the bed, showered, and dressed.

She found Tom still in bed when she came out of the bathroom. He raised himself on one elbow. "Not spending the night?"

"I want to go home. I'm going back to the hospital early tomorrow."

His mouth took on an unpleasant twist. "I know your sister's been through a lot, but frankly I don't see why you can't spend more time with me."

He had a point. Lately, between her job and the hospital, she'd hardly seen him at all. She only came tonight because he insisted. She looked him square in the eye. "You know my sister comes first right now."

"So she's getting more tests?"

"More chemotherapy and they're going to check her lungs."

"I've got a surprise for you."

"Good. I could use a nice surprise right about now."

She was standing in front of his dresser mirror, running a

comb through her hair. He got out of bed and walked to her, wrapping a towel around his trim middle. Standing behind, he slipped his arms around her waist and looked over her shoulder into her mirrored eyes. "I'm buying a company plane, a Beechjet."

"Your own jet? How neat. How big is it?"

"Big enough to go wherever you want to go. Just think, we can go skiing any season we like, anywhere in the world. We'll head for New Zealand in July, do powder eights down the Tasman Glacier."

"What about that place in Argentina?"

"Bariloche? A long weekend."

"Or closer to home?"

"Big Sky? White Fish? We can buzz up for the day."

"Tom, that's marvelous."

Was it? She tried to make herself care but just couldn't. She hated being such a fraud. How strange that only a few weeks ago she would have been ecstatic over Tom's news. But now…she must keep up the pretense. When Karlin got better, when things got back to normal, then she would care about Tom again, and the Caribbean honeymoon, Beechjet and skiing down the Tasman Glacier. All of it, but not right now.

Her shoulders sagged as she left the Larrimer Towers. The chemotherapy had been devastating. Her sister was sick and weak. Her hair was gone, even her eyebrows and eyelashes. The constant threat of metastasis in her lungs hung over them. No wonder Karlin's spirits had sunk. And damn, not a word about Lucky.

Chapter 21

St. Francis Hospital

Karlin's eyes were closed when Jillian entered the hospital room and tiptoed to the bed. How pale her sister's face was, how gaunt. Dark circles ringed her eyes. To hide her baldness, she was wearing the bright red ski hat she'd worn at Winter Park that sunshiny day when she'd raced like the wind down the mountain on two good legs, back before the cancer, a lifetime ago.

Karlin's eyelids fluttered open. "Oh, hi, Sis." The whiteness around her mouth was pronounced.

"So did you have many visitors tonight?"

She turned her head away. "I got a text from Dennis."

"You did?" Uh-oh, this was going to be something bad.

"Take a look."

Karlin's smartphone lay on the nightstand. Jillian picked it up and read Dennis' message.

Sorry, can't see u anymore. Not u it's me. Can't stand to see u suffer. Pls forgive.

"I can't believe this." Jillian sank into the chair by the bed. "I never thought he could be that rotten."

"A text message. He didn't even care enough to tell me in person."

Oh, Karlin, I am so sorry."

"Not your fault."

"It isn't that he doesn't love you, it's just...some people aren't strong enough to be supportive."

"My hair is gone, my leg is gone. I'm ugly and I'm going to die."

This was almost unbearable, watching her sister suffer and not a damn thing she could do to ease the pain. But she must stay strong. "Your hair will grow back."

"My leg won't."

"You've been so very brave. No wonder you're feeling

down, what with all the drugs in your system, but you know you're going to get better. Dennis is just stressed. Maybe, when he thinks it over…"

Swiftly, Karlin turned towards her, pride blazing in her eyes. "I wouldn't want him now."

"Good. I'm glad you said that. Who needs the little bastard?"

Karlin smiled through her tears. "Sometimes, sister, you are so funny. You're right, who needs him?" She started to cry. "I'm such a mess. Sorry, I can't stop crying." She reached up and touched the red ski cap. "I hate losing my hair. Hate it! I'd rather lose my leg than lose my hair."

"Now, Karlin—"

"There's something else. How could I forget?"

"What else?"

"Dr. De Leon was in a while ago. He says I have to have another operation tomorrow. He said there's a single metastatic growth in my lung. They'll do a bit of surgery to remove it. Like a secondary tumor is nothing, he says, but I know better."

As if a giant hand were pressing on her shoulders, Jillian slumped back in her chair. "You're just full of good news tonight, aren't you?"

"I am getting so scared." Karlin spoke barely above a whisper. "Last night I woke up and the room was pitch dark. I felt this terrible sense of aloneness. It's like the dark is associated with death, and I have the feeling that I'm going to die alone, in the middle of the night, and nobody will care."

"You know that's not so."

"I know, but try to convince me of that at two in the morning." Anguish pinched her exhausted little face. "Why me? I keep asking myself that, over and over again. What did I do wrong? Why does God hate me so much He even took my dog away?"

Karlin's words struck like a knife to her heart. "I am so sorry about losing Lucky."

"I don't blame you, but it isn't just dying I worry about in the middle of the night, I think about Lucky, too. Hour after hour, I lie here and wonder, where he is and if he's cold, if he's hungry, if he's dead. Oh, Sister, I want my dog back. What if I die without seeing Lucky again or even knowing what happened to him? I don't think I could bear it."

8 a.m.

Jillian parked her Camaro in the garage and stumbled like a zombie into her condo. It had been a hard, nightmare of a night. She'd spent it by Karlin's side, helping her through the "two a.m. syndrome" as her sister had so grimly named it. Never had she seen her sister so sick, frightened and despairing. She would return directly to the hospital as soon as she showered and changed clothes. Weariness enveloped her. She was so tired her nerves throbbed. She absolutely must sleep, just for an hour or two. When she left the hospital, Karlin was finally asleep, so it would be okay. The surgery wasn't scheduled until this afternoon. First she'd better call work. Her job seemed so unimportant alongside what Karlin was going through, but she forced herself to call her office, tell her boss she wouldn't be in, probably not for the rest of the week. If he didn't like it, he could fire her, but of course he understood. As she hung up the phone, she noticed she had voice mail. Why bother? She was beyond caring, but then, it could be important. She punched in her code and listened.

First came three new messages, two from friends, another from a charity. Then the recorded voice asked if she'd like to hear her saved message. Whatever it was, she'd better delete it, but maybe she should hear it again first.

"Hi, my name is Tiffany Clair and like, I live in Encino and I've got your dog, Lucky. Call me at area code 818-555-5950."

Jillian's eyes went wide. Did she hear what she thought she'd just heard? She punched for the repeat and played the message again. It had been there several days. My God, how could she have missed it? She grabbed the telephone and dialed the number Tiffany left.

A woman's high, baby doll voice said hello.

"Hello, my name is Jillian Dahl. I'm calling about a dog named Lucky. I'd like to speak to Tiffany."

"Tiffany doesn't live here anymore."

Oh, no. "Is there any way I can find her? I'm anxious to find my dog."

A long silence. Jillian held her breath waiting for the woman to speak again. "Well, I suppose I can give you her new number. She's back with her mother now."

"Yes, please." Jillian grabbed a pencil and wrote down the number the woman dictated. "Thank you, and could you tell me, do you know anything about Lucky?"

"I think it best you talk to Tiffany. Will there be anything else?" The baby doll voice had definitely gone frosty.

"No. Thanks, goodbye." Jillian quickly dialed again. After only one ring, a young girl's lively voice answered. "Is this Tiffany?" When the girl answered yes, she continued, "This is Jillian Dahl in Denver. You called a while back about my dog?"

A shocked silence, a surprised squeal, and then, "Where have you been? I called you ages ago."

"I just now found your message on my voice mail. So could you tell me—?"

"Gee, I wish you'd called me sooner."

"What do you mean?"

"I don't have Lucky any more. My stepmother gave him away."

The way she hissed out *stepmother* made the picture clear. Jillian sagged into the chair by the telephone and covered her eyes with her hand. "Where is he now?"

Tiffany told her about the day Lolly Birdsong took Lucky away and how suspicious she and her stepbrother, Jason, had been. "Like I don't know what exactly, but something was wrong."

"So you didn't like this Lolly Birdsong?"

"She didn't seem real. And like, you know, she said she was from San Diego, but Jason saw the name on her license plate and it said Santa Marta. And she had a 408 area code. That's north, not south."

"I don't suppose you remember the number."

"Gee, no. It's gone, for sure."

"So where do you think I should look first?"

"You're going to try to find him?"

"Oh, yes."

"Jason thinks she lied about San Diego. I do, too. I'd look in Santa Marta first. I'd maybe look in the phone book and see if there's a Lolly Birdsong listed, or a Sunnybrook Farm."

"I've heard of Santa Marta, but where is it exactly?"

"It's a city about a two hour drive south of San Francisco.

"Tell me, I'm curious, where did you find him?"

"On the south fork of the upper Kings River. That's in the Sierra Nevada Mountains."

"I can't imagine what he was doing there."

"We found him close to where a car had gone into the river. He was all muddy and wet, so that's probably where he came from, but we never knew for sure."

By the end of the conversation, Tiffany had related the whole story of finding Lucky and how she fought to keep him. "I sure did love Lucky. He was such a neat dog."

What a nice girl, and bright, too. "You've been a real help, Tiffany. I'm so glad you called and left that message."

"You can thank Jason for that. He's the one who remembered your phone number after Lucky's collar got lost."

"You mean he's not wearing his collar now?" Another blow.

"It got left by the river. Gee, I'm sure sorry "

"Never mind. It doesn't matter." It did matter.

"I hope you find him. Will you let me know? I think about him every day and wonder if he's okay."

"It's awful, isn't it, worrying over a lost pet? Of course I'll call you when I know."

"Thanks loads." Tiffany's voice suddenly brightened. "My mother says I can have another dog. We're going to the animal shelter this weekend. I want to find a black Lab, just like Lucky."

"Wonderful! I'm so glad. Well, goodbye, Tiffany, and

thanks again."

Now what was she going to do? In her stockinged feet, Jillian paced the living room. On the one hand, she should be at Karlin's side, now, today. The operation was scheduled for this afternoon. Absolutely no way could she run off to California and leave her sister, but on the other hand…

Karlin was heartbroken about losing Lucky. Getting her dog back would be just what she needed to lift her sagging morale, especially after what that jerk Dennis did. Should she stay with Karlin or should she fly to California? And even if she did fly to California, how did she know she'd find Lucky? Damn, but life was full of hard choices. She stopped pacing. *So okay, get yourself in gear and make up your mind.* Her fatigue forgotten, she reached for the telephone and called Martha Trimmer.

"Hello, Martha, it's Jillian again."

"Jillian? I've so appreciated your phone calls. Where are you?"

"At home in Denver. I wasn't sure you'd be in San Francisco."

"We just got back from filming in Arizona. I haven't had that much fun in ages. Guess what? Garth and I are going to get married."

"Wonderful. I'm so happy for you."

"Thanks, but I'm sure you're not calling just to see how I am. So tell me, how is your dear sister? And have you found Lucky?"

"My sister is…hanging in there. And no, I haven't found Lucky. That's why I'm calling. Can you do me a favor?"

"Well, of course, dear, anything."

She told Martha what had happened. "This little town of Santa Marta is about a two hour drive south of San Francisco."

"I know it well," Martha replied. "I was born and raised in Fresno, which is a straight shot inland from Santa Marta. I have friends there."

"Could you maybe have them check and see if there's a Lolly Birdsong in Santa Marta? And a Sunnybrook Farm?"

"Hmm, somehow those names ring a bell. Something I've read in the papers lately...now what was it?"

"I'll get back to you in about an hour."

"Fine, I'll get right on it."

Jillian hung up and dialed again. "Hello, Tish?"

"Jillian! I was about to call you. I just heard you're not coming into work today. Is it Karlin?"

"Can you duck out of work and meet me at the hospital in an hour?"

"Sure. May I ask…?"

"I'll give you a hint. This comes under the *what are friends for* category."

"See you in an hour."

Before she left for the hospital, she packed a small bag, this time remembering to throw in an extra pair of low-heeled shoes.

Jillian shivered as she hurried through the front doors of St. Francis Hospital. Although it was April, the day was cold and crisp. Snow covered the ground, but she wasn't dressed for snow. Tish was waiting for her just inside the entrance. "Hi, kiddo, what are you up to?"

"Depending on a phone call to San Francisco, and what Dr. De Leon says, I'm going back to California."

"Tell me what's happening."

"You wouldn't believe what that little weasel Dennis has done. And wait 'til I tell you about the message on my machine. First I've got to make a phone call."

Tish sighed, crossed her arms and leaned against the wall as Jillian pulled out her smartphone and dialed a number. "I hope you appreciate the splendid good humor and enormous patience of your dearest friend."

"Believe me, I do." Jillian spoke into the phone. "Martha? Have you found out anything?"

Martha Trimmer's voice quivered with excitement. "Indeed I have. I called my friends, and they checked and found a Sunnybrook Farm in Santa Marta. I called and got no answer.

Then I got a hunch and called the Santa Marta Humane Society, just to see if they knew this place, and Jillian, I hate to tell you, but it's awful what I found out."

Jillian gripped the phone and prepared for the worst. "So tell me."

"The place is owned by bunchers."

"What on earth is a buncher?"

"They're middlemen who sell animals to laboratories. That's what they do at Sunnybrook Farm. It's all quite legal, but when I mentioned Sunnybrook Farm to this lady at the Humane Society, she just about had a fit. It seems the place is owned by a man named Johnny Valentine who has a terrible reputation for cruelty to animals. An old woman helps him run it. Guess what her name is?"

"Lolly Birdsong."

"Right. The Humane Society has been trying to shut Sunnybrook Farm down for years. This lady told me that conditions on that farm are abominable. She said the pens are filthy and sometimes the dogs and cats go for days without food or water. Some have been so neglected they starved to death. If they're sick, nobody cares. They get no medical attention."

"Are you trying to tell me Lucky is there?"

"Yes, but no. The lady told me that this Johnny Valentine is a legitimate kennel operator who sells animals to researchers. Would you believe he's licensed by the United States Department of Agriculture? She said he's got a Class 'B' license, which means he sells random source animals. That means people's pets. He gets some animals from pounds, some from other dealers, but the worst is he's already been convicted twice of picking up animals by illegal means."

"Like putting an ad in the newspaper, offering a good home for your pet?"

"Exactly. And answering "free to good home" ads. Getting a pet through trickery is what it amounts to. Then he turns right around and sells the animal to a laboratory for maybe a hundred dollars each, or even more. Isn't that awful? That's why I recognized the name. It's been in the newspapers about how the Humane Society's trying to shut Johnny Valentine down. It'll happen soon, the lady said. But I must tell you the rest. Right now, there's not a dog left at Sunnybrook Farm."

"Lucky's not there?"

"No. This lady from the Humane Society checked and called me back. She's got her sources, apparently. She says all the dogs were sold to a laboratory to fill a special order. They were shipped out yesterday."

"You mean a research laboratory? The kind where they do experiments on—" she took a sudden intake of breath as the horror struck her "—*dogs?*"

"Yes, I'm afraid so. Wait a minute. I wrote it down. It's the Linderman Research Laboratories in Santa Marta, California. It's run by Dr. Harvey Linderman, the famous scientist and researcher. Have you heard of him? He's won quite a few awards. I'll bet you anything, that's where Lucky is."

Jillian found Dr. De Leon studying a chart at the nursing station near Karlin's room. He looked up as she and Tish approached. "Oh, Jillian, I wanted to talk to you. I heard about Karlin's boyfriend getting cold feet, and I'm sorry. You'd be surprised how often that sort of thing happens."

"I wanted to see you, too, Doctor."

"You've heard about the surgery?"

"Karlin told me. I need to know what you would say if I wasn't here."

"I'd say you'd better have a good reason. Karlin needs you now, but you knew that already."

"I just found out her dog's been sold to a research laboratory in California. You know what that means."

Dr. De Leon looked suddenly stricken. "Oh, my god. As if she hasn't been through enough already, now this."

She looked deep into the eyes of the man with the stone cold heart and saw pain mixed with tenderness and passion. Why hadn't she seen before? Why hadn't she realized? "You care about Karlin, don't you?"

"How could I not care? She's the bravest, smartest,

most…" His jaw tightened. "I'd like to forget that oath I took and wring Dennis's neck, that lowlife bastard." He put on his mask of indifference again. "I've said too much."

So the man had a heart after all. Clearly he cared for Karlin. And here she'd always thought the worst of Dr. De Leon, never understanding what he was all about. Later, she'd sort it all out, but not now. "I've got to go to California. Tish will stand in for me. She'll be here for Karlin 'til I get back. I don't want to go, but—"

"You don't have a choice. Karlin loves that dog. Go to California. Find Lucky. If you don't…" As if he could say no more, Dr. De Leon turned and walked away.

Leaving the hospital, Tish asked, "What about Tom?"

"Tom? Oh, yes…Tom."

"Are you going to call him?"

"I guess I'd better let him know, don't you think?"

Tish rolled her eyes. "This is the guy you're going to marry. You're supposed to share your problems and sorrows. He's supposed to be helping you through all this mess, but he's not. You're handling it all by yourself. Correct me if I'm wrong, but I get the feeling Tom's being incredibly selfish. Looks like he resents all that time you're spending away from him."

Tish was dead-on. Jillian searched for an answer, some way she could defend Tom, but nothing came to mind.

Tish continued, "You didn't even think to call him. Look, far be it from me to sound like I'm on Tom's side, but if you're going to marry the guy, you've got to start including him in your plans."

"You're probably right."

"If you want to stay engaged, you'd better call that turkey."

"I keep telling you, Tom's not all bad. He's buying a company jet, you know. Just think we can go skiing anywhere in the world, any time we please."

Tish eyed her with scorn. "Another fine reason for getting married."

"Don't be ridiculous. I keep telling you, I love Tom."

"Then why do you keep talking about that animal activist guy, that Travis Kerrigan?"

Her heart lurched at the sound of his name. "Oh, him. What about him?"

"Are you going to see him when you get out there?"

"I'm going to Santa Marta, not San Francisco."

"So what's your plan?"

"Simple. I'll just walk into the Linderman Laboratories and ask for my dog."

"What if they won't give him back?"

"I won't give up. Karlin's going to have her dog back if it kills me."

"They might say no."

"Then I'll keep demanding, go right up the ladder if I have to, to the man at the top, this Doctor Harvey Linderman. I don't know him, but he's a doctor, isn't he? Aren't all doctors kindhearted and compassionate? So how could there be a problem?"

"All I know is you'd better call Tom before it's too late."

"Hello, Tom?"

"Jillian, how's it going?"

"Good and bad. Karlin's got to have another operation this afternoon, but the most exciting thing, I got a phone message about Lucky—"

"You found him?"

"Could you drop everything and come to California with me? I've just learned Lucky's in a research laboratory. I've got to get him out. I–"

"Drop everything? Are you insane? I've got clients here. We're nipping up to Loveland this afternoon for a half-day's skiing. Tomorrow I won't be able to squeeze out a minute, let alone...how long will you be gone this time?"

"I have no idea."

"Not even a seat-of-the-pants guesstimate?"

"No."

"Well, keep in touch. When you get back, we'll try out my new bed again."

Chapter 22

Santa Marta

Gretchen was gone.

Dr. Harvey Linderman managed only the barest of civil "good mornings" as he swept past Bonnie, his dignified, white-haired secretary, and entered his office. "No calls." Seated at his desk, door firmly closed, he slumped forward, placed his forehead in his hands, and whispered softly, "Jesus."

He had called Gretchen early to make plans for the evening. She didn't answer. Slightly alarmed, he drove straight to her apartment (damn it, *his* apartment), only to discover an empty closet and empty drawers. His latest love had fled without a word, without a note. Only last night he'd taken her to an Armenian restaurant for dinner, spent close to two hundred dollars plus the tip for rack of lamb marinated in pomegranate juice and a bottle of Domaine Chandon Brut. Back at the apartment, he failed again.

Harvey shook his head and groaned. He could hardly believe his eyes when he toured the apartment in the bright, unforgiving, morning light. An absolute pigpen. The kitchen was full of unwashed dishes and smelly garbage. In the bedroom, a clutter of empty bottles and tubes, spilled powder and smeary lipsticks desecrated the polished surface of his Bergamo dresser, and—that bitch!—she'd spilled an entire bottle of frosted purple nail polish on the fine oak finish. She'd left trash everywhere, but by far the most infuriating sight was the obscene object that lay crumpled on the floor by the bed. Gretchen's parting message—a used condom.

She must have called a boyfriend after he left last night, some young buck who could get it up and keep it up, not like… He closed his eyes and groaned again. Ungrateful bitch. They were all bitches, especially Connie after her astounding phone call.

I've decided to stay here, Harvey. I'm not coming home.

Incredible. How could a woman of her sensitivity and breeding degrade herself that way? How could she choose to live in that stinking neighborhood on the wrong side of town? But then, she was a woman and you never knew what women would do, illogical and inferior as they were. They were bitches, each and every one. He hated them all.

Later in the afternoon, he sat at his desk, reflecting it had been a busy day. With the arrival of the dogs from Johnny Valentine's, the heat stroke experiment was underway. Tomorrow all forty dogs would be shaved and made ready. On Friday, Group "A" would be pretreated with antibiotics, "B" with cathartics, and "C" with enemas. Group "D" would have nothing at all. They would all be anesthetized and the circulating water blankets applied. The results should be exciting. Already the framework of his article was forming in the back of his mind. He'd call it "Increasing the Survival Rate in Dog Heatstroke after Reduction of Gut Flora." Yes, that had a nice ring to it. Tired though he was, he was thankful for the diversion of his newest experiment. Sometimes minutes would go by when he wouldn't think of Gretchen, Connie, the humiliation he'd suffered at their hands.

Bonnie buzzed on the intercom. "I've got a bit of a problem, Doctor. There's a young lady here who's being rather persistent."

"What does she want?"

"She says we've got her pet dog here. She wants it back."

"You know our policy. We can't accommodate pet owners who claim their animal is here. It's too late."

"I know, but—"

"Tell her no and send her packing."

"Yes, sir."

One minute later, she buzzed him again.

"What is it now?"

"She won't go. Insists she wants to see you."

"No!" Here was yet another bleeding heart pet owner, claiming their pet was held captive by Linderman Labs. "Get her out of here, Bonnie. Call Security if you have to." He slammed down the phone.

Moments later, his door swung open so hard it banged against the wall. A lithesome young woman with long, honey colored hair strode purposefully across the room and stood, face flushed from her boldness, gazing down at him. He dropped his pen, jerked up in his chair. What a beautiful woman. Great figure. She knew how to dress in those smooth fitting slacks, high-heeled sandals, tweed jacket and cashmere sweater, a silk scarf knotted at her throat. Gucci bag slung over her shoulder. Classy, like Connie used to dress. His eyes locked on the two round, full, enticing mounds shoving against the soft cashmere. Just like those of that bitch of all bitches, Gretchen. "How dare you come in here?" He jabbed a finger towards the door. "Get out."

She stood her ground, her eyes drilling into his with keen intensity. "Doctor Linderman, I presume?"

Bonnie hovered nervously behind. "Doctor, I'm so sorry. She got to your office on a visitor's pass and then she barged right in. Shall I call Security?"

"You don't need to do that," the woman explained rapidly, her smoothly modulated voice well under control. "I'm not here to cause trouble, I just want my dog. Doctor Linderman, will you hear me out? It won't take long."

For a long moment, Harvey Linderman stared at her as she stood, tall and proud, and not the least bit afraid, waiting for his response. How he disliked this boldness in women. *Assertiveness* they called it nowadays—gave classes in it, the fools. Most definitely, this woman needed to be put in her place. Indeed, a little cat-and-mouse might teach her a good lesson. With studied casualness, he leaned back in his chair, pressed his fingertips together. "Who are you?"

She flipped back her hair and tilted her chin. "My name is Jillian Dahl and I'm from Denver. Sorry to intrude like this, Doctor, but I had to see you." Her eyes flicked to a chair. Oh, no. This bitch was going to stand. He picked up his pen, tapped it impatiently on the desk. "I'm a busy man, Miss Dahl."

She took a deep breath. "I'm looking for a dog named

Lucky. He isn't my dog, he's my sister's dog. Lucky's been lost for some time now, and...my sister is very ill. She's in the hospital and she—"

"What has that to do with Linderman Laboratories?" His gaze slid insolently over her breasts.

"I'm getting to that. My sister has cancer. She's very sick. She's already lost her leg, and I'm afraid she's getting worse."

"Get to the point." He continued staring at the front of her sweater.

"The point is, Lucky's here."

"Oh? What makes you think so?"

"I found out he was picked up by Johnny Valentine." She stretched out her hand. "Look, you don't know my sister, but she's brave, a fighter, and she's had such a tough time. Now, on top of everything else, her dog is gone. She's grieving for her dog. I can't tell you how much it would help if she got Lucky back. I'm sure he's here. Won't you let me take a look?"

"That's out of the question. It's Linderman's policy that once we buy an animal, that animal is not redeemable for any reason whatsoever." He looked forward to her response. It was time for her to beg. Her desperation showed but only in her eyes.

In a remarkably calm voice she replied, "Look, I'll pay you what the dog is worth, plus whatever more you ask. Surely, just this once, you could break your rule? It would mean so much to my sister."

In answering, he articulated each word carefully, as if he were speaking to someone who wasn't very bright. "No. Absolutely, unequivocally, no. Do you understand, Miss Dahl? The answer is no." Now what would she do? Hysteria was next, he should imagine.

She surprised him. Though her face flushed with anger, she said in a reasoning way, "I can't believe this. Surely, you don't mean to be so heartless."

He shrugged and addressed his words to her chest. "Rules are rules."

"Then I'll go to the SPCA, the Humane Society, there

must be something I can do."

"Not really. This is my laboratory. Those animals are mine. I own them, just as I do my house and my car. They have no rights at all. Legally I can do whatever experiments I please. Trust me, I've been through all this before. Besides, there's hardly time. The dogs from Johnny Valentine's are slated for an experiment. There will be no survivors. So if I were you, I'd forget about Lucky."

She blanched at his words. "You're telling me Lucky's going to die?"

"Yes, but for science, Miss Dahl. All for a noble cause."

"But that's horrible. To take someone's pet—"

"Had you thought of simply getting your sister another dog?"

She exploded then. Amazing it took her so long. "You arrogant sonofabitch! Have you no heart? Why are you treating me like this? You could break your own rules if you wanted to."

About time. With a look of mock astonishment, he looked toward his secretary. "Call Security, Bonnie, this woman's hysterical." To his great disappointment, she did not shed the tears he'd anticipated. Instead, a look of understanding spread across her face, as she realized, and (give her credit), rightly so, he was goading her all along and her case was hopeless.

She was no fool. In fact, he could almost admire her as she backed away from his desk, gathered her dignity about her, and said in a throaty, scornful voice, "There's no need to call Security. I'm leaving." With head held high, she walked to the door and turned. "Did you enjoy staring at my tits, you bastard?"

She spun around and was gone. He flushed with embarrassment. Damn her. How dare she insult him that way, and in front of his secretary. Another humiliation at the hands of a woman. He felt Bonnie's gaze upon him. He looked towards her and wished he hadn't. His long-time secretary's lips were tight with anger. Loathing filled her eyes. So what? Why should he give a damn? In fact, it was rather amusing, watching her struggle with her desire to tell him off versus the gold twenty-year pin and generous bonus she was scheduled to receive in two months' time. Which would win? "Do you have a problem, Bonnie?"

She stood silent, fists clenched, while her battle raged within. "No problem, Doctor." She turned and walked swiftly out of his office.

Good. He had just killed two birds with one stone. Or had he? His amusement ceased as he thought of Jillian Dahl. The bitch. Was she laughing at him now, aware how she'd humiliated him with her parting remark? Well, no matter. Maybe she'd won that round, but in the long run, she was the loser. Her sister's dog would die on Friday, Saturday at the latest if he was one of the unlucky ones who survived the first eighteen hours.

Jillian drove the rented car out the gates of the Linderman Laboratories, pulled over to the curb and sat stunned behind the wheel. She'd expected a kindly old Doctor Linderman who would gladly return her dog and apologize for the misunderstanding. Not in her wildest, most far-out scenario, had she pictured a scene like the one she'd just gone through. She must calm down, pull herself together. Like Tom would observe, *your ducks are not all in a row, sweetheart*. According to that horrible man, Lucky was slated to die on Friday. It was now late Wednesday afternoon. Not much time to rescue Lucky, but at this point what could she do? She'd burned her bridges with Dr. Harvey Linderman. The guard had allowed her in on a visitor's pass, but he'd surely be informed not to do it again. She would never get back in…legally. She turned in her seat and peered through the back window at the entrance gate. The guard wore a gun. He carefully checked every car that came through. She looked at the high metal fence that surrounded the entire complex. No way. How ridiculous even to think of sneaking in.

Only one person could help her now, the man who'd haunted her thoughts since the day they'd met, whom she vowed she'd never see again. He was her only hope. If there was any possible way to save Lucky, he would know. She reached for her smartphone and looked up the number for

Travis Kerrigan.

In her small apartment on Polk Street, Terry Woodard hummed through her evening chores. All was in readiness for tomorrow night. Each room sparkling clean—pink ribbons adorning the necks of her three cats—two newly bought Waterford crystal wine glasses waiting to be filled. A new, black, slinky dress, size ten, hung on a satin hanger on the bedroom door where she could gaze at it fondly whenever she passed. She'd done it! Lost twenty pounds just like she vowed she would. The wonderful dream was about to come true. After the banquet Thursday night, she was going to make love with Travis Kerrigan. She still wasn't sure how she'd break the ice and get him into her bedroom, but when the time came, it would all work out. At long last he would realize what a fool he'd been, how blind not to see they were made for each other. He would ask her to move in with him, and she would. She'd refer to him as her "significant other" and not even mention marriage, but when she accidentally got pregnant, he would insist she marry him. By then he'd know he could never, ever live without her. She would give him one child, maybe two. They would live in Marin County—San Anselmo would be good—and work together for the animals for the rest of their lives.

Terry ran her hands over the newly defined indentation of her waist, down over her flat stomach and around to her now-svelte hips. All was in readiness for Travis. How could he resist now that she was thin?

Fort Mason, Wednesday Evening, 7 p.m.

Dear Supporter,
Alone in the dimly lit office, tie loosened and white shirt sleeves rolled up, Travis Kerrigan stared at the two words he'd typed half an hour ago. The rest of the screen was as blank as his mind whenever he tried to formulate his latest fundraising letter.

Dear Supporter,

Where were the lively, compelling sentences that usually flowed so swiftly that his typing could hardly keep up? Where were the zest, the spark, which had always sustained him in his battle for the animals? The life of an activist was never easy. He'd been jeered, reviled, criticized, cursed, spat upon, arrested and thrown in jail. Yet not once had his courage flagged. Never had he even considered choosing another, easier path. Nor was he considering it now. A lifetime of work lay ahead, but somehow, for a reason he couldn't explain, his enthusiasm had drained away, leaving him wallowing in a state of melancholy from which he couldn't seem to escape. He could pinpoint precisely when it happened—that night he put his arms around a beautiful, vain and frivolous woman in a mink coat and pink tennis shoes, had kissed her soft lips while the foghorn sounded and the lights from the bridge sparkled like jewels across the bay. The feeling he had when he was with her was like no other he ever felt before. It was just so right, that night when he walked off, alone, into the fog.

Try as he would, he could not get Jillian Dahl out of his mind. He'd behaved like a lovesick teenager, even copying her phone number from the Pet Finder's card. Again and again, his hand had been on the phone, about to dial her number, but each time, pride and logic stopped him cold.

She was engaged. Therefore, she belonged to another man. Not honorable to try to steal her away. What if she didn't remember him? *Travis Who?* Although he knew his kiss had stirred her, perhaps it was only a physical thing, long forgotten now she was back in Denver with her hotshot fiancé. What could he suggest if he did call? A spot of dinner? A day of skiing? They lived a thousand miles apart and he didn't ski. And what, in the long run, could he offer her? A lifetime of picketing and chaining herself to fences? So why had she called? She hadn't said, only that she'd explain when she saw him. Why was she on her way to see him right now?

Dear Supporter,

He heard brisk, light footsteps out in the hall. His back was to the door as it opened, and when he heard the soft, "Hi,

Travis" his heart was pounding.

He got up to greet her, caught his breath when he saw her standing there. For a moment, words escaped him. "Hello, Jillian Dahl."

She smiled in return, tilted her chin, and regarded him in that proud, assured way he remembered. "So you didn't forget my name."

"No, I didn't forget." She was as beautiful as he remembered, her long legs in slacks this time, still the flimsy high-heeled sandals, her hair falling in long silky curls, and that velvet skin of hers so flawlessly white against the coral of her sweater. Drawing closer, he saw that her face was drawn into tight, anxious lines. He looked deep into her long-lashed eyes. For one brief, heart-stopping moment, as his gaze locked with hers, he thought he saw...but no, he was wrong. Worry filled her eyes, and yes, a certain anguish, but nothing more. He wanted to put his arms around her but took her hand instead and shook it firmly. "It's good to see you again. Come in and sit down." He indicated a chair, removing his suit coat from the back, tossing it over another chair.

She sat down and said in a teasing way, despite her obvious distress, "A suit? White shirt and tie? Travis, you've gone corporate."

"You caught me. Today's my lawyering day. I do occasionally have to earn a few pennies towards the rent and groceries."

He leaned casually with his back against the desk, grasped the edge in his hands and commanded his heart to stop pounding. "How's your sister?"

Her face tightened. "Karlin's holding her own. She had another operation today, to remove a...something from her lung. I called a while ago and she's out of the recovery room and doing all right."

"Did you find her dog?"

"No...yes...well, that's why I'm here."

He knew without asking. "You need my help."

"You're the only one I can turn to."

He listened attentively as she told him the story of what had happened to Lucky. And when, with anger spilling out, she described her disastrous scene with Linderman, he was hard put to conceal a smoldering rage of his own. "There must be something I can do," she cried, her desperation breaking through. "Isn't there a way I can get in there? I can't just let Lucky die in that horrible way."

Linderman's, dear God. For a moment he had to turn his face away. "You can't. I only wish...the trouble is..."

Her eyes beseeched him. "You can't help?"

He got up and began to pace back and forth from the desk to the Xerox machine. "WEELA's been trying to get into Linderman Laboratories for years. We've picketed, leafletted, asked to come in and inspect, but Linderman won't hear of it. You've met the man, so you know his contemptuous arrogance. He'd like to take WEELA, everyone in it, and boot us all into orbit. He hates our guts."

"He's a hateful man."

"Exactly. We've been working on a scheme to break in and steal every animal in the place, but it's tough. So far, we haven't figured how to get past their security."

"I see...so there's nothing else?"

The words stuck in his throat, but he had to say them. "There's nothing else, at least that WEELA can do."

She stood up, reached for her purse, and with a heavy sigh slung it over her shoulder. "Thanks anyway. You were my last hope. Tomorrow I'll drive back to Santa Marta, try the Humane Society." Her laugh was bitter. "Make my last-ditch stand." Her footsteps dragging, she started towards the door. "Sorry I bothered you."

"Don't go." He uttered the words before he even had a plan, but he couldn't let her get away. He had an idea, a long shot, ninety-nine percent doomed to failure but worth a try. Anything was worth a try rather than see her walk out the door with that look on her face. "Wait a minute." He hesitated, decided he could trust her. "We have someone working at Linderman's, a spy you might say, someone inside who's been trying to find a way around their security."

"And?" Jillian looked at him hopefully.

"So far, no luck. She called a few days ago and confirmed what we already knew. The place is like a fortress. There's no way we can get in."

"Is she still there?"

"Working at Linderman's? Yes, though she'll be leaving soon." He reached for the telephone. "Don't get your hopes up, but I'll check with her again. Who knows? Maybe she's turned up something new."

Jillian returned a faint but grateful smile. "You will? Good! Please call your connection, it's worth another try."

"I like that," he said as he dialed, "our Santa Marta Connection. Sounds like something from a spy story, doesn't it?"

"I suppose." Her smile faded. "Only this is for real."

When he got Latonia on the phone, she confirmed what she told him earlier. "Sorry, Travis, there's nothing new. I've racked my brain, trying to find a way, but it's hopeless. We can't get in, baby. Period. Case closed."

"Thanks for trying. Thought I'd double-check. I've got a pet owner here who's traced her dog to Linderman's."

"Is she sure?"

"Her dog was picked up by Johnny Valentine."

"Oh, lord. I hope it's not one of the ones...tell me what the dog looks like. I'll check tomorrow, but I have to tell you, if her dog's in the latest batch from Sunnybrook Farm, there's no hope."

"She heard he was picked up just the other day."

"Yeah, forty dogs were just sold to Linderman's. You don't want to know the details."

"Hang on." He asked Jillian to describe Lucky and then returned to Latonia. "A male Labrador retriever. No collar. Small paws. All black except for three white paws and a white tip on his tail."

Jillian touched his sleeve. "And a white star on his chest, and tell her Lucky is very good-natured, very friendly, and..." her voice wavered "...loves people." She bit her lip and turned her face away.

Travis gave Latonia the rest of the description. "So you'll check tomorrow?"

He heard a deep, frustrated sigh. "Yes, for what good it will do. Sorry I can't be of more help, Travis."

"You've done all you can."

By the time he hung up the phone, Jillian had regained her composure. "It doesn't look good, does it?"

"No. Latonia confirmed what I already told you. There's no way in." He looked at his watch. "Have you had dinner?" She wasn't going to escape again.

She looked surprised, as if the thought of food hadn't crossed her mind. "Dinner? No. I hadn't even thought."

"Of course you haven't. I live not far from here. Follow me to my place. I'll give you dinner and maybe even a glass of wine."

"I don't want to put you out."

"You're not." He turned off his computer. "Come on, let's get out of here."

Halfway down the stairs, he remembered and cast her a warning glance. "Don't expect steak. In case you've forgotten, I'm a vegetarian."

"That's all right. Nobody's perfect."

Jillian was surprised when she stepped into the small living room of Travis's fifth floor apartment. "You lied to me."

"I did?" Travis laid down his keys and turned on a stereo. Soft symphony music filled the room.

"Your apartment, remember? You told me it was trashy. I pictured bundles of old newspapers stacked to the ceiling, and bags and bags of garbage. Obviously you exaggerated." It wasn't bad at all. She looked around the living room at the floor-to-ceiling shelves crammed, but neatly crammed, with books, magazines, and stereo components; at the worn but comfortable furnishings; the fine etchings of antique automobiles hanging above his couch. She walked to a large window at the far side of the room and found a dazzling view of the Bay

Bridge and distant city lights across the bay.

Travis stood beside her. "Not a bad view, is it? Here, let me take your jacket, and you can relax while I start dinner. I'll get you that glass of wine."

She sank down wearily on his couch, wishing she hadn't come, wondering why she felt so awkward and miserable. But after a day like this, how else could she feel? It had all gone wrong, starting with the frustrating scene with Doctor Linderman, ending at Fort Mason, with Travis telling her that there was nothing he or WEELA could do to save Lucky. Karlin's beloved pet was going to die. No, don't think of it! Think about Travis, only he was bad news, too. Ever since she walked into his office this evening, he'd been so formal, so terribly polite that it was obvious he had no special feelings for her at all. How dumb could she get? What was, after all, one kiss in the fog by the bay? How could she possibly have spent the past three weeks dreaming about it night and day like some love-struck schoolgirl? To him it hadn't meant a thing, probably his standard "welcome-to-San Francisco" greeting to every halfway attractive female he met.

And what was she doing here, anyway? Engaged to one man, yet fantasizing about another. Wasn't it obvious Travis was just being polite when he'd invited her to his apartment for dinner? It was only out of kindness and perhaps a touch of guilt because he couldn't rescue Lucky. She could always tell when a man wanted her just by the look in his eyes. She saw nothing but compassion in Travis's. He was far too noble, too engrossed in saving the animals ever to have a lustful thought.

She'd eat and run, drive back to Santa Marta, find a motel, and then in the morning decide what to do.

"You're going to love vegetarian." He headed towards the kitchen.

She forced a smile. "So what's the menu?"

"Veggie burgers with cheese gravy, a rice and bean salad, and my specialty for dessert—tofu cheesecake."

"I can hardly wait."

"I'll get the wine."

He was back a minute later with a glass of plum wine. She took her first sip and felt the warmth of the wine inside her. It was really good. "Are all animal activists vegetarians?"

"Mostly, although some are closet meat-eaters. Some are vegans. I'd never go that far."

"So what's a vegan?"

"Vegan is a contraction of sorts. People got tired of saying 'total vegetarian.' A vegan diet is one that avoids eggs and dairy products or anything that's from an animal."

"You are kidding."

"Oh, no. You see, for many people veganism goes beyond just being a vegetarian, It becomes an entire philosophy of consciousness. Your most devoted vegans make full-scale lifestyle changes and give up things like leather, cleansing solutions that contain animal products, even honey."

Give up steak and lobster—omelets—leather shoes—cheeseburgers? No wonder this man wasn't interested in her, she wasn't nearly noble enough. "That's real dedication."

"I'll start dinner."

He had failed her. Out of sight, in the kitchen, Travis spread his hands wide on the kitchen counter and stared down at the makings of dinner. It had been a mistake to invite her to his apartment. She was only being polite. Obviously, that kiss had meant nothing. No doubt she could hardly wait to get back to Tom and his fucking Mercedes. It would have been nice if he'd been able to rescue her dog. He could picture it—breaking into Linderman's, finding Lucky, carrying him out and laying him at Jillian's feet. But Captain Marvel he was not. Hero dreams would get him nowhere.

The telephone rang and he went to answer. "Travis?"

His brow lifted in surprise when he heard the voice. "Latonia?"

"Travis!" He could not mistake the vibrant undercurrent of excitement in her voice. "You're never, ever, in a million years going to believe what's happened. Let me tell you..."

Chapter 23

Santa Marta
The Santa Marta Women's Rehabilitation Center

Another day without alcohol. Connie Linderman curled up on her bed and opened *The Big Book*, AA's bible. Thank God she decided not to go home to Harvey. In this rundown old house with this ragtag assortment of women, she was piecing her life together again. Soon the evening's AA meeting would start downstairs. Tonight she was going to tell her story, how she got hooked on alcohol. No lies, no excuses, she'd tell it like it was. At the first few meetings the words stuck in her throat, but tonight she wouldn't hesitate. "My name is Connie and I'm an alcoholic."

She had just settled back and turned to the first page when Latonia, who'd gone to answer a phone call, burst into the room, grabbed up one of her teddy bears, and flung herself on her bed. "Damn, damn, damn!"

"What's wrong?"

"That phone call? It was from a guy named Travis Kerrigan. Ever hear of him?"

"Uh...yes, I believe so. He's an animal activist, isn't he?" She would like to have a nickel for every time she heard Harvey ranting and raving about Travis Kerrigan.

"You've got it right, honey, he's the activist. That man has done so much for animals you wouldn't believe, and now, when he really needs my help, I can't do anything." With sudden fury, Latonia hurled the teddy bear against the wall.

"Oh, Latonia, whatever did he want?"

"He wanted to know if I was positive there's no way they can break into Linderman Labs."

"But why?"

"He's got some poor woman there who's traced her Labrador retriever to Linderman's. She found out that on Friday her dog's going to die, and she's right. They're going to do this vile experiment that'll wipe out forty dogs. 'Trash dogs' they're called. Can you believe that? I've given my notice. Friday's my last day. I can't stand anymore."

Connie had never seen Latonia so upset. "Why didn't that woman go to the Linderman Laboratories and simply ask for her dog back?"

"She did. Travis says she barged right into Linderman's office."

"But surely...didn't he—?"

"He laughed at her, gave her a hard time. I tell you, the man's a monster."

Connie walked to the window. For a few moments she stared into the darkness. "So they want to break in?"

"Yes, but I had to tell Travis it can't be done. First of all, there's an armed guard on duty at the front gate, twenty-four seven. Then there's that eight-foot fence that runs all the way around. It's not an ordinary fence. It's a welded mesh fence with the gaps so close together it would be impossible to use a wire cutter or a bolt cropper. Not only that, three strands of barbed wire run around the top. They're treated with anti-climb paint."

"Ye Gods, what's that?"

"A slippery stuff with an acrylic finish. But you know what really hangs us high and dry? Linderman just sprung for a new, two hundred thousand dollar computerized proximity access control system. Nobody can get past that sucker. Each employee has a plastic key card, but this isn't one of those old put-the-card-in the-slot deals. Oh, no! There are no slots. They've built a sensor into the wall by each door. All you have to do is put your card near it and the door will open—if you've got the right code on your card, of course."

Connie turned from the window. "But you work there and you've got a card. Couldn't you just—?"

"It's not that easy. The catch is this system is like an electronic Big Brother. They've installed heavy sliding steel and glass doors to all the buildings and along all the corridors. The cards are programmed with limits so that each employee can open only certain doors, at certain times. Take me, for instance. There's a back gate that's card controlled, but I'm not programmed to use it. I have to go in the front, past the guard. Then I can only go into Building One, Corridors A and B, and only between 7:30 a.m. and 5:30 p.m. Otherwise, the card doesn't work. Of course the system tracks everything I do. From what I hear, Linderman gets a listing on his desk each day that tells which employees are absent, which employees are at work, what time they got there and all that." Her lip curled with disgust. "Basically we're back to time clocks, only now they're high tech time clocks."

"But isn't there a card that would open everything?"

"*Sans doute.* Dr. Osborne probably has one and, of course, Linderman. You can bet he's got the open sesame card that takes him through the back gate into any building he chooses, down any corridor into any lab he wants, any time he wants. Oh, yeah, I'd sell my soul for Linderman's card."

From the beginning, Connie had wanted to tell Latonia the truth but held off. When the right time came to tell, she would know. She'd been right. The time was now. She sat down on the bed again and looked across the room at her friend. "That won't be necessary."

"What do you mean, that won't be necessary?"

"I mean, you won't have to sell your soul to get Linderman's card."

"Meaning?"

"Meaning I'll get it for you."

"*What?*"

"It's time I told you my last name. I'm Connie Linderman. I am the wife of Doctor Harvey Linderman."

It was even better than she'd imagined, seeing Latonia, always so unflappable, with her mouth dropped open, eyes grown big as saucers, hearing her gasp, "*You are married to Doctor Harvey Linderman?*"

"You've got that right, honey."

"Latonia, are you sure?" Travis's heart spiked as he

grasped the import of her words.

"I'm sure."

"You're saying this Mrs. Linderman—Connie—can get her husband's key card?"

"She's positive. It makes sense because she still has her own key to the house. She might be in rehab, but she still lives there and has every right to enter. She says he puts his wallet on his dresser in his bedroom every night like clockwork. She'll know right where it is."

"So tomorrow night—?"

"Connie says the doctor's a creature of habit. Thursday night is his TV night and he's almost always home. At nine he watches *Grey's Anatomy*. At ten, he watches *Scandal*. After that, he might watch a movie. She'll wait until he's in his robe and pajamas watching his programs in the den. She'll slip in with her own key, nip into the bedroom, and voila! make off with the magic card."

"Too easy. There's got to be a catch."

"There isn't. Accept it, Travis, we're getting a fantastically lucky break. I mean do you realize the wife of Harvey Linderman is on our side? She doesn't give a shit about him and his great humanitarian research. She just wants to help our cause. This is the chance of a lifetime. We'll break into Linderman's, rescue what animals we can, and take pictures." Her voice filled with emotion. "Oh, Travis, the things I've seen in there—the filth, the neglect, the unspeakable cruelties, the...the..." Silently, he waited for her to pull herself together. "So what do you think? Shall we go for it?"

Dear God. This was moment-of-truth time. This wasn't picketing Saks or leafletting the North Korea Consulate. This was breaking, entering, stealing—all illegal as hell. Linderman would have his ass, all their asses, if they got caught. For himself it didn't matter. He'd risked prison so many times he hardly thought about it anymore. But the others.... "You know the consequences if we get caught. They won't just slap our wrists. If we're convicted—"

"This is my life, Travis. Whatever happens, I'll be involved and so will the others. It's what I want. It's what everyone in WEELA wants, so what do you say?"

Latonia was right. His dedicated WEELA members were as ready as he to sacrifice their freedom for a cause they believed in. It's what they'd fought for all along. It could all go wrong, but did he really have a choice? "We'll do it."

"Right on!"

He could picture Latonia thrusting a triumphant fist in the air. No time to lose. "We'll need a safe house, a truck and a van, maybe two, and a detailed layout of Linderman's. That's your end, aside from getting that card, of course."

"No problem with the first two. Don't worry about the card. I'll be with Connie when she swipes it. Oh, and Travis, she wants to be in on the actual raid, too. She made that very clear." Latonia stopped to chuckle. "It cracks me up. To think, for weeks I've been living with Mrs. Harvey Linderman and didn't know it. And she's going to help. I wish I could see the look on Harvey Linderman's face when he finds we broke through his precious security. If we're careful, he won't ever suspect it was Connie. He'll wonder 'til his dying day how we got his key card."

Travis hardly heard. They were short on time and he had a lot to do. "The first priority for me is to call everyone and let them know the plan. We'll get Terry, of course. What about Bernadette? Can we possibly do without her?"

"She'll kill if we leave her out."

"Okay, and Sparrow and his camcorder."

"Absolutely. We want to record every inch of Linderman's so the public can see."

"We'll have Mrs. Bagley too, if she's up to it."

"I don't know, Travis. She's such a nice old lady. I'd hate to see her tossed in jail."

"If we do this right, nobody will get tossed in jail."

"Who else?"

Travis thought for a moment. "Larry, of course. Krista and Josh from Berkeley and that's enough. It's got to be a small group. So we've got you, me, Connie, Terry, Mrs. Bagley, Sparrow, Bernadette, Krista, Josh, Larry, and let's see—"

"And me," a firm voice came from the couch.

He covered the phone. "You?" Jillian nodded vigorously. This was no time to argue. "And one more, Latonia. Let's see…dark clothes and ski masks, of course."

"And another thing." Latonia's voice grew somber. "We'll need vets standing by for the animals we rescue. Some of them won't be in very good shape. I need to know where we're going to take them."

"We'll go north."

"Our friends in Napa County?"

"Can you let them know?"

"I'll take care of it. Anything else?"

"I'll talk to you tomorrow, early. Count on us arriving in Santa Marta by five in the afternoon at whatever safe house you've provided. After that, we'll make our final plans and then wait while your Connie Linderman 'borrows' her husband's card. One more thing, when you go to work tomorrow, see if you can find Lucky, okay? You've got his description."

"Sure, Travis." A wary note crept into Latonia's voice. "What if I don't find him? Will you cancel the raid?"

Another moment of truth. But again, there was only one answer. "And pass up an opportunity like this? Maybe we can't stop Linderman's parade of horrors, but we'll sure as hell slow it down." Travis turned to Jillian as he hung up the phone. "Dinner's going to be late. It seems I have to make some phone calls."

Laughing, she walked toward him. "Thank you!"

Despite the heavy load on his mind, his pulse raced as she lightly brushed his cheek with her soft lips. Their warmth lingered as she stepped away. "You realize I'm going with you on this raid."

"That's not a good idea. The risks are high. We know what we're doing, but you—"

"Don't waste your breath. Who else can identify Lucky? I'm going with you." Quickly, before he could argue further, she changed the subject. "I'll do dinner while you make your calls. Just tell me, how do you fix a veggie burger?"

He reached for the phone. "Any way you can."

The dishes were done. The dinner she fixed could best be described as "adequate," but Travis hadn't said a word. Now Jillian sat curled on the couch, feet tucked beneath her, watching Travis Kerrigan in action. What a charming, charismatic man he was, and so efficient. Tie discarded, sleeves rolled up, making notes while he hunched the phone between shoulder and ear, he had, in the space of a few hours, devised a master plan with details falling neatly into place. On the phone he'd been funny, wise, and ever so tactful.

"No graffiti, Bernadette. We are not going to spray-paint 'Torturer' on Linderman's office door. We are not going to trash the place, either. Leave that to the AFL."

"Yes, Sparrow, bring the camcorder. Make sure you've charged the batteries."

"You're sure now, Mrs. Bagley? You feel up to it? Okay, tiger, you're on the team."

His conversation with the young woman named Terry had Jillian puzzled. What was it in his voice? Regret, of course, but more, a certain sadness when he said, "Oh, my God, Terry, I forgot the banquet's tomorrow night. I'm sure you could catch another ride. You don't have to... you do? Look, don't feel obligated...but of course I want you with us. Great, see you tomorrow."

At midnight, he put down the phone. "Done, at least for tonight." His face relaxed as he rolled down his sleeves. "Glass of wine?" He headed towards the kitchen.

"Love it. Some more of that plum stuff would be good."

He brought back two full glasses and set them down on the table in front of the couch. "I'll put on some music, okay?"

"Fine, but I hope you've got something besides symphonies." Barely audible, the stereo had been tuned to a classical FM station all evening.

He thumbed through a stack of CD's. "How about a little George Michael's 'Faith'?"

"Great." "Faith" was one of her favorites, not that she'd say so. That would sound too phony, even though it was true.

He set the CD's to play, sat easily on the other end of the couch, picked up his glass and toasted her. "Here's to the lady from Denver. Thanks for doing dinner. Great veggie burgers."

"You're very kind. It's hard to burn a veggie burger but I managed." She took a sip of wine. "When I finish this, I'll go. I've got to find a place to stay."

"Midnight in San Francisco and you're going to hunt for a hotel? Come on, you're staying right here. My fault, I just assumed...I should have mentioned it sooner. You're taking the bedroom. I'm sleeping on the couch."

She couldn't help laughing. "That sounds straight out of an old Doris Day movie. I believe you, but really, I don't want to put you out." He was just being polite, and she would have none of it.

"But why? Wouldn't Tom approve?" His easy manner had disappeared.

"Tom?"

"Tom, your fiancé, the guy with the Mercedes."

She set down her glass. "Why do you men always identify people by the kind of car they drive? Women don't do that."

He didn't laugh. "You haven't answered my question."

She lifted her chin in the most aloof manner she could manage. "I don't need Tom's approval for anything I do. Not now, not after we get married either."

"So when's the wedding?" He sat, seemingly relaxed, as he waited for an answer, yet the gray softness of his eyes had disappeared, replaced by a gray steel of piercing intensity. This was how he must look in court when he cross-examined a hostile witness.

"We haven't set a date yet."

"Why not?"

Those eyes! She shifted her glance away before she answered. "Lots of reasons, like Karlin and Lucky, and now there's Doctor Harvey Linderman..." Her voice wavered. "So many things happening, I'm just not sure."

He moved closer. His arm shot out, and he clasped her hand firmly in his, holding it high, towards his chest, almost as if they were arm wrestling. "Tell me, Jillian, why isn't Tom here helping you? Why did you have to go through this hellish day all by yourself?"

"Tom's awfully busy. He owns his own company, so he has to do a lot of traveling, and...well you see, he operates on such a demanding schedule that he doesn't have time for…" That sounded ridiculous, even to her own ears.

The expression on Travis's face, a mixture of anger and disgust, revealed how unconvinced he was. "Demanding schedule, my ass. The man's a selfish fool. If you were my fiancé, I'd be moving heaven and earth to find that dog. What's he doing back in Colorado today? Skiing?"

"Actually, he is, but it's not what you think. He's with clients, so that makes it..." Why finish when she had no further desire to defend her selfish fiancé? Travis had just revealed he cared. Otherwise, he wouldn't sound so jealous of Tom. Always before, she'd waited for the man to make the first move, knowing he would, but tonight there'd be no game playing with Travis Kerrigan. Her eyes met his. She gripped his hand tighter. "I want to tell you something."

"What?" He knew. Already his breath was coming fast and shallow, she could tell.

"That night you kissed me? You remember?"

"Of course I remember."

"I've been thinking about it, and you, ever since. I tried to put you out of my mind because I was engaged. I figured in time I'd forget all about you, only it didn't work. Then came the thing with Lucky and I had to turn to you for help. Deep down, I was glad. I really wanted to see you again."

He pressed her hand against his chest. She could feel the pounding of his heart. "What about Tom?"

Goodbye, Mrs. Mayo's Wedding World. Goodbye, jet trips around the world. Goodbye, yacht in the Caribbean, ski lodge at Aspen. Goodbye, Tom. "He's history."

With a sharp intake of breath, and such a cry of gladness

she could not believe, he took her in his arms and crushed her so tightly she gasped, and would have called, "Hey!" except his lips were hard on hers with a need so compelling she melted into his arms and totally forgot about Lucky, Harvey Linderman, WEELA, the raid, and everybody and everything except being in the arms of Travis Kerrigan.

Her first thought when she awoke in Travis's bed the next morning, still entwined in his arms, was, last night was awesome. The feelings Travis awakened in her were feelings she'd never had before. Her second thought was, today could be the day she'd find Lucky. Her third thought, what am I doing?

Today was the day she was going to break the law, the day that she, up to now the most honest and respectable of citizens, could very well get herself arrested. Today could be the most terrible day of her life.

Or the best.

Black male Lab with a touch of terrier. Small paws, three white, one black. White tip on tail. White star on his chest.

Latonia silently recited the description of Lucky as she and Bobby Joe approached the cinderblock building where the dogs were kept. Latonia had never been inside before. Called the Annex, it stood behind the main building of Linderman Laboratories, well hidden from public view.

They entered a small lobby where Bobby Joe held up his key card to activate a glass and steel sliding door. They walked down a long corridor. "Where are they doing this experiment?"

"Upstairs." Bobby Joe carried two pairs of electric clippers. "There's lots of laboratories up there where they've got experiments going. Downstairs is where they keep the animals." He opened another door. They stepped into a room where two rows of narrow, floor-to-ceiling chain link cages were divided by a walkway built over a bare cement floor. Though each cage was large enough to house only one animal comfortably, dogs of all sizes and descriptions were packed together, at least four in each one. The room reverberated with ear-shattering barking.

Latonia wrinkled up her nose. The smell was overpowering, and no wonder. Filthy cages, no food bowls, empty water bowls. In the first cage, a poodle laid limp and panting in the corner. She pointed. "That dog is sick. Has a vet seen it?"

Bobby Joe snickered. "Are you kidding? Why bother? If it's real sick, they won't use it in the experiment. They'll kill it right away."

"Where's their food and water?"

"They're not supposed to have any food, on account of the experiment. Besides, it saves the doctor a few bucks. He's always for that, if you know what I mean." After he winked knowingly at Latonia, an expression of annoyance crossed his face. "Jeeze! I'll be deaf by the time I get outta here. We should have debarked these mothers."

"You've got a heart as big as all outdoors, Bobby Joe." Latonia started down the narrow walkway between the cages.

"Hey, come back here. We're gonna start the shaving."

"In a minute." The first and second cages had no black dogs. The third cage held a black cocker spaniel. The fourth held a black Labrador retriever, but it was female. In the fifth cage, an old, arthritic white terrier and two mixed breeds stood yapping at the front. Another dog lay quietly on his side at the back, not barking frantically like the others. Latonia looked closer. Black male Lab with small paws, three white ones and a black. Black tail with a white tip and a white star on his chest. His ribs showed through his dull, matted coat. "Lucky!" At the sound of his name, the dog's head jerked up. He looked bewildered. His head flopped down again. "Lucky, over here. Come here, boy, I won't hurt you." The dog slowly rose to his feet and limped with a faltering gait, partway across the cage. He stopped and regarded Latonia with wary, frightened eyes. "Come on over here. I'm your friend, okay?" For a few more seconds, Lucky hesitated, as if deciding whether or not this strange woman could be trusted. He hobbled the rest of the way and stood at the front of the cage, head and tail drooping, eyes wary yet with a pleading look. He was trembling.

How could they do this to someone's pet? Latonia opened

the door of the cage and stepped inside. "Don't you worry, Lucky. We're going to get you out of here." She looked at the other occupants of the cage—the two mixed breeds, both young and frightened, the feisty old terrier, still barking bravely. He had to be somebody's pet because he wore a brown leather collar and tags around his neck. With slow-motion speed, Latonia reached out to touch Lucky's flank. At first the dog cringed away, but when Latonia touched him gently, he whimpered softly, finally recognizing a friend, and licked the outstretched hand. His eyes flooded with gratefulness, like this was the first kindness he'd received in a long time.

"Let's get started." Bobby Joe's nasal twang broke the spell. "We don't have all day."

"All right, but first we're going to get these dogs some water."

"We don't have time."

Latonia stomped back down the walkway. "Listen up, white boy. We're going to get those dogs some water before we start. Is that clear?"

"Yeah, sure, Latonia. Don't get mad."

After they filled the water bowls, they began shaving the dogs. Latonia had to force herself. Never had she done anything so repulsive, so against what she stood for. If it weren't for the raid, she'd walk out right now, but for the moment she had no choice. She looked at her watch. Two o'clock. They'd be leaving San Francisco right about now.

Dressed in dark slacks and sweater, clutching a small overnight bag with her ski mask inside, Terry Woodard felt excited, happy and wonderfully skinny as she stood waiting in front of her apartment house for Travis. She'd be sitting next to him all the way to Santa Marta. She would help him plan the raid. He would listen attentively and respect what she said.

Here he came, pulling his Prius to the curb. Someone she didn't recognize sat on the seat beside him. She covered her disappointment and hopped into the back beside Mrs. Bagley. "So where is everybody?"

"Sparrow's driving his van with the others."

Travis pulled into the traffic. He nodded towards the woman beside him. "You remember Jillian Dahl don't you, Terry?"

Seated directly behind the woman on the passenger side, Terry could see only that she was tall, with a lot of gorgeous hair. But oh yes, how could she forget? The one who wore a fur coat and fainted, the one Travis seemed so taken with. She leaned forward. "Hi, Jillian. Sure, I remember you."

Jillian glanced around. Her beautiful face lit with a friendly smile. "Hello, Terry. It's a pleasure seeing you again. I remember how nice you were to me that day I fainted in WEELA's office."

"Did you ever find your dog?"

Travis broke in. "Guess I forgot to mention Jillian's the one responsible for this raid. She found out Lucky is at Linderman's, slated to be used in an experiment tomorrow, unless we can rescue him."

"Oh, I hope we can," Jillian said fervently.

Travis reached out and touched her knee. "We will, Jillian, I know we will."

Oh no. The gentle, special way he'd touched her knee…his voice when he said, *Jillian,* letting each syllable fall lovingly from his lips. Terry could almost feel the vibrations zinging back and forth between them. "How did you find out Lucky is at the Linderman Lab, Jillian?" She tried to sound natural, like her whole world hadn't just fallen apart.

Jillian turned in her seat and told her about Tiffany and the lost message, Johnny Valentine and Sunnybrook Farm, the horrible confrontation with Linderman. "It was then I realized WEELA was my last chance. That's when I drove to San Francisco to see Travis." She tossed him a loving, playful glance and laughed ruefully. "I was feeling about as low as a person can feel, as you can imagine. Travis was so great. He took me in, gave me dinner and a place to stay."

And that's not all he gave you, is it? He made love to you, didn't he? There, in his apartment, in his bed where I wanted to be. Terry turned her face to the window, grateful Travis was busy driving through traffic and Mrs. Bagley had started chattering at Jillian. Maybe they wouldn't notice the tears in her eyes and the way she was having to gulp to keep down the hurt. All her carefully laid plans, those stupid plans. Starving herself to lose twenty pounds, the expensive dress, the wine, the pink bows on the cats, useless now. What a fool she'd been, loving him so much she was positive she could make him love her, too.

Travis had never loved her. He never would.

They were halfway to Santa Marta when Mrs. Bagley looked at her strangely. "Terry, you're being awfully quiet. Are you worried about tonight?"

Somehow, with whatever strength she had left, she must stop feeling sorry for herself and salvage her pride. There'd be time enough later to grieve for her lost love, but for now, what did her own feelings matter compared to the suffering of the animals? At last, here was her golden opportunity to do something truly significant. If done right, a raid might even close Linderman's down completely. She turned from the window and smiled. "I'm fine, Mrs. Bagley. It's a great opportunity, isn't it? I'm betting it's a night we'll never forget."

At ten o'clock that night, a battered, rusted-out old van with two women inside rolled up stately El Dorado Boulevard in the heart of Westwood Oaks, Santa Marta's most fashionable neighborhood. Connie Linderman, seated on the passenger side, turned to the driver. "Where on earth did you get this dreadful van?"

"Borrowed." Latonia shot a warning glance. "Don't ask where." Her long, lean frame looked catlike in black, tightfitting leotards and black sweater.

Connie, also in black, sniffed scornfully. "It looks as if it's got a case of leprosy, the way the paint's all corroded." She poked a finger into a large hole in the seat. "Just look at this upholstery."

"Hey, you want to get out and walk?"

"Certainly not. Only, it simply isn't the kind of vehicle

you'd expect to find in Westwood Oaks. We'll stand out like a sore thumb."

"You worry too much."

"I'm not worried at all. This is going to be a lark. Imagine, sneaking into my own house!"

Latonia flashed Connie a questioning look. "Why are you doing this? You didn't have to volunteer to get the card. You didn't have to tell me who you were. You could have kept your mouth shut and no one would ever have been the wiser."

Connie thought a moment. "I'm doing this because I don't like the way Harvey treats those animals, and I want to do something about it. Really, I had no idea how awful it was until you told me. There's another reason I'm doing this. It's hard to explain, but I needed to do something on my own. I can't believe the years I spent under Harvey's thumb, not doing a thing without his approval. He even approved of my drinking, not that I'm trying to shift the blame. He didn't force it down my throat, but in all those years, he never, not once, asked me to stop."

Latonia gave an understanding nod. "He enjoyed the power he had over you when you drank. You know that now."

"There's yet another reason I'm doing this, a bad reason. It's hard to put into words."

Latonia sniffed. "The bad reason is you'd like to get even with the jerk for all the crap he's dumped on you, right?"

"Let's just say, Harvey's had his way far too long. Now I can see how he rides roughshod over people—doesn't give a damn about anybody but himself. He needs to be taken down a peg or two, or three or four."

Latonia's shoulders started twitching and she broke into laughter. "Oh, Jesus, I keep telling myself this is not funny, but it's funny."

"You, too? Part of me is scared, but part of me wants to laugh. I keep thinking, 'What if Harvey catches me?' And then I think, so what? I can't be arrested for opening my own front door with my own key, can I? Is there a law that says I can't?"

"Not that I know of."

"Harvey will be furious. I just wish I could see him when his face turns all red and he about explodes trying to figure out who took his card. Turn right next street. You go two blocks to Blackwood Road and turn left. Then you park this...this disgraceful wreck of a vehicle in the darkest spot you can find, because we, my dear, are in the classiest part of town, and despite what you say, we do not want to be noticed."

"*C'est du gateau*, my dear."

"Piece of cake indeed. Just be careful."

They guided, lights out, to a stop two houses down the block from the Linderman residence. Latonia swung down from the van. "We'd better make sure he's there."

"That's easy to find out. He never pulls the drapes in the den. Shall we go peek through the window?"

With stealthy steps, the two black-clad figures crossed the expansive lawn and crept to a window at the side of the house, squeezed past some shrubbery and peered through a window. To their left, a scene from *Grey's Anatomy* played on a giant flat screen. In profile to their right, Harvey Linderman, dressed in a rumpled robe, slumped in his La-Z-Boy recliner, martini in hand.

He's getting old. Connie stared through the window at the man she'd been married to for over half her life. Harvey had aged, and in such a short time. The once taut muscles of his body were relaxing into a loose fleshiness. The beginnings of a pot showed where his once trim waistline used to be. Ugly bags puffed beneath his eyes. His jowls sagged. Even his hair looked thinner. What was that on top? A bald spot! He'd always been so vain about his looks—his trim body, movie star face, wavy blond hair. He was no Adonis anymore, this man she loved or thought she loved, had been positive she could never live without. Harvey was growing old. How he must hate it, but that was his problem. She didn't care anymore.

Latonia touched her arm. "Okay, he's there, come on, let's go get that card."

They backed away from the window and went around to the front door. Connie reached in her pocket for her key. Her knees were shaking. This wasn't a lark anymore. "I'm getting a bit nervous."

Latonia laid a hand on her shoulder. "You'll be okay. Your husband looked half zonked to me. He's not going to hear anything. Don't forget, this is your home, too. You've got every right to be here."

"I keep telling myself that, but the truth is, if Harvey catches me, I shall about die on the spot. If that happens, you must run. I'd have enough trouble explaining me, but you? Of course, it would almost be worth it, just to see the look on his face."

"Very funny, but that's not going to happen. Okay, I'll be right here by the front door waiting. Now hurry."

Connie slid the key into the lock and turned it. She opened the door and slipped inside. Oh, dear, the hall light was on. She hadn't thought to bring a flashlight—a fine burglar she'd make—so she'd better leave it on. Her heart pounded as she tiptoed down the hallway towards Harvey's bedroom. She reached the den and peered through the half open door. Harvey still sat slumped in his chair, still watching TV. Continuing on, she passed her old bedroom and couldn't resist a peek inside. Even in the semidarkness she could see it hadn't changed a bit. Bed unmade, blankets and linens still piled on the floor. The trash lay where she had left it, even an empty vodka bottle in the corner. The pink velvet chair—the TV—the place where the spiders had crawled out—all the same. Never again. The poor, pathetic creature who lived in that room was gone forever.

She continued down the hallway to Harvey's bedroom. Once inside, she closed the door, switched on the light and swiftly made her way to his dresser. His wallet lay on the right front corner, exactly where she knew it would be. She opened it. There, in its plastic container, as she'd been positive it would be, was Harvey's key card. Mouthing a silent thanks, she removed it and replaced the wallet in the exact same spot. She hurried to the door, turned off the light, and began retracing her steps down the hallway. *I'm going to make it.* She had almost reached the front door when she banged against the small table in the entryway. Oh, God, she'd made a noise. Harvey must have heard. She froze in her tracks, her whole body pulsing with terror. Any second now he'd come charging down the hall and all would be ruined. Moments passed. No Harvey. She opened the front door, quickly stepped outside and closed it softly behind her. Latonia stood waiting in the shadows. "Got it! Let's get out of here fast."

The van rolled, at high speed now, back down El Dorado Boulevard, headed towards the safe house where the others were waiting. "Here it is, the magic card." Connie waved it in the air.

"Way to go, girl. Any problems?"

"Of course not. I was laughing all the way." She punched her friend's arm. "Why ever did I think my life was over? Do you realize I am only forty-five years old? My life's just beginning. I've got lots of good years ahead. I feel fabulous!"

Harvey Linderman heard a noise from the hallway. He half rose out of his recliner and was about to go check it out when the commercial ended and *Grey's Anatomy* began again. Oh, well, it was probably nothing. He settled back in his chair and forgot the noise.

Chapter 24

A Safe House in Santa Marta

"Hello, Tish? It's me, Jillian. I—"

"Jillian! Where are you?"

"Is Karlin okay?"

"She's still pretty depressed, thanks to that rotten Dennis, but she's sure got her hopes up about Lucky. Did you find him?"

"Not exactly. I've hit a snag."

"Why are you whispering?"

"Because I'm in the back bedroom of a safe house. They don't want me make calls right now, but I just had to check on Karlin."

"Okay, let's back up a little. What's a safe house?"

"This one's a dumpy old house on the outskirts of Santa Marta. It's well back from the road, so it's the perfect spot to hide our truck and vans."

"What are you talking about?"

"It's a place you hide out when you're doing something illegal."

"And you're doing something illegal?"

"Yes, very."

"Like what?"

"Like breaking into the Linderman Research Laboratories tonight to rescue Lucky."

"Oh, my God."

"It's a long story, Tish, but believe me I have no choice. If we don't rescue him, he'll die. He will literally be roasted to death."

"Oh, my God."

"Don't tell Karlin. She's not to know any of this until it's over. Maybe not even then, depending on whether or not we're successful."

"Of course, but Jillian, breaking into a lab? What if they

catch you? Couldn't you be sent to prison?"

"Actually, I could. This evening while we've been waiting, I've been remembering every women's prison movie I ever saw."

"How about TV? *Orange is the New Black?* You might become a lesbian."

"No chance of that."

"Will you please tell me what's going on?"

"Sorry, got to run. Travis is about to go over the plan."

"Travis?"

"Yes, Travis. That's another thing. I'm breaking it off with Tom."

"You're *what?*"

"Bye, bye, gotta go. I'll call as soon as I can. There's so much to tell, but for now, keep your fingers crossed we don't get caught."

Jillian hurried back to the shabby living room and found a place in the corner of a dusty old couch. The air thick with tension, WEELA members, all in dark clothing, waited for the final word from Travis. Earlier they'd been relaxed, had even played a boisterous game of monopoly. When Sparrow brought in two jumbo vegetarian pizzas, they ate heartily, down to the last tiny bit of pepper and splinter of cheese. As the departure time grew closer, the easy laughter died away. Who were these people who were about to risk their freedom? She'd met them all by now, including cool, articulate Latonia, the one who saw Lucky in Linderman's Lab. *Don't worry, we will definitely get him out.* What a dynamo of a woman—tall, black, and beautiful, a natural born leader. To look at her, you'd never believe she was an alcoholic.

Petite Connie Linderman carried herself with style, like an elegant little bird. She didn't look nervous at all. In fact, she had a sort of inner glow, like she'd just discovered life can be beautiful. Or maybe it was just because she finally found the guts to defy her husband.

Bernadette. The woman had been smoldering for hours. Must be her usual condition. A diabolical light glowed in her eyes. It grew brighter whenever Travis said, "No trashing." Had anyone else noticed?

Brave Terry with her Alice-in-Wonderland hair. How confident and strong she was, encouraging the others, her pretty face glowing with excitement. Only in the depths of her eyes could Jillian see the mass of hurt. *You don't know how sorry I am, Terry. I can't tell you because you don't want me to know, but it's so plain you love Travis Kerrigan. On the trip down I could tell how badly you felt, but what can I say? I love him, too.*

The rest of them, such good people. Krista and Josh, the students from Berkeley—Mrs. Bagley—Larry the vet—nervous Sparrow clutching his camcorder, sticking close to Travis's side.

Travis. He'd ignored her for hours, so busy planning the raid he hadn't even looked in her direction. Last night she'd lain in his arms. He'd drawn her to a height of a passion she'd totally, totally never known before. He'd…*How could I? Hold on! A serious moment like this and you're lusting after Travis.* Later, when she could sort through her thoughts like a rational, untroubled human being, she would decide what to do. She would tell Tom, of course, that much was for sure. She'd never marry him now, no matter what. Travis lived in San Francisco, she in Denver. How that would work out, she had no idea. Right now she must concentrate on the raid, then getting back to Karlin fast as she could. She was about to risk years in prison, but it didn't matter. Nothing mattered except rescuing Lucky before that monstrous doctor roasted him to death.

When she looked at Travis again, he had turned toward the group, eyes on his watch. The room grew silent as he began to speak. "Okay, here's the plan. If you have any questions, stop me and ask." He pointed to a layout of Linderman's, tacked on the wall. "Here's the lab. Here's the back gate. There are only a few houses along that back road. It's mostly an open field. All we need worry about is the Safe-T-First Security patrol that drives by that gate every hour, just about on the hour. So at 1:05 a.m., or as soon as that patrol goes by, we drive to the back gate. I'll be driving one van, Latonia the other. Sparrow, you've got the truck." Travis looked at Latonia. "By the way, thanks for the vehicles. Where did you get them on such short notice?"

"Various resources," Latonia answered with veiled eyes.

Terry burst out laughing. "Various resources, spelled A-L-F."

Travis suppressed a grin. "If we're getting a little help from the ALF, so much the better. Okay, back to business. We open the gate with the card Mrs. Linderman has been kind enough to obtain. We drive in and park between the main building and the Annex. That way, we'll be hidden, should the patrol come by unexpectedly. Then we begin phase one. That involves the main building. We use the card, get inside, and—listen carefully now—while Sparrow takes pictures of everything he sees, we clear out as many laboratories as we can. It won't be easy. Some of the animals will have to be tranquilized, am I not correct, Larry?"

The vet nodded. "We'll need time to get them out of their restraints."

"We'll allow as much time as we possibly can. We'll carry them to the vans. When the vans are full, Krista and Josh, you'll each drive a van and leave. Someone, make it Terry, will open the back gate. You'll drive straight through and on to the safe house."

"And the rest of us?" Terry asked.

"That's phase two. We hit the Annex. First, the dogs." He looked at Jillian. "Lucky and the rest. Depending on time and room in the truck, we'll take whatever other animals we can find. Sparrow, you'll still be taking pictures."

"What about the guard at the front gate?" Mrs. Bagley asked.

"He shouldn't come around, not at that hour. He'll make his next rounds at 2:30 a.m. We'll be gone by then."

"There's nobody else there?"

"The animals are left alone after eight o'clock at night."

"You mean they just leave those poor animals unattended? Even the sick ones? All night long?"

"I'm afraid so, Edith."

"Now I know we're doing the right thing."

Travis went on, "When the truck is full, we leave, by two o'clock at the latest because that's when the patrol will be coming around. That gives us an hour. Can we do it?"

Shouts of "yes!" filled the room.

"We return here. Then Latonia's 'resources' will begin coming by, to help get the animals up north."

Arms folded, Latonia leaned against a wall. "It's all arranged, sort of an underground railroad for animals. I guarantee you my connections will make sure every animal gets whatever medical treatment it needs. After that, we'll do what we can to find the adoptable ones a new home."

"Excellent. Meantime, we'll have it all on video to show the world."

"You bet we will, Trav." Sparrow held up his camcorder. "We'll be sending copies to the media, congressmen, senators and everyone else we can think of who might help."

"Good." Travis nodded approvingly, paused for a moment, looking down at the floor as he gathered his thoughts. "I have a few final words. Be aware we're crossing a line we've never crossed before. Nonviolent civil disobedience is one thing. Breaking, entering and stealing is another. Make sure you know what you're doing and the consequences. You can still back out, no recriminations." He paused and looked around the room.

Terry got to her feet. "You all know how I feel, but I'll say it again. I'm not sure there's such a thing as reincarnation, but if there is, I'd like God to put me on a planet where there's no cruelty to children, or animals, or anyone or anything. Meanwhile, since I'm stuck on this planet, I will do what I can to stop the suffering, and I don't care what the cost."

"Well put, Terry. Anyone else?" Travis waited, but no one else spoke. "Okay, boys and girls, we're about to become criminals in the eyes of the law."

Sparrow's voice rang out, "But not in our eyes."

"Agreed, not in our own eyes. We won't be saving a huge number of animals, but what we do tonight may get us worldwide publicity. We want people to see the immoral barbarism in these labs. But one thing I want to make perfectly clear." His eyes met Bernadette's. "There will be no wrecking of the laboratories. Got that?"

"You're making a mistake, Travis." Bernadette spoke in clipped tones. "If ever there was a lab that deserved to be trashed, it's Linderman's."

"That has nothing to do with it. The public doesn't understand vandalism. We'll end up harming our cause. Better to take the animals, record it all on video and leave the rest alone."

Bernadette raised an eyebrow. "If you say so, Travis."

His eyes hardened as he looked at her. "I do say so." He looked around the room. "Is everyone carrying bail money, just in case?"

Terry spoke up. "We've all got our money, but we're not going to need it."

Travis relaxed and smiled. "I believe it. One more thing. Mrs. Bagley, did you get enough money out of our bank?"

"Yes, Travis, five hundred dollar bills, just like you asked. They're in my pocket."

"Fine, keep it handy."

"You think we might have to bribe someone? That's not too likely, is it?"

"No, but we're covering all bases." Travis took a deep breath. "So anything else?" He waited. "Okay, then. Get your ski masks. It's time to go."

Jillian was standing by the back of the van, waiting her turn to get in, when she felt Travis beside her. "Jillian, over here," he said softly. Cupping his hand beneath her elbow, he guided her into the darkness of the yard. Standing close, he asked, "Are you all right?"

"Of course I'm all right."

"Still want to go through with it? This is your last chance to back out."

"Never."

"You're sure?"

She could barely see him in the near-darkness of a quarter

moon. "I've been remembering a day not too long ago when I was skiing at Winter Park and thinking how magical the day was, how great my life was, how much fun I was having and how much fun I was going to have. That was all that mattered."

"Before Karlin—?"

"Before Karlin got diagnosed with cancer and lost her leg. I've changed a lot since then. 'Fun' isn't at the top of my list anymore. Rescuing Lucky—seeing my sister smile again—that's what's important. So back out? Never." She rested her hands lightly on his shoulders. "I'm not a quitter, and I'm not just another pretty face."

"Of course you're not." His arms went around her, drawing her close. "A friend of mine recently informed me that at least once in my life I should have a raging passion for a woman. She would love to see me smitten, lifted on the wings of love, weak with longing. I told her not to hold her breath." He buried his face in her hair. "She was right. Whatever happens, know that I love you, Jillian Dahl."

Sparrow's voice cut through the darkness. "Hey, Trav? Where are you? It's time to go."

"Coming, Sparrow." Travis stepped away, took Jillian's hand and held it close to his heart. "You haven't seen the last of me."

Three vehicles halted at the back entrance of Linderman Laboratories. Connie Linderman, key card in her hand, hopped from the back of the van and walked to the side of the gate. She held up the card. The gate slid open. With silent elation, she whirled and ran back to the van. "It worked, Latonia." She scrambled back inside.

"Did you think it wouldn't?"

Mrs. Harvey Linderman tilted up her nose. "*C'est du gateau.*"

Three vehicles rolled through the gate and silently parked behind the main buildings of The Linderman Research Laboratories.

* * *

Phase one went so quickly that after Jillian, heart pounding, jumped from the van, she had only the vaguest impression of sliding steel doors, long corridors and swiftly moving, masked members of WEELA with animals in their arms. A few poignant scenes stood out, like Connie Linderman lifting the infant stump tailed macaque monkey from its cage. Only slightly larger than Connie's hand, the tiny creature's skull and face were covered with surgical tape. A sonar device was implanted in his head. "How could Harvey do this?" Connie asked of no one in particular. She gently carried the tiny monkey to the van.

Travis dangled a cage of white rats from each hand. "Rats too?" Jillian asked.

"Rats, too. Did you know what remarkably curious creatures rats are? Intelligent, sensitive and gentle, both to human beings and one another."

She rescued lots of cats, trip after trip, hauling them to the waiting van—cats with electrodes in their brains, wires embedded under their skin, tubes implanted in their stomachs. She pointed to a Persian with a severed spinal cord. "Is there any hope for this one?"

"Bring it," Latonia commanded fiercely. "We'll take care of them all."

She remembered Sparrow taking his pictures with tears in his eyes. "I'm getting it all, Trav, getting it all, only, it's hard, Trav. I never knew it was this bad."

Most of all, she remembered creeping into a dark, eerie lab with Larry and Latonia where a large chimpanzee sat strapped into a metal chair, confined so tightly it couldn't move. "How could they do this?" Latonia's voice shook with anger. "Day after day, month after month, they've made him sit there." She bent and looked into his staring eyes. "I've come to get you, Charlie. Tranquilize him, Larry, quick, will you?" She reached for the restraining bands. "Help me, Jillian. Let's get him out of there."

Jillian would never forget the sight of a tall, triumphant woman racing down the hallway with an unconscious chimpanzee in her arms, calling to Travis as she passed by, "I got Charlie!"

Within twenty-five minutes, Sparrow's pictures were complete. Both vans were loaded full with cats, rats, monkeys, rabbits, mice, ten pigeons, two opossums, the infant monkey and Charlie, the chimpanzee.

"That's it," Travis softly shut the back of the second van. "Go, Krista. You follow Josh out." He turned to the others. "Let's go get the dogs. Twenty-five minutes more and we're home free."

After he watched *Scandal*, Harvey Linderman made a quick trip to the bathroom. Heading back to the den, he formed his "things to do" list for tomorrow. The experiment would occupy most of the day, of course, and what else? Ah yes, dinner with Clarence at Reuben's. Would he need any cash? Probably not, but to be on the safe side, he'd stop by the ATM. Or need he bother? How much cash did he have? He went back to his bedroom, picked up his wallet from the dresser and looked inside. Something wasn't right. Something was missing... *My God, the key card.* He couldn't have left it at work. He couldn't get out of the building without the card. Maybe he dropped it somewhere, but that was impossible. The card never left his wallet. There was never a need to take it out.

Harvey strode around the bedroom, gaze sweeping the floor. Nothing. Where the fucking damn hell was his card? What could have happened? *The noise.* Only one explanation. Somebody sneaked into his house and stole his card.

At this very moment, someone could be breaking into the lab.

He grabbed the bedside phone, looked up a number, and dialed the guardhouse. No answer. Where was the guard? Should he call the police? If he was wrong, he'd look like a fool. Better check for himself. He threw off his robe, pulled his trousers up over his pajama bottoms, threw a jacket over the pajama top. Bending forward to pull on his shoes, he nearly lost his balance. Damn, he'd drunk too many martinis, but nothing he could do about it now.

1:35 a.m.

Through the vacant streets of Santa Marta, a red Lincoln MKZ sped through the night towards Linderman Labs. Doctor Harvey Linderman, half-drunk and extremely agitated, bent grimly over the wheel.

In the guardhouse at the main entrance of Linderman Laboratories, Elpidio Delgado had sat studying *The Security Guard's Bible*. Silently he mouthed the words while his forehead furrowed in concentration and his finger traced carefully along each line. After a time, he paused and looked up from his book. A pleased little smile flitted across his broad, brown face. He considered himself a lucky man and never tired musing about the astonishing improvement in his fortunes that had recently occurred. For Elpidio, life had been about as bleak and lonely as a man could stand. He'd tried to earn a living in his native land, and failed. To feed his wife and child, he was forced to leave his home in Chihuahua, swim the Rio Grande (and nearly drown), and find work in The States. For several years, with only a few sneaked visits home, he toiled at stoop labor in the fields, living in constant fear of deportation because he didn't have a green card. He learned the bitter loneliness of living in a land of strangers, where people didn't give a *mierda* if just another wetback lived or died.

At long last, God smiled on Elpidio Delgado, like He suddenly discovered a terrible mistake had been made, and this hard worker, good husband and loving father was getting that end of the stick he did not deserve. To make up for it, God made Elpidio a winner in the U.S. Department of State's yearly green card lottery.

Now, because he had taken the trouble to learn English, because his cousin worked there, and because they were short-handed, two days ago he was hired by Safe-T-First Security Services of Santa Marta, California. So here he was, the second night of his assignment, night guard at the front gate of the

Linderman Laboratories. What luck! What joy! He had his precious green card and soon could send for his family. Before long, he'd be playing with his small son, Juan, making love with his fiery wife, Josephina. Not as soon as he would like, though. Ten dollars an hour wouldn't go far, especially with the gun and uniforms he had to buy and what the government would take for taxes. He would have to save money for their bus fare. He would need to rent an apartment, put down a security deposit, a utilities deposit, buy furniture. And in America, you had to have a car.

Elpidio sighed. It would be months before he had enough, but his thoughts never lingered on the dark side. Proudly he looked down at his new, crisply pressed khaki uniform with the Safe-T-First patch on the sleeve and the shiny, official looking shield over his front pocket. He reached to touch his cap. It looked just like a military cap with its large Safe-T-First badge directly over the bill. He adjusted it to a jaunty angle. Too bad it was the middle of the night and no one was around to see how good he looked.

He shrugged, and started to read again. Firearms was next. He turned the page, patting the .38 caliber, 4-inch barrel revolver, the "police special" he had just purchased, that hung in a holster at his side.

Section I. NOTE: Many deaths and injuries have been caused by "warning shots." The bullet could ricochet. The officer could stumble. In all circumstances, warning shots are a NO-NO.

The distant sounds of dogs barking intruded into his thoughts. *Dios.* Those animals were restless tonight. He heard them last night, too, but tonight the barking seemed sharper somehow, like they were barking at something. Elpidio stood up, set his new cap squarely on his head and stepped outside. He heard another noise, a kind of muffled clang. Should he leave his post? Go see what it was? His regular rounds weren't until 2:30 a.m. He hated to disrupt his routine, but what if someone was trying to break in? What were the regulations? What would an experienced security guard do?

Elpidio patted his 38 police special. Clearly, his duty was to go investigate the noise. Section I of *Firearms* forgotten, he pulled his gun from its holster.

At last they were headed for the Annex where Lucky was held. Jillian was racing ahead of the group until Travis quietly called, "Wait, I want to do a head count. Someone's missing. Let's see...Krista and Josh are gone. That leaves Jillian, Terry, Latonia, Connie, Mrs. Bagley and Sparrow. Where's Bernadette?"

"I don't know," Sparrow replied. "She was in the main building a minute ago. Do you suppose she's still there?"

Travis uttered an oath beneath his breath. "She must be, and doing God knows what. I'll go back for her as soon as we get the dogs."

They were at the front door of the Annex when a sharp yell broke the silence.

"Halt!"

Jillian stopped in her tracks. "Oh, gee!" came from Sparrow.

The rest stood silently frozen as a short, Hispanic-looking guard, gun drawn, came rushing towards them through the darkness. "Put up your hands!"

They all put up their hands. "Oh, dear me," Mrs. Bagley gasped.

Jillian's heart sank. To be this close to saving Lucky and fail? It couldn't be.

Travis stepped forward. "Buenas noches, senor."

The guard eyed him suspiciously. In thickly accented English he asked, "Why are you here? Why do you wear those masks?"

"We mean no harm. We're merely rescuing some animals that are being cruelly treated here."

The guard pointed his gun directly at Travis. "You are all under arrest."

Travis's gaze focused on the gun. "Put that down. Surely, you don't mean to shoot anyone."

The guard looked confused. For a brief moment, he lowered the gun. Reconsidering, he raised it again. "I must arrest you all. You are tres…tres… "

"Trespassing. Yes, but for a good cause." Travis nodded towards the main building. "They do bad things to animals in there. You look like a man with a heart. I'm sure a man like you can understand."

The guard hesitated. His eyes flicked to the building and back again. "I have my orders. In the book, it's clear." He waved his gun again. "March ahead of me, all of you."

Jillian's knees wobbled. She'd never had a gun pointed at her before, never realized how frightening it was. But they couldn't give up now. "Travis, can't we do something?"

Travis's eyes were on the guard. "Let's discuss this. Perhaps we can arrange something. Tell me, how much to you earn here as a guard?"

"That is none of your business, senor."

"Whatever it is, I'm sure you could use a little extra. I have a proposition for you, if you'll allow me to lower my arms for a moment."

"What kind of proposition?" The guard looked interested.

"May I?" Travis asked as he slowly lowered his arms. He stepped to Mrs. Bagley's side. "Put your hands down slowly, Edith. Dig out one bill."

Mrs. Bagley reached in her pocket and pulled out a hundred dollar bill. She handed it to Travis, who offered it to the guard. "Here's something to help you forget you saw us."

The guard shook his head. "One hundred dollars? An insult. I cannot be bribed. Raise your hands."

"Not enough? Then let's see…Mrs. Bagley?"

As Elpidio Delgado walked briskly back towards the front gate, he tucked the bills carefully away, deep into his pocket. Five hundred dollars, a fortune he could not refuse. Nothing to worry about. If he acted dumb, said he hadn't heard a thing, how could he be blamed? How had those strange, masked people got in? Not through his gate! Clearly, he was not responsible. Soon as he got off duty, he would call home. He would tell

Josephina to buy tickets for the next bus out of Chihuahua. Soon he'd be playing with little Juan. Soon his wife would be in his arms.

They stood like statues, looking after the retreating guard until Travis said, "Let's get the dogs and get out of here, just in case he changes his mind."

"Let's go." Desperately anxious now, Jillian raced ahead, up the steps to the Annex, the others close behind. She opened the outer, unlocked door and they stepped inside. Connie held the card to an inner door. It immediately slid back. They ran along a wide hallway. Halfway down, Latonia took the card and held it to a door marked LABORATORY 12. She cast a warning glance at Jillian. "He's in here. You may not recognize him."

Almost there. Jillian wanted to laugh, wanted to cry. A big lump swelled in her throat. "I'll know him."

Almost at the end of a long row of cages, Latonia stopped and pointed. "Is that Lucky?"

Jillian peered into the cage crowded with dogs, all of them shaved, shivering, and utterly miserable, not only because of the cold but because the shaving had been a terrifying, degrading experience. She saw a dog at the back of the cage. White star on his forehead—white tips on three of his small paws.

"My god, I've found him."

Lucky shivered like the rest. With the exception of his head, tail, and legs, all his hair had been shaved from his body, leaving his sensitive pink skin naked and defenseless against the cold. Jillian fought back her rising, scalding rage. Time for that later. She softly called, "Lucky, here, boy. Yes, it's me." He lifted his nose. "I've come to get you."

Lucky sprang to his feet, limped as fast as he could to the front of the cage and let out the loudest, most welcoming howl Jillian ever heard. Latonia swung open the cage door.

Jillian ripped off her mask and stepped inside the cage. As she knelt, Lucky flung himself into her arms and licked at her face. She looked up at Latonia. "See? I said I'd know him." She could say no more.

The Lincoln screeched to a halt by the guardhouse. Doctor Harvey Linderman, wild-eyed and disheveled, caught sight of Elpidio. "Let me in, you fool. Why aren't you doing something? Don't you know they've broken in?"

Elpidio placed an innocent, wide-eyed look upon his face and took time for an elaborate shrug. He pressed the button that opened the gate. The Lincoln roared through and stopped again. The doctor reached to open the passenger door. "Get in, hurry up!"

Elpidio got in the car. Before he had even shut the door, the car shot forward, headed around the Main Building toward the Annex in the back.

Terry, who had also pulled off her mask, was the first to break the spell. Although her face reflected Jillian's joy, she shouted above the barking of the dogs, "Hey! We've got to get out of here fast."

Travis nodded. "You're right. Everybody grab a dog. Be careful you don't get bitten. Time's getting short." He looked down at Jillian. "He's a big dog. I'll take him."

"No, I want to carry him." Jillian picked up Lucky and stood up straight. He was heavy, but she wasn't about to complain.

Connie reached for a tiny chow. "Poor little thing, so strange looking without its hair."

"I'll get this one." Terry picked up the old arthritic terrier that still wore a collar. Her face beamed. "Look here, tags! We can get this one back to its owner."

Travis reached for the two crossbreeds that cringed but didn't snap. "Let's go. We've got fifty feet to carry them to the truck. Then we'll see if we've got time for more."

Holding Lucky tight in her arms, Jillian raced back down the hallway, out the Annex and started towards the truck. The others followed close behind. Out of the darkness, a large car loomed. It screeched to a halt and two men leaped out. Latonia cried, "It's that guard again and Doctor Linderman. Run, everyone run!"

Jillian began to run, her footsteps awkward and slowed by Lucky's weight.

"Halt!"

No way would she stop. Her feet flew across the open yard towards the truck, Lucky clutched tight in her arms.

Linderman's voice rang out. "Fire a warning shot!"

A gun shot shattered the night, so loud Jillian's ears rang from the roar. She stopped in her tracks and began to turn.

"Keep going, go, go!" Travis's voice. "Jillian, GO!"

She heard another shot and started to run again. The truck seemed far away. Her lungs began to burn, her arms to turn numb from their heavy burden, but she didn't stop until she got to the truck.

She heard Travis' voice far behind her. "Latonia, get out of here. Don't worry about us. You get in the truck and you go."

Eager hands pulled her and Lucky into the open back. "Let's roll!" someone shouted.

"But wait," she cried, "where's Travis?"

Sparrow arrived. "Travis said we've got to leave without him." He jumped in the back.

Latonia climbed into the front seat and took the wheel. "If Travis says go, then we go." She started the truck and drove to the gate. Connie Linderman got out, held the card to the sensor, then scrambled back in as the gate opened. The truck sped through.

Bouncing in the back, Lucky clutched in her arms, Jillian tried to catch her breath. She looked around. Connie was there, and Latonia, Sparrow, and Mrs. Bagley. But what had happened to Travis? Where was Bernadette? Someone else was missing, too. "Where's Terry?"

Terry's ears had been deafened by the roar of a gun, while, at the same moment, something struck her in the back. Suddenly she stumbled. And then…what was she doing on the ground? Why did she feel so strange, so lightheaded, as if she were floating? Why was Travis shouting, "Keep going, go, go! Jillian, GO!" Why was he kneeling beside her asking, "Where are you hurt?"

"Am I shot?" She could hardly talk. "The little dog...?"

"Don't worry, Sparrow took it." He gathered her in his arms. He must have felt something because he pulled his hand back and took a close look. "My God, blood. This wasn't supposed to happen."

She couldn't see his face in the near pitch-blackness, but she heard the anguish in his voice. He cared. Maybe he didn't love her, but he cared. She could hardly lift her arm, but she managed to reach up and touch his face. "Now they'll notice us, won't they?"

"Of course they'll notice us."

She had to gather her strength to speak once more. "I'm going to that perfect place now—the one where there's no cruelty to children or animals, where everyone's kind and...and...ah, Travis."

She felt a tear upon his cheek. He understood her and would never forget. Her hand fell away as she died in the arms of Travis Kerrigan.

Epilogue

From the San Francisco *Clarion*

RESEARCH LAB HEAVILY DAMAGED SLAIN ANIMAL ACTIVIST IDENTI-FIED. TWO ARRESTED

SANTA MARTA – In the wake of Thursday night's break-in at Linderman Laboratories, two animal activists have been arrested. A third, who was shot and killed by a security guard, has been identified as Theresa Marie Woodard, twenty-four, of San Francisco. She was a full-time employee of WEELA, the group that staged the raid in order to "free" animals used in research at the laboratory.

Two activists were arrested on the scene. Travis Kerrigan, 35, head of WEELA, was found next to the body of Woodard. Bernadette Lawrence, 49, a self-employed accountant from San Francisco, was found locked inside the main building where extensive damage to laboratory facilities was done.

Doctor Harvey Linderman, Director of Linderman Laboratories, arrived at the scene during the raid. He said the shooting of Woodard was accidental. "They were all scattering, running toward their trucks where the security guard first encountered them," he stated. "The guard drew his gun and fired a warning shot in the air. Then he stumbled, and the gun went off again."

According to Samuel Reese, Santa Marta Police Chief, charges against the activists are pending. Charges against Elpidio Delgado, the security guard who reportedly fired the fatal shot are under investigation.

From the Santa Marta Sentinel

HISPANIC COMMUNITY COMES TO SECURITY GUARD'S DEFENSE

Members of La Raja and other groups affiliated with Santa Marta's large Hispanic community today announced a "Save Elpidio Delgado Defense Fund" has been established for the security guard accused of murder in the April killing of animal activist Terry Woodard at Linderman Research Laboratories.

Delgado claims the shooting was accidental. He says he was told to fire a warning shot by Doctor Harvey Linderman, director of Linderman Laboratories when they were in pursuit of a group of animal activists who broke into the lab. "Doctor Linderman ordered me to shoot," Delgado claims. "I shot in the air. Then I stumbled and the gun went off again. When he said the girl was dead, I cried. I will never forgive myself, but it was an accident."

Linderman has not been charged.

From the One World Section of the San Francisco *Clarion*

WHY I'M STILL AN ANIMAL ACTIVIST
Exclusive interview with Travis Kerrigan, head of WEELA

Animal Activist Travis Kerrigan will never forget the night he held his dying friend in his arms. "Terry Woodard was one of the special ones," he says. "Kind, generous, with a love for animals that encompassed all else. I will never forget her. Though her death in that raid is a tragedy, she'd be the first to say that if it helped the animals, then her death was not in vain."

Although Kerrigan faces charges for breaking and entering

Linderman Laboratories, it appears WEELA's raid was a success. None of the stolen animals has been recovered. Their whereabouts remain unknown. The Linderman Research Laboratory has experienced severe difficulties. Because of Woodard's death, worldwide publicity has focused on the facility. During the raid, cameras recorded many violations of the Animal Welfare Act, now being investigated by the U.S. Department of Agriculture. These recordings were widely distributed to the media, as well as members of congress. As a result, the National Institute of Health and the American Cancer Society have withdrawn their funding. Other agencies are considering following suit.

Doctor Clarence Osborne, spokesman for Linderman Laboratories, confirms the company is having financial difficulties. "Thousands of dollars' worth of damage was done in our Laboratory facilities," he states. "An untold number of experiments were ruined. We are being sued by the parents of Terry Woodard, the young woman who was killed in the raid. We have lost much of our funding. Bankruptcy is a definite possibility, but we are looking at all our options."

Kerrigan remains unrepentant. "We accomplished what we set out to do. Despite the tragedy, the parade of horrors at Linderman Labs has been stopped, and for that we are grateful."

From the San Francisco *Clarion*

ANIMAL ACTIVISTS CONVICTED. LINDERMAN LABORATORIES DIRECTOR OUTRAGED

SANTA MARTA – Two animal activists were found guilty yesterday of breaking and entering Linderman Laboratories in April and causing extensive damage to their facilities.

Travis Kerrigan and Bernadette Lawrence were sentenced by Judge Hubert Crandall to time served, plus one hundred hours of community service each.

Doctor Harvey Linderman, director of Linderman Laboratories was present in the courtroom when the verdict was read. "These sentences are a travesty of justice," Linderman declared. "They should have been sent to prison for life, or better, lined against a wall and shot." After the verdict was read, Linderman had to be restrained and was forcibly ejected from the courtroom.

From the San Francisco *Clarion*

SECURITY GUARD
FOUND NOT GUILTY

SANTA MARTA – Elpidio Delgado has been found not guilty of second degree murder in the shooting death of animal activist Terry Woodard at the Linderman research Laboratories. Amid a cheering throng of supporters, he was borne on the shoulders of friends and family from the courthouse.

A defense fund of many thousands of dollars was collected to aid Delgado. At a victory celebration at El Torito Restaurant, Delgado announced plans to open a tortilla factory with money left from the defense fund. "My wife and I will run it, along with our parents who will soon arrive from Chihuahua, Mexico," he stated. "Every day I thank God that I live in America, the land of opportunity. My factory will be small at first, but who knows where it will lead?"

Excerpt from *Holly's World of Fashion* Blog

MAIDEN LANE, SAN FRANCISCO – *C'est du Gateau* is definitely the most popular boutique in town. If you haven't bought your latest outfit there, you are so not *de rigueur*. Latonia Jones and Connie Linderman (wherever did they come from?) opened this little treasure of a shop a year ago. It's been THE

PLACE ever since.

If my high school French hasn't failed me, C'est du gateau means "Piece of Cake." (Explain that, Latonia and Constance?) The shop features everything from fashion fun items to elegant evening wear from throughout the world. "We travel a lot," says tall Latonia. "Rome—Paris—London—we'll travel anywhere to find just the right fashions for our customers."

Tiny, bubbling-with-enthusiasm Connie agrees. "It's loads of fun," she says. "What could be better than making money at something you love to do?"

From the San Francisco Clarion

ANTI-VIVISECTIONISTS ARRESTED IN BERKELEY PROTEST

Seventy-one animal rights demonstrators, many carrying gruesome posters showing dissected cats, were arrested by University of California police in Berkeley yesterday. As portable tape players yelped out the cries of what protesters claimed were laboratory animals in pain, the anti-vivisectionists tried unsuccessfully to gain access to research labs.

Most of the protestors were arrested on or near the Berkeley Campus. They were cited for trespassing and released. Charges of interfering with police officers were dropped.

The protests were led by Travis Kerrigan, a lawyer who is also president of WEELA (We Especially Love Animals.) "Our aim is to get university officials to show they are sincerely attempting to move away from relying on animals for scientific experimentation," Kerrrigan said.

Kerrigan's wife, Jillian Dahl-Kerrigan, who heads the Theresa Marie Woodard Animal Foundation, was also present. She made an impassioned plea to the crowd gathered on the grass near the entrance plaza on U.C's system-wide headquarters on Oxford Way. "Most of U.C's research history is fraught with irresponsibility and negligence, callousness and indifference,"

Dahl-Kerrigan said. "If it takes a lifetime, we won't give up until the last animal is removed from U.C.'s research labs."

From the San Francisco Clarion
Financial Section

LINDERMAN RESEARCH LABORATORIES LIQUIDATION PLAN

SANTA MARTA – A spokesman for Linderman Laboratories of Santa Marta said today they plan to file for voluntary liquidation. The research laboratory filed for Chapter 7 bankruptcy protection in December. No details of Linderman's financial condition were released, but the company was previously reported to have been heavily in debt.

Doctor Harvey Linderman, head of Linderman Laboratories, was unavailable for comment. He was recently the loser in a civil law suit brought by the parents of Terry Woodard, the young woman killed during a raid at Linderman Laboratories nearly two years ago. Although the settlement amount was undisclosed, reliable sources state the amount was in the neighborhood of twenty million dollars.

From The Denver Post
February 20, 2018

WINTER OLYMPICS A GOLDEN MOMENT FOR DISABLED SKIERS

PYEONGCHANG, SOUTH KOREA – Karlin De Leon was age twenty when her right leg began to hurt while on a ski trip. Days later, doctors told her the cancerous leg must be amputated. "Will I ever walk again?" she asked her older sister, Jillian. Yes she would! Last Wednesday, Karlin skied up a storm, leading a 1-2-3 U.S. sweep in the disabled women's giant slalom at the 2018 Paralympics, held in conjunction with the regular Olympics.

Jillian Dahl-Kerrigan, a full-time animal activist from San Francisco, fought back tears as her ecstatic sister received her gold medal—not an Olympic gold medal, to be sure, but as meaningful as the real thing.

Shivering in the bitter cold, Dahl-Kerrigan took deep breaths, struggling to put that golden moment into words. "We weren't sure she would live, and now look at her. How lucky we are."

Several months after the amputation, still weak from chemotherapy, Karlin De Leon returned to Winter Park and started skiing again. "Right away, we knew we had a maverick on our hands," says her sister. "To this day, Karlin rejects the favored out-rigger ski worn by many disabled skiers. She has a closetful of artificial legs but seldom wears one."

A popular champion, Karlin De Leon, now twenty-four, is married to prominent oncology specialist, Dr. Richard De Leon. She will soon graduate with her own degree in medicine. "I plan to specialize in Oncology," she says. "You can guess why."

Disabled skiing made its debut at the 1998 Olympics in Calgary, Alberta, Canada, at an exhibition.

The End